A Lullaby to Love's Sweet Embrace...

Slowly, inexorably, he bent and kissed her, his mouth warm and soft upon hers, yet insistent and demanding.

"Cara, Cara." His words were thick and mumbled. "God, I want you. I can't remember wanting another woman this badly...I wasn't going to call you or see you again, but I couldn't stop thinking of you. I tried to write, but the words wouldn't come. Whatever I did, there you were, soft and tempting, smiling with those lips that..." Suddenly Chris broke from her and stood, reaching down to lift Cara up. He sank his hands into her hair, holding her head fixed as he gazed deep into her eyes. "You're so young. This is probably the worst mistake I've ever made. But I have to..."

Dear Reader:

We trust you will enjoy this Richard Gallen romance. We plan to bring you more of the best in both contemporary and historical romantic fiction with four exciting new titles each month.

We'd like your help.

We value your suggestions and opinions. They will help us to publish the kind of romances you want to read. Please send us your comments, or just let us know which Richard Gallen romances you have especially enjoyed. Write to the address below. We're looking forward to hearing from you!

Happy reading!

The Editors of
Richard Gallen Books
8-10 West 36th St.
New York, N.Y. 10018

Summer Sky

KRISTIN JAMES

PUBLISHED BY RICHARD GALLEN BOOKS
Distributed by POCKET BOOKS

Books by Kristin James

The Golden Sky
The Sapphire Sky
Summer Sky

 A RICHARD GALLEN BOOKS *Original* publication

Distributed by
POCKET BOOKS, a Simon & Schuster division of
GULF & WESTERN CORPORATION
1230 Avenue of the Americas, New York, N.Y. 10020

ISBN: 0-671-44695-9

First Pocket Books printing June, 1982

10 9 8 7 6 5 4 3 2 1

RICHARD GALLEN and colophon are trademarks
of Simon & Schuster and Richard Gallen & Co., Inc.

Printed in the U.S.A.

For my sidekick, Stacy

Summer Sky

Chapter 1

Cara Stone settled into her chair, adjusting the card file on her lap. The day nurses ranged themselves around the small lounge to listen to the third-floor-patients review before she went off duty. Cara was a night nurse, and every morning she reviewed the condition of the patients for the incoming day shift. Quickly and concisely she began discussing the patients, methodically going from chart to chart, adding personal observations to the written data. The day supervisor listened carefully, nodding her head in approval now and then. Initially she had had her doubts about Cara, who was fresh out of nursing school and came from a wealthy, lei-sured background. However, Cara had proved to be an excellent nurse—intelligent, compassionate, competent and sure of herself. Mrs. Dorsey, the head nurse, had come to rely on her completely.

One of the day nurses made a laughing comment, and Cara smiled. Cara would not meet the usual standards of beauty in a woman. Her facial structure was too strong and her coloring too vibrant for that. Her long, thick hair, which she wore up during work, was a glossy black. Her eyes were blue with the faintest hint of green, the color of a clear stream running over mossy stones. The thick lashes that ringed her eyes were black, as were the straight, uncompromising brows above. Her skin glowed with natural color. She had a determined chin and broad, high cheekbones, but the sharp planes of her face were softened by a pleasant dimple and a wide, generous mouth. Her waist was narrow and her breasts full. Though she lacked classic beauty, there was something arresting about her, a sensuality and vibrance that drew a man's gaze back for a second look.

"Now, Mrs. McAlister, room 314—" Cara's words were cut off by an imperious knock at the door. Everyone turned as it was flung open and a white-coated doctor appeared in the frame.

"Why, Dr. Cummings." Mrs. Dorsey half rose, one hand going nervously to her chest. "What—"

The doctor ignored her as he shot a fulminating glance around the room. "Which of you incompetents forgot to give Mrs. Delanoy her pain medication last night?"

Cara stood up smoothly, depositing the loose charts on the chair behind her. Of all the hospital staff, she alone had never shown any fear of this man. He was influential at the small suburban hospital, and most of the staff quaked before his authority. Although he was a skillful physician, he was unable to admit a mistake. Anything that happened to one of his patients was invariably a nurse's fault, never his, and he and Cara had clashed more than once.

"Dr. Cummings, I was unable to give her the medication because you left no orders for it."

He grimaced. "Don't be absurd. Of course I did."

Without another word Cara pulled Mrs. Delanoy's chart and handed it to the doctor. As Cummings flipped open the metal cover and began to peruse the sheets, Mrs. Dorsey frowned. She obviously felt that Cara should tone down her remarks and smooth over the situation. Cara glanced away. She knew what the head nurse wanted, but she wasn't about to play the little games with him that the other nurses did in order to soothe his inflated ego. Calm, confident, with more than a streak of Stone stubbornness in her, Cara was one who didn't back down easily.

The man snorted and handed back the chart. "All this proves is that you forgot to write down what I prescribed."

"I'm sorry, Dr. Cummings," Cara replied, her face controlled. "I distinctly remember your instructions, and pain medication was not among them. I started to ask you if you wanted to order it, but then I realized that she shouldn't have enough pain to require one."

"That sort of judgment is not up to you to make!"

"I agree that it's your decision. I'm simply pointing out that I remember your instructions clearly."

"Better than I do myself?" he inquired sarcastically. "Miss Stone, I don't know why you're lying, but the next time I suggest you own up to your mistake." Quickly he scribbled on the chart, thrust it back at Cara and strode from the room.

For an instant Cara stood motionless, clutching the chart. Fury surged in her, and red swam before her eyes. Suddenly she slammed the chart down on a counter and hurried after Cummings, who was waiting for an elevator. She stormed up to him, heedless of the avid curiosity of nearby hospital staff and patients.

"Just a minute, Doctor!" she barked, and he turned toward her, his eyebrows lifting in surprise. "I've put up with a lot from you since I came to work here. You're an overbearing sexist, but I've endured your moods and tantrums. I've put up with the way you place the blame on anyone but yourself. I even stood by and made no comment the times you made a joking remark about my figure to one of the patients. It was demeaning and degraded both me and my profession. However, I let it pass because older, more experienced nurses advised me to keep the peace.

"But I'm not afraid of you like most of the people around here. And I'm sick and tired of your attitude. The rest of us were not put here to bear the brunt of your ill humor and vanity. I'm a reliable professional, and I expect you to respect me as such. If there was a mistake last night, it was yours. I am not a liar, and don't you dare ever call me that again!"

Cara faced him boldly, her hands firmly on her hips, her chin outthrust. He stared at her, mouth open, his face a picture of stunned amazement. The elevator doors slid open, and without a word he stepped inside, and the doors closed after him. Cara turned and became aware for the first time of the curious, astonished faces of her co-workers. She realized then what she had done: humiliated publicly one of the most powerful doctors on the hospital staff. No doubt he would go immediately to the director of nursing and demand that she be fired. Some doctors would be too sensitive to the inordinate amount of power they wielded to use it in an argument with a nurse. Others would be too reluctant to get rid of a good nurse. But not Dr. Cummings. Competence threatened him, and he enjoyed using his power.

She walked past the interested gazes and reentered the nurses' lounge, picked up the charts and resumed her seat. Uncomfortably the other nurses followed. Mrs. Dorsey frowned and began uncertainly, "Cara, we don't really need to finish this . . ."

"It's perfectly all right," Cara assured her, although her fingers still trembled from rage. "After all, this is probably the last thing I'll do here."

"Cara, if you'd just go to the director and explain what happened . . ."

Her eyebrows peaked in disbelief. "You know the director considers herself more an administrator than a nurse. She'd never take my side."

"No, but she could help smooth things out. If you apologized to Dr. Cummings, I'm sure—"

Fire flashed from Cara's blue eyes. "I'll never do that. Perhaps I shouldn't have attacked him so publicly, but I meant every word I said. I won't apologize for speaking the truth."

The older woman sighed and fell silent as Cara took up where she had left off. When she had finished, she stood and calmly replaced the charts in the nurses' station just outside the door. Picking up her purse, she ran lightly down the stairs to the first floor and headed straight for the office of the director of nursing. Mrs. Dorsey hated conflict and didn't want to lose a good nurse. It was simply wishful thinking on her part to suggest that the director might solve the problem. Cara would be lucky to get out her words before the woman launched into a tirade of recrimination. Funny, after all the time she'd spent wanting to be a nurse, studying, dreaming of helping people, here she was about to quit her first hospital job. She had foreseen many hazards in medicine, but she'd never imagined any direct conflict with her integrity. What in the world was she to do now?

Cara marched past the secretary and through the open door of the director's office. The woman behind the desk looked up inquiringly, blinked and rose, her face flushing alarmingly. Cara almost smiled. Dr. Cummings had obviously been here before her. The director opened her mouth, but Cara forestalled her. "Don't bother. I came to say I quit."

She swung on her heel and left the room, grinning at the choking, gobbling sounds behind her. Well, at least there was one good thing to be gained from this. She'd be able to go with the others to Ginny's fiftieth birthday party in Washington, D.C., next week.

Cara's stepfather, Wilson Decker, held an admonitory finger up to his lips as he quietly pushed open the kitchen door and peered around it. Swinging it wide, he went inside, motioning to the group behind him to follow. Cara, holding the large cardboard box with the cake inside, slipped in next, then her two sisters and their families. Wilson made more comically unintelligible gestures and vanished through the swinging doors into the breakfast room. Cara set the cake down on the table and unfastened the carton, then pushed in the large numeral candles 5 and 0. Alexis slid open drawers searching for a large knife while her stepson, Paul McClure, put his hand over his mouth to stifle his nervous giggles. Typically, it was Morgan who found both the silver server and a crystal cake plate. Once they were ready and the candles lit, Cara picked up the plate, Nick threw open the swinging doors, and Cara marched through, following the sound of her mother's voice to the elegantly furnished living room.

Ginny sat with her husband on the couch, her familiar, still-lovely face lit with animation as she talked to Wilson. At the sound of footsteps she turned, and her mouth went slack with astonishment. "Cara! What on earth . . ." Her gaze traveled from the elaborate cake in her daughter's hands to the group trailing after her. "Alexis! Morgan!" She sprang to her feet, tears glistening in her clear green eyes. "Where . . .what . . . oh, I'm so happy to see you!"

She rushed forward to hug Cara, narrowly missing the cake, then turned to embrace her other two daughters in turn. Cara set the cake down on the low ashwood coffee table and watched the exuberant greetings. She was struck, not for the first time, by the similarity between Alexis, Morgan and their mother. Morgan's hair was a deep, luxuriant auburn; Ginny's and Alexis's hair was red-blond; Ginny's was streaked with gray. All three were tall and slender, with the same fair skin and delicate features. Cara was the only one to resemble their father, Alec, whose hair was coal-black and whose eyes were a bright, piercing blue.

Ginny released Alexis and turned to Alexis's tall husband, Brant McClure. "Brant, how nice to see you. And Paul." Ginny shook Brant's hand warmly, then bent to give his son a hug.

Paul smiled up at Ginny, his brown eyes gleaming and unexpectedly large for his Oriental face. Paul's mother was Vietnamese, and he had been trapped there for several years until Alec Stone had used his considerable influence to get the boy into the United States in return for a gas lease from Brant. It was this lease—and their mutual love for Paul— that had originally thrown Alexis and Brant together. When Paul arrived in America, he had been short and underweight. But under the healthy diet of the past two years, Paul had grown like a weed, and his sudden height bespoke Brant's parentage.

"Nick." Ginny turned to the man who stood beside Morgan with a baby in his arms. "Oh, and my darling Matthew." She kissed Nick on the cheek and scooped up the baby.

"Well, that's the last we'll see of him," Nick joked, his dark eyes glinting with laughter. He had known Ginny and her daughters since he was a child, and had long been Ginny's favorite choice for a son-in-law, although initially Ginny had picked him for Alexis, not Morgan. Darkly handsome, easy going and at home in any social situation, Nick was a far cry from the quiet, intense rancher Alexis had married.

"Your candles are melting," Wilson interjected dryly. Ginny whirled with a horrified gasp. Quickly she bent and blew out the tiny flames, and there was a ripple of pleased cheers.

"Cara, will you cut the cake for me?" she asked, reluctant to let go of her grandson even for a moment. Cara went to get plates and forks. As she left, she could hear Ginny accusing her husband with mock indignation, "Wilson, did you know about this?"

"Who do you think met us at the airport?" Alexis said with a laugh as Wilson turned up his hands in a resigned, guilty gesture. "In fact, it was all his idea."

It took Cara a few minutes to find the dishes in the unfamiliar kitchen. When she returned, the others had all settled down in the chairs and couches and were happily talking. ". . . big day for Matthew Fletcher," Nick was joking as she entered. "His first chance to cry in an airplane."

"I thought he was a perfect angel!" Alexis protested.

Nick smiled wryly. "You would. There's nothing quite as deluded as a doting aunt."

"Stop trying to sound cynical." Morgan gave Nick's hair an affectionate tug. "You know you're so proud of this baby it's disgusting."

Brant smiled and shot a speaking look at his wife. Alexis

nodded and said softly, "Okay." She raised her voice. "Listen, everybody, I have some important news. I've saved it until we were together, so I could tell everyone at once."

The others turned inquiringly toward Alexis, and Ginny urged, "Honey, what is it?"

Brant slipped a loving arm around his wife's shoulders, his golden-brown eyes glowing with pride. Alexis grinned, happiness suddenly bursting across her face. "We're going to have a baby."

"Alexis!" Morgan shrieked and jumped up to hug her. "That's terrific!"

"When's the happy date?" Nick shook Brant's hand and bent to place a peck on Alexis's cheek.

"November fourteenth. Since this is only the end of April, I'm a long way away." Alexis beamed as the rest of the family added their congratulations.

"I'm going to be an aunt again!" Cara exclaimed. "But how am I going to visit this one as often? Barrett is so far away! You know, it's weird. I used to hardly have a thought about babies. I mean, they were kind of cute and fun to hold, but that's all. But I've fallen in love with Matthew. Whenever I hold him, I get a crazy glow all over. And now I can hardly wait for yours, Alexis."

"I think it's called the maternal instinct," Morgan said with a laugh. "I know what you mean. I've been the same way. There must be a wellspring of motherhood hidden in us Stones somewhere."

Seven-month-old Matthew had had his fill of being quiet and began to squirm and whimper in his grandmother's arms. Before long he worked himself up into a full-fledged rage and let out a loud squall. Morgan sighed and held out her arms for him. "I think he's probably hungry as well as wet. I'll go upstairs to change and feed him. What room are you going to put us in, Ginny?"

Ginny rose with alacrity. "I'll show you."

The two women left the room, happily absorbed in the baby, and Cara began to cut the cake. It was funny, she thought, watching her family, to see them laughing and talking amiably, considering the undercurrents of passion that had disturbed them in the past. Alexis's early relationship with Brant had been a stormy one, and Nick had once burned with hopeless love for Alexis. At Ginny's wedding, Morgan had feared that Nick and Brant would come to blows. But now here they were, cheerful and friendly as any set of in-laws, Alexis happily pregnant after long months of disappointment, and Nick and Morgan very much in love and the proud parents of a healthy boy.

Cara handed Paul a large piece of cake and affectionately ruffled his hair. "How ya doing?"

"Fine," he answered shyly.

"Are you pleased about the baby?"

"Oh, yes. Allie says I can help her take care of it."

"I bet you'll enjoy that."

He nodded and swallowed a large mouthful of cake. "Did you see me hold Matthew on the plane? Morgan let me, and you know what? He grabbed my finger!"

"That's because he liked you."

"He didn't cry the whole time," the boy assured her gravely.

"That's good. I'm sure your baby brother or sister will be just as happy with you."

"Probably," he agreed serenely. "He'll know I'm his brother, so he won't be as scared."

Cara smothered a grin. "That's true."

"He's not exactly lacking in confidence, is he?" Brant chuckled. "I wonder where he gets that."

"I'd say he probably sees a lot of it around the house," Cara replied dryly. She felt awkward joking with Brant. Cara hadn't been around him very much, and his silence and tanned, unreadable face did little to encourage friendliness. She was much more used to Nick, having spent more time with him. Before he and Morgan were married, Morgan had confided in Cara about their tumultuous affair. In fact, it had been Cara who had called Nick and forestalled Morgan's disastrous plan to marry Mike Durek, their father's icy business partner.

Nick now slid his arm around her shoulders and gave a squeeze. "How's my favorite little sister-in-law?"

"How about your only little sister-in-law?" Cara countered.

"Don't be picky," Nick reprimanded. "Say, Brant, what do you say to our taking Paul sightseeing tomorrow? That'd give Ginny a chance to spend some time alone with her daughters."

"And you wouldn't have to be bored listening to us talk," Cara added.

"Such cynicism in one so young." Nick shook his head in mock sorrow.

"Sounds good," Brant replied. "What do you say, cowboy?"

"Great!" Paul mumbled enthusiastically around his mouthful of food.

"Good. It's a deal, then."

Paul swallowed. "Can we see the White House? And the Capitol? I want to go all the way up in that tall pointy thing."

"The Washington Monument," Cara supplied.

"Yeah. And I want to see where they have all the planes and the spaceships and stuff."

Brant groaned. "I can tell it's going to be a long day tomorrow."

"Chicken," Cara teased.

Ginny reappeared in the doorway. "Morgan's putting Matthew to sleep. Nick, he is the most beautiful baby. Just think, I have two grandsons, and pretty soon I'll have another grandchild." She squatted down beside Paul and gave him a hug. "Who would have thought I'd be happy to be a grandmother?"

"Well, you're a very pretty grandmother," Cara put in.

"Thank you, sweetheart. I haven't even thought to ask—how did you get off work to come here? That was awfully nice of the hospital."

Cara grimaced. "It's a long story. I'll tell you tomorrow. The guys are going to go sightseeing, so we'll have plenty of time to talk about it then."

"Why, that sounds wonderful." Eyes sparkling, she smiled at her sons-in-law. "You two are so sweet. Now, don't eat too much cake. We're going out for dinner to an absolutely elegant restaurant. You know, I've always dreaded my fiftieth birthday, but look what fun it's turned out to be!"

Cara set Matthew down on the carpet, then stood. "Anyone else want another cup of coffee?" It was mid-morning, and the four women sat at the table, their light breakfast long past, sipping coffee and lazily talking.

Morgan and Ginny shook their heads. Alexis hesitated, then sighed. "I guess not. I'm trying to cut down on caffeine now that I'm pregnant."

Cara went into the kitchen and returned a moment later with a full cup, carefully stepping around Matthew, who was crawling across the floor. Ginny bent as he neared her chair and ran a loving finger across his silky black head. "He has hair like Cara," she remarked. "Morgan and Alexis were almost bald, and what you two did have was too fine and blond to see. But Cara had a nice head of thick black hair."

"Daddy said the same thing," Morgan replied. "I was amazed he had noticed the color of our hair when we were babies, or Matthew's, either. But he's convinced that Matt's hair is exactly like his, ignoring the fact that Nick's is that color, too."

Alexis and Ginny laughed. "That sounds like Alec."

"He's crazy about Matthew," Morgan continued. "I never thought I'd see Alec positively drool over a baby. He drops by a least once a week. And the gifts! Matt's room looks like a toy store."

"He finally has the boy he always wanted," Ginny explained softly.

Morgan glanced at her anxiously. "Ginny, I'm sorry. I didn't mean to—"

"Oh, no." Ginny waved away her apology. "It doesn't bother me. No matter how much Alec wanted a boy, he didn't blame me for not having one. Alec had many faults, but that wasn't one of them. And now that I'm married to Wilson, nothing about Alec affects me. I think of him as someone I was once close to and loved, but all the hurt is gone."

"Good."

"I can't imagine Daddy acting like that," Alexis commented.

"Believe it," Cara told her. "I've seen him. He's absolutely mushy."

"He even accepts Nick, since he played some small role in the production of this wonder. The other day Alec patted Nick on the shoulder. I nearly went into shock."

The front doorbell rang, cutting into their conversation. Ginny sighed. "Oh, dear, I wonder who that could be. I look terrible. I haven't even put on my makeup yet."

"You want me to get it?" Cara offered.

"No, thanks. It's probably someone I know." Ginny reluctantly left the room. There was the sound of voices, and Ginny returned with a middle-aged woman dressed in an expensive pale mauve pantsuit. Her hair was iron gray and stiffly set, and her face was well made up. She was a heavy woman, but the extra weight gave her a stately look. However, the touch of dignity expressed in her clothes and features was nullified by the avid look of curiosity that glittered in her gray eyes.

"So these are your girls," she enthused as she entered the room.

"Yes, these are my daughters: Alexis, Morgan and Cara, my youngest. Girls, this is my next-door neighbor, Lucille Caldwell." Ginny's smile was forced as she made the introductions, and Cara suspected that Mrs. Caldwell's visit was not welcome.

"My, my, such a beautiful bunch of girls. Of course, I might have known your daughters would be gorgeous."

"Thank you, Lucille. Won't you sit down? Could I get you a cup of coffee?"

"Well . . ." The woman hesitated, then plopped into a chair. "Yes, coffee sounds nice, thank you. I hate to disturb your family reunion. though."

"Nonsense," Ginny replied perfunctorily.

As it turned out, Lucille managed to be persuaded to stay for another cup of coffee and a piece of the leftover birthday cake. For thirty minutes she regurgitated the gossip of Washington, D.C., commenting about this senator's well-publicized divorce, the affair of another senator's wife with his own aide and every other juicy tidbit she could dredge up. Cara stifled a yawn and noticed with amusement that Alexis's eyes were glazing over. She was about to make an excuse to get away from the table when the woman finally sighed and remarked sadly that she had to leave.

"I'm due at a luncheon in thirty minutes, and I must tidy up first. But I hate to go. It's been such a lovely talk. Nice to meet all of you. Ginny, I'll call. 'Bye, now."

Ginny walked her to the door and returned a moment later, sagging comically against the door frame. "I thought she'd never leave! I swear, that woman knows everything about everybody. Arlington, Alexandria, D.C.—she does nothing except run around gleaning all the latest pieces of scandal."

"How do you stand her?" Alexis asked bluntly. "She'd drive me crazy."

Ginny shrugged. "Sometimes Lucille can be interesting. And if I ever need to know anything about someone, she's the woman to ask. But I have to admit I've hidden from her more than once." She flopped into her chair and turned toward Cara. "Now, I want to hear this 'long story' about your job. Why were you able to come see me in the middle of the week?"

Cara sighed. "Well, the hospital didn't allow me to come. I'm no longer working there."

Only Morgan seemed unsurprised. "What happened?" Alexis asked.

"I either quit or was fired, depending on how you look at it," Cara admitted ruefully.

"Fired!" Ginny repeated in a stunned voice. "Cara, I can't imagine that."

"They were about to fire me, but I beat them to it." Cara launched into a full account of her angry confrontation with

Dr. Cummings, ending with a sigh as she said, "The question is, what do I do now?"

"Quit nursing," Morgan advised decisively, and Alexis chimed in her approval.

"I've thought of it," Cara admitted, her brow knotting with a frown. "That specific incident triggered my explosion, but there was a lot more behind it. Not just my problems with Dr. Cummings, but the attitudes of so many doctors and nurses. I was prepared to have to spend a lot of time on administrative work and less with the patients. What bothered me was that so many doctors look upon nurses as their handmaidens. Why, I've seen nurses jump up and give a doctor their chair when one came behind the nurses' station. What's more, a lot of doctors expect that kind of treatment. I've had them ask me to run get them a Coke or look for a chart they've mislaid, as if I were their servant. They had no respect for my brains or skills."

"That's a pretty common attitude of men everywhere," Alexis sympathized.

"I know, but I wasn't prepared for it. I think it was the way I was raised. Daddy was so forceful, and you were always such an achiever, Alexis. I didn't have the same kind of role models a lot of girls did. Plus growing up in Highland Park and always having everything I could want materially, I got used to people thinking I was somebody important. It was a real shock for me to find that the doctors didn't think I was anybody. The only important things about me were my figure and my face."

"Do you think you'll leave nursing?"

"I'm not sure." Cara sighed and shoved a hand through her long black hair. "I'm so confused right now."

"I still think you should apply to medical school."

"I know you do. But I don't want to spend a lot more time in school, then internship, then residency, before I could actually practice. Besides, I don't want to be a doctor. I like nursing. I enjoyed my relationships with the patients. You know, it's really the nurses who keep the patients alive. We're the ones who are with them all the time, who monitor, feed and bathe them and make sure they don't die. I feel useful. When I think about quitting altogether because I can't put up with some doctor's attitude, it seems pretty cowardly. I can't make up my mind. I'm considering going back to graduate school to get a higher degree."

"Why, honey, I think that's a marvelous idea," Ginny exclaimed. "You could go to school here in D.C. There are several good universities here, and I'd love to have you close to me."

Cara blinked. "Well, I suppose so. I'd thought about going somewhere besides U.T., for the change."

"Well, think about going here, please. It would be perfectly marvelous."

Cara shrugged. "My first problem is whether or not to go back to school at all. Maybe I'm copping out."

"What would you major in if you went?"

"Obstetrics or pediatrics. I've loved being around Matthew so much, I know I'd want to work with children."

"Sounds good to me. Why are you debating it?"

"Becuase I'm afraid the doctors aren't going to change simply because I have another degree. I'd still be a nurse. A lot of nurses go back to school, then teach nursing. I don't want to teach. I want to be with the patients. So I'm dithering around about it."

"I think the best option is graduate school. You'll be in the field of your choice," Alexis ticked off the points on her fingertips. "You're more likely to get the doctors' respect. And if you don't—if you can't take it and have to leave nursing—at least you'll have given it the extra effort. It won't be any worse to quit then than now, will it?"

"No, that's true. Maybe you're right."

There was silence, the group's spirits dampened by Cara's doubts and confusion. Morgan leaned forward, smiling, and patted her younger sister on the arm. "I know what will brighten you up. Let's go shopping and get you an absolutely gorgeous new outfit."

Alexis laughed. "That sounds like you, Morgan."

"Oh, no," Cara protested. "I'm not too crazy about shopping."

"Buying a stunning new dress is bound to perk you up," Morgan explained reasonably.

"Besides, there's a perfect occasion for it," Ginny added. "Your coming practically drove it out of my mind, but Friday night I'm having a party. You'll need a special dress for your first D.C. party. I'm so glad you're here. I can show off my beautiful daughters."

Cara shook her head ruefully. "You two are something else. All right, I give up. Let's go shopping."

Chapter 2

Cara revolved slowly before the mirror. Morgan had been right. On their shopping trip the afternoon before, Cara had quickly found two or three dresses she liked well enough to buy, but Morgan and Ginny had held back. Cara had grown tired and would have preferred to come home empty-handed, but Morgan had dragged her into one last shop. She had gone to a rack as if she had radar and pulled out a dress excitedly.

"I think this is it," Morgan exclaimed, turning to Cara. "Try it on."

At the time Cara had hardly cared what it looked like and bought it simply because it satisfied Morgan and Ginny. But now she had to agree that it was stunning. Of a royal blue color that turned her eyes vivid blue, the dress had a low, square-cut neckline that tantalizingly revealed the creamy tops of her breasts. The waist was tightly belted, and the material then fell in a soft swirl about her hips to sway enticingly as she walked. With her dark hair swept up in a soft chignon, a touch of makeup on her cream-and-roses complexion and the final touch of sapphire studs in her earlobes, Cara looked elegant yet sensual.

A knock sounded at the door and Cara called, "Come in."

Morgan stuck her head inside the room. "You ready? It sounds as if the party's in full swing downstairs. Nick's already there, but I had to stay to feed Matthew."

"Yeah, I'm ready."

"You look absolutely gorgeous," Morgan assured her as they went down the stairs. "I knew it would look that way on you."

"And you were right, of course."

Morgan laughed. "When it comes to clothes, I usually am. I never could quite match you and Alexis in school, though."

"Better make that only Alexis," Cara amended. "I'm no genius, either. And speaking of looking gorgeous, you're pretty sparkling yourself. I thought new mothers were supposed to be scraggly and tired."

Morgan wore a sea-green dress that set off her green eyes and dark red hair. She was the beauty of the family and had exquisite taste in clothes, making it a certainty that she would capture every eye when she entered a room. Cara was amazed that Morgan had managed to remain as warm and unspoiled as she was. She smiled now at Cara's words. "Thank you. I bought it a couple of weeks ago at Loretta Blum's. Believe me, when your husband is as handsome as Nick, you can't afford to look scraggly and tired."

They paused at the foot of the stairs. The party was going on all around them, flowing from hallway to living room and through the folded louvered doors into the formal dining room, even onto the small brick terrace. There a small band played, adding to the noise of laughter and conversation. "Good heavens, what a crowd," said Cara with a sigh. "And I don't know anyone."

"Think what opportunities it presents for meeting people. There's Nick. What did I tell you? He's already surrounded by women."

Cara gazed in the direction Morgan pointed and saw Nick

chatting with three middle-aged women. She laughed. "I don't think you need to worry about the competition."

"If only all the women who chased him were their age."

"Come on, you know Nick's crazy about you. I bet he doesn't even notice other women."

"Oh, he notices. He just doesn't do anything about it . . . and I intend for it to remain that way. There are Alexis and Brant, looking thoroughly bored."

"They dislike parties more than I do. I'm sure they wish they were safely back on the ranch. Shall we join them?"

"Cara! Morgan!" Ginny spotted them and fluttered across the room, the long, loose jacket of her blue satin pants outfit flowing out behind her. "I'm so glad you're here. I was beginning to think you weren't going to show. Let me introduce you to everyone. They're so anxious to meet you." She took each of her daughters by the hand and led them into the living room, a coolly elegant place decorated in chrome and white, with touches of apricot for warmth. "I'm not sure about this room. Morgan, what do you think?"

"It's very lovely."

"I know, but do you think it looks a trifle cold? When I thought of it, it seemed perfectly beautiful, but when it was done, I thought it might be a bit too perfect. You know what I mean?"

"Don't worry, Ginny," Cara told her. "You'll redecorate it in a few months anyway."

A peal of sparkling laughter broke from Ginny, and she squeezed Cara's hand. "You're probably right, my love. Oh, I want you to meet the senator. Senator, these are my other two daughters, Morgan and Cara. Girls, this is Senator Cramer."

The tall, white-haired man smiled charmingly and shook their hands. "Mrs. Decker, your daughters are as lovely as I expected. Knowing you, how could they be anything else?"

They chatted for a few moments about nothing, Cara smiling and contributing little to the conversation. She felt bored and socially inept, but at least with Morgan and Ginny around, she didn't have to worry. They could carry the conversation very well without her support. As they talked, she felt uneasy prickles run down her back, as if someone was watching her. She glanced around the room, trying to appear casual, stopping with an almost physical jolt as her eyes met the dark, searing gaze of a man leaning against the far wall. He was of medium height, craggy, almost rough-looking, and he would have appeared forbidding except for the faint smile on his lips. His mouth was wide and firm, as were all his features, from the broad forehead and predominant cheekbones to the square, stern jaw. His brown hair was a bit long and shaggy about the ears and collar, and he was dressed more casually than the others in brown slacks, beige turtleneck sweater and tweed jacket. Cara's stomach tightened inexplicably, and she swiveled back to the conversation quickly.

Who was he? And why had he chosen to stare at her? She could still feel the force of his magnetic gaze on her, but stubbornly she refused to look at him again. Moments later she realized that the pull was gone and turned. He was not there, and though she scanned the room, she did not see him anywhere. A curious disappointment struck her. The senator excused himself and moved on to another group. Ginny leaned toward her daughters confidentially and muttered sotto voce, "Most insincere man I ever met . . . but he's always good for the ego. Let me see, I can't introduce you to everyone. Wilson invited some of these people, and I'm afraid there are quite a few whose names I don't know. Isn't that terrible?" She spotted someone and waved. "Jean! Don't go yet. Come here and meet my daughters."

A short, dumpy, blond woman came toward them. She was not attractive, and the blaze of jewels she wore at her throat and wrists did little to soften her looks. But her eyes were bright with intelligence, and her face betrayed a humorous interest in life and people. Ginny held out a hand to her. "Jean, these are my girls, Cara and Morgan. This is Jean Littleton. She's the head of some administrative agency or other. I never can keep them all straight."

Morgan soon left to rescue her husband from the clutches of the middle-aged ladies, and Ginny floated away to greet more of her guests, leaving Cara alone with Jean. The woman was as unusual as her looks implied—funny, warm, down to earth, yet undeniably powerful—and Cara enjoyed talking to her. Abruptly Jean halted in mid-sentence and glanced over Cara's shoulder. Cara turned her head and saw directly behind her the man who had been staring at her earlier. Her heart jumped and began a thunderous beating. She realized with embarrassment that the color had risen in her face, and she was perversely irritated with him for causing her to react so.

"Hello, Jean," he addressed Cara's companion, and his voice held the tinge of a Northern accent. "Aren't you going to introduce me? I came over just for that, you know." His gaze returned to Cara, scorching her with its heat. She had the indistinct impression that his eyes were dark before she turned her own away, unable to meet his.

"Careful, you'll wound my ego," Jean retorted dryly, warm laughter bubbling in her voice. "I figured that's what brought you, but I wanted to make you suffer a little. Cara, this is Chris Wozniak. And don't say you've heard of him or it will puff him up worse than ever. He used to be one of the best newspaper reporters around, but since his book sold a million copies, he's become a bum."

"Now, Jean," he protested, grinning, "I do still work, you know."

"Free-lance." Jean dismissed it with a wave of her hand. "There's not enough of it, just an article every couple of months. I liked reading your stories in the paper every day."

Cara extended her hand to him, schooling her face and voice to a cool disinterest. "I'm Cara Stone. I do think I've heard of you. You did an exposé on graft and waste in government agencies, didn't you?"

"Yes, that's me." He held her hand a moment longer than necessary before he released it, his skin warm against hers. A tremor raced up Cara's arm, and she was relieved when he unclasped his fingers. "Unfortunately I wasn't able to get anything on Jean here."

"I'm sure that must have been a severe disappointment," Cara responded tartly.

His eyebrows rose slightly at her tone, and Jean laughed.

21

"I don't think Cara likes reporters, Chris." She winked at Cara. "Good idea. Never trust a news hound, that's the best advice in D.C."

"What do you have against reporters, Cara?" he asked, his warm brown eyes intent upon her.

Cara had the feeling he couldn't have cared less about her reasons. And since she had spoken off the top of her head, saying the first sharp retort that came to her, Cara was at something of a loss herself to explain her reasons. She could hardly say that he bothered her, made her uncomfortably aware of her body and set it tingling beyond her control every time he looked at her. Quickly she marshaled her thoughts and replied crisply, "I don't like the pushing and prying into people's lives. When I see photographers and reporters all over someone who's just suffered a tragedy, even if it's something he brought on himself, I feel sorry for him. After the press gets hold of you, nothing in your life is private anymore."

"The people I deal with—politicians, national figures— put themselves voluntarily in the public eye. They shouldn't unless they can stand up to the scrutiny." His mouth twisted and he made a dismissive gesture with one hand. "Or do you think the public doesn't have a right to know when their elected officials are engaged in bribery or other wrongdoing?"

"No, of course they're accountable to the people."

"And how is the public to know unless there are reporters sniffing around digging it out?"

Cara bit her underlip. She would have liked to have made a cutting remark, but she could think of nothing to say. In her desire to best him and shake his strange power over her, she had worked herself into a hole. In truth, she believed more in his side of the argument than hers. He smiled at her, his eyes twinkling, and she realized that they were not brown but a green-hazel that changed with his mood. Cara had the suspicion that he was fully aware of the real reason for her antagonism and was amused by it.

"Now don't start in on her," Jean came to her rescue. "It's her father you should be after."

"Your father?"

"Yeah, she's Ginny's daughter."

"You mean Wilson is your father?"

Cara laughed. "No, my stepfather. Daddy's name is Alec Stone."

He paused, his brows drawing together in thought. "You mean . . . your father is Stone Oil?"

"That's Daddy," Cara agreed. "In fact, I can't think of a better way to describe him."

"Chris is doing an exposé of the oil companies," Jean volunteered.

"Don't worry, I won't pump you for information," he promised Cara. His smile warmed her to the bones and softened the harsh lines of his face.

"It wouldn't matter. I couldn't reveal a thing, anyway. I have nothing to do with the company. I'm a nurse."

"My doctor never had a nurse like you." He paused. "Could I get you a drink?"

"Yes, thank you. A gin and tonic, please."

"Back in a minute." He left them, striding through the crowd to the bar at the far end of the room.

Cara turned to Jean. "I never thought I'd meet a famous ace reporter."

"Chris is a nice guy—a little tough sometimes, and once he's on the trail of something, he hangs on like a bulldog— but still he's nice." She paused, chewing uneasily at her lip. For a moment she seemed about to add to her statement, but then she shrugged, and her face cleared pleasantly. "I have to go now. I was about to leave when Ginny stopped me. It's a lovely party, and I've enjoyed talking to you, but unfortunately I have to sit in on a hearing tomorrow morning."

"It was nice to meet you," Cara said sincerely, and Jean raised a hand in a farewell gesture as she wound through the crowd.

Chris returned a moment later and handed Cara a frosty glass. Cara sipped at her drink, even more uncertain with this man now than before. What was it about him that unsettled her so? Having been around her sisters, she was used to older, sophisticated men. He was powerful, but once again, she had grown up around men with power and money. "Why don't we move into the other room? I think I spot a couple of empty chairs in there."

He pointed in the direction of the less-crowded dining room and, without waiting for her answer, put his hand beneath her elbow and guided her forward. A shiver ran up her arm and through her body at the touch of his hand, and Cara knew why he disturbed her so, although she hated to admit it. He possessed a magnetic sexuality that was perceivable clear across the room, and she had been drawn to him even before she heard the low, rough timbre of his voice or felt the touch of his sinewy fingers on her flesh. Hardly knowing him, Cara had responded to him, her own sensuality stirring involuntarily. It was surprising, almost frightening, to feel the reaction of her body to him, practically against her will. She had always prided herself on her cool control, and the ease with which he destroyed it set her on edge.

They sat at a corner of the long table, a good distance from the small group at the other end, and turned toward each other. Cara smiled at him—the calm, detached expression with which she greeted strangers—hoping to establish a certain distance from him, but she found herself distracted by his eyes. This close, she could see the shading from hazel to clear green and the startling sunburst ring of gold around the pupils, and she was mesmerized. He spoke, pulling her from her trance. "So tell me about yourself, Cara Stone. Who and what are you besides an oil heiress?"

She shrugged. "I don't think of myself that way. I'm a nurse. I was working at a small hospital in Dallas, but now I'm thinking of going to graduate school."

"Why?"

Cara related her struggle with Dr. Cummings and her subsequent doubts about her career plans. "Ginny wants me to go to one of the universities in D.C. She's been urging me to stay a few days longer and look at the colleges here."

"And are you?"

24

"I don't know." She glanced away, suddenly aware of how very much she wanted to stay in Washington for a few more days.

He changed the subject easily, sensing her confusion. "But you must be something more than a nurse. Tell me about your family."

"Well, Alec Stone is my father, and Ginny's my mother. My oldest sister is Alexis. That's her in the pale yellow dress talking to the white-haired man. And Morgan is my other sister, the beautiful woman in green sitting on the love seat. Alexis is the brains of the family, very bright, hard-working and ambitious. But Morgan is the beauty. She loves clothes and parties. She's Ginny's girl, and Alexis is Daddy's."

"And where do you fit in with this family group?"

Cara paused for a moment, her head cocked to one side in thought. "Actually, I don't think I fit very well with them. I'm the odd one out. I'm five years younger than Morgan, and when we were children, I was too young for Morgan and Alexis to want me around. I never had a role, like the others. Daddy once said he didn't understand me at all. He could see being an achiever like Alexis or ornamental like Morgan, but to want to be a nurse!"

Wozniak laughed. "Definitely a low form of life."

"Absolutely. Helping people is not Daddy's idea of a job."

"You're an unusual woman."

"Why do you say that?"

"I expected you to be shallow and self-centered when Jean said who you were."

"Ah, the typical oil heiress. Tell me, how many oil heiresses do you know?" Her tone was lightly mocking, her eyes twinkling.

His mouth drew down grimly. "Not many. But believe me, I've had some experience with rich girls, and you're a welcome change."

A wave of warmth swept over Cara at his words, and she felt suddenly shy. She realized how intimately she had been talking with him, telling him things about herself she had never mentioned even to close friends. She glanced down into her drink and aimlessly stirred the swizzle stick. "I don't know why you don't think I'm self-centered. I've been chattering on about myself like an idiot. Tell me about you."

"Me?" He hesitated, then began slowly. "I'm from Pennsylvania. A small factory town, the sort of place where the wealthy lived in one spot, and the workers lived across the tracks—the Polish here, the Italians there, the Czechs in another area. Dad worked in the factory all his life, and my mother did her best to raise nine kids."

"Nine children! Oh, the poor woman."

"Yeah, but at that time and place it wasn't unusual. All our neighbors had big families, too, although nine was a bit excessive. Mama died three years ago of cancer, and Dad didn't last long afterward. I was the ambitious child. I wanted to get out, be somebody, do something. I went to a small Catholic college in New York, and when I graduated, I worked on a newspaper in Albany. I zeroed in on the political news, and after a while I managed to get a job on the *Post*. So here I am. A rather dissimilar background to yours."

"Yes, I guess so. But tell me more about your family. Big families fascinate me. How did your mother handle it? What was she like?"

"She was tough, and she ruled us with an iron fist. We knelt and said the rosary every morning before breakfast, no matter what. Mass every Sunday and holy-day, confession every Saturday, and if the nuns reprimanded me at school, I'd get a whipping when I got home for making trouble for the sisters. The Poles believe in suffering on earth and getting your reward in heaven . . . or at least my mother did. She was from the old country and came to the States on an immigrant ship when she was three or four years old. Her family were refugees from World War One."

"What kind of man was your father? Hard like your mother?"

Chris frowned in thought. "He could be, but he was more a quiet, retiring man who once in a while would fly into a temper. He was always serious, grave and not at all expressive or affectionate. But when I graduated from college, he hugged me and had tears in his eyes." A faint smile touched his lips. "There, you probably know more about me than anyone in this city. Usually I'm the one who gets the information."

"That's because you're easy to talk to."

Slowly he ran his forefinger along the line of her cheek and jaw, and Cara's breath caught in her throat. There was something dark and unreadable in his eyes, smoldering and almost pained. Abruptly he removed his hand. "Would you like to dance?"

Cara nodded, and they went outside. She was intensely aware of his square, hard hand against the small of her back, propelling her onto the dance floor. Then he pulled her into his arms, and she could feel the rough tweed of his jacket against her skin, smell the delicious male scent of him. It was a slow dance, and he held her closely. Her breasts pushed against his chest, their legs pressed together, and the closeness made her tremble. The dance finished, but he did not release her, and Cara glanced up questioningly. His face hovered above her, eyes blazing down at her, his heavy, sensual mouth moving closer. Cara knew he was going to kiss her, and she closed her eyes in anticipation, offering up her soft mouth.

Suddenly he released her and stepped back. Cara opened her eyes in astonishment. Chris's face was grim, his mouth tight. "I . . . I'm sorry, but I have to leave now. I'm afraid I have another commitment."

Cara stared, trying to marshal her scattered wits. "Oh. Well . . . uh, I enjoyed meeting you."

"Thank you for your conversation and your company." He clasped her hand tightly for a moment and smiled with an expression that did not reach his eyes. Then he turned and was gone, leaving Cara staring after him.

* * *

27

The following day Cara went with the rest of her family on a quick tour of Washington, ending with a visit to the Smithsonian Institution. She could not keep her mind from straying to thoughts of Chris Wozniak. He had seemed interested in her, and she had been immediately attracted to him, uncomfortably so. Yet after their pleasant, revealing conversation, he had left abruptly, almost as if he wanted to get away from her. She told herself not to worry about it, that she hardly knew the man, and whether he liked her wasn't a matter of importance to her. But then she would see him again in her mind's eye—the strong, rough face; the green eyes; the mobile mouth; and she would remember the shock that ran through her when he touched her hand.

"Cara, where are you?" Morgan's amused voice cut into her thoughts.

"What?"

"You've been staring at Mamie Eisenhower's inaugural dress for five minutes. Surely you aren't that interested in the fashions of the fifties."

"Oh." Cara felt a betraying blush creep up her throat. "I was thinking about Chris Wozniak."

"Who?"

"A man I met at the party last night." Cara replied as casually as she was able and sauntered past the glassed-in case of first ladies' inaugural gowns toward Alexis, Paul and the two men who were far ahead of them.

"You mean the man who was talking to you in the dining room?" Morgan pursued the point, quickly on the trail of romance. "Brown hair and a tweed jacket?"

"That's him."

"Who is he? I couldn't decide if he was a member of the Mafia or an F.B.I. agent."

Cara laughed. "Oh, Morgan, he doesn't look mean."

"Well, he has a sort of rough-and-tumble appearance, like Tommy Lee Jones. Kind of sexy, but I'm not sure I'd want to get mixed up with him. Of course, my taste runs more to playboys than the dangerous type."

"For your information, he's an investigative reporter. He wrote a book about graft in government agencies."

"I knew his name sounded familiar. *Inside Job* was the name of the book, wasn't it?"

"Yeah. And a few months ago I read a magazine article of his about an embezzlement at a large bank. It was awfully good."

"An investigative reporter, huh? Well, that could fit his face. Tell me more about him. Are you interested in him? Is he after you? What went on?"

Cara chuckled. "Don't blow it up into a big romance, Morgan. Honestly, you're as bad as Ginny. I'm sort of interested in him. He's . . . different."

"From what?"

"Oh, from the men I'm used to—college guys, professors, Daddy's friends, the kids I grew up with. He's Polish-American and grew up in a factory town in Pennsylvania."

"Aha! A Yankee. This may be serious. I always knew you'd fall for a Yankee. You've had a crush on Dustin Hoffman since you were thirteen," Morgan teased gently.

Cara grimaced. "Come off it. Anyway, he's unusual, out of the ordinary. He intrigues me, but I don't think I've *fallen* for him."

"Is he going to call you?"

"I don't know."

"That's what you were concentrating on awhile ago?"

"Yes, I was thinking about it," Cara replied with mock exasperation.

"If you're going back to Dallas tomorrow with the rest of us, seeing him again could be difficult. Maybe you ought to take Ginny up on her suggestion and spend a few days with her."

"On the off chance that a man I scarcely know may call me?"

Morgan shrugged. "What's the harm? Unless you honestly don't care whether you see him again. Ginny would love to have you stay. If you need an excuse you could look at the colleges around here to see if you'd like to apply to one of them. It's not as if you had to get home quickly."

"Maybe. I might be interested in the graduate schools, and since I'm in a state of confusion about what to do, I could be confused here as easily as at home."

"Sure. Ginny would be thrilled."

"Okay. I'll think about it."

The more Cara considered Morgan's idea, the more it appealed to her. By the time they returned to Ginny's house, Cara had decided to stay. Ginny beamed and insisted that Cara immediately call the airline to change her reservation. The next afternoon Ginny and Cara took the others to the airport and waved them off.

When the rest of the family was gone, Ginny squeezed Cara affectionately. "It's easier to watch my other children leave when I know you're staying. We'll have such fun. We can run down to Virginia if you want and look at some of the old plantations. And you can explore the colleges. Maybe we'll even go on another shopping spree."

Cara groaned. "Not that. Anything but that."

Ginny laughed. "Unnatural child."

They left the airport and drove back to Ginny's Arlington home, battling the thick Washington traffic. When they reached the house, it was time for supper, and Ginny whipped up a quick tuna salad for the two of them, explaining that Wilson would not be home until late that evening. After they ate, Cara scraped the dishes and stacked them in the dishwasher, then glanced at the clock and sighed inwardly. She couldn't deny that she was waiting for Chris to call.

No matter how she chided herself, Cara would jump whenever the phone rang, her stomach fluttering in anticipation. But he had not called, even though two days had elapsed since the party. Face the fact that he isn't going to phone, her inner voice commanded sternly. After all, you didn't stay here just to see him. There were lots of good reasons. Yet she drooped with disappointment. Had she been mistaken about the interest in his eyes? Had he merely been passing time at a party?

The telephone on the wall close by trilled loudly. Cara jumped. Firmly she pushed down her hopes, set the last glass in the washer and strolled into the den, where Ginny had answered the phone. Her mother turned toward Cara with a bright expression. "Just a minute. Here she is." She extended the receiver to Cara, one hand across the mouthpiece. "It's Chris Wozniak. Do you know him?"

Cara's heart began to pound furiously, and she swallowed. "Yes, I met him at your party." She took the receiver with trembling hands. "Hello?"

"Cara. I wasn't sure you would still be there. I thought you might have gone back to Dallas."

"No. I decided to spend a few more days with my mother and visit the universities here."

"Good. That's why I was calling. I'd like to show you around, if it's all right with you."

"Yes, I'd like it very much," Cara said, struggling to suppress the eagerness in her voice.

"Great. Tuesday? Wednesday?"

"Either would be fine."

"Tuesday morning, then. I'll pick you up, say, at ten o'clock?"

"Yes. Great." Mentally Cara cursed herself for sounding like an idiot. Why couldn't she think of anything to say?

"Good-bye."

"'Bye." There was a click and a buzz on the other end of the line, and Cara set the receiver back in its cradle.

"What was that about?"

"He wants to take me to the colleges."

"Well, how nice. He's someone Wilson knows. I'm not sure I've met him. He was at the party?"

"Yes. He was . . . very nice."

"And he's interested in you?" Cara shrugged, and Ginny continued. "Of course he is. I hope you're interested in him, too. If I can't persuade you to stay here, maybe he can."

Cara smiled perfunctorily. Inside she was a strange combination of hot and cold, and she wanted to dash up to her room to select an eye-catching outfit for Tuesday. Chris's call had sent her sensible barriers tumbling, and Cara was flooded with excitement. In two more days she would see him again!

"You know, Ginny, maybe we should go shopping tomorrow."

Chapter 3

Cara dressed carefully in the blue slacks and light blue short-sleeved sweater she had bought the day before, applied touches of lipstick and mascara and brushed her long hair one last time. The outfit showed off her figure and enhanced her eyes. Wetting her lips nervously, she went downstairs to await Chris's arrival.

Ginny, who was sitting in the den reading her mail, looked up and smiled. "My, you look pretty. I always longed to have color like that in my cheeks and never could achieve it. Yet you and Alec have it without even trying."

"Luck of the draw, Ginny," Cara replied a little breathlessly.

"Are you all right? You sound nervous."

"I am."

"Why? Usually you're as unflappable as Morgan."

"I don't know. Maybe because he's older than the men I usually date. And he's different. I feel like I need to be on my toes."

33

"Maybe it's because you like him better."

"I swear—you and Morgan! You two must have radar where romance is concerned. Am I that obvious?"

"No. Like you said, I have radar."

The doorbell rang, cutting off whatever else Ginny might have said, and Cara sprang up gratefully. She hurried to the foyer, stopping to take a deep breath before she pulled open the heavy oak-and-glass door. Chris lounged on the doorstep. He was dressed in jeans, a white shirt and a dark green sleeveless pullover sweater. When he saw her, a smile burst across his face, changing and warming it. Cara's heart lurched, and she wondered why she hadn't remembered exactly how green his eyes were, or the long lines beside his mouth that deepened almost into dimples when he smiled.

"Hi," she said inadequately, her bright face betraying the excitement her greeting didn't express. "Would you like to come in? Ginny would love to meet you. She didn't get a chance at the party."

"All right." He followed her into the den and was introduced to Ginny, then waded through a few minutes of obligatory chitchat. Afterward they went out to his car, a banged and battered Volkswagen. "Hope you don't mind the rattletrap," he commented as he opened the car door for her. "I use it for driving in town. I figure, why expose a beautiful new car to Washington traffic? I can take the fender-benders in this one, and I get good gas mileage."

Cara laughed. "I don't mind. I've never been much on fancy cars myself. In fact, I drive a Rabbit."

"I thought we'd go to Georgetown and George Washington universities first. They're the most likely prospects. I don't know if American has graduate studies in health. And Catholic University is mostly theological."

"Whatever you say."

"Nothing like an agreeable female." He paused and looked at her. "You know, you put one over on me the other night."

"What do you mean?" Cara glanced at him, surprised.

"I mean, the other night I thought you were a woman, but now I see you're a child."

"Oh." Cara's sparkling laughter rang out. "Well, I'm not a child. I *am* a full-grown woman, and a nurse, and I've been to college. So I couldn't be *that* young."

"How old?"

"Twenty-two," Cara admitted reluctantly.

He raised his eyes heavenward. "Just a babe."

"Any complaints?"

He shot her a quick sidelong look. "No. A few doubts, maybe."

"About what?"

He shrugged and changed the subject. "Have you done much sightseeing?"

"Some. We went to the Smithsonian and looked at a bunch of monuments—the Washington Monument, the Jefferson Memorial, the Lincoln Memorial, et cetera—and we drove around the Tidal Basin, but the cherry trees had already bloomed."

"We can go to East Potomac Park, if you like. It's lined with cherry trees that blossom a couple of weeks later than the Tidal Basin ones."

They went first to George Washington University, which lay in the heart of the downtown area, and walked around the campus, picking up application materials and a catalog at the administration building. After a brief lunch at a busy downtown delicatessen, Chris maneuvered through the heavy traffic, pointing out the various government buildings as they drove. Cara glanced over at him surreptitiously, her eyes drawn to the clean line of his thighs in the tight-fitting jeans. She had spent all morning looking at him and trying not to, wanting to reach out and caress his arm or let her hand drift through his thick brown hair. She literally ached for him to touch her and hold her molded against his lean body as he had the other night when they danced.

At the party he had stared at her with hot, hungry eyes and held her in a way that left no doubt that he wanted her. Frustratingly, he had made no move toward her today, not even taking her hand as they strolled over the campus. It was bewildering. Once she had turned to him suddenly and caught him watching her, the golden ring around his pupils blazing and his face a study in longing. Swiftly his expression had gone blank and his eyes become unreadable, changing so immediately to friendly interest that Cara wondered if she had merely imagined the previous look. It was crazy, she admonished herself, to be so drawn to this man. He obviously thought their relationship that of acquaintances, perhaps friends at best. She would be returning to Dallas soon and would probably never see him again. It was silly to wish for anything between them. And yet . . . her stomach tightened with desire when she looked at him, and she wanted very badly for him to kiss her.

Chris entered a tricky traffic circle that made Cara close her eyes. He chuckled. "What's the matter? I thought you were a city girl."

"I am. I can take expressways. It's this wild downtown driving that gets me."

"Washington traffic is tough," he admitted. "But in what other major city do you have such parks and wide expanses of land between buildings?"

"Not to mention stately buildings, statues and places of historical note," Cara added teasingly. "I agree. There is something very appealing about it."

"When I came to work here, I thought I'd landed in heaven." His hazel eyes unexpectedly sparkled. "The city, the politics, all the stories running around begging to be written, the cosmopolitan people—" His eyes darkened, and he halted abruptly. "Enough reminiscing. We're entering Georgetown now. Would you like to drive around and look at the houses? There are some beautifully restored homes here. Then we'll hit Georgetown University."

Cara craned her neck to peer at the homes they passed, while Chris threw in bits of historical information and named the more famous residents of some of the houses. "You know everyone," she marveled.

"That's my business—to know everybody and everything that goes on."

"That's what you said about your mother."

He grinned. "You caught me. Had enough?"

"I think so. I'm beginning to get dizzy from looking."

They drove along a row of quaint shops and parked so they could walk to the picturesque Georgetown University campus, which sat on a bluff overlooking the Potomac River. As they strolled past the old buildings, Chris related some of the college's history. "This, in case you don't know it, is the oldest Catholic college in the United States. It's a Jesuit school and of course once was all-male, but now it's coed. I believe their nursing program is one of the best in the country."

"I've heard. Whew! Let's sit down for a minute." Cara sank onto a stone bench, and he joined her. "I enjoy sitting and watching people walk by. People fascinate me. Everyone is so different, so singular. I like to watch their faces and mannerisms and speculate about their lives and families. I see some couples and wonder what in the world they like in each other. They appear so different from each other, ill suited, and yet some quality brought them together."

"Insanity, probably," Chris stated flatly.

Cara grimaced. "No, I think, no matter how dissimilar a couple appears, deep down there must be a similarity or a . . . a matching of qualities that makes them love one another." His fingers touched her hair in a feather-light caress, and Cara turned, startled. Quickly he snatched his hand away.

"Spoken like a twenty-two-year-old." He continued lightly, "More likely they see what they want to, imagine things that don't exist in the other person, but the blinders fall off after it's too late. Then they realize they've made a ghastly mistake, which they'll pay for for the rest of their lives."

Cara stared at him, surprised by the gravity of his tone. There must be a bitter incident in his past that provoked his words, Cara thought, but after one look at his closed, set face and darkened eyes, she shut her mouth on her questions. Anything she asked now would seem unwelcome prying to him. Instead she countered lightly, "Thus speaks the cynic. It must be the newspaper reporter in you."

"I suppose." He smiled at her, although the tightness did not entirely leave his face. "It's hard to escape reality when you report the news. Particularly the kind I write—it's all scandal and corruption. You can't believe what anyone says, even the people who are your sources. As likely as not, they're after someone for personal gain."

"It doesn't sound very attractive."

"There is satisfaction in the job. I enjoy being a detective, sifting through things to find the truth. Sometimes it's tedious, even boring. I'll follow a lot of wrong leads and come up with nothing. But when I hit it, when the big story suddenly unfolds in my head or I get the missing piece of information I need, there's nothing quite the same."

"Is that why you do it? For the excitement?"

"Partly. I enjoy it. In fact, I think I need it. Does that make me hard? I guess I am. I'm not particularly inclined to pity. I leave that to people like you, who want to take care of everyone." A smile softened his face, and he reached out to run a finger along her jawline. "Don't get me wrong. I'm very glad there are people like you, or the rest of us would suffer."

A tingle ran along Cara's skin where he touched her. For a moment her breath stopped, then picked up again in quicker spurts. "Somehow," she said breathlessly, "I don't think you're as tough and cynical as you like to make out."

"Oh?" He quirked an eyebrow sardonically at her. "That's probably just as well for me. Tell me, is there some cowboy back in Texas waiting anxiously for you?"

"Not that I know of," Cara replied honestly. "For one thing, I don't know any cowboys. Anyway, there's no one waiting for me."

"No panting young man after you? I find that hard to believe."

Cara shrugged. "I'm scarcely a femme fatale."

"Maybe not. But you're very desirable." The golden ring around his pupils darkened as his gaze went to her mobile mouth.

Cara's heart began to trip wildly within her chest. ". . . Thank you. I've always considered myself the ugly duckling."

"Why on earth?"

"You've seen my sisters, especially Morgan. My hair was the wrong color, and I wasn't tall and slim enough. I hardly dated in high school. I wasn't pretty like a teenage girl is supposed to be."

"You're striking."

"Tell that to a seventeen-year-old. When I went to college, I discovered that I was attractive to some men—older ones like seniors or graduate students." She chuckled. "One of my professors tried to date me. Maybe men have to grow into my kind of looks."

"You're probably too much of a threat to the young male psyche," Chris agreed with a grin, rising from the bench. "But believe me, you appeal to more mature men."

Cara stood up also, the heat rising treacherously in her face. They strolled back across the campus and out to his car. When they were settled inside, he pulled into the traffic and spoke without looking at her. "My apartment is nearby. Would you like to come up for a drink? Then I thought we might go out to dinner."

"All right." Surprisingly her voice remained calm, but inside, Cara's nerves danced with tense excitement. She had dated frequently in college, but none of the men there had prepared her for Chris. She couldn't figure out what he wanted from her. At times his voice was low and intimate and his green eyes caressed her, and she'd be positive he wanted her. Then, abruptly, he would become distant, remote, almost unaware of her. What did he intend by inviting her to his apartment? Simply a friendly drink? Or would it lead to something far more delightful . . . and, she suspected, dangerous?

His apartment occupied the second floor of an old three-story town house in Georgetown. It had been renovated inside and out. The aged brick was painted a creamy beige and highlighted by tomato-color wooden shutters on the windows. Fan-shape stairs led to the stoop, and the front door was a heavy oak affair with leaded glass panes in the top quarter. Chris opened the door and led her up antique mahogany-banistered stairs to the second story.

His apartment retained the original hardwood floors, gleaming with the patina of age. A large blue-toned Oriental rug adorned the living room. The place was sparsely but tastefully furnished with heavy antiques. Cara exclaimed over the rich mahogany furniture and followed him on a tour through the small apartment. A massive wardrobe in his bedroom caught her attention, but she quickly averted her eyes from the high, colonial-style bed. He had turned the other bedroom into a study, which was dominated by a large oak roll-top desk. A bank of glassed-in legal bookshelves adorned one wall of the study, and an oak library table stood by the window. It was covered by a profusion of scattered papers, pens and a large typewriter.

"It's beautiful," Cara said honestly. "Do you refinish your own furniture?"

He laughed shortly. "Hardly. I'm afraid I don't have the skill or the patience. I like to look at antiques, though, and this part of the country is a collector's dream. But you haven't seen my prize possession—an old pie safe I've turned into my bar."

Cara followed him into the living room and saw, against one wall, the antique pie safe with its holed doors. "It's lovely."

"For some reason I love these things. This one was in better condition than most I've found." He caressed the wood almost lovingly, then opened the door to reveal rows of bottles and glasses doubled by the mirror on the back wall of the cabinet. "Would you like a drink? It was gin and tonic, wasn't it?"

"Yes, that's fine. I'm surprised you remember."

"I probably should say that I hung on your every word, but the truth is I always remember details." He handed her the drink and turned back to the bar to mix a Scotch and soda.

Cara wandered from the cabinet to the grouping of furniture on the Oriental rug and sat down on the dark blue couch. "I notice your couch is the only concession to modernity," she commented, settling into the thick, lush cushion.

"Yes. Antique sofas are damned uncomfortable—hard and about six inches off the floor." He came to stand before Cara, studying her for a moment before he sat down.

She shifted uncomfortably, suddenly shy and unable to think of anything to say. "Thank you for the tour today. It was very nice of you," she began, then could have bitten her tongue for the stilted, almost prim sound in her voice.

"It was my pleasure, I assure you."

Cara looked at his rough, hard face. There was no answer to her questions there. His eyes were hooded and unreadable.

"You're very different. When I saw you at the party, I couldn't take my eyes off you. I had to meet you. You intrigued me."

Cara fought the embarrassment and pleasure that flooded her at his words, striving for a cool, unconcerned interest. "Really? Why?"

He grinned. "Not for your icy sophistication."

Cara set down her drink. "I'm sorry. Do I amuse you? Is that why you asked me out today? So you could make fun of my naivete?"

"Hold on. Don't get carried away." He placed his glass beside Cara's and grasped both her hands in his. "I mean it's you as you are that interests me, not some role you try to play."

"I wasn't playing a role!" she protested. "I didn't know how to reply to your statement. I hate to appear a complete fool. You obviously think I'm young and naive and—"

"And refreshing." Slowly, insidiously, his thumbs stroked

41

the insides of her wrists. "You aren't jaded and hard. Your cheeks glow, and your face changes with every feeling you experience." He raised her hands to his lips and softly kissed the palm of each, and the thin skin inside her wrist. Cara knew he must feel the swift beat of her pulse against his lips. She trembled at the soft brush of his mouth. "Your eyes are the brightest, clearest blue I've ever seen, and your hair—God, your hair is lovely. Shining and thick. The other night I wanted to unpin it and bury my face in it."

He released her wrists and smoothed his hands down her hair, cupping her face and neck below her jaw. Gently his forefingers teased at her neck and ears while his eyes roamed her features hungrily. The blood hammered in Cara's ears as she watched him, waiting, tremulous. Slowly, inexorably, he bent and kissed her, his mouth warm and soft upon hers, yet insistent and demanding. She responded eagerly, opening her mouth to the hot possession of his tongue, and his kiss deepened. His hands slid down her neck and shoulders, caressing her with velvet desire. They slipped inside the neckline of her sweater, spreading fingers wide over her bare skin. His mouth left hers to travel across her cheek to her ear, and he nibbled gently at her sensitive lobe. His lips trailed down the tender flesh of her throat, tasting, nipping, until the edge of her sweater stopped him. With a groan he buried his head against her breasts.

"Cara, Cara," his words were thick and mumbled. "God, I want you. I can't remember wanting another woman this badly . . . I wasn't going to call you or see you again, but I couldn't stop thinking of you. I tried to write, but the words wouldn't come. Whatever I did, there you were, soft and tempting, smiling with those lips that make me ache to kiss you, beckoning me, tormenting me." Suddenly Chris broke from her and stood, reaching down to lift Cara up. He sank his hands into her hair, holding her head fixed as he gazed deep into her eyes. "You're so young. This is probably the worst mistake I've ever made. But I have to . . ."

His lips swooped down, cutting off his words, grinding

into her, discovering her mouth anew with lips and teeth and tongue. She clung to him, dizzy with passion. Wrapping her hair around one hand, he pressed Cara even closer to him, molding her body against his iron chest and muscled legs. His molten lips covered her face and neck while his hands crept lower to squeeze and caress her buttocks. White-hot flames burst in Cara, and she shook from the force of it. "Chris," she moaned. "Oh, Chris."

Quickly he stripped off her sweater and bra and fumbled at the waistband of her trousers, his eyes riveted on the rise and fall of her breasts. Under his gaze, her full, pink-brown nipples rose and hardened, pointing with desire. When at last Chris unfastened her trousers, he whisked them off and carried her easily into the bedroom. There he laid her tenderly on the bed and slipped the pale blue wisp of underwear from her body, revealing every soft, lush inch of her skin to his hungry eyes. His hot gaze did not stray from her as he tore off the remainder of his own clothes and joined her on the bed. "Cara, you're so beautiful," he whispered, his voice almost reverent.

Slowly, savoring every moment, Chris ran his hands over her flesh, cupping her breasts and sensuously tracing her nipples with his thumbs, trailing his fingers down the flat plane of her abdomen and slipping in between her legs. Cara sucked in her breath at the magic of his touch and closed her eyes, luxuriating in the delightful sensations he sent shooting through her. He bent to take one nipple in his mouth, rolling it between his lips, and all the while his hand never ceased its exploration. His lips left her breasts to roam her body, scorching her skin and stoking her passion until she thought that she would explode with pleasure. Cara stroked his firm back and shoulders helplessly, digging her fingers into him as she writhed beneath his ministrations. "Chris, please, please take me. I want you."

A groan sounded low in his throat, and Chris covered her, filling the aching void of her desire. Cara rotated her hips beneath him, her hands clutching at his back. His breath came hot and ragged, and his skin was slick with sweat.

He buried his face in her hair as he thrust them faster and faster into ever-spiraling delight. With a hoarse cry he reached his shuddering peak, and the movement ignited the powder keg that had been building inside Cara. A white-hot explosion thundered through her, and she arched against him. Chris wrapped his arms around her tightly until the wave washed over them and receded. Then, sighing, he rolled from her, sliding one arm beneath her head to cradle it in the hollow of his shoulder. They did not speak, still lost in the shattering pleasure they had experienced. He ran his hand through her long, tangled hair and twined it around his fingers. Softly they slid into sleep.

Cara awoke in Chris's arms, her head nestled on his shoulder, her hair streaming across his chest. For an instant she blinked uncertainly. Then the memories of the afternoon flooded in upon her, hot and sweet. She smiled and blushed at the same time. Although she was not totally inexperienced, she remembered nothing that had shaken her like Chris's lovemaking. Her entire world had trembled, and for a moment she had felt an utter peace, a complete oneness with him. Gently she disentangled herself from his arms and sat up, her arms clasped around her knees, remembering and savoring each precious moment. Her thoughts were interrupted by the light touch of Chris's hand upon her bare back. Lightly he traced the ridge of her backbone.

"A penny for your thoughts."

Cara turned to him with a grin. "I was thinking that we never did make it to see the cherry trees today."

He chuckled. "I can't say I'm sorry. You are one exciting woman, Cara Stone. Nobody else ever turned me inside out the way you do."

"Is that good?" she teased lightly.

"I don't know." He grasped her shoulders and pulled her down for a long, thorough kiss. "Mmm. If I weren't starving to death, I think I'd ask for a repeat."

Cara smiled sensuously, her teeth catching her full underlip. "Is food so important to you?"

Chris growled low in his throat and reached out to fondle her full breasts. She bent to touch her lips to his chest, the curtain of her hair spilling across his skin. She entangled her fingers in the thick mat of hair covering his chest and kissed his throat and chest, drifting from the plateau of ribs to the softer flesh of his stomach. He quivered involuntarily beneath her mouth, and the muscles in his arms bunched. Finally he sank one hand into her hair and forced her head up. "Vixen," he muttered, his eyes glowing green. "You've just forfeited your dinner."

His mouth consumed hers in a burning kiss that left Cara breathless. More leisurely this time, he caressed her with hands and lips and tongue, arousing her to the height of rapture, then letting her drift down from the peak to be raised once more. Cara moaned and twisted under his expert hands, twining her legs around him and raking her fingernails across his unyielding back, until at last she could stand the exquisite torture no more and begged him to take her. Then he came into her, hot and demanding, driving them both to the shivering unity of desire.

Chapter 4

Cara ran the brush through her hair while Chris leaned against the doorjamb, watching her as he buttoned his shirt. "All right, enough primping," he commanded, his words belied by the satiated softness of his usually stony face. "This time I have to eat or I'll start chewing on the bedpost."

She giggled, flashing a brilliant smile at him in the mirror. "I thought you said I'd forfeited my dinner."

"Ah, but not mine."

"Oh, I see." Cara made a face at him and turned. "I'm ready whenever you are."

They left the apartment and drove to a restaurant not far away. They said little as they rode, but Cara didn't mind. She was bathed in a warm glow, and the heat that had thrilled her veins went beyond words. At the moment she needed nothing more than to be with Chris and know that whenever she looked at him, the same spark leaped between them. He took her to a seafood restaurant that was casual enough so their attire did not seem out of place, but that served delicious food.

"Mmm," Cara commented, digging into her oysters. "You can't get oysters like this in Texas. The shrimp is good, but the oysters don't have the taste these do."

"Chesapeake Bay," he explained. "They're the best. I didn't know they had seafood in Texas."

Cara wrinkled her nose at him. "Ignorant Yankee. Texas borders on the gulf."

"That's true. Weird—Texas connotes the wide open spaces and scrub brush to me."

Cara laughed. "Not the part I'm from."

"The only experience I've had with Texans has been with politicians. You're delightfully different."

"How?"

"Aside from the fact that you're far prettier, you aren't wily and defensive. I have trouble getting past their barriers—you know, the good-old-boy camaraderie that doesn't reveal a thing."

"What sort of people tell you the most in interviews?"

"Hard to say. People who feel really guilty, usually. They're so uptight about *not* revealing something that they invariably let it slip out one way or another. It's too much on their minds. Then there are those who are proud of what they've done. They think they've been so clever or strong they can hardly bear not to tell me how well they did. One guy I talked to was very resistant at first, but I could tell he was about to burst with news. I started talking about something else, not touching on what he had done, and he grew impatient. I could see him shifting in his chair and cracking his knuckles. Soon he began to lead *me* toward the subject. He didn't say anything outright, but he kept hinting. By the time I slipped in some questions about his request forms for typewriters that weren't really bought, he answered easily. He was almost relieved that I'd finally gotten around to what he had done. He was very proud of the scam he'd been operating for years."

As they finished their meal, Cara noticed a man in the bar looking in their direction, peering around the rail separator. "Chris, there's a man who keeps staring at us. Is he someone you know?"

Chris half turned in his seat, scanning the bar area. Suddenly he smiled and gestured at the man, motioning him toward their table.

The man waved back, picked up his drink and came quickly. He was in his forties; his curly, dark hair was streaked with gray; very tall and slender, he walked with a slouch that made him appear both gauche and endearing. His smile was warm and lit up his kindly brown eyes. "Chris, how are you?"

"Hello, Dean. Cara, I want you to meet a friend of mine, Dean Lowenstern. Dean's an editor at the magazine that publishes most of my articles. Dean, this is Cara Stone."

"Cara." He nodded at her, his look openly curious and admiring but not offensive. "It's nice to meet you. How did you wind up with a bum like this?"

She smiled as Chris joked, "You're a real friend. Next time I'll leave you in the bar by yourself. Here, sit down and finish your drink with us. What are you doing out so late without Cynthia?"

Dean folded his lanky frame into a chair and answered sorrowfully. "She's deserted me again. She flew to Detroit to some kind of meeting Ford's having for its lawyers."

"Cynthia is Dean's wife," Chris explained in an aside to Cara. "She's with one of the best law firms in Washington."

"My second wife," Dean continued. "My ex couldn't have spelled *litigation* let alone done it. Jeannie is a beautiful woman but no Rhodes scholar."

They talked casually for a few moments, Chris and Dean reviewing people they knew and current events in the Capital. After a while Cara excused herself and made her way to the ladies' room. Dean observed her back with interest as she walked away. "Beautiful girl. Where in the world did you find her?"

"At a party Wilson Decker gave. She's his stepdaughter. Her father, by the way, is the Stone of Stone Oil."

"Don't try to tell me your interest in her is purely for the sake of your story."

Chris laughed. "Hardly. I haven't yet turned over anything Stone's done."

There was a pause, and Dean asked, "What about Monica?"

Chris shot him a dark look, his mouth tightening. "What about her?"

"Does she know about Cara?"

"No. How could she? And she's not going to know."

"Don't get me wrong," Dean began hastily. "Nobody who knows you and Monica could blame you. She's a class-A bitch and has given you hell for years." He raised a hand at Chris's glowering look. "I'm sorry. I'll quit. You're aware of my opinion on the matter. But I'm glad to see you with this girl. You haven't looked this relaxed since I've known you."

"Dean, someday that mouth of yours is going to get you into trouble," Chris remarked, but his tone was pleasant, almost disinterested.

"Here she comes. Well, I'll leave you two alone." Dean rose, politely held out Cara's chair for her and said his good-byes before he ambled back to the bar.

"I hope I didn't scare your friend off," Cara said anxiously. "Was I rude?"

Chris laughed shortly. "No. Besides, Dean is an ex-reporter. His hide's too thick to be pierced by mere rudeness. Let's say he was hit with an unexpected case of tact. He thought we might prefer to be alone."

They soon left to drive back to Ginny's house. Chris held her hand, now and then casually rubbing it against his cheek, but Cara sensed that his mind was elsewhere. "Are you chasing down a story in your head or what?" she asked lightly.

He turned toward her, his eyebrows going up. "What?"

"You seemed very far away."

"Oh. I was thinking about this weekend. Have you been to Virginia?"

"No."

"How would you like to take a weekend trip with me? We could drive into Virginia, look at all the spring flowers and trees, go to some of the old Tidewater plantations. We could see Williamsburg, Jamestown, Richmond, whatever you want."

Cara's heart swelled in her chest. With difficulty she managed to get out, "Yes, I'd like to very much."

"Good." He squeezed her hand. "I'll pick you up late Friday afternoon . . . if I can make it till then." He pulled into Ginny's driveway and cut off the engine. Raising Cara's hand to his lips, he gently kissed each fingertip. "You do something to me I can't describe." He closed his eyes and a sigh escaped his lips. "Oh, baby, I'm ten kinds of a heel. You'd be better off if you returned to Dallas and never saw me again."

"But I don't want to," she retorted. "I like it exactly where I am. Why are you such a heel?"

"Can't tell you, or then you *would* go back to Dallas." His grin was lopsided, curiously appealing yet almost bitter. He ran a hand over her hair. "I want you so much. Even now I'd like to drive back to my apartment and make love to you all over again. Cara . . ." He hooked his arm around her neck and pulled her to him. His mouth was eager and hot, and she wrapped her arms around his neck, content to stay in his arms forever if he wanted it. Finally he released her and swung out of the car.

They strolled to the front door, and again he took her in his arms, molding her body to him as his lips branded her in a lingering kiss. "I don't want to leave you," he murmured hoarsely. "I think I could make love to you all night and wake up in the morning wanting you."

Cara's laugh was throaty, beckoning. "I wouldn't mind."

"Don't tempt me." He gave her a quick, firm kiss and stepped back. After an instant's hesitation he swung on his heel and strode to the car. Cara watched him go until his car disappeared from sight. With a sigh that was part happiness, part loss, she unlocked the door and went inside. Friday seemed ages away.

* * *

"Cara, are you sure about this?" Ginny asked, her usually sunny voice tinged with worry. "You hardly know the man, after all." They were seated at the breakfast-room table, the remnants of lunch on the plates before them. Ginny absentmindedly ran one finger around the rim of her iced-tea glass, a frown creasing her forehead.

"I know it's not something a girl would have done in your day," Cara began patiently. "But going for a weekend trip with a man isn't the end of the world anymore."

"No, honestly, it's not that. I've tried to adjust to modern times. I knew about Morgan and Nick's affair, and I didn't come unglued."

"That was different because it was Nick."

"Of course I like Nick. But the important thing was that Morgan knew him. She understood the situation. You've barely met Chris. I'm afraid you're getting in too deep too quickly."

"Wilson knows him. He invited him to the party."

"All Wilson knows is that he's an influential reporter. You can invite a person to a party without thinking he's a suitable date for your daughter. Chris is quite a bit older than you are. He's thirty-five or thirty-six, and you're twenty-two. You haven't dated anyone that mature or sophisticated, have you?"

"No, but you're making it sound as if he's some dirty old man luring an innocent maiden into his lair. That's not the way it is at all. Thirteen years' difference isn't terrible. I don't have a father complex. I've always liked people who are older than I am, probably because I used to tag after Alexis and Morgan, trying to be the same age they were. Anyway, I feel comfortable with him."

"You always were mature for your age, I'll admit. But honey, I'm afraid you have more invested in this relationship than he does. You may be just another girl to him, but to you it's something special and wonderful."

"It *is* special and wonderful," Cara retorted. "I think he believes it is, too. But even if he doesn't, that's the way

I feel. So why should I deny myself the joy of this trip simply because later I might get hurt? I don't have stars in my eyes, Ginny. I'm not expecting him to fall madly in love with me and marry me. But I want to enjoy this experience to the fullest."

Ginny studied her daughter, thoughtfully chewing at her underlip. After a moment she smiled, although the worry lingered in her eyes. "If that's the way you feel, then I suggest you go up and start packing. It's past noon, you know. When's he coming?"

"I'm not sure. He said late this afternoon, but who knows exactly when that is?" Cara whisked the plates off the table and stacked them in the sink, then ran lightly upstairs to her bedroom. She did not pack quickly but took her time choosing her clothes. For one of the few times in her life, what she would wear seemed terribly important. She selected two casual slacks outfits, one pale pink and one bright red, that complemented her skin tones and hair, added a slinky nightgown she had spent several hours shopping for the day before, then tossed in accessories and underwear.

When she finished, Cara took a long, hot shower, emerging rosy and damp, toweled herself dry and slipped into soft, lacy blue underwear. She pulled on tight-fitting jeans and a pale yellow shirt that tied under her breasts and left her midriff bare. Next she combed out and dried her nearly waist length hair, a tiring process that often made her contemplate cutting it. When it was dry, she braided it in a single plait down her back, intertwining the strands with a yellow ribbon to match her shirt. She slipped into her sandals, put on lipstick and a touch of mascara, then checked to make sure she had packed everything. A quick dash of perfume at her throat and wrists completed her toilette. She carried her bag downstairs, joining Ginny in the den.

Chris arrived an hour later, dressed in blue jeans and a casual dark blue shirt. He looked lean, tough and thoroughly desirable, and when Cara answered the door, she retreated a step, suddenly shy. "Chris." What if his passion had waned? What if it had not been as strong as she imagined?

He smiled, his broad face lifting at the sight of her. "Is that all I get after three days?" He hooked one hand behind her neck and pulled her close for a deep kiss. Cara stood on tiptoe, pressing up into him, her lips clinging, her tongue exploring, remembering. When he released her, her cheeks were glowing, her mouth soft and full with awakened desire. "That's more like it." His eyes glittered, the gold rings flaming.

"I'll get my bag," Cara offered breathlessly and hurried into the den to fetch it. Waving a happy hand, she called good-bye to her mother and rejoined Chris at the door. He took the suitcase from her, and they left the house. A forest green Jaguar stood in the driveway. Cara stopped in astonishment. "You've got a different car!"

"I told you the bug was what I use for city driving. But on the road—now that's a different matter."

"It's gorgeous," Cara commented as she slid into the padded leather seat.

"Thank you." He stowed away the bag and slammed the trunk lid shut, then slid into the driver's seat and turned the ignition. The engine came to life with a purr. "Sounds a little different from the Volkswagen, too." They backed out of the drive and were soon headed south.

"Where are we going?" Cara asked as they left Arlington behind. Around them the countryside blossomed with tender new leaves and delicately flowering trees and bushes. The fragile white dogwood and red-purple redbuds shimmered in the breeze, and lavender wisteria hung draped like veils over the tall trees. "Oh, Chris, this is beautiful!"

"Isn't it? There's nothing like Virginia in the spring. We're going to a small country inn along the James River. It's hundreds of years old and once was the main house of a tobacco plantation. The family fell on hard times in the twentieth century, and a few years ago someone bought the house and turned it into a showplace. They give tours of it, and one wing was turned into a hotel."

"It sounds delightful."

"Tomorrow you have your choice of things to do. We

can see Jamestown, visit some of the old houses along the river or go into Williamsburg. We won't be far from Richmond, either, and there are hundreds of things there if you're a history buff."

"I don't know if I'd qualify as that, but I do love to look at old houses. And they're so amazingly old here. Except for San Antonio, everything in Texas has been built in the last hundred and fifty years. To see houses like some of those in Georgetown that are two or three hundred years old simply astounds me. I'm sure I'd like to do any of those things. You decide. You've been to them."

"We'll see how things go and make up our minds as the mood strikes us. Who knows—I might want to spend all day tomorrow in bed." He glanced sideways at her, his eyes dark and heavy lidded. Cara warmed under his gaze and unconsciously wet her lips. "My work went lousy this week," he went on. "I kept thinking about you, remembering our lovemaking, and all I wanted to do was take you to bed again."

"Why didn't you call me? I could have been persuaded to visit you."

"I was trying to exercise a little discipline. But I regretted it. In fact, right now I'd like to pull over to the side of the road and strip off every stitch of your clothes."

"That might provide quite a sight for the other cars," she teased, but her voice was tremulous.

"Then I'll have to wait until we reach the inn. But it's going to be far too long." He paused, his eyes intent on the road, his hands gripping the steering wheel until his knuckles whitened. "Let's change the subject or I may *have* to stop before we get there." Cara flushed and looked out the window. His desire for her was all too evident. "Tell me about your childhood, your parents or something."

She complied quickly, and they were soon deep in a discussion of their childhoods and growing up, conversing with the eagerness of strangers who want to know each other immediately and completely. It was only later that Cara noticed that she had done most of the talking, especially regarding the more recent past. They stopped for supper at a restaurant built to resemble a colonial tavern, staffed by waiters and waitresses in colonial dress. Every room had a fireplace, rustic wooden tables and pewter dishes hanging on the walls. The food was primarily hearty beef dishes, delicious but far too substantial for Cara, who finished only half of what was on her plate. However, she managed to make room for the hot homemade bread and some delicious old-fashioned pudding.

An hour or two later they approached the inn on a narrow, winding road closely edged with trees and redolent with the sweet smell of flowers. The two-story house was built of faded red brick and comprised three separate wings—the main rectangular edifice and a wing running back from either end. There was a chimney at each end of the wings. The steep roofs ended abruptly at the walls, with no overhang, and dormer windows were set into the slope of the roof. The dormers and shutters were painted white, and a small, white-columned porch jutted out from the main door. It was a plain, squarely built house, pure Williamsburg style, with no outcroppings or ornamentations. Yet there was a certain beauty to its austere simplicity, a quiet stateliness that spoke of age and craftsmanship.

"This is actually the rear entrance. The other side is prettier, has a more elegant door. The house was designed to face the river, where all the traffic came from in colonial times," Chris explained. "The center section is the original house. It was built in the early 1700s. The other two wings are quite new, merely dating from the 1840s. The right wing is the hotel. The rest of it is open to tours. We can walk through it tomorrow if you like. The guides tell numerous romantic legends about the place and the surrounding countryside. Most are palpably false, I'm sure, but they lend an aura to the house."

He drove around to the side, where a line of trees concealed a gravel parking lot for the guests. They parked and entered the side door, which led into the small, antique-furnished lobby. A woman in a mobcap and colonial-style

Summer Sky

dress showed them to their room, a small, high-ceilinged bedroom dominated by a massive four-poster pine bed.

"Look!" Cara cried, enchanted. "The bed is so high there are little steps to climb up into it."

Chris closed the door, smiling. "Yes. The rooms here are furnished with genuine antiques. What's more, they're all for sale."

"Really?" Cara scanned the room with interest. "Aren't they worried about people causing damage?"

Chris shrugged. "They have a select clientele."

"And they let us in?" Cara mocked.

"Imagine that. But you'd better be careful or they might kick us out."

Cara gave a deep sigh of pleasure as she walked to the bed and lay back on the mattress, contemplating the plaster-molded ceiling. "Why did they used to make ceilings so tall? Especially since the people were shorter?"

"I'm a reporter, not an architect," Chris retorted, walking to the bed. "Maybe it was cooler that way." Leaning over, he slid one hand across her bare stomach and up under the brief top, stroking and kneading her breasts. Cara closed her eyes, reveling in his rough hand upon her bare flesh. "No bra?"

"Can't wear one with this blouse."

He paused to unfasten the buttons and shove the two sides of fabric away, revealing her creamy breasts with their taut pink crowns. He stood watching her, his breath ragged in his throat. Cara unfastened the snap and zipper of her jeans and, arching her pelvis, slowly slid them down her legs. Chris's eyes gleamed but he made no move, enjoying the tormenting pleasure of looking at her slowly undress. With a kick Cara shed her sandals and sent the denim trousers to the floor. Only the flimsy blue panties remained, and she leisurely drew them off as she had the jeans, never rising from the bed, only thrusting up her buttocks to slip them past. With a low noise Chris reached and dispatched the scrap of material. "Tease," he said without animosity. Cara smiled and stretched, pulling her stomach and breasts tight.

Quickly Chris divested himself of his clothes, adding them to the heap on the floor. He straddled Cara, covering her breasts with his hands, his face flushed and rapt above her. Sliding his hands beneath her, he lifted her and buried his face in her breasts. His mouth ran free across her, nibbling at her neck and ears, kissing and teasing her breasts until the nipples stood hard and proud, and finally his mouth came to rest on her own, dominating, commanding. Cara wrapped her arms around him, thrusting her body against his, pressing bone to bone and sinew to sinew. His desire was hard upon her soft flesh, and its touch aroused her. Cara wiggled her hips, circling and stroking, until he moaned and ground his pelvis into her.

"Cara, Cara." He kissed her deeply and rolled from atop her, his hand seeking the tender, responsive flesh of her womanhood. Gently his fingers aroused her as his tongue did her mouth. Cara's legs moved restlessly, and she burned to feel his strength inside her, but he did not fulfill her immediately. Instead his hand continued its sensual massage as his mouth moved lower to seek a rose-tipped breast. Heat built in Cara, focusing on the caress of his hand, swelling and demanding, until she trembled all over, her need swirling away every other thought and feeling. She was hunger only. Outside her nothing existed but the hand that pleasured and denied her. She arched her back, seeking the satisfaction only he could give, and at last the joy erupted within her. She stifled her cry against his shoulder, her teeth sinking heedlessly into his flesh.

The tiny stab of pain aroused Chris further. He lay back and moved her on top of him, impaling her on the thick, throbbing shaft.

"Slowly," he whispered, and she obeyed, moving gently, almost infinitesimally upon him, pulling up and sliding down, weaving from side to side, each movement deliberate and slow. His face contorted, and he sank his hands into her hair, wrapping the silken threads around his fingers and wrists. Sweat popped out on his brow, and a groan escaped him. "Oh, baby. Sweet—" His chest heaved, and his hair glistened and curled damply. Cara bent down, her hips still rotating rhythmically, and circled one nipple, then the other, with her tongue. He gasped something unintelligible, and she took the hard button of flesh in her mouth, sucking and stroking. Chris gave a hoarse cry and thrust up hard. Cara clung to him and moved against his strokes, further igniting his passion until at last it burst in a cataclysm of delight that shook them both, leaving them trembling and weak.

Chris cradled her in his arms as their breathing slowly eased. Cara released a shuddering sigh and brushed her lips against his skin. It took all her will to bite back the words that rose to her lips. "My love."

The next morning they ate a hearty breakfast in the restaurant on the ground floor of the hotel, downing salty Virginia ham and fresh hot biscuits dripping with butter and honey. "I feel guilty," Cara moaned, eyeing the dwindling food. "It'll take a week of dieting to repair this damage."

"We'll tramp around Williamsburg today and work it off," Chris promised. "What would you like to do first?"

"After this breakfast? Take a nap," Cara said and laughed. "No, I think I'd like to tour the house first. It looks like the epitome of an early Virginia plantation home."

They walked around to the front of the building and joined a tour. Their guide was another woman dressed in white mobcap, long gown and long white apron, although the modern hairdo showing beneath the cap spoiled the colonial effect. "Colby House was built in 1654 by John Emerson Colby, the founder of the Virginia family. He was awarded a substantial land grant by the king and sailed to Virginia in 1644 with his wife Elizabeth and their two children. Elizabeth caught swamp fever soon after they arrived and died within the year. In 1646 John remarried, this time to the young daughter of a neighboring family, Mary Ann Chastain. Mary Ann and John had six children. The original house was located about a hundred yards downstream, where the dock is. Later John built this home as a showplace for his fast-growing wealth. We are now standing in the foyer of Colby House. You will notice the hand-painted porcelain doorknob and matching keyhole cover. These were added in the 1840s by Hyram Colby, the wealthiest of the clan. Let us go into the front drawing room . . ."

The woman maintained a continuous chatter as they passed from room to room, pointing out the colors of the walls and the antique furniture and adding gossipy bits of information about the various inhabitants of the home. In one small bedroom she paused dramatically and informed them, "This is known as Miss Cressy's room. It was intended as the nursery for the children of Cressida and Benjamin Colby, but all three of their children were stillborn or died shortly after birth. Cressida, known to her family and servants as Miss Cressy, also died bearing the third child. It is rumored that in later years her ghost would walk down the hall into the room and weep over her lost babies."

Cara shivered, and Chris grinned at her. "Probably apocryphal."

"Well, it gives me the goose bumps anyway," she whispered back.

The tour wound through the upstairs rooms and ended with a trip down the back stairs and through the kitchen to the river side of Colby House. The guide pointed to the small outbuildings necessary for the upkeep of the plantation: the stables and smithy, the icehouse, the smokehouse, the cooking kitchen, the underground vegetable cellar and the cistern. When the hostess finally released them, Cara sagged against Chris. "Whew! I'm exhausted."

"You want to go back to our room and rest?"

She shot him a doubtful glance. "Somehow I don't think I'd get any rest there."

He chuckled. "Probably not. Shall we return?"

Cara smiled and linked her arm through his. "Why not?"

Chapter 5

Later that afternoon they drove to the small town of Williamsburg, where they walked through the reconstructed colonial town that had been financed by John D. Rockefeller. Except for the other tourists, it was like stepping back in time. The shops, the houses and the people who worked in them looked authentically colonial. After they finished their tour of the village, they strolled across the tree-shaded campus of William and Mary, soaking in the aura of the old school. Following a leisurely dinner in Williamsburg, they drove back to the inn. Cara leaned back, watching the darkened trees rush by, filled with a joy that was both excited and peaceful. Ginny was right. She was falling in love. No, it had gone further than that. She might as well admit that she was already lost, head over heels in love with Chris Wozniak. It was utter bliss to watch him talk, to see the movement of his long, thin fingers and the quirk of his mouth. Right now she could ask for nothing more than to be with him and happily anticipate the night ahead.

They parked in the gravel lot and walked among the trees
to reach the inn, Chris's arm casually, securely around her
shoulders. Cara reached up with one hand and covered the
hard, sinewy hand that rested on her arm. "These don't feel
like a reporter's hands," she teased.

"No?" He grinned quizzically: "And what do a reporter's
hands feel like?"

"Not rough, like someone's who's worked with his
hands."

"Oh, I see. Well, I wasn't born a reporter. It's only in
recent years that I've led a soft life. When I was a teenager,
I worked at the factory. And I was athletic. I was planning
on playing third base for the Pirates."

"So you were a baseball player, huh?"

He chuckled. "Until reality intruded on my dreams—
namely having to get a job."

"How'd you go from baseball and the factory to jour-
nalism?"

"I went to college and found my niche, I guess. Jour-
nalism and athletics require similar characteristics—com-
petitiveness and stubbornness."

"I suspect you have both qualities in abundance," Cara
told him with a mischievous grin. They entered the lobby
and climbed the wide, curving staircase. On the landing she
paused and leaned against the banister to gaze down upon
the antique lobby. "Isn't it lovely? I can't remember when
I've been this happy." She turned to Chris and caught him
watching her intently, his green eyes boring into her as if
to lay bare her soul. "Why are you looking at me like that?"

He frowned slightly and did not answer. His lean hands
came up to cup her face. "You're beautiful. I want you so
bad it scares me. Cara, I never thought, never dreamed . . ."
He broke off suddenly and bent to kiss her, his mouth
scorching, hungry. After a long, blood-pounding moment
he pulled away and took her hand to lead her upstairs. They
ran into their room and shut the door. Cara lifted her arms
to Chris, and he seized her in a fierce embrace. His lips
played across her face and neck, sending tremors of spar-

kling desire through her. Quickly they tugged off their encumbering clothing and tumbled onto the high bed, arms and legs entwined, suddenly as hot and impatient as if they were coming together for the first time. Chris covered her with the weight of his body, and she accepted him eagerly. Afloat on a molten wave of lovemaking, they surged ever higher, exploding at last in shattering unity.

Afterward Cara lay quietly in Chris's arms, and his hand strayed through her hair, parting the strands and letting them slide through his fingers. "Oh, Cara," he sighed.

"What?" The faint sadness of his tone disturbed her bliss.

"Nothing. Just wishing we could stay like this forever."

She smiled indulgently. "Don't you think it might become a trifle boring, even for us?"

He kissed the top of her head. "Perhaps. I don't suppose we'll have the chance to find out."

She snuggled against his shoulder and drifted into sleep.

The next morning Chris was quiet, almost withdrawn. They drove to the site of the original settlement of Jamestown and walked across the grassy area, reading the historical markers. Once Cara turned to find Chris standing several feet away, studying her, but when she smiled at him, his response was only the barest twitch of his lips. Puzzled, she strolled on, her mind busily exploring the possible reasons for his behavior. Had she somehow offended him? Or was he simply moody? Perhaps his mind was elsewhere, working on a story. Maybe he had become bored with her, realized she was young, inexperienced and too shallow for him. Firmly she suppressed the thought. If there was something wrong, surely Chris would tell her sooner or later. And if it didn't concern her, she shouldn't pry. Better to leave it alone and let him work it out. After all, everyone was entitled to a bad mood now and then.

Leaving Jamestown and the Tidewater behind, they drove back to Arlington. The friendly ease between them had vanished, and Cara tried several times to begin casual conversations, only to fail miserably. Finally she lapsed into silence and eventually slipped into an uneasy sleep.

She awoke some time later with a start and glanced over at Chris. He drove with one hand on the wheel and the other elbow resting against the door, his index finger thoughtfully tapping his lips. Lines furrowed his forehead, and he seemed unaware of Cara's existence.

"Hi there," she began tentatively.

His head jerked toward her, startled, and Cara saw a brief flash of pain in his eyes. He summoned up a smile. "Hello. Have a nice nap?"

"Fine, thank you. How long have I been asleep?"

"I don't know. Close to an hour, I imagine." The ghost of a grin touched his eyes. "Apparently you didn't get much rest this weekend."

"You're one to talk. Are you . . . do you feel all right?"

"Sure. Why do you ask?"

"You've been awfully quiet this morning."

He shrugged. "Just thinking about something. I hope I haven't been terrible company."

"Of course not."

"We're almost to Arlington," he stated formally, and the conversation died again.

Cara was glad when they entered the city. Chris was not a particularly talkative man, and they had sat together in companionable silence before. Why, then, was this quiet so uncomfortable, so strained?

Soon the Jaguar pulled into the driveway of Ginny's house and stopped. Chris hauled her luggage out of the trunk and walked Cara to the door. She paused awkwardly on the doorstep. "I . . . it was a lovely trip. Oh, that sounds trite and meaningless. It was much, much more than that."

Chris put down the bag and grasped her by the shoulders. Cara turned her face up to his and was surprised to see his eyes aflame with anguish. She opened her mouth to speak, but Chris stopped her words with a kiss, his lips grinding fiercely into hers, intensely alive and burning. His arms wrapped around her tightly, and for a brief moment he rested his cheek against her hair. Abruptly he released her, and his voice was grim. "Good-bye, Cara."

She stared after him as he jumped into his car and slammed it into reverse. Her mouth tingled from the rough pressure of his kiss, and her brain buzzed around his words. "Good-bye, Cara." No mention of seeing her again, no casual farewell. And what had caused the despair in his eyes?

"Cara?" Her mother's soft voice intruded on her thoughts, and Cara whirled. Ginny stood in the open doorway, staring at her. "What are you doing, dawdling out here? Come in and tell me about your trip."

Cara forced a smile and dismissed her worried thoughts. They were ridiculous. Chris had simply said good-bye and left, not a very unusual or startling thing. She was reading too much into his words. The weekend had been heavenly, and it would be better to remember its sweetness instead of dwelling on foolish doubts. "Oh, Ginny, it was absolutely wonderful . . ."

Happily Cara recounted the trip and her feelings for Chris, and Ginny, the eternal romantic, squeezed her daughter's hand and joined in her glee. Cara's attempt to think only of the weekend and not the strange good-bye worked successfully for a day or two. The following day she filled out and mailed in an application to George Washington University. After all, she told herself, it was a good school, and she didn't want to go there solely because of her infatuation with Chris. Then a giggle escaped her. Who was she kidding? Perhaps she would have applied there if she hadn't met him, but the school interested her no more than a hundred others. She wanted to stay where Chris was. In fact, she admitted, she could not envision going anywhere he wasn't.

Ginny merrily helped her daughter plan her move to Washington, even looking for an apartment close to the school. "Ginny, I've just applied," Cara pointed out laughingly. "You're acting as if I'd already been accepted."

"Well, it's a foregone conclusion, isn't it? How could they turn you down?"

Cara grinned indulgently. "I don't imagine they have quite as much faith in my ability as you do."

As the days slipped by and no call came from Chris, Cara's mood lowered, and she could no longer ignore the peculiar way the trip had ended. Could he have really meant good-bye? Maybe he didn't intend to see her again. But why? Why would he drop her so abruptly after the heady excitement of their trip?

A week passed with no word from him, and Cara drooped. Ginny saw the change. "Honey," she began one morning, clasping Cara's hand and leading her to the couch. "Can you tell me what's wrong? Did something happen between you and Chris? Is that the reason you're so gloomy all of a sudden?"

Cara smiled wanly. "I don't know what happened. We had a marvelous time in Virginia. I don't think I've been so happy or felt so close to any other man. Oh, Ginny, it was so special. But Sunday Chris turned almost morose. I don't know why, but he began to act differently. When he dropped me off here, he looked so . . . so unhappy! He said good-bye and hugged me tightly. I didn't understand it. But since he hasn't called me in a week, I'm afraid he was telling me good-bye permanently."

"But why?" Ginny's forehead creased. "If you had a wonderful time, why would he decide not to see you again? It doesn't make sense."

"I know. I'm afraid something's happened to him, but I haven't the nerve to call and find out. Or maybe he's tied up with a story and can't break the mood."

"Even for a phone call?" Ginny remarked skeptically.

"Sounds stupid when I say it. But I don't know what his work habits are. He might get so wrapped up in his stories that nothing else is important to him at the time."

"It's possible, I suppose. Alec was like that. He'd concentrate completely on a problem at work and ignore us."

"On the other hand," Cara went on, "I keep thinking he simply doesn't want to see me again. Maybe he specializes in one-night stands. What if you were right? Perhaps I went too fast, let myself get too involved. This weekend I realized I had fallen in love with Chris. At the time I didn't care. It seemed the greatest thing in the world. Now I'm not so sure."

Ginny sighed, her face saddening empathetically. "Honey, don't think that way. Remember, you said that even if it didn't turn out right, the feeling was too precious to kill before it started."

The doorbell rang, cutting into their conversation. Ginny rose to answer it. For one hopeful moment Cara held her breath, aching to hear Chris's voice at the door. Her shoulders sagged when Ginny reappeared with her neighbor, Lucille Caldwell, in tow. The woman's gossip had bored and irritated Cara the other day, and she had no desire to hear any more of it. She started to leave the room, but a thought stopped her. Mrs. Caldwell seemed to have the lowdown on everybody. Perhaps she knew Chris Wozniak, too, and could give her some information that would explain his actions. So Cara smiled at the woman and politely listened to her chatter for a few moments, waiting for a chance to ease in a question about Chris.

There seemed to be no subtle way to do it, and finally Cara plunged into a brief pause that opened in the conversation. "You know everyone here," she told Lucille admiringly.

Lucille preened, visibly pleased. "Oh, yes. I've lived here all my life."

"I was wondering about someone I met at a party the other night. Chris Wozniak."

"But of course!" Lucille flashed a toothy smile. "He's quite a charmer, if you like the quiet, brooding type. Not handsome exactly—too earthy—but compelling, don't you think? Actually, though, I am better acquainted with his wife. She's from Alexandria, a very fine family."

Cara was stunned, as paralyzed as the time she had fallen from the willow tree as a child and had the air knocked out of her. Suddenly her hands and face were cold, and her heart seemed to stop pumping. She saw Mrs. Caldwell and heard her voice, but the words were unintelligible. Slowly the world came back into focus, and feeling returned to Cara's numbed body. Her hands began to shake, and she quickly clasped them together.

"I . . . I didn't realize he was married," she forced out, striving for a normal tone.

"Oh, my dear, most people don't. They have a home in the Virginia countryside, where Monica lives. Chris only goes there on weekends. During the week he lives in an apartment in Georgetown. Of course, you can imagine what goes on there."

"No, what?"

Lucille shrugged expressively. "When a man has a separate apartment, which his wife never visits, it's obvious what he uses it for."

"You mean he . . . he's . . ." Cara could not choke out the words.

"A philanderer," Lucille finished for her. "Well, do you think any man who looks like he does would be spending his nights alone?"

"No, I suppose not."

"I hope *you* weren't interested in him." The woman made it almost a question, her eyes glinting with curiosity. "You looked awfully pale when I mentioned his wife."

"Did I?" Cara summoned up a brittle smile. "I guess I was surprised. He certainly didn't seem to be married."

"That's the problem," Lucille concluded decisively.

"Lucille," Ginny interjected brightly, "it was so nice of you to visit us, but I'm afraid Cara and I have to leave in a few minutes. I promised Sarah Cavini I'd meet her at three," Ginny said, calmly inventing a friend as well as an appointment to get rid of the woman.

"Sarah Cavini," Mrs. Caldwell repeated thoughtfully. "Do I know her?"

"I don't think so," Ginny replied without elaborating and

rose. Lucille had little choice but to stand and take her leave. Cara murmured a polite good-bye, smiling until her lips ached, and Ginny escorted Lucille to the front door.

Cara melted into a chair, the muscles that had held her tautly upright collapsing like putty. Chris was married! Molten tears sprang to her eyes. Married . . . and indulging in a brief, meaningless extramarital fling. She remembered the bitter remarks he had made concerning marriage that day at Georgetown University and his reticence about certain times and events of his life. No wonder he hadn't called her. It made obvious, horrible sense now. He was cheating on his wife . . . and Cara had fallen in love. A shudder tore through her, and hot tears spilled down her cheeks.

"Oh, baby," Ginny said as she hurried back into the room and threw her arms around Cara. "I'm so sorry. If only I'd known . . . Damn Wilson! Why didn't he realize that man was married?"

"Apparently it's something he keeps well hidden," Cara gulped between the sobs that racked her body. "What an idiot I was! I assumed he was a bachelor or divorced. Yet he even hinted to me about it. He said he wasn't any good and I'd be better off without him."

"Well, for once he was telling the truth," Ginny agreed grimly.

Gradually the storm of tears subsided. Cara drew back, wiping at the tears staining her cheeks, and pulled in a deep, shaking breath. Ginny watched her anxiously, and Cara managed a watery half smile. "I guess I'm younger and more naive than I thought. If you don't mind, I'll go sit in the backyard for a while."

"Do you want me to come with you?"

"No. I'll be all right. Really. I simply want to be alone for a while."

The rest of the afternoon Cara sat motionless on the stone bench, staring down at the small lily pad before her.

Finally, almost three hours later, she returned to the house, her face set and pale. When she spoke, her voice was toneless, almost indifferent. "I'm flying back to Dallas tomorrow."

"Cara!" Morgan cried happily when she answered the doorbell and found her younger sister on the porch. "When did you get back? I thought you were still in Washington."

"I came back yesterday."

"Come in and tell me all about your visit." Morgan led her into the large family room, then stopped, head cocked, listening to the wails from upstairs. "Sounds like Matthew. I'd better get him. Nick is up there but he's in his studio, and he'll never hear Matt if he's concentrating on painting."

"I'll go with you," Cara offered, following Morgan up the carpeted stairs.

"So, did you hear from the man you met at the party?" When Cara didn't answer, Morgan turned to look at her. "Cara, are you okay? You look kind of sick or something."

"Thanks a lot," Cara retorted, avoiding the question.

Morgan entered the nursery and pulled the squalling Matthew from his crib. "There, there, it's all right. Look who's here to see you—Cara! Yeah, how about that? You know her, don't you?" Babbling soothingly, Morgan laid the baby down and changed his diaper. Gradually his sobs vanished. Cara lifted him, and he leaned against her familiarly, one hand firmly clutching her long hair. Morgan stepped back, folded her arms across her chest and studied Cara. She did look pale and different somehow—there was a strange sadness lurking in the clear blue eyes. "You haven't answered my question," Morgan prodded. "Is something wrong?"

Cara buried her face in Matthew's fat, wrinkled neck and breathed in the sweet smell of baby powder. How comforting it was to feel his soft body in her arms. Perhaps if she held Matt for a while, she would be all right. But Matt began to squirm, tired of inactivity, and Cara set him down on the floor to crawl to his toys. She glanced at Morgan, who waited for an answer, and sighed inwardly. Cara had expected to tell Morgan about Chris, hoping it would relieve her of the awful feelings boiling inside her, but now she found she couldn't say anything.

"No," Cara replied. "I'm okay. Why should anything be wrong?"

Morgan frowned, certain that Cara was lying, but she didn't pursue it. If Cara didn't want to reveal something, nothing could pry it out of her. She was even more stubborn than Alexis. "Well, let's go downstairs and talk. Come on, Matthew." Morgan swept him up and started toward the stairs. "Would you like something to drink? Iced tea or a Coke?"

"Iced tea sounds nice."

"Good. I think Maria made some. Did I tell you I was returning to my decorating business part-time?"

"No. That's good. When?"

"Next week. I convinced Maria to work all day and watch Matthew for me in the mornings. Now that Matt's eight months old, I decided I've been a full-time mother long enough." She set the baby down and went into the kitchen for glasses of tea. "What about you? Have you decided what you're going to do?"

"I'm going to graduate school. I've applied to U.T., and I'm sure I'll get in there. The problem is how I'll occupy myself this summer. I'd like to do something, but where could I get a job for just three or four months?"

"Nursing?"

"Yeah. It wouldn't hurt to have more experience."

"Well, I could call Suzie and see if she knows anything. Her husband's a plastic surgeon, and he might know a doctor who needs a temporary nurse. Would that be okay?"

"Sure, if you don't mind asking," Cara agreed carelessly. She knew it would be better if she had a job to take her mind off Chris, but she felt indifferent to everything. She had hoped that seeing Morgan would cheer her up, but it hadn't worked. It was comforting to hold Matthew, but she could hardly carry the baby all day long.

Morgan dominated the conversation, discussing Nick's work, Matthew and the most recent news from Alexis, who was progressing splendidly with her pregnancy. Yet, even

Morgan found it difficult to conduct a conversation single-handed, and soon they drifted into silence. Cara glanced guiltily at her sister and murmured, "Sorry. I haven't been saying much, have I?"

"Not exactly," Morgan replied dryly, and her brilliant green eyes searched Cara's face. "I wish you'd tell me what's bothering you. And don't bother to deny it, because I wont't believe you."

Cara grimaced. "You're right. Only . . . I can't seem to talk about it. I probably shouldn't have come."

"Don't be silly. Of course you should have. And you're going to stay for dinner."

"Oh, no, thank you. I like Nick, but tonight I couldn't stand his teasing."

"Nick's very perceptive. He'll know there's something wrong and won't tease you, I promise."

"You're sweet to want me to stay and cast gloom over your dinner. But really, I'd rather be alone." Cara rose and crossed to Matthew, who was concentrating earnestly on the plastic rings he was banging together. She bent down to hug him, and he gurgled up at her pleasantly. "Bye-bye, Matt. I think I'll run home, Morgan. Don't worry about me. I'll be all right."

Morgan trailed Cara to the door, her eyes shadowed with doubt. She squeezed Cara with affection. Cara ran lightly down the shallow steps and along the stone pathway to her car. She jumped into the Volkswagen and started the engine, blinking away the treacherous tears that had started when Morgan hugged her. Morgan was so kind, and Cara knew she wanted to help. But her very kindness, like Ginny's, made Cara feel more hopeless, more bereft, more lonely. Morgan was too close to her. Cara hated to expose her stupidity and pain to Morgan's quick, loyal sympathy. Besides, some idiotic softness in her could not bear to reveal the kind of man Chris really was.

Cara pulled into the traffic and headed toward her North Dallas apartment, brushing away the tears that spilled onto her cheeks. She simply had to live through this ordeal alone. Before long she would get over him. After all, she despised Chris now, and her hatred would kill the vestiges of love lurking within her. It was a silly schoolgirl infatuation and would vanish as quickly as it had come. She would be all right. But Cara could not still the voice within that wailed: when?

Chapter 6

A cheerful, faintly familiar voice bubbled through the telephone. "Hi, this is Suzie Holland. I don't know if you remember me. I'm a friend of Morgan's."

"Of course I remember you," Cara assured her, the voice falling into place in her memory. "You used to come over when I was a kid."

"Ah, yes, many years ago," she sighed with mock nostalgia. "I spoke to Morgan yesterday. She told me you're a nurse now and you want a job for the summer."

"Yes, I'd be interested in one."

"Well, I asked Phil, my husband, and he said one of the doctors in his office building needs a nurse for a couple of months. His name is Daniel O'Hara, and he's an obstetrician-gynecologist. His nurse is about to have a baby—poetic justice—so he's been looking frantically for someone to take her place. She's close to term now, and she wants to take off for a month or so."

"That'd be fine. I'm returning to school in the fall, so I wouldn't want anything that would last past July."

"Well, this will probably be perfect. You want Dan's number?"

"Sure." Cara grabbed a pencil to jot down the telephone number on the back of an envelope. "Thank you, Suzie. It's very nice of you."

"Are you kidding? Dan will kiss me for finding you. And once you see him, you'll understand that that's payment enough."

Cara dialed the doctor's office, and his receptionist immediately connected her with Dr. O'Hara. His deep voice was almost pathetically eager when Cara explained that she was interested in a very temporary job, and he asked her to come for an interview that afternoon. She agreed to arrive at three. She went into her bedroom and took a severely cut light gray skirt and jacket and a blouse to match from the closet. After a quick shower she applied a touch of makeup and pulled her hair up into a demure knot atop her head. She dressed and stepped into plain low, black heels, then studied herself critically in the mirror. The plain suit hid her lush figure, and the restrained hairdo aged her a few years. Cara had found in other interviews that it was better to look older and less attractive than she was. Her first interview after she had received her state nursing certification had been with a middle-aged doctor who shook his head regretfully and explained that his wife would have his head if he hired a nurse who looked like Cara.

At five minutes to three Cara arrived at Dr. O'Hara's office in a four-story, blue-glass medical office building on Walnut Hill Lane. The receptionist greeted her with a friendly, amused twinkle in her eye and escorted her to the doctor's office. A few minutes later he bustled in in a swirl of white coat. Cara understood at once what Suzie had meant when she said Dr. O'Hara's kiss was payment enough. He was tall and slender, with bright blue eyes, golden-blond hair and a full blond beard that glistened with highlights of red. He smiled at Cara, exposing a dazzling set of teeth. He stroked his beard, a nervous gesture Cara was soon to become familiar with.

"Miss Stone, I'm Dr. O'Hara." He extended a hand to shake. "Sorry I'm late. That's the way it is in this place." He chatted with her for a few minutes, asking about her credentials and schooling, explaining once more the temporary nature of the job and informing her of the hours and pay. "Now, have I left anything out? Any questions?"

"No, not really." Cara shook her head.

"Good. I hate to seem eager, Miss Stone. May I call you Cara? We run an informal office."

"Of course."

"You have good credentials, even though you don't have any experience in the field. Since you're considering entering obstetrics, this would certainly be a good spot for you. Frankly, I'm desperate. When you meet Leslie, you'll see why. She's only two weeks from her due date. When Phil told me this morning he'd found me a nurse, I practically hugged him."

Cara grinned. "Having met Phil, I imagine that would have gotten quite a rise out of him."

Dr. O'Hara laughed. "You're right. Fortunately, I didn't. Anyway, I'm offering you the job on the spot, and please say you'll take it."

"All right." Cara could not keep from smiling at his pleading look. She suspected that Dr. O'Hara usually got what he wanted, one way or another. "It sounds like a perfect job for me."

"Terrific. Next question—can you start tomorrow? Leslie would love to get away from here as soon as she can, but she'll have to familiarize you with the routine first. So if it's not too inconvenient . . ."

"That's fine. I'll be here at . . ."

"Eight o'clock," he answered her unspoken question. "Now, let me introduce you to Leslie. Believe me, she'll be delighted to meet you."

Ushering her down the hall to the receptionist's office, he introduced her to Fran Ward, the receptionist, and to Leslie Meacham, a tall, dark-haired, very pregnant woman in her early thirties.

Leslie grinned and clasped Cara's hand warmly. "Hurray," she laughed. "Am I ever glad to see you! I was beginning to think I'd still be working when they wheeled me into the labor room. By the way," she turned to the doctor with friendly ease, "Mrs. Campbell's in the blue examination room, and I wish you'd see her right away. She left her two kids in the waiting room, and they're about to tear the place down."

"Okay," he agreed with a chuckle and backed out into the hall.

"Well." Leslie returned to Cara, her brown eyes warm and sparkling. "I can't tell you how this relieves my mind. Dan was going crazy. He's convinced he couldn't make it for a month without a nurse. He might be right. He goes at such speed that he needs someone to make sure he has everything and is headed in the right direction. But it's not a demanding job, like working in a hospital."

Cara smiled back, already liking the woman. "Dr. O'Hara seems very nice."

"He is. Not stuffy like a lot of doctors. He'll have you calling him Dan in a couple of days, I guarantee. Are you coming in tomorrow?"

"Yes."

"Good. Then you can explore the office early before the patients arrive. I'll show you all the ropes, and hopefully you'll be settled in before Junior here decides to make an appearance."

"I'll see you at eight, then." Cara smiled, said good-bye to Leslie and the receptionist and reentered the waiting room, where two children were climbing over furniture and shrieking at the top of their lungs. Cara glanced toward the receptionist's window. Fran rolled her eyes heavenward in mock despair. Cara suppressed a giggle and hurried out into the Dallas sun. As she got into her car, it occurred to her that for the past few minutes she had felt almost cheerful.

Cara was the first one at the office the next morning, and she had to sit on a bench in the hall outside the locked door until Leslie came a few minutes later.

"A key!" Leslie exclaimed when she saw Cara. "That was stupid of me. I swear, my mind is going. One of Dan's patients told me she is positive that either pregnancy or delivery kills off some of one's brain cells. I'm beginning to believe her. We've got a spare key in the drawer. I'll give it to you right now, so you won't have to wait again tomorrow."

She opened the door, switched on the light and vanished into the receptionist's area. She rummaged through several drawers before triumphantly holding up a key. "There you go. The first thing I do when I come in, if I'm the first one here, is turn the air-conditioning cooler. We leave it warmer at night." She peered at the thermostat and nudged the dial. "Okay, where shall we start?"

Quickly she gave Cara a tour, pointing out the small lounge, which contained a couple of comfortable chairs and a small refrigerator, as well as the two examining rooms, one blue and one dusky pink, where Leslie went through the cabinets and drawers in great detail. She turned to the metal examining table, which was padded on top for comfort. "The doctor's instruments are in the drawers beneath the table. A heater keeps them warm. That's another thing I do when I come in—flip on the heater switch." She did so, then led Cara into the small room behind the receptionist's office. "This is where I spend most of my time when I'm not with a patient. I do some simple lab work here, as you can see." She waved a hand at the equipment against one wall. "But we send most of our work to the pathologists in the next building down. Here's their address. I usually run it over there by hand. They'll send a girl to pick it up, but she's dreadfully slow. She's also bad about bringing back the results, so when I want to know quickly, I call them on the phone. Now, these drawers contain our booklets. Here's the pamphlet for pregnant women, and here are a bunch of other papers on pregnancy. These are about birth control, and over here is the V.D. drawer." She pulled open drawer after drawer and handed Cara samples of the contents.

By the time they were finished, both the doctor and the

receptionist had arrived, and at eight-thirty the first patient was there. Leslie showed the woman's file to Cara. Inside was a medical history, a weight chart and several sheets beginning with her first visit after the positive pregnancy test. Flipping through the sheets, Cara could see that she was here for her fourth-month visit, that her weight was steady and that her blood tests had shown no sign of V.D., diabetes or anemia. She followed Leslie as she called the woman in, took her weight and blood pressure and did the urine test. Leslie's manner was easy and friendly. She introduced Cara and chatted for a few minutes about what was going on in the patient's life.

"That's about it," Leslie said after they left the woman. "When they come in at their third month, I take blood samples—the lavender-topped vial. It has anticoagulant in it. And we take them again the sixth month and the ninth. Some doctors don't give blood tests as often, but Dan feels it's safer. I agree. Sometimes diabetes won't show up in the simple urine test."

Cara stuck to Leslie's side all day, through a variety of patients, some of whom had come for yearly checkups, one white-faced woman for a lump in her breast and several in various stages of pregnancy. Leslie knew most of the pregnancy cases since they came in so often, and she was careful to explain to Cara anything that was unusual about them. "This lady," she told her, pointing to a name on the afternoon's appointment list, "had a miscarriage about eight months ago, and she was very depressed. She's pregnant again, and every time she comes in, she has a new worry. She's scared something will go wrong, even though she's into her fifth month and well past the time she miscarried before. So I spend a little extra time with her, talking about a new symptom or an article she's read on birth defects and reassuring her that nothing's wrong. She's very nice, just scared. If I talk to her, she won't take up so much of the doctor's time."

"Sure. I understand. I promise I'll talk to her."

"Good. Sometimes I think I do as much for the patients' mental well-being as for their physical."

Cara smiled. "I know what you mean. But I enjoy it. When I was at the hospital, I hated the administrative work keeping me from talking to the patients as much as I should."

"Me too."

As the day wore on and was followed by more days of Leslie's teaching, Cara discovered that she liked her very much. Many of their beliefs were similar, and Leslie had a warm, calm nature that was both soothing and fun. She and Cara ate lunch together every day, and soon they were discussing bits and pieces of their personal lives, things from the past and humorous incidents. Forming the new friendship and learning the office routine helped keep Cara's mind off Chris most of the time, although nothing drove him from her thoughts in the evening, when she was alone. However, as she grew more familiar with her job and concentrated on it less, she was not as successful in forgetting him. One day at lunch, as she and Leslie sat in a small Mexican restaurant waiting for their order, Cara gazed absentmindedly at the tinkling fountain in the foyer, and suddenly she remembered the cool quiet of the Virginia inn's lobby.

"What's the matter?" Leslie asked.

"What do you mean?"

"You look sad."

"I was thinking about something—a place I visited not long ago." Cara paused and then, to her amazement, the whole story of Chris came rushing out of her, from their meeting to Lucille Caldwell's statement, which had split her like a knife. Her eyes were riveted on the table as she talked, and her words tumbled out breathlessly as she traced a nervous design on the tablecloth with her fingernail.

"I'm so sorry," Leslie said as she frowned in concern and put her hand sympathetically on Cara's wrist.

She looked up, tears flashing in her sapphire eyes. "It isn't only the heartbreak. I was in love with him, and to know I'll never see him again really hurts. But there's more. I feel betrayed, used. Someone I put my whole heart and soul into, even if it was just for a short time, lied to me— worse than lied. The man I loved doesn't exist. He was a fabrication of my imagination and Chris's lies. The real man is a liar and a cheat, a seducer who wanted nothing but to have me in his bed for a few days. I didn't expect him to love me . . . I knew I was being carried away by my emotions. But I believed he had some feeling for me. Yet he cared so little that he wouldn't tell me the truth. If he had said, 'Cara, I'm married, but I want to make love to you,' I'd have more respect for him. I thought he was honest, whatever else he might be! The hard-hitting investigative reporter who has no patience with or sympathy for deceit and cover-ups—what a joke! He was nothing *but* deceit."

She sighed and leaned back in her chair. "I guess I was pretty stupid, huh? I'm sorry for dumping this on you. I couldn't even tell my sister, but for some reason it came out when I started talking to you. No wonder Dan's patients tell you their worries."

Leslie smiled. "I do have that effect on people, but I'm glad. I think you chose the right person. You must have known instinctively that you'd found a kindred spirit. I've been through the same thing myself."

Cara stared. "You? You're joking. But you're so level-headed, so calm."

"Believe me, it's hard won. When I was first out of nursing school, I worked on the surgical ward of a hospital in Oklahoma City. I fell in love with one of the surgeons. I didn't have your excuse. I knew he was married from the start. But I loved him, and I thought he loved me. So he told me. He had a wife who didn't understand him, the whole bit. He'd divorce her and marry me, but first he had to wait until one of his kids got through an illness. Then it was another thing, and after that another. Finally I realized that he wasn't going to divorce her. I told him it was over between us, which killed me. I was miserable. A few weeks later he came to me begging me to take him back, saying the same old stuff. I wanted to believe him, so I did. It continued for almost three years, on and off. I consoled myself with the thought that even though he stayed with his

"Sure. What time? Say, this isn't anything fancy, is it?"

Morgan laughed. "No. Would I put you through a formal dinner party? It's casual. Come in shorts if you want. But I wouldn't be a good sister if I didn't warn you . . ."

"What?"

"Somebody else is coming—a person of the male sex."

"A blind date!" Cara wailed. "Morgan, how could you? When did you take up matchmaking?"

"Oh, I've always enjoyed it. But it isn't a blind date or matchmaking, honey. He's just a friend of mine, and another man balances the table."

"You sound like Ginny." Cara paused, then continued suspiciously, "Have you been talking to her, by any chance?"

"No. Should I?"

"I thought she might be behind the blind-date idea."

"No. And it's *not* a blind date. Really, he's a very nice, amusing young man who directs one of the live theaters here. He's funny, intelligent and interesting—a nice dinner companion. That's the only reason I invited him."

"Oh, all right." Cara sighed. Even if Morgan was trying to arrange a romance for her, she had promised that she would date more.

The following evening Cara found that Barry Sommers was exactly as Morgan had described him. Of medium height and slenderly built, he had dark curly hair, a trim beard, gray eyes and an intense, energetic manner. He told humorous stories about his theater work but also spoke with serious enthusiasm about the next play he was putting on. Cara, less interested in the arts than Morgan and Nick, was not as enthralled as they were by his anecdotes. More than once she found her mind wandering to something at work she needed to do. Much as she liked Morgan, she was glad when the evening wound to a close and she was able to make her escape.

Sommers offered to drive her home, but Cara replied with relief that she had brought her own car. She smiled at him, careful not to suggest any friendliness or encouragement. There was nothing wrong with Barry, but she knew she didn't want him to ask her for a date. No matter what Leslie advised, she simply could not stand going through another evening like this, close to boredom and filled with tension from pretending to enjoy the company and the conversation.

Cara turned to Morgan and Nick. "Thank you, it was a delightful dinner."

Morgan smiled wryly. "I hope you enjoyed it."

"Of course." Impulsively Cara hugged her sister and whispered, "I know you mean well."

Cara stepped back, and Sommers began his good-byes. Nick looped an arm around Cara's shoulders and walked her out the front door and down the sidewalk to the car. "Morgan's worried that you're unhappy," he said bluntly. "If I can do anything . . ."

"I know, Nick. You and Morgan are very sweet."

"You helped us when we needed it . . . and boy, did we need it."

Cara grinned at her brother-in-law. His eyes were black in the darkness, but concern glowed from them. "I wish other men were as nice as you," she blurted out.

"Ah, then Morgan is right. Some man has treated you badly. Unfortunately not all men are the paragons that I am. Now, what did this guy do to you?"

"He was married, but he didn't bother to inform me of the fact."

"Oh. I'm sorry. A guy in Washington?"

"Yeah. A 'brief fling.' I've been moping about it longer than it lasted. It's more hurt pride than anything else. Somehow I haven't been able to tell Morgan about it. It's just something I hate to talk about."

"That's understandable. I'll tell her to lay off the inquisition. Okay?"

"Okay."

He opened the car door for her. "But if you get lonely, remember to call us. We're an old married couple with a kid now, and we're always at home."

"I doubt that," Cara retorted good-humoredly. "But thank you, Nick. I'll remember."

"Good night."

"'Bye." Cara started the engine and turned the car toward home. Everyone was so nice and understanding, so eager to help her. Cara felt guiltily that she wasn't making enough effort herself. But how did you force yourself to get over a heartbreak?

Chapter 7

Cara glanced up from her desk and smiled at Dr. O'Hara as he walked into the office. "Good news," he boomed jovially. "Leslie delivered last night."

"Really?" Cara's voice and the receptionist's rose in chorus.

"Yeah. A six-pound-eight-ounce girl."

"I'll have to go see her."

"I'm sure she'd like that. She's as giddy as if she'd never seen a baby before."

That evening Cara went to the hospital. She stopped with other visitors to gawk at the babies lying asleep in their cribs. Cara searched the cards hung on the cribs for the one that read: Baby Girl, Mr. and Mrs. Robert Meacham. She found it on the bed containing a tiny, red-tinged baby with such fine blond hair that she appeared to be bald. Tilting her head, Cara studied the infant and decided judiciously that she was an attractive child, even if she didn't possess the thick black hair that had stood out like a brush all over her beloved Matthew's head when he was born.

Finally she left the nursery and made her way to Leslie's room. Leslie was propped up in bed, lazily watching television when Cara entered. She emitted a cry of welcome and quickly turned off the set. "Cara! I'm so glad you came. Did you see her?"

"Sure. She's beautiful, but I never doubted that. What did you name her?"

"We're vacillating. The nurses come in every fifteen minutes to ask me if I've decided on a name yet. But we're really stuck between two—Jennifer Marie and Amy Kathleen."

Cara sat down beside the bed, and they chatted happily about names for a few minutes, then went on to the many wonderful and distinct qualities of Baby Girl Meacham. Finally Cara stood up. "I'm afraid I'll tire you with so much talk. You'll need your rest when you take her home."

"That's the truth. I'm glad you came by. How are things at the office?"

"So far, running smoothly." Cara crossed her fingers in a hopeful gesture. "Now if I can just keep it that way until you come back."

"Give me one more month. By then I'll probably be screaming to get back to work."

"Likely story." Cara smiled and left, circling back to the nursery for a last look at the infants.

The days crawled by as summer hit the city with full force. The unusually mild, rainy days of May and early June vanished, replaced by hot, sweltering weather. Cara enjoyed her work, but Chris still pervaded her dreams. She realized now that forgetting him would take much longer than she had thought. How could one week have made such a lasting impression on her life?

A month later Leslie phoned to say she would return to work the next week. The thought depressed Cara. It was the end of June, and there would be six more lonely weeks before school started. When Alec called her the next day, it was a welcome relief from her troublesome thoughts.

"Cara?" her father's voice vibrated strongly across the telephone wires, so vital that she saw in her mind's eye his crisp black hair and piercing blue eyes, slim and straight as a ramrod, no doubt reading a letter or signing papers as he talked to her. "I had to get your number from Morgan. I didn't know you'd left the hospital."

"Yeah, I quit over two months ago."

"I'd like to see you. When can you come to my office?"

That was Alec for you—always *when*, not *if*. "Anytime, I guess. Today at lunch?"

"Good. I'll see you at noon."

"A few minutes after, Daddy." Cara hung up the phone and frowned in puzzlement. Alec had worked closely with Alexis, and he had often taken Morgan out for a social lunch, but his relationship with Cara had not been close, and he rarely invited her to his office. Uneasily she wondered what he was after. One thing was sure: Alec wouldn't have called unless he wanted something.

She left for lunch a few minutes early and navigated the thick traffic down Central Expressway to the blue glass building that housed Stone Oil. Her father's office was on the top floor, along with a plush boardroom and a few other executive offices, including that of his new partner, Michael Durek. Cara stepped off the elevator and strode across the thick carpet to Alec's reception area. She glanced with distaste at the doors leading to Durek's office. She had met the man only once or twice, and she did not like him. His gray eyes were cold and hard as flint, and Cara was certain he didn't have a feeling in his entire body. Look at the way he had been eager to marry Morgan without love or passion, simply to obtain a controlling interest in the company after Alec's death.

Mrs. Jenkins, her father's middle-aged secretary, smiled at her politely. "Miss Stone, it's so nice to see you. You haven't been here for quite a while."

"No." Cara returned the smile stiffly. She was always intimidated by the woman's calmly efficient air. Nothing short of a tornado blasting through the door would faze Mrs. Jenkins . . . perhaps not even that. "Is my father in?"

"Oh, yes, he's expecting you. Go ahead."

When Cara walked in, Alec was seated at his desk, frowning down at the papers before him. He glanced up, his face tight with anger, and visibly forced a smile when he saw her. "Cara." He rose. "How are you?"

"Better than you at the moment, I think," she returned lightly.

"What? Oh." He smiled ruefully and sat back down. He did not leave his desk to hug her, and Cara didn't expect it. She curled up in the massive chair close to his desk. "I was reading a letter from the district manager in Canada. He's been having problems with one of the wells. First the bit broke, and now someone's vandalized some of the equipment."

"Oh. Sorry."

He shrugged as though putting the matter from him. There was a long pause, and Cara shifted uncomfortably. She and Alec rarely had anything to say to one another. He had been a rather misty, superhuman figure in her life, one who grew vaguer with her parents' divorce. He was almost a stranger to her. It would have surprised Cara to learn that Alec felt as awkward as she. His youngest daughter was an enigma to him, unlike anyone else in the family, and he had the uneasy feeling that he had never handled her well.

"Did you . . . want to tell me something?" Cara prodded, remembering that she had only an hour for lunch.

"I wanted to speak to you about your career. Uh . . . this nursing idea. Morgan told me you were dissatisfied at the hospital. Personally, I didn't like the idea of your working there anyway. However, I'm not sure a job in a doctor's office is any better. Cara, don't you want to do something with your life?"

"Nursing is something."

"I mean more important, more—"

"More prestigious?" she supplied.

"Well, yes, if you want to look at it that way. A career appropriate to your background, your life-style."

"You mean *your* life-style. Actually, Daddy, except for the clothes Morgan bullies me into buying, I manage to live on my salary. That may surprise you, but—"

"No, it doesn't," he replied, his brow contracting thunderously. "I've talked to your trust officer. You've hardly taken out a dime from either of your funds, mine or your grandparents', since you finished college. I can't understand why you don't want pretty clothes, a nice car . . ." He stopped and visibly pulled himself away from the topic. "However, that's not what I wanted to discuss with you. If you choose to live like a pauper, it's your business."

"I'm not living like a pauper. When I need something, I get it. I'm simply not crazy about buying things."

"All right, Cara. It's beside the point, as I said. There's more to the issue than money. The fact is you're wasting your potential. You have a bright mind. If you want to remain in the health-care field, why not go to medical school? There should be a lot of opportunities for a female doctor. There are for any doctor. Most people would give their eyeteeth to be in the position you are—young, intelligent, plenty of money to attend med school and set up practice."

"I don't want to be a doctor," Cara replied, setting her jaw mulishly. "If you and Alexis don't forget this doctor business, I'll scream. If I wanted to be a doctor, I'd become one, but I don't. And nothing you say is going to convince me."

"I'm more aware of that every day," he remarked dryly.

"If it makes you feel any better, I'm going to graduate school to get my master's. I'll specialize in obstetrical nursing. Will that satisfy you?"

She could tell from the frown creasing his forehead that it would not, but Alec temporized. "Well, it's certainly better. At least you'd have a higher degree, more chance to use your abilities. Besides, once you're back in school, you may find another field more interesting."

"There's always hope."

Alec ignored her mild sarcasm. "But why obstetrics?"

"I've been working in an obstetrician's office and I'm enjoying it. Of course, I'd prefer to work in the hospital delivery room. I got the idea of specializing in either pediatrics or obstetrics when Matthew came, because he's so terrific."

A smile lit Alec's face at the mention of his grandson, and he was easily derailed to the new subject. "Have you seen Matt lately? Laraine tells me he's standing now."

"Yeah. He's pulling himself up at the coffee table and chairs."

"He's a fine boy. You know, I always wanted a son, but I never guessed I'd be as silly about Matthew as I am. Morgan is convinced I've flipped my lid."

Cara smiled faintly. "It *is* a new side of your character."

He stared into the distance, his gaze abstracted. "I was a builder when I was young—still am, I suppose. But I had a goal. I wanted to build a business for my son, an empire he could take over one day. Then I didn't have a son. Oh, I loved you girls, of course. I was never disappointed in any of you. Still, it wasn't the same as a son—someone like me. I could have taken him places, done things with him that— Well, it doesn't matter. It's all in the past." He turned his attention to Cara, his blue eyes devoid of the emotion that had lurked in them briefly. "I'm learning that you don't get everything you want in life. It took me awhile to accept it."

Cara stirred, pierced by an unfamiliar sympathy for her father. "But you have Matthew now."

He smiled. "Yes, I have Matthew. It's not the same as my own son, but I'm satisfied. Now, about you. I'm glad you're going back to school. UT?"

"I've applied there and have been accepted. For a while

I considered going to a different school, just for the experience." With a pang Cara remembered her application to George Washington University. She stood up quickly, banishing the thought. "I have to get back to work now. I have only an hour for lunch."

"Of course. I'm glad you came in." Alec's voice was formal, and his eyes flickered to the papers in front of him. Cara knew that before she was out the door, he would be absorbed in some project. She strode to the heavy wooden door and slipped through it, then froze, her eyes fastened on the man seated in the outer office. Chris Wozniak.

Cara gripped the door handle behind her, suddenly faint. It couldn't be. Her mind was playing tricks on her. She swallowed and closed her eyes, then opened them again. He was still there, his attention focused on the yellow pad on his lap. Cara ran her eyes over him hungrily, noticing the changes. She hadn't seen him in the tailored blue three-piece suit before. He seemed thinner than she remembered. His thick brown hair was a trifle shorter and less shaggy. He glanced up, and their gazes locked. His green eyes widened and his hands clenched involuntarily on the pad. A muscle in his cheek jumped and stilled.

"Cara." He rose from the chair, lean and spare, his hard body and stony face painfully familiar.

"What are you doing here?" she spat out.

"I'm trying to interview your father for my story on the oil companies."

"I thought you said the story didn't concern Stone Oil."

"At the time it didn't. Since then I've discovered something I'd like to check with Mr. Stone. Unfortunately, he's a rather difficult man to see."

Mrs. Jenkins interrupted smoothly, "I was just explaining to Mr. Wozniak that Mr. Stone's schedule is quite full this afternoon."

Cara smiled thinly. "It usually is. You might as well give up on him, Chris. This time you've found a worthier opponent."

"Worthier?"

"Than, say, his daughter."

"I wasn't aware you were an opponent."

"Neither was I . . . at first. But it occurred to me later that it must have been a contest, since there was a winner and a loser."

A shadow touched his eyes. "Cara, don't . . . I'd like to talk to you."

"I'd rather not. If you'll excuse me, I have to leave." She smiled artificially at the secretary.

Cara walked past Chris, ignoring his gesture toward her arm as if to stop her, and strode rapidly toward the elevators. It seemed an eternity before the doors opened with a slow, elegant whoosh. Cara waited on pins and needles for fear Chris would follow her to continue the conversation. But he didn't and she was able to step into the mirrored box and punch the button for the underground parking level. She gripped the cold metal rail behind her back and stared at her reflection on the opposite wall. Her face was pale, her eyes huge and dark and her stance rigid with unspent tension. Chris Wozniak. Damn him! Why did he have to show up in Dallas? He should have stayed in D.C., where he belonged, not intruded on her territory.

It made her feel curiously vulnerable. Dallas had been her refuge when she fled Washington, and now it was no longer safe. Great tears welled up in her eyes and refused to be blinked away. She barely made it to her car before she lost the battle and gave way to a storm of tears.

Cara moved through the rest of the day like an automaton. More than once Dr. O'Hara had to repeat himself before she heard him. When the day was finally over, she thankfully left the office and fought the traffic to her apartment It was a small place but neat and tastefully decorated in shades of peach, pale yellow and light blue. The fruitwood furniture of simple, clean lines lent an air of lightness. Usually it seemed to her a quiet haven, restful and comforting. But tonight she hardly noticed the surroundings as she mechanically made a salad and a quick frozen dinner. She found that she could force very little of the food down and soon gave up the effort. She cleaned the dishes and went into the living room to read. Yet, Cara was unable to concentrate on the words, and she tossed the book onto the end table with a snort of disgust. Closing her eyes, she stopped fighting the thoughts of Chris that had been hammering at the back of her mind all afternoon.

Suddenly there was a sharp rapping at the door. She jumped in surprise. After a moment she slowly rose, smoothing down the white uniform she hadn't bothered to remove. Her stomach was in turmoil and her mind calmly fatalistic. She knew who it was before she opened the door. Chris was framed in the doorway. He wore the same slacks and off-white shirt he had worn earlier, but he had discarded the pinstripe jacket and tie. His shirt was open at the throat, revealing a patch of curly dark hairs. Cara quickly averted her eyes and stepped back.

"I might as well let you in," she snapped, "since I know it wouldn't be any use trying to keep you out."

"Probably not," he agreed with equanimity and moved into the apartment. "I don't suppose you'd offer me anything to drink."

"Not if you were half dead in the desert."

He sank heavily into one of the yellow chairs across from the couch and rubbed his face. "Christ," he muttered wearily, without heat. "Ah, Cara, I wish everything had been different. Do you hate me?"

"Rather."

"I can't really blame you. I shouldn't have left you without a reason. It's just—"

"That you're a coward," she finished for him.

"I suppose that's as good an explanation as any," he agreed. "But I didn't come here to discuss what happened or to try to justify my actions. It's over and done with. Can we talk on a purely business plane?"

"I can't imagine what we could talk about."

"I need some information for my story."

94

"I see. You think you can use me for something."

Chris glanced up sharply, his eyes bright and hard. Cara noticed for the first time the tiredness on his face, the deep grooves that bit into the flesh on either side of his mouth. For a moment she thought he was about to protest, but he shrugged and replied, "Put it any way you want."

"I'm afraid you've come to the wrong person. Even if I wanted to help you, which I don't, I know nothing about Stone Oil. You might as well leave."

"This is a personal matter as well. A couple of years ago a young boy, the illegitimate son of Brant McClure, came to this country from Vietnam. McClure had been trying to get him out of Indochina for several years, but with no luck—until he agreed to sign a gas lease with Stone Oil on some very valuable property. After that it was a matter of months before the boy showed up. It's rumored that your father did some fancy pulling of strings, not to mention a little judicious bribery and blackmail, in our own government and quite a few others, in order to get Paul McClure into this country. That's what I'm investigating—the power play your father pulled in return for McClure's signing the lease."

Cara stared at him, stunned. "You can't be serious!"

"I am. Surely you know about the situation."

"I know Paul and Brant. I know that my sister is married to Brant McClure and is crazy about her stepson."

"And that's it?" His upper lip curled in disbelief. "You're not aware of the shady dealings to obtain Paul?"

"No, I'm not. Why do you think there were any? Of all the things to choose to investigate! Isn't there anything more scandalous than rescuing a small child from the hands of a hostile government?"

"Oh, I've found no lack of scandal in any of the areas I'm investigating. This is just one of many."

"Then concentrate on them. This one isn't worth your while."

"Why don't you let me be the judge of that?" His response was cool, his face a mask.

"Fine! You've obviously appointed yourself judge of

quite a few things. But you can pursue your godlike judicial tasks somewhere else. I don't want you in my apartment."

"Cara, all I'm asking for is some simple information."

"Look: number one, I wouldn't tell you if I knew. Number two, I was away at college at the time. Number three, I've never been involved with Stone Oil. And I don't know anything about Paul's getting out of Vietnam!"

"I don't expect you to give me the details of the deal. All I want is information about your sister and her new family. Where does she live? Alexis McClure is the one I want to talk to."

Fear curled in Cara's stomach. "Stay away from Alexis!" she hissed. "She's happy and pregnant, and I refuse to let you harass her!"

"Being pregnant doesn't make her an invalid, surely," he retorted. "I merely want to ask her a few questions. From what I've heard, Alexis is a tough corporation lawyer, not a fragile Victorian flower."

"Of course she's not an invalid, but I won't have her upset because you want to whip up a little sensationalism."

"Not sensationalism. Truth."

"You have an odd set of standards!" Cara lashed out. "Truth is some kind of god to you when it concerns other people. Then it doesn't matter who gets hurt, whose lives you invade, how many people are ground into the dirt. But when it comes to yourself . . . ah, that's another story, isn't it? Truth isn't so sacred then. It's okay for you to cheat and lie for a few hours of gratification, just like it's okay for you to use people or hound someone for a story to boost your career. The world revolves around Christopher Wozniak, and everyone else is here to serve his ambition or pleasure."

His mouth whitened under her attack. "Damn it, Cara, that's not true."

"Not true! You mean you didn't lie to me? Surely any omission of truth is a lie, and you neglected to inform me of one minor detail—the fact that you're married!"

He looked at her for a moment without speaking. Sighing, he crossed the room to stare out the window. "Who told you?"

"Does it matter? The point is . . . you didn't."

"No, I didn't."

"Why?" Cara's bitter frustration boiled up. "Why didn't you tell me?"

"I should have." He shrugged, his gesture weary, defeated. "I started to a hundred times. But I couldn't. I wanted you so badly I'd have done anything—illegal, immoral, insane, I didn't care. Probably you won't believe it, but I do have principles. What I did to you tore me up inside, and yet," his voice lowered almost to a whisper, "I couldn't stop myself."

"Mmmm, like an alcoholic, no doubt." Her voice was brittle and flippant.

Chris whirled, his eyes dark and wounded, his face etched with bitter lines. "Cara, please . . . don't paint me worse than I am."

"That would be pretty difficult." She sank onto the sofa, suddenly tired. "Look, I understand that having extramarital affairs can be an addiction, like drugs or alcohol. They call it nymphomania in a woman. Does it have a name in a man, or is it just good clean fun? Rationally I'm able to say you have a . . . a problem, but I don't enjoy being the victim of your weakness."

"It isn't that way. You weren't the latest in a string of girls. I'm not compulsively driven to have affairs. I'm not trying to excuse myself, but I want you to know you weren't a cheap interlude for me. You were something very different, very special. When I saw you at the party, I suddenly felt seventeen years old again. My palms started to sweat, and I was aching to touch you, kiss you." Cara turned her head, her throat closing treacherously at the raw need in his voice. "I knew I was acting crazy, and finally I managed to get out before I went in over my head. But I couldn't stop thinking about you. I told myself it wouldn't hurt to see you again, just to talk and enjoy your company. So I called you and took you to the colleges. But of course it

wasn't enough simply to see you. Everything about you—
your hair, your perfume, your body, the delicious way you
laughed—made me want you worse than ever. I justified
it by saying you were part of a generation that was used to
casual affairs. One or two nights would mean nothing to
you. You would go back to Dallas in a few days, and it
would have a natural end. Nobody would get hurt."

"Aren't you forgetting your wife?"

He sighed and ran one hand through his thick, straight
hair. "Monica has nothing to do with it."

"Nothing to do with it?" Cara echoed in astonishment.

"You don't know her. All she cares about— It doesn't
matter. Believe me, there's no love between her and me.
Don't imagine her sitting at home weeping because I might
be in bed with another woman."

"That's hard to believe."

"Then believe what you want!" he flared. "Damn it, I'm
trying to explain that I didn't mean to hurt you! I thought
it was nothing but a strong physical attraction. I thought if
I had you once, it would be enough. Obviously I was de-
ceiving myself. I was so hungry for you I would have lied
to anybody, including myself. After we made love, I discovered I wanted you even more. I kept getting in deeper
and deeper, and finally I realized I had to stop it immediately
or I wouldn't ever be able to stop. I could tell I was beginning to mean something to you, and I knew how desperately you'd be hurt if we continued. As for me, even I
couldn't fool myself any longer. It was no casual affair,
could never be casual. For both our sakes, I had to cut it
off.

"When I left Sunday, I swore not to see you again." He
gave a short laugh. "I can't tell you how many times I
almost broke my resolution. Once I went so far as to call
your number, but I hung up before you answered. One day
I saw Wilson and asked him how you were, and he turned
frosty as January and said you'd gone back to Dallas. After
that I had to live with it, and I did. I guess I'll continue

to." He broke off and strode rapidly to the front door, then turned. "It was stupid to come here. Good-bye, Cara."

The door closed behind him with a soft, final click, but Cara continued to stare at the blank wood, still seeing him poised there—the turn of his head, his long, thin fingers wrapped around the knob, the line of his shoulder, chest, and legs. Another picture of him to store away with all the others, another memory she would be unable to forget.

Chapter 8

Cara remained on the couch for a long time after Chris's departure. The wound to her feelings seemed as fresh as the first time. Bitterly she brooded over what he had said, scorning his explanations and coloring every word darkly. He had lied to her again, talking about how greatly he desired her, how he had stopped the affair to cause her no further pain. And yet at the remembered passion in his voice, her abdomen curled with longing. Angrily she tried to push away the feeling. How could she let him affect her so after all that had happened? She ought to be thinking about Alexis and Paul. It was her sister he intended to hurt now with his ruthless ambition... and a child who had already gone through enough pain for a lifetime.

She marched decisively to the phone and dialed. When the line was answered, she plunged in. "Alexis? This is Cara."

"Why, how nice! What—"

"Listen," Cara interrupted, "I have something important

to tell you. Do you remember the reporter I was talking to at Ginny's party in Washington?"

There was a pause, and finally Alexis asked uncertainly, "The one Morgan teased you about?"

"Yes, him."

"I don't remember him exactly, no. I mean, I recall Morgan speaking about it, but not the man himself."

"His name is Chris Wozniak, and he's a free-lance investigative reporter. He's written a very successful book and several magazine articles."

"I'm familiar with the name."

"You'll be more familiar with it. I saw him today in Daddy's office, and it seems he's doing an article on the misdeeds of oil companies."

"He's after Stone Oil?"

"Partly. He's investigating Paul."

"Paul?" Alexis's voice rose slightly.

"Yes. He came to my apartment tonight and asked where you lived. He wants to talk to you about how Daddy got Paul into the United States. Apparently Chris thinks Alec bribed and blackmailed everybody he could find."

A short, vivid expletive broke from her sister's mouth. "I can't let him near Paul. I don't want anything to remind him of Vietnam. He hasn't had a nightmare for a long time, but merely the mention of Vietnam might bring one back."

"I didn't tell him where you were, of course, but he'll find out another way. He's very persistent. So I thought you and Paul could come visit me. Chris has been here, and I doubt that he'll return."

"Okay. I'll pack tonight and fly in tomorrow morning. Will you be at work?"

"Yeah, but I could pick you up at lunch."

"Don't bother. I'll call Morgan."

"All right. See you tomorrow."

"Yeah. Thanks for calling. 'Bye."

"'Bye."

* * *

It was after one the next afternoon when the receptionist called Cara to the phone. Morgan's breezy voice said, "Mission accomplished."

"You picked up Alexis and Paul at the airport?"

"Sure did. And guess what? Our slender sister is beginning to show a tiny bit. Paul is cute as ever and knows nothing of the purpose of the visit. I felt like somebody in a spy novel, checking my rearview mirror to make sure no one was following me and all that. Nick thinks I'm crazy."

"I'll drop by on my way home from work to pick them up."

"I could make dinner for us all. How would that be?"

"Super. I'll be there after six."

It was one of her longest days at the office, and as it turned out, it was closer to seven than six when Cara stopped in front of Morgan and Nick's elegant Highland Park mansion. Nick waited for her at the door, a tall, cool drink in hand and a grin lighting his face. "You look like you could use this."

"Could I ever!" she exclaimed. "Leslie's coming back Monday, and frankly, after today I don't feel a bit of regret."

Nick handed her the drink and motioned down the hallway. "Morgan and Alexis are in the den talking. I'm in the game room with Paul, teaching him the finer points of pool. Take your choice."

She smiled. "I'm too tired for pool. I'll stick with the women."

Her sisters rose from the couch at her entrance, and Alexis came forward to hug Cara. "Thank heaven you got here," Morgan exclaimed, one hand to her stomach. "I was about to die from hunger. I stopped nursing Matt, so I've had to cut back on my eating. It seems like ten hours since lunch."

"Sorry. Some of us have to work, you know."

"Well, now that you've arrived, don't sit." Morgan linked her arm with Cara's and propelled her in the direction of the dining room. Alexis called Paul and Nick to the table, and soon they were seated at the elegant burl walnut dining table, ladling out Morgan's delicious supper. Cara could almost see the wheels spinning in Alexis's head as she selected her vegetables. Morgan chuckled. "Honestly, Alexis, you're so organized even about being pregnant. She maps out her whole diet each day—two servings dark green leafy vegetable, two eggs, four slices of bread, etcetera. Then she spends the rest of the day calculating where she is on the plan—what she needs more of and can this be substituted for that."

"You should talk," Nick put in. "I remember you poring over your books, trying to decide whether you could sneak a potato in as a vegetable or as bread."

"That's because I was trying to cheat," Morgan retorted serenely. "At the end of the day, I tried to make what I'd eaten fit into the diet categories. But Alexis plans the diet in the morning and then follows it."

Alexis smiled and began to recount the difficulties of her suddenly enormous appetite. Cara concentrated on her food, thinking miserably of the separation between her and her sisters. No matter how much older and closer to them she became, a gulf always seemed to appear in some form. She remembered talking to Chris about her sense of being on the outside looking in. It was the night she met him, when they were seated at Ginny's dining table. Cara swallowed and glanced around, looking for something to take away the memory. Her eyes fastened on the sideboard, remarking to herself how excellent Morgan's taste was and how right the classic piece of furniture was for her sister. But Cara's mind skittered obstinately from the furniture to the heavy antique table in Chris's apartment, and tears welled in her eyes. Since his reappearance, she had done little but think of him. It was silly, crazy, even self-destructive, but she couldn't stop herself.

"Cara?"

She heard her name and came to with a start. "What? I'm sorry. I had my mind on something else."

"That's the understatement of the year. What I said was, 'Have you heard anything from Barry?'"

"Barry?"

"I don't know whether to cry or laugh." A resigned chuckle escaped Morgan. "The guy who was here the night you came for dinner."

"Oh!" Cara's eyes twinkled. "You mean the guy who wasn't my blind date but merely a friend of yours?"

"Is Morgan matchmaking again?" Alexis laughed. "Sister dear, you ought to give up. Your judgment in such matters is unfailingly wrong."

"What!"

"Well, let's see," Alexis began to tick off items on her fingers. "First, you tried to get Nick and me together. Next, didn't you fix yourself up with Mike Durek?"

"Okay, okay, I give," Morgan interrupted hurriedly, a blush staining her fair skin. Nick began to chuckle. "I'll retire from matchmaking."

"Hurray!" Cara clapped her hands in mock delight.

After supper they dawdled over coffee and amaretto until Paul's eyelids began to close. Alexis laid her hand tenderly on his dark head and suggested they leave so she could put him to bed. He protested valiantly, blinking and struggling to stay awake, but Cara agreed, and they made their way to the Volkswagen. Nick followed to stuff Alexis's luggage in the little trunk. As they drove home, Paul leaned his head against the window of the backseat and was soon asleep.

Alexis looked around her and sighed. "I forget what the traffic's like in Dallas. Do you realize how long I've lived in Barrett? Two and a half years! I'm practically a country girl."

Cara glanced at her sister. Alexis's face was relaxed, her blue eyes dreamy. The sharp, anxious expression that had once marred her features was completely gone. "You really are happy, aren't you?"

Alexis nodded. "It's funny. I've discovered that the things I used to want aren't the things that make me happy. When I think of the time I wasted chasing shadows, I get furious. But if I hadn't been the way I was, I wouldn't have met Brant or Paul. And that's what turned my life around."

"I could shoot Chris!" Cara slammed her knotted fist

against the steering wheel. "Why does he have to come along now and upset you?"

"Don't worry about me. I may have changed, but I can still take care of myself. I'm the tough one, remember? If it was just me, I wouldn't bother with this hole-and-corner business. I'd see him and get it over with. But I don't want him to ask Paul any questions or disturb him in any way. He's come too far."

"I'll do everything I can to help," Cara promised.

"I know you will." Alexis patted her on the arm in an unusually affectionate gesture. "You're the most loyal person. I feel bad sometimes when I think how mean Morgan and I could be to you when we were young."

Cara shrugged. "I wanted to be with you all the time and play all your games. Of course, I understand now why you didn't want me tagging along."

"Children are cruel. Thank God we grow out of it. But no matter what, you always took up for us. One time we weren't watching you like we were supposed to, and you fell out of a tree. Scared me to death. You only had the wind knocked out of you, but I was sure you were dead. When Ginny came running, you managed to talk and assured her that we'd tried to stop you."

Cara laughed. "I remember it. I was scared you would be mad at me for getting you into trouble and then you wouldn't let me come along anymore."

"You were game for anything."

"I never stopped to think first, that was my problem." Cara sighed a little wistfully. "I guess it still is."

Cara and Alexis stayed up until the small hours of the morning talking and would have been glad to sleep late, but Paul woke them early, eager to visit the apartment-complex swimming pool. Alexis groaned and stumbled out of bed, but Cara walked into the guest room and motioned her back under the sheets. "You need more rest than I do. I'll take him swimming. Tell me, Paul, are you part fish or what?"

He giggled and ran to put on his trunks. Cara sleepily

dressed in a turquoise bikini that revealed much of her slim hips and ripe breasts and grabbed a bottle of tanning lotion. Normally she acquired a good tan, but this summer her job had kept her indoors and woefully pale. She had avoided the pool during her time off because she found it difficult to deal with the come-ons of the men who usually gathered there. Fortunately very few people would be there this early.

They strolled down to the kidney-shape aqua pool. It was designed more for appearances than for swimming, since it was too short and curved to be useful for doing laps, but Paul didn't mind. His main enjoyment was diving or jumping in and immediately climbing out to dive again. Cara swam for a while, then emerged and smoothed on tanning oil before stretching out on a webbed lounge chair. Soon she drifted into a light sleep.

A sudden shadow across her body awakened her. Cara opened her eyes, groggy and disoriented, squinting to see the features of the man who stood over her with the sun behind him. "Chris!"

"Yes, it's me," he answered, tight-lipped. "No doubt you hoped I was running around Barrett looking for your sister."

Cara sat up uneasily, thinking of the amount of bare flesh her skimpy swimsuit revealed. She wished she had something to put over herself to conceal her from Chris's hard, penetrating stare. Did he remember, as she did, how well he knew her body beneath the thin strips of blue-green cloth? She wet her lips and strove to keep her voice calm. "Why should I hope that? I thought I made it clear I didn't want you to see Alexis."

"You did. But you knew I'd be able to find her, so you warned her off. When I got to Barrett yesterday afternoon, I discovered she had left early that morning."

"Brant, too?" Cara shaded her eyes with her hand, struggling to maintain a casual look. Please don't let Paul grow curious and come to find out who this man is, she prayed silently. His Oriental features would give him away in-

stantly. She forced herself not to glance at the water to
check on him.

"Oh, no, the husband was there. I tracked him down in
the middle of a pasture. He kindly told me that if I set foot
on his ranch again, the best I could expect was the sheriff
hauling me off to jail for trespassing."

Laughter bubbled up from Cara's throat. "Poor Chris.
Wouldn't anyone allow you to invade his privacy? It must
have been quite a blow."

"Damn it, Cara, I only want to talk to Alexis. I'm not
going to harm her."

"Your talking can do a great deal of harm!" Cara spat
back, rising to face him. It was too overpowering to sit
practically at his feet while he glowered down at her, arms
akimbo. Even standing, she had to tilt her head to look at
him. She felt exposed and curiously vulnerable in the brief
bikini. To combat the feeling she thrust out her chin and
attacked. "I know you. You want to browbeat Alexis into
telling you something damaging about Stone Oil."

"I have no intention of bullying her. I just want to ask
a few questions. If nothing wrong happened, it shouldn't
upset her."

"That's a specious argument if I ever heard one. You're
very glib, Chris, but you won't slip past me with your
arguments about freedom of the press, justice and the people's right to know. Nobody has a right to pry into Alexis's
life. There is no great moral principle that demands my
sister expose every detail of her life and her stepson's to
the public."

"I don't care about the details of their lives," he thundered, his hazel eyes glittering green. "I only want to know
about the deal."

"The deal, the deal," Cara repeated scornfully. "How do
you know there was a deal? Alec helped get an innocent
child out of a hostile country and reunited him with his
father. It hardly sounds like an evil scheme to me. And
what if the things you say are true? What if Alec pulled a

few strings? Isn't a boy's life worth it? Is it so terrible to rescue a child from hell? When Paul arrived, he was plagued with nightmares. His mother had been killed by a bomb. He had no home, no family. If he'd been left in Vietnam, he would have starved to death or become a thief or a beggar in order to survive. Yet you dare to condemn my father for taking him away from such a life. No doubt it would have been more just to leave Paul there to die. Then there wouldn't have been any questionable deals."

"Sometimes I'd like to shake some sense into your head," he growled, and for a moment his face was so dark with anger that Cara feared he might actually do what he said. "You sound as if your father were the white knight who selflessly went charging off to save a child. That's hardly the case. He used Paul against his own father. He forced McClure to sign a gas lease by promising to give him the one thing he would have done anything to have—his son. That's real kindness and compassion for you."

"How do you know? There's nothing to prove it."

"You can't be so naive. Alec Stone wouldn't go a step out of his way for someone unless he got a payoff."

It was a thought Cara had often had about her father, but coming from Chris, the words prodded her anger to a white-hot pitch. "You ought to know, because you're exactly like him. You cheat and lie to get what you want. You're both so power hungry you don't care what happens to the people in your way."

"Power hungry!"

"Yes! Oh, you may not seek it in a multimillion-dollar business the way Alec does, but you use your pen to force everyone to knuckle under. You hold the power to destroy a person or make him a hero. Influential men quail when they hear you're after them. And you love it, don't you? What does it matter if a boy's life is ruined, as long as you get your story? Paul's forgotten his past. He hasn't had nightmares in almost two years. But you insist on talking to him about it. You're going to send him back into that hell . . . so you can take a potshot at Alec Stone."

For a long moment Chris stared at her speechlessly. "Is that what you think? That I want to dredge up old, painful memories for a child? I didn't say I wanted to talk to him. It's his stepmother I want to see."

"Why should I believe you?"

"My God, Cara, do you honestly believe I'm so ruthless? Is that the impression you received from our lovemaking?"

"How dare you bring that up?" Cara went rigid with rage. "It has nothing to do with the subject."

"It has everything to do with it. You're so furious with me that you aren't thinking rationally. I hurt you. Therefore, you hate me and will do anything to thwart me. That's the reason for your actions, not a desire to protect your sister and nephew."

"All roads lead to Chris Wozniak, don't they?" Cara's mouth twisted bitterly. "I've never met a more self-centered person. You aren't the only man in my life, you know. I've slept with others . . . before and since."

His brows contracted, but before he could speak, they were interrupted by a cool, feminine voice. "Excuse me. I'm Alexis McClure. I think I'm the one you wish to speak to."

Cara whirled to see Alexis standing a few feet away, her hand on Paul's shoulder. "Alexis!" Cara exclaimed. "Don't—"

"It's all right. Mr. Wozniak is obviously very determined to see me. Paul ran upstairs to get me, saying a man was yelling at you. Of course, I guessed who it was. I might as well talk to him and get it over with. If you'll take Paul upstairs with you . . ."

Paul turned to her worriedly. "But Allie—"

"It's okay, honey. You know nobody can outshout me, including your father." A reluctant smile touched the boy's face. "You go with Cara and fix lunch. I'll bet you're starved. I'll be up in a few minutes."

"Alexis, are you sure?" Cara lingered.

"Of course. I've handled worse than this at negotiating tables, believe me."

"Okay." Cara took Paul's small, cold hand, and they walked through the open iron gate of the pool. Resolutely Cara did not turn to look back.

"Now." Alexis turned briskly to Chris, looking every inch a capable, experienced attorney despite her shorts and loose top. "What was it you wanted to ask me?"

Cara and Paul were on pins and needles until Alexis returned to the apartment, although Cara could not express exactly why she was nervous. She knew her sister to be smart and capable, a match for anyone. Nor was Cara worried, as Paul was, about Chris physically harming Alexis. But some boiling emotion inside her warned that Chris was too treacherous for even Alexis to deal with.

She made tuna sandwiches and warmed a green vegetable for Alexis, chattering all the while to Paul about ordinary things. Though she tried her best to appear cool and unconcerned for Paul's sake, she jumped with relief when Alexis finally knocked on the door and Paul ran to open it.

"Great, you've got lunch ready," Alexis said as she came into the kitchen smiling. "Let's eat. My appetite is ridiculous these days."

Cara was slightly annoyed at her sister's breezy attitude and eager to hear what had passed between Alexis and Chris, but she could hardly blurt out her questions in front of Paul. So she had to wait patiently through lunch before Alexis sent him to play outside and they could sit down for an uninhibited conversation. "Well, what happened?" Cara prompted.

"Oh, nothing much. First he assured me he didn't want to talk to Paul, and I assured him he wouldn't be allowed to. We sat down, and he asked me a bunch of questions. I answered a few and squirmed out of some others. And that was that. He's a very persistent man, but he didn't find what he was looking for. I presume he'll try to get it from someone else."

"I'm sure. He'd dig it out of a grave if that was the only way he could get it."

Alexis glanced at her sister, her eyes clouding in puzzlement. "Why are you so down on him? He's determined and stubborn as a bulldog, but overall I thought he was a pretty sharp guy. Rather charming."

"Oh, he's charming, all right. He's also devious and deceptive. He doesn't care who gets hurt as long as he succeeds. If he didn't want to talk to Paul, it was only because Paul was of no use to him."

Cara's vehemence brought another sidelong look. "Obviously you know more about him than what meets the eye. What did he do to earn such contempt?"

"He's trying to drag you and Daddy through the mud. Isn't that enough?"

Alexis smiled. "Our father is hardly lily-pure. Alec's deals could stand a little investigating. Not that I'd like him to be in trouble, but I can't fault a reporter for trying to bring his tactics to light. I don't know exactly what Daddy did to get Paul. I was careful not to inquire too closely. Wozniak is right. I don't really care about Alec's methods, because they brought Paul home. And I'll do my best to protect Daddy. Still, I don't despise Chris Wozniak for not seeing things the way I do. Besides, I have the funny feeling his investigation of Alec isn't what turned you against him."

Cara sighed. "No. I—oh, Alexis, I made an idiot of myself over him in Washington. After you all left, I went out with him, even took a weekend trip with him. He was... I thought he was the most wonderful man I'd ever met. Ginny warned me to be careful, but I wouldn't listen. I was too starry-eyed."

She paused, staring fixedly at her clasped hands. Alexis finished for her. "Then you found out he was married."

Cara's head snapped up. "How did you know?"

Alexis shrugged. "Educated guess. Most men in their thirties are either married or divorced, and I didn't figure divorce would upset you so. It had to be something terribly wounding. Besides, there's a haunted sort of look in his eyes, as if he were torn."

"Torn? I hardly think so. He didn't tell me he was married. He pretended he was single, and when he got tired of the game, he dropped me."

"No explanation?"

Cara made an inelegant snort. "I wouldn't believe a word he said. His excuse was that he was 'carried away by desire for me.' I'm not that gullible... at least not anymore."

"No, now you're so bitter you'd cut off your nose to spite your face," her sister retorted, not unkindly.

"Alexis! Why are you defending him?"

"I'm not. I want you to be happy, and you won't be as long as you store up this anger inside you. I'm not claiming to be an expert in the romance department. But I've worked with men a lot, and I've found they're usually just as human, emotional and inept as we are. But they're poorer at expressing it. Fewer things are done from sheer wickedness than from stupidity or unrecognized and uncontrolled emotions. Maybe he's a villainous liar who coldly set out to deceive you. On the other hand, maybe he *was* carried away. It can happen—I know. He could have feelings for both you and his wife, or be so confused he doesn't know what he wants. Perhaps he's in a marriage he can't break free from."

"Nowadays? Come on, Alexis, nobody suffers through a bad marriage anymore. Most people get divorced at the slightest disagreement."

"I don't know him. I have no idea what his motives or morals are," Alexis admitted. "But I know from my own experience with Brant that you only make yourself unhappy by denying how you feel, by pretending to hate a man when you really love him. And the worst mistake in the world is making assumptions without giving him a chance to explain. I almost lost Brant because I assumed he'd been in Amarillo with an old girl friend, and I left him flat. Actually he'd been there to buy an engagement ring for me. If he hadn't given it one last try, I'd still be miserable and alone today."

Tears flooded Cara's eyes. "Sometimes my anger and hatred eat me up inside. I ought to get rid of them, but I know if I do, all that's left is the hurt and...and love." Her voice dropped to a whisper. "When I saw Chris in Alec's office, I knew the weeks in between hadn't helped. I hated him for the depression I've been feeling, yet I wanted to throw myself into his arms. I still want him. I still love him. And I don't know how I can bear to live with that!"

Chapter 9

Chris paced the floor of his hotel room. He knew it was time to leave Dallas. He'd gotten as much information out of the Stones as he'd expected—almost nothing. Alexis had been as tight-mouthed as a clam, and when he'd finally managed to see the old man, Alec had made her look chatty. As for Cara ... well, he really hadn't hoped for anything from her, not after what had passed between them. Besides, he doubted that either she or Morgan was privy to Stone Oil secrets. Fortunately, during the past week he'd found a couple of employees who had inadvertently revealed some information. At least he'd scraped up enough to provide some leads in Washington. He knew he would find nothing more here.

The intelligent thing to do, therefore, would be to call the airport and make a reservation on the next flight to D.C. So why wasn't he doing it, he asked himself. The answer wasn't hard to find. Cara. He was hoping for an excuse to see her one last time. It was stupid, of course, dangerous and a half dozen other negative adjectives. But reason and

safety had nothing to do with what he felt. He kept picturing
Cara as she had looked the other morning at the pool, her
ebony hair spread out against the bright yellow of the lounge
chair, her luscious body clad in a skimpy turquoise bikini.
The suit had revealed every line and curve, the soft swell
of breasts and hips, the sharp contrast of the jutting collar-
bone and the delicate pulsing triangle nestled at the bottom
of her throat. Her attire left almost nothing to the imagination, and his memory knew enough to supply in detail
what little was concealed. It had required all his control to
keep his hands off her. Since then, through all the wearying
interviews and tracking down of personnel of Stone Oil, he
hadn't been able to erase her image from his mind.

It was sheer insanity. Chris was fully aware of that. He
had been crazy to touch her in the first place. He'd realized
it the instant he set eyes on Cara at Wilson Decker's party.
She threatened the careful shell of numbness he had built
around himself over the years. There was no future in it,
never could be. Monica was an unchangeable fact. It would
have been better all around if he had left without speaking
to Cara. But she had set him on fire, and caution had paled
beside her ripe body and cornflower blue eyes. He had been
compelled to meet Cara, then to see her again and finally
to possess her fresh vitality in his bed.

Chris would exchange nothing for the memory of his
nights with Cara. Unfortunately their impassioned couplings
had only made him want her more, until at last he realized
he must give up Cara or be lost forever. He couldn't do it
to her...could not turn her into a married man's mistress
or lie to her trusting, smiling eyes. He could never have her
openly. It was a nightmarish situation, one that worsened
when he came to Dallas and discovered how deeply Cara
had been hurt by his foolhardy passion. It was inevitable
that she'd learn he was married. He was wrong not to have
told her himself. It was not a surprise that she hated him.
But the painful intensity of her hatred had startled him...and
sliced through him like a knife. Yet, despite the pain and
anger, Chris wanted her, dreamed of her, ached to touch

her again. She awakened every nerve ending in his body, and the thunderous exchanges between them only aroused him more.

He pulled his suitcase from the closet. He should stop mooning around over the girl, should pack and catch a plane. He flicked open the catches and laid the bag open flat on the bed. Slowly he began to fold his clothes into it. About halfway through he flung the case shut with a resounding curse and grabbed the keys to his rented car. At least he could see her before he left. Surely there was no harm in that.

After having a salad and a glass of white wine for supper, Cara settled onto the couch with another glass of wine and searched the entertainment page for something to watch on TV. Her apartment seemed much lonelier following Alexis's return to Barrett a week ago. The knock at Cara's door was a welcome interruption. Quickly she rose to answer it, realizing as she did so that the wine had made her a trifle light-headed.

She opened the door to find Chris standing before her. Perhaps it was the wine that made her bolder. She didn't care to examine her other reasons. But instead of slamming the door in his face as she had promised herself to do should he ever dare to come to her, Cara stepped aside to let him in. Chris walked past her without a word and sat down on the couch. He rubbed wearily at his face, then gazed up at her.

"You look beautiful, as always."

Cara glanced down at the faded denim shorts and yellow halter top. "Comfortable, maybe. Beautiful? Hardly."

A ghost of a smile flickered across his lips. "Perhaps not to you. They say it's in the eye of the beholder. And what I behold is that your attire sets off your . . . uh, attributes well."

Cara made an impatient move with her glass. The dark heat in his eyes made her uncomfortable, not the less so because it tightened the knot in her stomach. "Why did you come here, Chris? Surely by now you've realized you won't get any information from me."

"I didn't come for information. I came—I'm not sure, really. I suppose to say good-bye."

"That's your forte, isn't it?" Cara commented dryly.

He sighed. "I wish I could explain it better, make you understand I never meant to hurt you."

"So you've said. Even if I believed you, tell me, what good would it do? You'd still be married, wouldn't you? I'd still be out in the cold."

Chris didn't answer. The heavy silence was response enough. Cara turned aside to hide the water that flooded her eyes. When she swiveled back, her eyes dry, she continued in a lighter tone. "Well, did you breach Stone Oil's defenses?"

"Certainly not your sister's or Alec's. But I managed to get enough information elsewhere."

"Enough for what? To blacken its reputation? Daddy's never been known as Mr. Nice Guy anyway."

Chris rose abruptly. "I don't know what I'm doing here. For some reason I thought maybe I could explain it better this time. Hell, that's not it. I simply wanted to see you again before I left."

He advanced, and Cara backed away rapidly, bumping into a small table and causing a lamp to sway wildly. Chris's hand whipped out to catch it, skimming Cara's arm and breast. Then suddenly his arms were around her tightly, molding her to the tough length of his body. For an instant Cara froze before she pressed into him involuntarily, flattening her breasts against his hard chest, her arms encircling his neck. His lips dug into hers, longing, demanding, and his hands rediscovered the curves and planes of her flesh, cupping her breasts through the thin cloth of her halter. Cara's nipples hardened traitorously at his touch, and her bones seemed to melt within her. Chris tore his mouth away to trace the clean line of her throat and jaw, mumbling against her smooth flesh. "Cara, Cara, I want you so. God, I've never ached so in my life. Cara, sweet, love."

Her blood throbbed through her veins, pounding hypnotically in her temples, and she clung weakly to him, her body alive after weeks of numbness. Chris fumbled at the knot of her halter, a brief curse escaping his lips as it refused to yield. For some reason the interruption penetrated the haze of desire that enshrouded Cara. She realized with horror that she was allowing herself to be seduced once more by the man who had hurt her so badly.

"No!" She thrust herself violently away from him. Chris started to follow, but Cara held out both hands to stave him off, her eyes wide with disgust. "No! Don't you dare come near me!"

"Cara . . ." His voice was low, desperate.

"You touch me again and I'll scream rape. It'll be on the front page of every newspaper tomorrow morning. I'll make sure of that."

Chris closed his eyes and drew a long, shuddering breath. "God, Cara, do you honestly think I'd force you?"

"I don't know what you're capable of! Obviously you believe you can fool me again, but I'm not *that* slow on the uptake."

His hands clenched and unclenched. He swallowed hard. "It was foolish of me to come here. Where you're concerned, I don't seem to have good sense."

"Are you saying it's my fault? What an old ploy. 'You're so sexy, I can't help myself. Therefore, you should feel guilty and leap into bed with me.' Well, I'm not falling for it." Suddenly she felt drained and weary. "Please leave, Chris. You're a bastard to come here and do this."

"I didn't do it to hurt you. Do you think it's easy for me? I feel as if I'm being torn apart limb by limb!" His eyes flashed, and for a moment Cara thought he'd reach for her again. She took a step backward, knowing she would be lost if he touched her again. Her movement stopped him abruptly. "Please. Don't be afraid of me. I couldn't bear it." He ran one hand through his hair, the rapid rise and fall of his chest slowing. "Okay. I'll leave now. I'm sorry. I promise you won't see me again."

Quickly Chris turned on his heel and left the apartment, closing the front door softly after him. For a moment Cara stood rigid, staring after him. Then she broke and ran to her bedroom to fling herself onto the bed sobbing. Damn him! How could she allow him to control her so? Why did she shiver at his touch and yield so easily, as if she hadn't a thought in her head or a bone in her spine! With a cry of rage she flung her pillow against the door. Worst of all was the weakness in her loins like hot wax, and the knowledge that only Chris could love it away. She knew she'd hunger for him the rest of the night.

The phone's ringing woke her early the next morning, and Cara groped for the receiver. "Hello?" Her voice came out a croak.

"Cara?" The familiar voice on the other end was uncertain. "This is Alec."

"Daddy?" She cleared her throat and pushed herself into a sitting position, stuffing a pillow behind her back. A persistent pain throbbed in her temples, and her eyes were swollen and stinging from the bout of crying the evening before. "Why on earth are you calling me at this hour? I mean—"

Alec briskly cut off her apology. "It's all right. Cara, I need your help."

"My help?" she repeated, her morning-numb mind wondering if she were going crazy. Her father rarely needed anyone's help, let alone hers.

"Yes. You see..." he paused, "Mrs. Jenkins tells me you know that reporter."

"Chris Wozniak?" This was growing stranger by the moment. "Yes, I know him."

"Good. Not in love with him, are you?"

Cara laughed mirthlessly. "I'd say it's more the opposite emotion."

"Fine. Honey, I need to speak to you. Can you come to the house right away?"

Cara fumbled for her alarm clock. "Daddy, it's only seven-thirty. And it's Saturday."

"I know. But this is urgent. I've been thinking about it all night."

"All right." Cara shrugged. She had no desire to get up now, but she could hardly refuse the first favor she remembered her father asking of her.

"Bring Wozniak with you."

"What!"

"He's staying at the Hilton on Mockingbird. It'll be easy for you to swing by there on your way."

"But I don't like the man! I just told you that. In fact, we're in a state of warfare at the moment."

"It doesn't matter," he snapped. "Just get him over here. Tell him I want to talk to him, and I guarantee he'll jump at the chance."

"I'm sure he will," Cara agreed. "But I don't want to drive him over there. He can find you himself. Why do you need me if you want to see Chris?"

"I want to see both of you. Together. Would you please call him and come over as fast as possible?"

Cara sighed. "Okay. I'll be there as soon as I can." She hung up the receiver and stared down at it. Without doubt that was the strangest phone call she had ever received. Why was Alec eager to talk to Chris? And what did she have to do with it? Now that she thought about it, her father's voice had sounded strange. There was an urgency in it that was totally foreign to his usual domineering tone. Frowning, she heaved the Dallas Yellow Pages from the bottom of her nightstand and flipped through the book for the number of the hotel. She had no desire to talk to Chris, let alone ride in the same car with him even for a few blocks. Especially after last night. Color sprang into her cheeks, and she wondered how low Chris's opinion of her had sunk when she'd started to give in to him so easily. He must think her weak and controlled by her desires. The awful thing was it was true.

She dialed the Hilton and asked for Chris Wozniak, hoping they'd tell her he had checked out. However, the operator merely buzzed his room, and after a few rings his gruff voice answered. Cara swallowed, unable to speak.

"Hello?" he repeated impatiently.

"Ch . . . Chris, this is Cara Stone."

"Cara!"

"Yes. I'm calling because my father asked me to."

"Not because you wanted to," he completed for her.

"That's right. Alec phoned me to say he wants to meet with us this morning."

"Us?" he repeated roughly. "You and me? Why? And why now, when I've been trying to get to him all week and he's refused?"

"I don't know!" Cara snapped back, grimacing. "I'm not in on Daddy's secrets. Maybe he's going to blackmail you by threatening to expose your affair with his innocent young daughter."

"That sounds like Alec Stone." Chris's voice was heavy with sarcasm. He sighed, and Cara could imagine his habitual gesture of running one sinewy hand through his thick brown hair. For some reason the picture brought the pang of tears to her throat. "I don't know why in the hell I'm doing this . . . but all right, I'll come," he agreed finally. "When will you be here?"

"Give me thirty to forty-five minutes. Traffic won't be bad, but I have to shower and dress. It can't be *that* urgent."

Chris was waiting beneath the portico when Cara stopped in front of the hotel forty minutes later. Her long hair was still wet from her shower, and she had pulled it up into a tight knot atop her head. She was dressed casually in pale pink shorts and a knit top. Cara noted with irritation that Chris's eyes slid over her appreciatively. It wasn't fair, she told herself, when she could hardly stand to look at him for fear of staring too long at the lean, muscled arms that emerged from his short-sleeved yellow top or at the clean line of his legs in the tightly fitting jeans.

She drove quickly to her father's house on Lakeside Drive. Neither of them spoke. The house was an impressive colonial-style mansion, separated from the boulevard by a wide, rolling green lawn. Cara hesitated in front of the house, almost stopping at the curb. Chris glanced at her oddly, and she turned into the driveway, gliding to a halt at the side portecochere.

Most of Cara's childhood memories were connected to this house, with its stately porches and stairways and the broad green lawn in back. Yet since her parents' divorce when Cara was thirteen, she had visited here very rarely. The last time she was here, Laraine, Alec's present wife, had redecorated it so completely that very little of the interior remained as it had been before. Cara felt almost a stranger in her former home.

Chris studied the house, then glanced at Cara, a faint smile curving his lips. "This is where you grew up?"

She nodded and slid quickly out of the car. Chris followed her, his eyebrows arching. "I think our childhoods were somewhat dissimilar. I always wondered what it would be like to live in a park." He gestured at the expansive lawns.

"It's not exactly an estate," Cara retorted and turned her back on him to knock at the side door. The thin white curtain covering the paned upper half was pushed aside, revealing Laraine's surprised face. The curtain dropped, and the deadbolt lock clicked. Laraine pushed open the door.

"Cara! Whatever are you doing here so early? Is something wrong?" Laraine's face and voice were as anxious as her calm, poised exterior allowed.

"No, not that I know of. I got a call from Daddy commanding my immediate presence. I told him I thought eight o'clock on a Saturday morning was a bit much, but he insisted."

Laraine's eyebrows rose and fell. However, she quickly recovered her manners and stepped back to let them enter the kitchen. Laraine was immaculate, every blond hair in place, her face already made up. Even the sky blue caftan she wore was neat and elegant. Cara was sure her stepmother did not possess a single robe with missing buttons or food stains down the front. "Would you like a cup of coffee? I just made it." She motioned toward the coffee maker, still steaming and filling the room with a delicious aroma.

"Yes, please," Cara said. "Chris?"

"Yes, if you don't mind."

"Oh, I'm sorry, Laraine. This is Chris Wozniak."

Laraine's eyes opened wider, and Cara suspected that Alec had made a few choice comments about the reporter dogging him. No doubt she was amazed at Alec's sudden decision to see him. Being Laraine, though, she didn't blurt out her doubts but smiled at Chris and poured two more cups of coffee.

Cara's feelings for Laraine ranged from indifference to faint dislike of the woman's careful control over her feelings, her face and her life. During the past few months, however, Cara had witnessed another facet of Laraine's character. If Alec was insane about little Matthew, Laraine was almost as bad. She knitted, crocheted and bought toys for him, pouring out on him all the maternal feelings she had never expressed before. Loving Matt had done a great deal to raise her in Cara's esteem.

"Sugar? Cream?" Laraine asked as she handed the steaming cups to them. Chris shook his head, preferring it black, but Cara helped herself to the cream in a delicate little pitcher on the counter. "Alec is in his study. I heard him come in a few minutes ago while I was upstairs. He must have gone to the office early this morning. Here, why don't you take him a cup, too?"

Cara accepted another cup of black coffee and led Chris through the mansion to the large study at the back of the house. The door was closed, and Chris rapped sharply on it.

"Come in," Alec's voice rumbled from inside, and they entered.

"Cara." He stood immediately and came forward. His gaze slid to Chris, and he nodded briefly. "Wozniak. Sit down, both of you."

"Here. Laraine sent some coffee." Cara extended the cup, and Alex took it abstractedly. He was dressed impeccably in a pale green golf shirt and cream-color slacks. Cara could not remember ever seeing her father actually play golf, and she suspected he wore the casual clothes more to show off his still-trim body than for any sporting purpose. This morning, however, he did not look quite himself, despite the crisp attire. There was a stiffness, almost a nervousness, in his manner. He returned to the heavy leather chair behind his desk and set the cup down. Cara noticed that he didn't touch it again. Leaning forward, he put his palms together and stared down at his desk.

"I don't know how to begin." He raised his hands and rested his chin on his fingertips, looking up at Chris as though he might give Alec an answer.

"Why don't you start by explaining why you asked us here?" Chris suggested impatiently. "After the way you've avoided me, I'm damned if I can understand it."

"And why we both had to come," Cara added.

Alec sighed and dropped his hands. "All right. I'll be as concise as possible. Stone Oil has an extremely important well in Canada. I think it will be the biggest one we've drilled since McClure Number One, maybe even bigger. Unfortunately there have been several delays. It's been a bad-luck well. First we lost a bit, and then fire destroyed some equipment. Finally vandals destroyed more equipment. Nevertheless, we've managed to keep drilling and aren't far behind schedule. We need that well. I'm certain there's a sizeable deposit there. I've practically staked my reputation on the well, not to mention sinking a lot of the company's money into it."

Cara frowned in puzzlement. "But Daddy, what does this have to do with Chris and me?"

"Someone's sabotaged the well, and I want to find out who's behind it. I'm hoping to persuade Wozniak here to investigate it for me." He smiled thinly. "Despite my dislike for his prying, I know he's good at ferreting out information. I need a man who's sly and subtle, who can worm things out of people without their even knowing what they revealed."

Chris gazed at him flatly. "Why me? Why not the police or a private detective? You couldn't possibly want me nosing around in your affairs after all the effort you've made to keep me out of them. You're hiding something, Stone. I don't know if you're trying to trap me or throw me off the scent or what, but it won't work. I won't do it."

Alec stared at him, his face slack with astonishment. "You refuse?"

"Give me one good reason I should do it. I can give you plenty why I won't. For one thing, what would I get out of it? A story on a sabotaged well? It doesn't impress me. Second, you're trying to pull something sneaky. You're concealing facts, and I won't go into something blindfolded. If you want me to help you, you're going to have to cough up something more. For once you're going to have to be honest. Tell me the *whole* story, and maybe I'll consider it."

Alec bit his underlip. "The reason I want you is because the last thing I want is an obvious investigation. I can't afford to haul in a blatant, flat-footed detective who would advertise his vocation all over the place. Since you've been snooping around trying to dig out dirt on me, it wouldn't appear suspicious if you went to the rig and asked a few questions." He paused and passed a hand across his lined forehead. "I'm not trying to pull a fast one on you. This is vitally important to me. You see, late yesterday evening I received a phone call in which a man demanded I close down the Canadian well." His voice rasped to a halt.

"I suppose he threatened you," Chris prompted.

"Of course. He told me if I didn't, we'd never see Matthew again." His last words tumbled out in a rush. He ran a trembling hand through his thick, gray-tinged hair. "He threatened to kill my grandson."

Chapter 10

Cara stared at her father numbly. A vision of her baby nephew, chubby and laughing, flashed across her mind, and she spluttered, "No...Daddy, you can't be...are you sure?"

He gave her a tight smile. "I know you find it difficult to believe. I did, too. But I assure you it's the truth."

"What exactly did he say?" Chris asked.

Alec closed his eyes. "I think he said, 'Shut down the Canadian drilling. Shut down Michaelson Number Two.' I said something belligerent along the line of I wouldn't do it. And he replied, 'If you don't, you'll never see Matthew Fletcher again alive. You want to see your grandson, Mr. Stone?' Then he hung up. At first I sat there like Cara, numb, not believing what I'd heard. Next I became curiously resigned and tired. I contemplated retirement. But gradually I came out of the fog, and I realized I'd have to fight it. If I give in now, he'll have me under his thumb for the rest of my life. I've never run scared from anybody yet, and I don't intend to start now."

"Oh, but Daddy, Matthew..." Cara wailed.

"No, Cara, he's right," Chris interjected. "You can't give up your whole life to another person's control. Besides, if Mr. Stone acceded to the man's demands, how could he be caught? You want someone capable of killing Matthew running around loose, free to do that or whatever other perversion comes into his head?"

"No, of course not. But how can you fight him without Matt being hurt?"

"Matthew's well-being is my primary concern. You must know that," Alec assured her. "I spent all last night thinking about it. I've hired the best private protection agency in the country to provide a personal bodyguard for Matthew around the clock. The guard's arriving this morning, and I'll take him to Morgan's immediately. Just in case, I'm sending another to Alexis, for Paul. That's as safe as I can make them. I've already explained the rest of my plan. I want Wozniak to find out who's behind the threat."

"Mr. Stone, this isn't right. Surely this is something for the police, not a newspaper reporter."

Stone quirked one eyebrow. "You're unduly modest all of a sudden. I'm passably familiar with your work, Wozniak. You've uncovered stories no law-enforcement agency even came close to. As soon as the law started poking into it, the extortionist would know what I was doing. However, you have a good cover. You're investigating *me*. I'll send Cara to Canada with you, to represent my interests. You can pretend she's my watchdog, or she's giving you entrée, or you're having an affair—whatever you like."

"No. Cara's not going," Chris ordered. "It's too dangerous."

"Surely you don't think I'd turn you loose on my well without my representative right on your heels."

"The men at the well will watchdog for you."

Alec shrugged. "I can't rely on them. Any one of them could be in league with this guy. It would be easy for one of them to have sabotaged the well."

"Then you'll have to trust me, because I'm not taking Cara."

"Look, mister, I don't trust anybody on this but a member of my own family. I'd talk Alexis into going, but she's pregnant. Cara is the perfect choice—no commitments till the fall, no husband or children to worry about. You finished that job, didn't you, Cara?"

"Yes, last week," she replied in a small voice. She had no desire to travel and work with Chris, but perversely, his adamant refusal of her company stung. "But Daddy, I'd probably just be in his way."

"Right," Chris agreed.

Cara shot him a fulminating glance. "I'm not that incompetent!"

He opened his mouth to reply, and Alec hastily interrupted. "Before you get any further into the argument, I want to say one thing. I make the decisions here, and I say she's going. I'll be damned if I'll sit around here with no idea of what you're doing. Cara's able and quick. She won't be a hindrance. Maybe you don't like each other, but you can put it aside for a few days. Cara, Matthew ought to be important enough for you to do this. As for you, Wozniak, I'll make it worth your while."

"I won't do it unless she stays here."

"You haven't heard my offer yet."

"You can't pay me enough money."

"Not money. Of course, I'll reimburse you quite adequately for your time. But I'm also offering something much more important to you—information. If you find out who's behind this, I'll spill my guts. I'll tell you every crooked and halfway crooked deal in the oil industry. You'll have enough material for two books. Forget the paltry article. I can give you names, places, dates—whatever you need."

"It's a tempting offer." Chris didn't add that merely the sight of Cara's white, terror-stricken face would have prompted him to track down the extortionist without any other inducement. "But I won't allow Cara to be placed in danger."

"What's this 'won't allow' business?" she demanded. "Since when do you have the right to allow or not allow me to do anything? I'll do whatever I please, and it's no concern of yours!"

His mouth tightened grimly. "I realize I have no rights over you. But I can hardly stand by and watch you rush into God knows what."

"You're going there! What's the difference? Daddy's not the male chauvinist you are. He knows his daughters are as capable as any man."

"Your whole family is impossible!" Chris exploded, jumping out of his chair. "Of all the pigheaded people I've met in my life, the Stones take first prize. We're talking about a man who is willing to kill an infant. Do you think he'll balk at destroying you if you get in his way?"

"I thought the idea was to be clever, so he wouldn't know you're investigating his threat."

"We can cover temporarily, but when we hit a nerve, he's going to guess the real purpose."

"You'll be in the same position as I will."

"I'm used to it. It's my business. I'm capable of taking care of myself, but I'm not sure I can protect both of us."

"You won't have to!" Cara rose and faced him, hands on hips, her small jaw outthrust.

Amusement tinged Alec's troubled face. "Cara, I've seen that expression in the mirror a hundred times. Careful, you'll turn out like your old man. Now, you two sit down. You're reacting so hysterically I'm not sure if either one of you is capable of the job. The only time I insist Cara be with you is when you visit the Canadian site. I presume you want to see it."

"Yes, of course. That's where I'll be most likely to find a lead."

"But it won't be your entire investigation."

"No, I doubt that what we find there will take us straight to whoever is planning this."

"I'll fly you to Canada. You and Cara visit the drilling rig. When you're through, Cara will return, and you'll be free to go wherever you need to. Greeson, who's in charge of the Canadian operations, knows Cara. He'll trust her a great deal more than you. She'll provide you with a cover before you touch that 'nerve.' When things start to get sticky, she'll be safe in Dallas. I'll insist she live at Morgan's house, where the bodyguard will be. How is that for a compromise? Provided you give me regular progress reports, of course."

Chris hesitated. Besides the danger, which had been his immediate thought, he was certain it would be nearly impossible to spend several days close to Cara without succumbing to his passion again. The time in Canada would be sheer hell on his nerves. Yet what Alec was offering was reasonable, and Chris couldn't afford to turn it down, for the sake of either the story he was promised or the fearful anxiety in Cara's eyes. "All right." He sank into his chair with a sigh. "I agree. Although I can't understand why you won't be content with my progress reports from the rig as well. I'll give you my word not to snoop into anything extracurricular."

Cara's lip curled. "He probably knows how much your word is worth."

"Don't start up again," her father warned sternly. "I'll call Greeson and tell him you're on the way. Can you leave today?" At their nods, he continued, "Greeson's a good man, but plan to leave him with the idea you're working on your story and Cara's overseeing you. The fewer people who know what's going on the better. But I'll order him in no uncertain terms to cooperate, and Cara, you reinforce that."

"Okay."

"Good. You'd better go pack a few things. I'll phone Anderson, the pilot, and he'll have the company plane ready to go. When can you reasonably get to Love Field?"

Cara shrugged. "In a couple of hours."

"I'll tell Anderson you'll be there at eleven. Here's some money for whatever essentials you need. The motel and restaurant will go on the company tab." He casually tossed Cara a thick envelope, which she stuffed into her purse without looking in it. She was sure that her father's idea of essentials greatly exceeded her own. "And I'll give my banker in Canada authority for you to draw on my account there, in case you need a large sum of money to encourage people to talk."

Cara was dazzled at the sudden acquisition of power and money. How was she to handle this? She wondered if Alec remembered it was his youngest daughter he was talking to, not Alexis. Buying information, keeping a watchful eye on Chris—good heavens, if Alec only knew how gullible she had been about Chris in the past. She turned to him uncertainly. To be alone with Chris, working closely with him—how could she endure it?

But Chris was not looking at her. He was jotting down notes on his ever-present pad. "Tell me, Mr. Stone, do you have any ideas about who could be behind this? Remote, unlikely, it doesn't matter. Just anything to give me a clue."

"My first thought was that it was a personal enemy," Alec mused. "But if so, why force me to shut down the well? That would hurt Stone Oil. We've put a lot of money and time into it. But it wouldn't ruin either me or the company, although the board of directors wouldn't like it very much. I ramrodded this well past the others, who were more cautious about it. I don't know. I'd lose face with the board, and perhaps he thinks the damage to my image would be enough."

"Who are these personal enemies?"

"I'm not sure. It sounds crazy, I know. I've stepped on quite a few toes in my time and probably didn't even realize I'd hurt some of them. It could be a person I don't know or don't remember. There's a banker I talked into a deal that later went bust. He's always disliked me. And let's see..." He enumerated a list of men who had reason for grudges, large and small, against him over the years, finishing, "But none of them seems capable of it. They aren't vicious. One possibility is another company that wants to obtain the lease and hopes I'll sell it if I can't drill. The well should be a good producer, and I know several men whose mouths would water at the idea of getting their hands on it. Again, I can't imagine any of them threatening Matt. Any oil company would have the most to profit by it."

"Okay." Chris flipped his pad closed and rose. "You're sure there's no one else who would profit by the well's closing?"

Thoughtfully Alec shook his head. "No. If I think of anyone, I'll let you know."

Chris glanced at Cara. "Let's get moving."

"All right." She paused uncertainly, gazing at her father. He looked grim and pained. She had never seen him like that before, and it was unnerving. For a moment she was tempted to put a comforting arm around Alec's shoulders, but she lacked the nerve to breach his defenses. Finally she turned and followed Chris out of the room.

By evening they were in Canada. The plane landed on a dirt strip near the small town of Bow Lake in Saskatchewan. Bill Greeson, a potbellied man with thinning hair and a perpetual frown, waited for them in a jeep beside the landing strip. When the plane rolled to a halt and the pilot let down the steps, Greeson hurried forward. "Hello, Miss Stone, nice to see you again."

"Thank you. Mr. Greeson, this is Chris Wozniak."

The two men shook hands, and Cara smothered a smile at the suspicion with which Greeson studied Chris. Despite her father's call, Chris might have trouble pulling any information out of this one. They piled the luggage in the back of the jeep and Chris climbed in with it, while Cara sat down beside Greeson.

"Shall we go to the rig first, or would you rather stop at the motel to freshen up?"

"Straight to the rig," Chris answered, although the question had been directed at Cara.

Greeson glanced at Cara questioningly, and she felt a smug satisfaction that he waited for her answer, no matter what Chris commanded. "Yes," she agreed, "the rig. We might as well get on it."

"Will the crew still be there?" Chris asked.

Greeson shot him a pitying glance at his ignorance. "Of course. We work three shifts. There's always somebody at the rig."

"I understand you've had some problems," Cara put in. The older man turned to her and then flicked his eyes uneasily in Chris's direction. Cara hastened to assure him. "It's all right. Chris knows about the problems. Didn't Daddy tell you to answer all Mr. Wozniak's questions?"

"Well, yes ma'am, but..." his voice trailed off uncertainly.

"But what?"

"I wasn't sure he'd mean this."

"Especially this, Mr. Greeson. That's one reason Daddy sent me along. He's concerned about what's happened here."

Greeson chewed nervously at his underlip. "So am I. It's been bad luck. First the bit broke. Next kids tore up some equipment one night, and we had a fire."

"I thought there were workers there around the clock," Chris interjected. "How could they get in to damage the equipment?"

"It was when we were shut down on account of the broken bit. We got the bit the next morning, but we still couldn't start because we had to replace the damaged equipment. The fire started over by the slush pit one evening when we were working. We were lucky it didn't spread and endanger the well. The wind had been blowing real hard toward the well, but it shifted and blew the opposite way. We put it out before it did any harm."

"What do you think about all these accidents?" Chris's question was soft, undemanding.

"The bit breaking? Well, that happens all too often. But the fire and the vandalism? I don't know. It sounds pretty fishy to me, that many things happening to one rig."

"Why would anyone cause the accidents?"

"You've got me. I don't know why or who. We were too busy fighting the fire to run around looking for who started it, although I suspect it was set. No one was there when the equipment was hurt, and they didn't leave any clues."

"Could it be one of the workers?"

He shrugged. "Could be. I don't know many of them personally. The tool-pusher can tell you more about the men than I can. He's in charge of them. I'm the company's representative. I oversee all the Canadian wells, and right now I've got three. I'm here only part of the time."

"What in the world is a tool-pusher?" Chris asked in amusement.

"It's the man who's in charge of drilling," Cara explained. "Don't ask me why they call him that. He's like a foreman."

"Tell me about this tool-pusher."

"His name's Ashe Harlan. He's young—twenty-seven, twenty-eight years old. He's the youngest tool-pusher who ever worked for me. But he's good. Tough and responsible. He never rests. From what I hear, he's very ambitious and is saving his money for a big business venture."

"Would you say he's reliable? Honest?"

"Reliable, sure. You can count on him to get everything done correctly. Honest? Offhand, I'd say yes. I think I can trust him. But frankly, I don't know him that well. He might be willing to do anything to increase his bank account."

"I'd like to talk to him."

"Sure. He's always there. He lives in a trailer close to the rig."

"He sleeps there? Why didn't he hear the vandals?"

"He was in town that night. He's the one who discovered the damage when he returned."

"I see," Chris replied, and his eyes darkened with suspicion.

They turned off the main highway and bumped along a dirt road. The jouncing ride precluded all conversation. Deep ruts revealed the passage of heavy trucks carrying drilling equipment and made the road almost impassable to smaller vehicles. They rounded a bend, and the drilling rig stood before them, towering above its metal platform. The long platform was raised and covered with heavy machinery. Eight or ten men moved around the machinery, apparently oblivious to the thundering noise. The metal platform and the steps leading to it were dark, royal blue, and the rig above it was painted bright yellow, a color scheme repeated on a nearby truck.

"Those are Stone Oil's colors," Cara explained to Chris. "See all the pipe stacked over there? Whenever I've visited a rig, it seems like they spend most of their time screwing the pipes together. Beyond it is the slush pit. That trailer is the tool-pusher's."

"I see they've put up a fence."

"Yeah, we did it after the vandalism," Greeson explained. "We also have a guard dog at night now." He left the jeep, and Cara and Chris followed suit.

Some of the men turned to look at the new arrivals. One called and gestured to a slender man in a hard hat, boots, jeans and a blue work shirt that was opened down the front and hanging loosely outside his trousers. He swiveled his head and glanced at them, finished talking to the other men, then strode across the platform and ran lightly down the metal steps to the ground. As he walked toward them, he pulled off the hard hat, revealing thick light brown hair, slightly curling and streaked blond from the sun. Although he was slender, his rolled-up sleeves and open shirt showed him to be all muscle, tanned and hard as iron.

"Mr. Greeson, how ya doing?" He stretched out his hand to the older man and shook hands firmly. He wiped the sweat from his forehead with the back of one arm and glanced incuriously at the two people who stood beside his boss. Cara noticed that his eyes, clear sky blue behind long sandy lashes, were startling in his deeply tanned face. He was handsome, she thought, but oddly stern and hard for one so young.

"Ashe," Bill returned his greeting. "I've got some people I'd like you to meet. This is Cara Stone, Mr. Stone's daughter. And Chris Wozniak."

Harlan's hand, which was already lifting toward her as

135

Bill spoke, suddenly froze in mid-air. His face went blank, and his eyes became hard as marbles. "Sorry. I'm too grimy for a lady." He turned over his hand as if to show her the accumulation of dirt and grease, then dropped his hand to his side without shaking hers. "Ma'am. Mr. Wozniak." He gave them a brief nod.

"I'd like you to help Miss Stone if you can, Harlan. She and Mr. Wozniak want to talk to you."

There was a slight hesitation before he replied. "Sure. I guess we'd better go into my trailer, where it's cooler."

"Fine. I'll take a look around while you talk," Greeson added.

"Okay. Here's my hat."

Greeson took it and walked away, settling the metal hat on his head. Harlan swept Cara and Chris with a cold blue gaze. "Come on. I'll take you inside." He turned and strode away without looking back to see if they were following.

Cara glanced at Chris, and he raised his eyebrows comically. "Not the world's friendliest, is he?" he whispered.

"Hardly."

The young man took the steps of the trailer in one long stride. Shoving open the door, he walked inside and folded his lanky frame onto the couch. He watched Cara and Chris expressionlessly as they entered. Cara sighed with appreciation as the air-conditioned air hit her. "Ah, this is nice."

"What can I do for you?" Ashe Harlan asked, his tone anything but helpful.

"I'm a reporter, Mr. Harlan," Chris began. He motioned Cara into a chair but remained standing himself. Cara suspected it was to intimidate the younger man, but she could see no signs of its effect. "I'm doing a story on Stone Oil."

"You want me to show you around the rig?"

"That would be nice. I'm more interested, however, in talking to your men."

"Why?"

"To get the feel of working on a drilling rig—the hours, the hard work, the loneliness, that sort of thing."

"My men are busy, Mr. Wozniak. They don't have time to stand around talking."

"Alec Stone has given me carte blanche to talk to the men."

"Is this a publicity job for Stone? Something to stick on TV or put in the shareholders' annual report?"

"Mr. Wozniak is an investigative reporter," Cara put in. "He's not paid by the company, nor is he in any way responsible to it. He's writing an article for a magazine and, quite frankly, he's more likely to attack Stone Oil than to do an advertisement for it."

"Then why does Stone want us to talk to you?"

"My father is bending over backward to treat Mr. Wozniak fairly. He doesn't want charges of a cover-up leveled at him."

"He must have hidden his tracks well."

"What do you mean?" Cara was stung by his obvious antagonism.

"Just that Stone wouldn't have risked Wozniak's coming here if he didn't know nothing would be found."

Cara's eyes flashed. "You don't sound like a very loyal employee."

"Loyal?" He raised his eyebrows quizzically. "I do my job and do it better than most. That's why Stone pays me. I get a good salary. That's why I work for him. Beyond that, I don't owe Stone Oil anything."

She started to retort hotly, but Chris held up a hand. "Cara." She clamped her mouth shut and settled back in her chair, crossing her arms defensively. Harlan's cold eyes left her and returned to Chris. "I'm going to interview your men. If you intend to be obstructive, I'll simply ask Mr. Greeson for authorization."

Harlan shrugged. "If Stone wants to waste his workers' time talking, by all means go ahead."

"First I want to talk to you," Chris added firmly, challenging the young man's gaze with his own hard green-brown eyes. Harlan stared back and finally wavered and glanced away. "Mr. Greeson tells me this rig's been plagued by accidents," Chris continued.

"We've had a few."

"Tell me about them."

"The accidents?" he repeated in puzzlement. "You're doing a story on them?"

"It seems an interesting sidelight to drilling—the problems involved."

Harlan shrugged as if to say he was not responsbile for the freakish interests of the reading public and began to describe at tedious length the breaking and replacement of the bit.

"What about the fire?"

"The night crew was on the platform, and I was in here asleep. Their yelling woke me up, and I ran outside. The slush pit was on fire. I phoned the fire department and then went to help fight the flames. The wind changed, and we managed to control the fire so it didn't hit the rig."

"How did it start?"

"I don't know. A match or a cigarette, I guess. The fire department couldn't find what started it."

"And the night of the vandalism—I understand you weren't here, although you usually are."

The look the young man gave him was long and measured. "What are you saying?"

"I'm saying Mr. Greeson told us you usually sleep here, but that night you were in town."

"If you're implying I did it, you're—" He quickly braked the first spark of emotion he had shown. "Why would I want to damage the equipment on my own well?"

"Money can be a powerful motivator," Chris replied. "But I'm not saying you did. It could have been any number of people who knew you were in town that evening. One of your men, say."

"Or anyone who saw me in the bar," Ashe pointed out. "Why do you want to lay it on one of us? Is that what Alec Stone thinks?"

"I don't know what he thinks. I simply like to consider

all the possibilities. Now would you tell me what you did that evening, so I can get a better picture of it?"

"We weren't drilling. It was after the bit broke. So we weren't working any shifts, and there weren't any problems for me to stick around here for. About eight o'clock I went into town for a few drinks. Most of my men were there, too, although I couldn't give you a detailed list. There's not much else to do in Bow Lake. About twelve o'clock I returned to the rig. I found the damage and called the police. You can ask anybody. I couldn't have left at twelve and called the police when I did and still have had time to tear up the equipment. Besides, it would take two men and a blowtorch, which I don't have."

"I see. You were at the bar till midnight?"

He shot an uneasy look in Cara's direction. "No. I was with someone . . . a lady."

"A good alibi."

"Alibi? You sure like to throw around mean-sounding words, mister."

"It's the way I make my living. Tell me something, Harlan, what do you think of the accidents?"

"What do you mean?"

"I mean don't you think three accidents at one rig are a little suspicious?"

Harlan's face was carefully blank as he returned Chris's penetrating stare. "Sometimes you have a run of bad luck. Haven't you ever done that playing poker?"

"Playing poker and crippling a rig are rather different things."

"Why would anyone want to cripple it?"

"I don't know. That's one reason I'm curious. Why do *you* think someone would want to?"

"I don't have any idea. It's your theory, not mine."

"Did you see anyone who didn't belong around the rig any of the days before the fire or the vandalism?"

"Not particularly. Sometimes local people come out to look, you know. I don't pay much attention to them. I have a job to do."

"Apparently you do it with singular concentration," Chris commented dryly.

"As a matter of fact, I do." He refused to rise to the bait.

"What about in town? The night you went to the bar, were there any strangers there?"

"There were other people besides my crew, but I don't know the townspeople. They're all strangers to me." Harlan rose abruptly. "If you're through questioning me, I'll take you out to meet my men."

Ashe walked swiftly from the trailer to the tall platform, and Chris kept pace with him while Cara trailed behind them. They were given hard hats and taken around to be introduced to each man. Chris asked extraneous questions about the rig and its operation to mask his intent, as well as the questions he had come for. None of the crew had the surly attitude of their boss, and they answered Chris freely. When they finished, Chris guided Cara down the steps to the jeep, where Greeson awaited them, his head tilted forward in slumber. He awoke with a start when they climbed in and, stretching, turned on the ignition. In a burst of dust they turned around and headed briskly down the rutted road. Cara glanced back and saw a tall, lean figure standing on the platform, staring after them.

Chapter 11

"Well, what do you think?" Cara asked before biting into a thick hamburger. They were sitting at a vinyl booth in the coffee shop adjoining their motel in the village of Bow Lake. After they had returned from the rig, Cara had discovered she was dying of hunger and realized that in her shock and excitement, she had forgotten to eat all day. As soon as they checked in, they headed for the restaurant. Now, feeling somewhat satiated, Cara was eager to review their progress.

"About what?" Chris replied infuriatingly, cutting into his meat.

"You know what," she exclaimed in exasperation. "About the investigation. I'll put my money on Ashe Harlan. He's mean as a snake."

Chris grinned. "He wasn't the picture of a gentleman, was he?"

"No, and he seems to have a grudge against Alec. I mean he didn't exactly encourage you to think Dad is an honest guy."

"He was also antagonistic toward you, which surprises me. It'd be easy enough for an employee to resent Stone Oil and its president. But it struck me as odd that a twenty-eight-year-old man, stuck way up here with little female companionship and presented with a very attractive young woman in tight slacks—"

"They're not tight!"

"Would you let me finish? In tight slacks and a well-cut blouse, should not only not fall all over himself trying to please her, but should be downright rude."

Cara shrugged. "I suppose so. Maybe he dislikes all Stones on principle. That's how Alexis's husband felt when he met her."

Something sparked in Chris's eyes. "Good. Then perhaps you'll be able to talk him around to marrying you." His voice dripped sarcasm.

"What's that supposed to mean? Do you think I'm trying to marry any guy I meet? I don't fall like an idiot for everyone, you know. I'm so selective I'm only attracted to married liars."

"All right. *Mea culpa.* I shouldn't have said that. Back to Ashe Harlan. He seems the likeliest suspect for a villain. But isn't he a little obvious? Would someone who's trying to destroy a well broadcast his feelings so? I would think he'd hide his antagonism better if he had committed the vandalism."

"Besides, he had a witness."

Chris smiled. "Ah, yes, the mysterious 'lady.'"

"So what's your decision on him?"

"I don't have one yet. He may have an idea who did the damage, although I suspect he didn't tear up the equipment himself. Given his attitude, it might not take much to bribe Harlan to occupy himself in town on a certain night, leaving the site accessible and providing himself with a nice alibi."

"Makes sense."

"One thing's for sure—I got the definite impression he's holding back."

"Did you? I thought he was just plain ornery." ·

"That, too. Which may be why he's holding back."

"You know, it's funny. I'd swear I had seen him somewhere before."

"Maybe you have."

"No. I asked Greeson, and he said Harlan was from Oklahoma."

"At your father's offices?"

"Perhaps," Cara replied doubtfully. "I don't know. I think it was his walk that looked so familiar. It's weird. You'd think I'd remember him more clearly if I had actually seen him someplace."

Chris studied her thoughtfully. "Well, try to remember if you can. It could be important. Maybe he reacted negatively to you because you might recognize him, and he didn't want that."

Cara wrinkled her brow. "I wish I could. Oh, well . . . it may come to me in my sleep." As soon as she said it, Cara felt self-conscious and wished she hadn't. It was a peculiar enough situation without her bringing up the subject of sleeping arrangements.

They finished their supper in silence, and as they rose, Chris announced, "I think I'll visit the bar Harlan spoke of. See if any of the townspeople remember strangers in there around the time of the fire or the vandalism."

"I'll go with you."

"I don't think so. If it's where the drilling crews hang out, I imagine it's too rough for you."

"Honestly, Chris, I'm not a child. I've probably seen worse honky-tonks at college."

"They weren't full of oil-field roughnecks."

Unconsciously Cara tilted back her head, glancing teasingly up at him. "Don't you think you can protect me?"

The air caught in his throat, the subtle provocation of her stance and curving, sensual mouth hitting him like a blow. He muttered hoarsely, "Damn, Cara, don't tease me. It's hell enough being here with you."

She swallowed, realizing she had flirted with Chris. Tears filled her eyes. "I...I'm sorry. I didn't know it was so awful to be around me."

"You know what I mean." His voice was low, tortured. "I want you. I'm a cad if I make love to you, but being around you and not being able to touch you is killing me. All day today, through the flight and the interviews, I was more aware of you than anything else. Your perfume, the thrust of your breasts against that blouse, your smile...God, Cara, I'm only human."

She trembled and looked away from the intensity of his eyes. He was trying to manipulate her, Cara told herself, making passionate speeches to stir her and convince her to fall into his arms. He didn't mean it. He was married. And yet...

"I'm sorry." Her voice came out frail and tiny, and she cleared her throat. He was too close; she wanted achingly to lean against his chest and be warmed by him, to hear the hammer beat of his heart and feel his lean, sinewy flesh beneath her fingers. "I...I'll go back to my room. I'll see you tomorrow morning."

Quickly, without looking at him, afraid of yielding if she did, Cara almost ran from the restaurant, digging in her purse for her key. Inside the motel room she locked the door and slid the chain lock across, then smiled wryly at her actions. The real danger wouldn't come through the outside door. It lay in the room next to hers, with its connecting door. That was Chris's room, and all she had to do was open her door and then she would be lost. Sternly Cara thrust the thought aside and began to get ready for bed. She occupied the time for a while by cleaning her face and unpacking her bags, then slipping into her thin nightgown. After that there was nothing left to do. She had not brought a book to read, and there was no television in the small, cheap room. She supposed they were lucky even to have a place to sleep in the tiny town. She turned out the lights and crawled into bed, but sleep would not come. She lay awake, straining her ears for the sounds of Chris's return.

Finally Cara heard the rasp of the key in his lock and his footsteps across the floor. She clenched her hands and listened to the sound of his movements as he prepared for bed, and she wondered how much he had had to drink. Had he learned anything? Perhaps she could knock on the connecting door and ask him. Just to find out the news. She grimaced. That was too shallow a lie to fob off even on herself. What she wanted was to go to Chris's bed and recapture the sweet, wild delight of his lovemaking. Pulling the sheet over her head, she lay taut as a bowstring until long after all sounds had died in his room, her heart tripping crazily, and her mind like a stuck record reliving the brief, passionate moments she had shared with him.

Cara's eyelids were heavy the next morning when her alarm dragged her from sleep. She stumbled into the bathroom and grimaced in the mirror at the bluish tint beneath her eyes. If she had to be around Chris much longer, she'd die of sleeplessness. Sternly she pulled her mind away from conjectures as to how well he had slept. She dressed in blue jeans and a cool, crisp blue cotton top. She had just finished tying her tennis shoes when a knock sounded at her door.

"Cara? You ready?" It was Chris, and Cara felt a perverse thrill of pleasure when she opened the door and saw that his face looked as if he had slept no better than she had.

"Yeah, just a second." She left the door open and went back to the mirror to pull her hair back and tie it at the base of her neck with a blue ribbon. Chris glanced at the rumpled bed, then quickly away.

Clearing his throat, he said, "Greeson left us his jeep. He's flown to another site and said he'd send the plane back for us."

"Good. What's on the schedule today? Did you find out anything last night?"

"The only thing I got out of last night was a ripping hangover." His fingers massaged his temples. "This morning we'll return to the rig and interview the day crew. After that we can canvass store clerks, gas-station attendants and anybody else we can find. If we're lucky, someone will remember and even describe a couple of strangers who were in Bow Lake at suspicious times."

They walked across the parking lot to the small diner for a greasy breakfast. Afterward they climbed into the jeep and, with Cara navigating, drove back to the drilling rig. Ashe Harlan was standing on the steps of his trailer, sipping a cup of coffee. As they drove up, his lip curled with annoyance. "He's as friendly as ever," Cara murmured under her breath, making Chris grin.

As always, Chris's smile gave life to his rough countenance, and Cara's heart twisted in her chest. It wasn't fair, she thought. Why did he still have the ability to attract her? She had thought, angry as she was at him, that he'd no longer appeal to her, that she'd see the defects of his character like sores all over him. Yet when she saw him in Dallas, she had been swept by yearning, and it seemed as if the more she was around him, the worse it grew, until her heart was a battleground torn by bitterness and desire. Quickly Cara jumped out of the vehicle and strode across to Harlan, not glancing at Chris.

Ashe tossed the coffee from his cup onto the ground and set the cup inside the trailer, then came down the steps toward them. "You back?"

"How could we leave when we knew what a hospitable reception we'd receive here?" Cara quipped.

The movement of the young man's mouth was more a grimace than a smile. "What do you want now?"

"We want to talk to the day crew," Chris replied. "Ask them the same questions we asked the others."

Harlan said nothing, merely shrugged, and led the way to the rig. Again Cara trailed along in Chris's wake, listening to his expert questioning, which, however, turned up few answers. To the crew, all the people they saw were strangers, and none had seen anything unusual around the rig at the time of either of the incidents. Cara's feet grew tired from standing and her ears ached from the noise of the drill. Her spirit began to sag within her. It was hopeless. How could they ever find the men who had committed the crimes, let alone trace them back to the instigator? They wouldn't be able to save Matthew. Her stomach twisted at the thought.

As they walked away from the platform an hour later, exhausted and dispirited, Cara suggested, "Do you think it would do any good to tell Ashe Harlan the truth? If he's involved, he knows anyway, and you said we'd start getting some action only when they realized we were on their trail. Maybe it would stir them up. On the other hand, if Ashe isn't in on the extortion but knows something about the vandalism, he might tell us if he understood it was a child's life at stake, not just the company losing some money."

Chris shot her a measuring glance. "I'm willing. We aren't getting anywhere this way. We have to do something." He turned and beckoned to Harlan, who stood on the platform watching them.

After a moment's hesitation Harlan swung off the metal walkway and clattered down the steps, his long strides eating up the ground between them. "Yeah?"

"We wanted to explain something to you," Chris began. "Could we go to your trailer?"

The other's eyes flashed a cold blue, and Cara expected him to refuse rudely, but he jammed his hands into his pockets and walked rapidly toward the trailer. As they followed him into the cool metal box, Cara asked impulsively, "Mr. Harlan, do I know you? You seem . . . familiar somehow."

He whipped around, his eyes searching her face suspiciously, and Cara unconsciously stepped back, bumping into Chris, who steadied her with his large, hard hands against her waist. An electric thrill ran through Cara at his touch, and she hardly knew which was worse, facing this cold stranger or being supported by Chris. Finally Harlan sneered, "No, lady, you don't know me. I never ran in the country-club circles."

"What gave you such a mile-wide chip on your shoulder?" Chris growled. "She asked you a perfectly innocuous question, and you react as if it were something criminal."

"Is this what you wanted to talk to me about? I have work to do, you know. I don't collect money for sitting around."

"Well, you may be sitting around permanently if you don't cooperate," Chris retorted harshly.

"What do you mean?"

"Alec Stone has been threatened and told to close down this rig. Would that please you?"

He shrugged. "There's no scarcity of jobs in the oil fields today. Besides, Stone wouldn't shut down. He's a meaner son of a bitch than anybody who threatened him."

"How do you know so much about him?" Cara flared in an unexpected defense of her father. "You've never met the man!"

"You don't have to meet the devil to know he'll scorch you."

"Look," Cara leaned forward earnestly, "I don't know why you dislike Stone Oil or my father. I don't really care, either. But there's another person involved in this. If Alec doesn't stop drilling, they've threatened to kidnap his grandson. My sister's child." Her voice faltered. "That's why it's so important to discover who's behind it, so we can keep him from harming Matthew. If you know anything about it, won't you please help us? It's to save him." Tears filled her eyes and Cara stopped, swallowing the sobs that threatened.

For a moment Harlan stared at her in surprise; then his face hardened and a blank stare shuttered his eyes. "Babies die every day, Miss Stone, and nobody gives a damn. Your father didn't care about—" He broke off and strode to the door. Turning, he spat out, "I don't give a damn about you or your nephew. It's no concern of mine what happens to any of you. I wouldn't step a foot out of my way to help a Stone."

Cara gasped at his vitriolic words. Chris stiffened and started forward, his fists clenched. A blazing light touched Harlan's eyes, and he tensed with almost delighted expectation. Cara flung herself at Chris, grabbing his arm with both hands. "What in the world are you doing?"

He halted and glanced down at her face. His jaw was set, and the gold ring around his pupils flamed. "You think I'm going to stand around and let that—" He jerked his head contemptuously at Ashe.

Cara interrupted quickly. "Starting a fight won't get us anywhere. You're a grown man, not a boy. A distinguished journalist doesn't go brawling in the oil fields."

He relaxed somewhat. "It's not the journalist who wanted to. It's the Polish mill worker."

Cara let out her breath. "Well, do you think you could control it? Let's leave." She stared at him pleadingly, and finally Chris allowed a faint smile. He brushed his fingertips along her jaw.

"Okay. I promise I won't revert." He turned his flinty gaze on the other man. "Harlan, you're working yourself into a precarious position."

Ashe's mouth twitched irritably. "I can take care of myself."

Chris's eyes spoke his disdain. "Come on, Cara, let's go back to town."

Doggedly Chris and Cara trudged through the few business streets of Bow Lake, asking over and over again the same question: had anyone noticed any strangers in town at the time of the incidents? Despite a break for lunch, Cara soon grew footsore and weary. No one could recall anybody out of the ordinary, except one aging gas station attendant. He thought a couple of men whom he assumed to be hunters had driven through about the time of the fire. Although he could easily describe their car, he had not noted the license plate and couldn't remember what the men looked like.

"No, sir," he told Chris, shaking his head. "They didn't say their names."

"How about credit cards? Did they pay with a credit card?"

"No, don't think so," he replied after much thought. "It was all cash. Only reason I paid any attention to them was 'cause I been wanting one of them Blazers like they drove."

"Thank you." Chris turned away with a sigh.

In defeated silence they drove back to the motel. When he stopped the jeep, Chris trailed Cara into her room and flopped into a chair. She wandered aimlessly about, too troubled to sit, fighting the tears that threatened to overwhelm her. Chris watched her pacing and finally remarked, "It looks like we've hit a dead end."

As if she had waited for his words to open the floodgates of her emotions, Cara whirled to face him, her eyes sparkling with unshed tears. "Oh, Chris, this is so horrible! When I think of Matthew, I could die! We haven't found a thing to help him."

"I know." Chris stared at Cara helplessly. He wished there were something he could say to take away the pain clawing within her. "They were too clever to leave any clues. Whoever it is did a good job."

"I'm positive Ashe Harlan knows something he's not telling. How could he be so callous? How could he stand there and say a baby's life didn't matter? He's hurting Matt, just like the men who are threatening Daddy, and I hate him!" The sobs Cara had been fighting swept her, racking her body in great shudders, and she raised her hands to her face to hide the tears.

Instinctively Chris rose and took her in his arms. Cara clung to him as she sobbed out her despair. He held her more tightly, stroking her head and back and whispering soft, meaningless words of comfort. Gradually, under his ministrations, her sobs subsided, but still she pressed into the strength of his rock-hard chest. Her ragged breaths steadied, and the tears slowly stopped. The touch of his hand on her hair was infinitely pleasurable, and in her misery Cara was aware of little else but his calming presence and the quiet peace that filled her.

"It's all right," Chris murmured against her ear. "I'll find him. I promise. I'll figure out a way to make Harlan talk. It will be okay, I swear." He nuzzled the silk of her hair, and she sighed and nestled closer. He kissed the tip of her ear and then the soft skin at the corner of her eye. She lifted her face to him, hardly aware of what she sought. His lips caressed her cheek and settled upon her mouth, tasting her slowly, tenderly. Cara arched up against him eagerly, and the banked fire between them burst into flame. Like a starving man too long denied, his mouth sank into hers, and she returned his kiss, hunger for hunger. "Cara." The word was a prayer upon his lips.

Chris plunged his fingers into her hair, tearing the ribbon away and sending the heavy mass flowing across his hands. A whimpering sound escaped Cara's throat as his tongue plunged into her mouth, plundering, caressing, possessing it as its master. His hands roamed down her back, squeezing her buttocks and pressing her into him so that his hard need pressed her eloquently. Chris released her to pull away her top and bra and lifted her off the floor to sample the honey of her breasts. Her nipples blossomed beneath his expert tongue, and she dug her fingers into his hair, tugging painfully. But he did not notice the sting, feeling nothing but the supreme delight of her passion-hardened nipples against his rough tongue. He eased Cara back onto her feet, sliding her body over him intimately. Cara stepped back, her face glowing with love, then turned to walk to the bed.

Chris watched the play of her hips in the tight jeans, his mouth dry and his eyes gleaming. She unfastened her trousers, and the rasp of the zipper sent the blood pulsing faster through his veins. He watched her ease out of the jeans and panties, his mind aflame, past reason or thought. His body knew all there was to know—that he wanted her, needed her with a yearning so deep and primitive it had no name.

Chris followed her, whipping off his clothes in a frenzy of impatience. Cara lay back upon the bed, holding up her arms to welcome her lover, and he covered her, his lips seeking hers again, then traveling down the satin expanse of her torso. His tongue delved into her navel and traced fiery circles across her abdomen. Cara moaned, her hands eagerly rediscovering his body. His skin was smooth, like satin laid over iron, and she learned again the joy of touching it. Chris murmured against her stomach. His mouth moved lower, seeking her feminine softness, and turned her veins to fire. Love burst quickly in Cara, and she cried out. He wrapped his arms around her tightly, holding her safe in the storm that shook her. When she quieted, she took him into her eagerly, impatient for the satisfaction of his filling desire. He moved within her with excruciating slowness, his face a mask of passion barely held in check. Again Cara felt the magic mushrooming inside her, and when Chris reached his peak, she came with him, adrift in the same blissful union they had once known.

For a time she floated in a dreamy euphoria, aware of nothing but the dazzling satisfaction of her senses after weeks of lonely hunger. Chris rolled from her with a deep sigh, and gradually, painfully, she returned to reality. Chris was still married. Nothing between them had changed, except that this time she had succumbed to him knowing fully what the situation was. He reached out to put his arm around her, and she scrambled to the far side of the bed and sat up, hugging her knees to her chest.

"Baby, I'm sorry." His voice was tired, defeated. "I didn't mean to. I had the best intentions, but feeling you in my arms like that, I—" He broke off, then continued in a voice devoid of emotion, "Don't hate me. I couldn't stand it."

"It's pretty obvious I'm incapable of hating you," Cara snapped. "I've tried hard enough, and look what happens."

"If I could just make you understand . . ."

"Understand what?" Cara demanded tearfully. "That I'm in love with a married man? That the only time I'm happy is when I'm with him? That the most beautiful thing I've ever experienced is cheating with him on his wife? I don't have the personality to be a one-night stand, let alone the other woman!"

"You aren't either of those. You're the best thing that's come into my life in eight years. I think . . . I think I love you." He reached across the bed to her, running his fingers lightly down her arm. She did not respond, but neither did she move away as she had before. "I'm not sure, since I've never felt it before." He laughed a little shakily. "Funny to think that this is the feeling I should have had when I believed I loved Monica."

"No doubt you're going to explain to me how your wife doesn't understand you, and you don't have a true marriage."

"I pay her bills, and we inhabit the same house most weekends. I haven't slept with her in over three years."

Cara turned toward him, her eyes dark with disbelief. "I don't want to hear any lies, Chris."

"Damn it, I'm not lying!" He sat up swiftly and grasped her by the shoulders, forcing her to look into his eyes. "I never lied to you. I didn't tell you about Monica, but everything I've said to you is the truth. God, Cara, can't you sense anything about my character? What I did to you was foolish and hurtful. I was acting out of desperation and desire, but the whole time I was fighting myself."

"Whatever you tell me about your wife, I won't hop into your bed anytime you want," Cara said, avoiding his questions, which she had so often asked herself. She sensed honesty and goodness in him, no matter how his actions had belied her instinctive trust. But her mind warned her not to believe him.

"I'm not asking you to. I'll go back to D.C. tomorrow and probably never see you again. I wouldn't ask you to become my mistress, because it's a dead-end situation for you. It wouldn't be fair. That's why I walked away from you the first time. I want to tell you about Monica because I hope it'll make you understand me a little, not judge me quite as harshly. All I'm asking is for you to listen, nothing else."

Cara contemplated him for a moment, striving to erect her defenses one last time. Finally she sighed and lay back down on the bed. "All right. Tell me about your wife."

Chapter 12

Chris sighed and linked his hands behind his head. Closing his eyes as if reseeing the past, he began, "When I met Monica, she was the beauty of the Capital, and I fell for her hard. I thought I was madly in love, but I couldn't imagine what she saw in me. She was lovely, wealthy, sophisticated. What I didn't realize was that she was also vain, selfish and possessive. Almost as soon as we were married, we began to fight. She had been intrigued by my background. I was a sort of sexual prize to her, the poor-boy Polack stud, good in the sack if not too bright in the head. My rough edges turned her on. But there was the added surprise and titillation of my being a reporter, still rough, but with a tinge of intelligence and sophistication. Yet after we got married, she tried to change me. She wanted me to become a slick carbon copy of the other men she knew. My job took up too much of my time. Why couldn't I take a regular job in an executive position like the one her father offered me? I was always gone, I didn't pay enough attention to her, etcetera. To retaliate she began to take lovers. The first time I was shaken to the core. After a while I began not to care.

"She also disliked my family and refused to visit them. They were too crude for her delicate sensibilities. She was jealous of every woman I spoke to, of every second I was away from her. I finally began to realize Monica was trying to keep me completely to herself. She didn't want me to have a life of my own."

Chris leaned over the edge of the bed, retrieved a package of cigarettes from his shirt and lit one, setting an ashtray on his bare stomach. He took a contemplative puff and continued. "I wasn't so easy to live with myself. I loved reporting. I spent a great deal of time at it. Probably any wife would have complained. Sometimes I'd feel guilty, and the more strained our relationship grew, the worse I felt. Because by then what she accused me of was true. I *was* staying at work longer than necessary to avoid being with her. I hated coming home. All we did was fight nonstop. The most innocuous thing would become the basis for a major battle."

"So why didn't you get a divorce?" Cara asked skeptically.

"I come from a very strict Catholic family. Divorce is anathema in our home. I was raised to believe that you stayed married forever. Besides," a twinkle momentarily lit his eyes, "I've always been stubborn. I was too obstinate to admit I'd made a mistake, which was intensified by the fact that Mother had warned me not to marry Monica. She'd put up a huge fuss about my marrying a *poganin*."

"A what?"

"Pagan," he translated. "For that read Protestant. She said it would never work, I'd be miserable. I'd have done almost anything rather than admit she was right. So we struggled along for five years. Monica got pregnant. I thought, here was the answer. We'd be a family. Monica would be able to love a baby unconditionally. She'd see a whole new side of life. I wanted children, always have.

Everything seemed brighter. We'd work things out. Then one day she told me she'd had an abortion."

"Oh, Chris." Cara reached out to him, touched despite her stern intentions.

His jaw tightened. "She hadn't even discussed it with me. She said she didn't intend to have any children. Our family was to be her and me. Just us, forever and ever. She was that possessive. I realized it was hopeless. We could never have a marriage, because all Monica wanted was to suck me dry, to completely obliterate my identity and merge it with hers. Unfortunately I waited to get a divorce. My mother was dying of cancer and had only a few months to live. Even though she disliked Monica, she would have been heartbroken if I got a divorce. She would've died miserable and angry at me. I told myself it wouldn't hurt to stay with Monica a few more months. After all, I had the rest of my life in front of me. So I moved out of her room but didn't divorce her."

"What happened?"

His eyes were bleak. "Monica was crippled. And it was my fault."

Cara stared. "Crippled! How? What do you mean?"

"I was writing a story on narcotics traffic at the time, and I had put myself on the wrong side of some pretty tough characters. One day Monica and I were standing on the front lawn of our home, in the middle of an argument. A car zoomed by and fired two shots at me." He extended his right arm and pointed to a small, puckered white scar. "That was one of them. The other hit Monica in the spine. The doctors saved her life, but she was paralyzed from the waist down. She's been in a wheel chair ever since."

Tears welled in Cara's eyes, and Chris smiled thinly. "I always knew you were a soft touch," he said.

"You're a peculiar man. A crippled wife would have been enough to make a lot of men leave. It made you stay."

"What else could I do? It was my job, the thing she hated so much, that did it to her. I had as good as crippled her.

I couldn't walk away and leave her to spend the rest of her life alone and bitter. At first I felt so guilty I tried to repair our relationship. But Monica hated me. All I heard from her was abuse and anger. Although I didn't think it was possible, our marriage grew worse. I took the apartment in town and began to return to our house outside D.C. only on the weekends. I pay for her support and give her two days a week of target practice on me. The rest of my life is my work—until you came along and blew it all to hell."

"Chris, you shouldn't do this to yourself," Cara began earnestly, her former resentment vanished beneath an onslaught of sympathy for the man she loved. "It's not your fault she was injured. What else could you have done? Were you supposed to quit your life's work because something bad might happen to your wife? Who could have imagined that she'd be paralyzed because of one of your stories? Should you have given up what you love and been miserable the rest of your life? It isn't rational. You could easily say you're to blame because you married her or because you didn't divorce her sooner. She wouldn't have been shot then, either."

He sighed and crushed out the cigarette. "Please, Cara. My mind is settled. I don't love Monica, but I can't leave her. I simply wanted you to understand that I don't pretend I love her and then cheat behind her back. She knows how I feel and why I stay. I'm not a philanderer. You are ... very special to me. I wish to God the situation were different." Chris sat up. "Let's not discuss it anymore. Are you ready for supper?"

Cara started to protest, then stopped. There was nothing else to be said. His mind was obviously set on its course. "All right. Let me shower first."

Later Cara couldn't have said what she ate. The food was as tasteless as sawdust in her mouth. They talked little and finished their dinner quickly. Afterward they walked back to their rooms, a tight awkwardness stretching between them. "Do you think there's anything more to be done here?" Cara asked formally.

"Not really. Harlan is the only one who appears to know anything, and he's not talking. The next thing to do, I think, is to go back to D.C. and follow up on some of the people your father thinks might be behind it. Perhaps I can dig up something suspicious on one of them."

"That sounds like looking for a needle in a haystack."

"It is, more or less. It would be easier if we had a name or a description. Then I could look for a link between the actual saboteur and whoever is responsible."

"Then we'll fly home tomorrow. I'd better inform the pilot."

"Yes."

They stopped in front of her room, and Cara's eyes asked the question her lips could not form: Will I ever see you again?

Chris shook his head sadly. "No, baby, this is the last time. It's better that way. You'll be happier someday if I don't intrude on your life again."

Cara removed the room key from her purse and unlocked the door. Chris bent to kiss the top of her head and slowly walked toward his room. "Wait!" Cara cried, and he turned. "If this is the last time we're together, let it be happy. I don't want to lie awake thinking about you and crying. I can do plenty of that in the future." She held out one hand. "Please, Chris, stay with me tonight."

He returned, his hand reaching out to clasp hers.

Cara glanced around the small motel room to be sure she had left nothing behind. It was the fourth check, and she already knew she was completely packed. It was simply a mental exercise to occupy her mind. She would rather think about anything than the fact that in a few hours she'd never see Chris again. There was a quick, imperative knock on the door, which she recognized as his, and her heart lurched.

"Ready to go?" he inquired brusquely when she opened the door.

Involuntarily tears sprang to her eyes. He spoke as if they were strangers. "Yes." She swallowed her tears.

His face softened. "Cara, I don't want to hurt you. I'm trying to . . . put us on a businesslike footing. Otherwise the trip will be pure hell. I've never believed in crying in my beer."

"I know. I'll get my bag." She went back into the room, and he followed to carry out her larger suitcase. As Chris stowed the luggage in the jeep, another blue-and-gold Stone Oil jeep roared into the parking lot and jerked to a halt in front of them. Ashe Harlan stepped out, tall and lanky in tight, worn denim trousers and a short-sleeved blue shirt, a straw cowboy hat tilted down over his forehead. Sunglasses obscured his eyes. Cara stared at him, and Chris straightened, immediately tense and expectant. "Harlan," he greeted him pleasantly. "Can we do something for you?"

The young man stood in silence for a moment, hands on hips. Finally he stated tersely, "More like I can do something for you."

"Let's go inside." Chris led him into Cara's room and she entered after them, closing the door behind her. Chris offered the other man a chair, but Harlan remained standing. "Now . . . you have some information for us?"

"I don't know what in the hell I'm doing here," Ashe began gruffly, removing his sunglasses and tilting back his hat. "If I was smart, I'd stay out of it. Let the Stones take care of themselves." He glanced at Cara, then down at the floor. "I don't owe you anything."

"But?" Chris prodded.

He sighed. "But here I am. I know the name of a man who . . . has something to do with the sabotage."

Cara sucked in her breath and had to bite her lip to keep from barraging Ashe with eager questions. But she reminded herself that Chris was the expert and she should leave it to him. Maddeningly, Chris said nothing.

The technique worked on Ashe. He continued. "I don't think he actually did it. He looks like someone who gives orders. Not the top guy, either. A sort of middleman."

"How'd you meet him?"

"I flew to Dallas for parts after the bit broke. Before I left Bow Lake, a guy called and asked me to meet him. He said he had a money-making proposition for me. I asked him what, but he wouldn't say. So I talked to him when I was in Dallas. He said his name was Vern Haskell, but I doubt that's his real name."

"It doesn't matter. It gives us a lead. What did he ask you?"

"He told me his boss had heard about the bit breaking and thought it was a good idea. He wanted the Michaelson Number Two to have more problems. He was willing to pay me ten thousand dollars to shut down the well. I could do it in ways where it wouldn't be obvious."

"What did you say?"

Indignation tinged the younger man's face. "Of course I said no! Would I be telling you otherwise?"

"Why didn't you? I hear you're always on the lookout for a buck."

"I like to make money, yeah. But I've never done anything dishonest for it."

"Yet you didn't report the offer, though you knew he would probably find someone else to sabotage the well. Even after the fire and the vandalism, you didn't reveal it. Why?"

"I wouldn't cheat my company. But I don't owe Alec Stone anything, either. If somebody else wants to work out a grudge on him, I'm not going to stop it." He moved impatiently. "I'm probably a fool to have come here today."

Cara could no longer contain her mushrooming curiosity. "Why? Why do you dislike my father so much? You seem to hate me, too, and yet you've never met either of us. Why are you so prejudiced?"

"Why?" he spat out. "I'll tell you why. While you were dancing at the country club and buying designer clothes, I was working—no chance for college, no chance for anything."

"I'm sorry about that," she retorted heatedly, "although

you have a pretty unrealistic view of my life. However, we don't have any choice about who our parents are. Most people aren't born rich, but they don't carry a grudge all their lives."

His blue eyes blazed. "No, you're right. I didn't have a goddamn thing to say about who my parents were, because believe me, I wouldn't have chosen to be Alec Stone's bastard!"

The silence following his announcement was profound. Cara's jaw dropped and she stared at him, stunned. Chris raised his eyebrows and studied the man before him. Finally she stammered, "You...you're Daddy's child?"

"That's right, lady. No doubt you find it hard to believe, but the same blood flows in my veins as in yours, or at least half the same. Of course, my mother was plain old Vicky Harlan, not a society queen like Virginia Stone."

"But how? When?"

"How?" He laughed shortly. "Same way it's always done. Your daddy was in Tulsa on a business trip, and my mother was a waitress in the hotel restaurant. Alec Stone took a shine to her. Why not? He was there for two weeks with nothing to do, and she was a pretty blonde...So he took her to bed, and when the two weeks were over, he left her with a ruby ring and a few hundred dollars he'd stuffed into her purse when she wasn't looking. Like a hooker! She loved him, and he paid her and forgot her. Nine months later I was born."

Cara blinked, still fighting the fog of surprise in her head. "But...if that's true, why didn't she tell Daddy?"

"She didn't want to put any pressure on him," Ashe sneered. "She was crazy in love with the guy, and she knew he was married. She wouldn't have made trouble for him."

"How can you be sure Stone's your father?" Chris asked quietly.

Harlan turned on him fiercely. "He was the only man she slept with! My mother wasn't some oil-field tramp."

"When were you born? I mean, when was it Daddy..." Cara trailed off, unable to think of a delicate way to express her question.

"Listen!" Harlan's voice was sharp and cold as a knife. "I didn't come here to prove I'm Alec Stone's son. I don't give a damn about it. You have no right to interrogate me. I don't need to justify myself to you or anyone else!" He burst out the door and loped to his jeep, shoving on the sunglasses as he ran. He swung into the vehicle and slammed out of the parking lot, not looking back to where Cara and Chris stood in the doorway, staring after him.

Shaken, Cara retreated into the room and sat down heavily on the corner of the bed. Her mind was whirling. "Chris, what do you think? Is it true? Can it possibly—" Her head snapped up as a new thought struck her. "Why, if what he said is true, he's my brother!"

Chris's forehead knotted. "I looked at him carefully, and I noticed something that I hadn't seen before. His coloring is different from yours and your father's because his hair is much lighter and his skin darker. But his eyes are very similar to Alec's, the same shade of blue, the same shape. They remind me of your eyes."

"You think he's telling the truth?"

Chris shrugged. "Who knows? I doubt he has any documentation. Obviously it's a story his mother told him. Although he believes her implicitly, we have no way of knowing whether she told the truth. Perhaps she met your father, even slept with him. After Ashe was born, she liked to believe it was Alec Stone's child, thinking it gave him a kind of secondhand power and importance, made him a cut above an illegitimate child. You know your father better than I do. What do you think?"

"It's quite possible Daddy had an affair with her. He cheated on Ginny innumerable times. That's why she finally got a divorce. In fact, Brant, Alexis's husband, hated Stone Oil because he blamed Alec for breaking up his parents' marriage." She realized with a guilty start that she had strayed into a subject heretofore forbidden between them, and her hand flew to her mouth.

Chris grinned. "It's all right. I won't use it in my article. Remember, I've got the promise of something bigger than the McClure lease from your father."

"That's right. It's why we came, isn't it?" Firmly she pulled her thoughts away from Harlan's startling revelation. "What about the name Ashe gave you? Will it help?"

"Are you kidding? It's like having a bar of gold dumped in my lap. This is a better lead than the description of one of the men who sabotaged the well. The middleman is a big step closer to the power. Now I have more to work with when I return to Washington. I have a few acquaintances in law enforcement who will check out his name to see if there's a criminal record on him." He paused, his eyes gazing off into the distance. "In fact, I know a police artist who could probably be persuaded—for a little cash—to fly to Bow Lake and draw a picture of Haskell from Ashe Harlan's description. Provided we can persuade that volatile young man to cooperate, of course."

"Then we'd better go, hadn't we?" Cara stood, striving for a matter-of-fact attitude. She had been stunned by Ashe's words, and her heart was torn in two, knowing that the sooner they left, the quicker Chris would be out of her life. But with Ashe's information, Chris might be able to save Matthew now, and she must not lose sight of the fact that Matthew was the vital concern in this whole thing.

"Good. I was afraid Harlan had knocked you for such a loop you'd want to stay to question him."

She shook her head as they again left the motel room. "No. I don't think he'd speak to me, anyway."

They drove to the airstrip, where the plane and pilot waited, and quickly scrambled into the small jet. On the long flight home Cara's mind skittered back and forth between Chris's departure and Ashe Harlan's claim of kinship. Deciding the latter subject was by far the less painful, she concentrated on that. At least it would break the heavy, awkward silence between her and Chris. "You said Ashe didn't have any documentation. How could you prove something like that?"

Chris shrugged. "I'm not too familiar with paternity suits. A blood test could prove Alec was *not* the father, but I don't think it can prove he *was*. Aside from that, I guess Harlan could show that Alec was in Tulsa at the proper time and had an affair with his mother. But how could he prove Alec was the only man she slept with? He was there only two weeks. It's hard to pinpoint conception to such an exact date. She could have been sleeping with someone else immediately before or after . . . or even at the same time. Unless Alec admitted at the time that he was the father of the child, made some sort of commitment to him."

"I'm sure he knew nothing about Ashe," Cara declared positively. "The one thing Daddy has always wanted more than anything else is a son. It's been the biggest disappointment of his life. He wouldn't have turned his back on a son, illegitimate or not. I'm sure of it. Daddy's not a villain. He would've supported the child even if it were a girl. And a boy! I think he would have given him everything—not just support but all the advantages. He'd have visited him, sent him to college, legitimized him if he could. He'd have viewed him as the heir to the throne of Stone Oil, the way he sees Matthew now."

"It hardly sounds as if he knew about the boy. So the question is, was Ms. Harlan as self-sacrificing as her son suggests, or was it that she knew her claim was false?"

Cara chewed her lip thoughtfully. "Well, the only person who has any idea if it's true is Daddy. At least he might remember if he was in Tulsa at the right time and if he had an affair with Ashe's mother. What year would it have been?"

"Either 1953 or 54, I presume. We don't know Harlan's exact age."

"Daddy made several business trips to Tulsa. It's an oil

town. And I'm not sure any business-trip fling would remain in his memory."

A faint smile curved his lips. "No wonder you so readily believe me to be a perennially cheating husband."

Cara swallowed and looked out the window. Huge wheat fields stretched out below them in a checkerboard pattern, blurring before her eyes. "Oh, Chris."

"I'm sorry, honey. I shouldn't have brought it up." He took one of her hands in his. "I don't want to leave you. But you'll be happier without me."

"And you?"

"I can't promise I'll be happier. But I'll get used to it after a while. Like they say, I made the bed."

Not looking at him, Cara traced the skin of his hand lovingly, caressing the slim, tough fingers and the hard palm, smoothing the fine, silky, black hairs on the back of his hand. He was right, of course. She couldn't waste her life as the mistress of a married man. It was doomed, hopeless. She couldn't be the "other woman." Not her, not good, sensible Cara Stone. With a sigh she blinked away her tears and released his hand. "Tell me how you'll look for this Haskell fellow."

They passed the remainder of the trip in strained, impersonal conversation. It was almost a relief when they at last landed in Dallas. While the pilot refueled the plane and filed a flight plan to Washington, D.C., Chris walked Cara to her car. As soon as the pilot was ready, he would fly Chris home. They were silent, heavily aware that they would not see each other again. When they reached the car, they turned to each other awkwardly.

Cara managed a weak smile. "I don't know what to say."

"There isn't anything to say." His hands cupped her face and he gazed at her hungrily, as if memorizing every feature. "What I feel can't be expressed." He bent and his mouth met hers in a final, demanding kiss. Cara moved her lips against his, and her hands clung to his shirtfront. She wished she could hold him to her forever. After a moment that seemed both endless and unbearably short, Chris tore his mouth away. His chest rose and fell rapidly, as if he had run a long race, and his eyes were bright crystals of pain. "Good-bye, Cara."

"Good-bye," she whispered. He whirled and strode away. Cara watched his retreating back, her hands clasped together in front of her in an unconsciously pleading gesture. He did not turn to look at her, and soon his form vanished into one of the airfield buildings. Cara sagged against the hot metal of the car. He was gone.

Chapter 13

When Mrs. Jenkins announced Cara to her father, Alec was so eager to see her that he opened the door to his office and ushered her inside. Cara seated herself in one of the chairs. He sat close to her instead of resuming his position behind the desk. Leaning forward eagerly, he began to question her. "What happened? Did Wozniak discover anything?"

"A little. We talked to everyone and couldn't get a lead on who committed the sabotage, but the tool-pusher gave us the name of a man who approached him with an offer of a bribe if he'd delay the drilling."

Stone's controlled face brightened. "Really? That's better than finding the men who set fire to it. What was his name?"

"Vern Haskell. Of course, it could be an alias. Chris is flying to Washington to search for a link between him and someone who might want to harm you. He'll check with law-enforcement officials and the regulatory agencies for a criminal record or a connection with an oil company. After that, Chris said, it would require digging into the backgrounds of your enemies to see if Haskell pops up in one."

"It could take months," Alec muttered and relaxed in his chair with a sigh.

"Did the guard for Matthew arrive?"

"Oh, yes. He's been here since you left for Canada. He seems competent enough, but of course Morgan's scared silly anyway. She and Nick are installing a fancy alarm in the house. There's nothing more we can do except wait and hope your reporter finds out something."

Cara stirred uncomfortably at his description of Chris as "her" reporter. "Daddy, we came on something else while we were up there—nothing to do with Matt."

"What?" His voice was devoid of interest.

"The name of the tool-pusher who gave us the information was Ashe Harlan." Cara watched him closely for any sign of recognition, but there was no change in his expression.

"Why did he wait this long to tell us about Haskell's bribe? Or was he responsible for the sabotage?"

"No, I don't think so. He swore he didn't take the money. He said he wouldn't harm his own well, and I believe him. He seems to be truthful to the point of rudeness."

"Then why the hell didn't he inform us? We could have jumped on the thing months ago, before it got this far."

"Apparently he's got a grudge against you, and he didn't want to go out of his way to help you."

"That's a fine way for an employee to act. I'll call Greeson and have him send the man down here. I want to talk to this Harlan myself."

"Wait—before you fly off the handle, let me give you the rest of it." She paused and drew a deep breath. "The reason he dislikes you is he thinks . . . he thinks he's your illegitimate son."

There was a moment of deathly silence as Alec gaped at her, his eyes wide with astonishment. Finally he gasped, "What? What are you talking about? I don't—"

"He says you had a two-week affair with his mother, and that she got pregnant as a result. But she never told you about the kid because she didn't want to interfere with your marriage. So he's bitter because he's your son but grew up poor instead of wealthy. He hates all of us."

"That's crazy. His mother's faced with having a baby and bringing him up alone, and she doesn't even ask me for money?" He rose and began to pace the office.

Cara, watching him, realized with a start why Ashe Harlan's walk had looked so familiar. "Daddy, he walks like you!" she exclaimed.

He swung on her. "What do you mean?"

"I just realized it. When I first saw Ashe, I thought I'd seen his walk somewhere before. I even asked him if we'd met. When you were pacing, I realized that it's very similar to your walk—long strides, but a little uneven. I can't describe it, but it's unique." Alec frowned at Cara and slowly, thoughtfully returned to the chair. "And Chris said Ashe's eyes were like yours and mine. They're the same color, anyway."

"Not much to go on."

"No. But it makes me wonder if it might be true. I'm sure Ashe believes the story. Chris pointed out, though, that his mother could have made it up to give Ashe a feeling of status. You're the only one who would have any idea if it's true. Do you remember a woman named Harlan?"

He closed his eyes for a minute, then shook his head. "No. I knew a man in Midland named Albert Harlan, but no woman. What was her first name?"

"Vicky, I think. When we started to ask questions, Ashe got mad and stormed out. Chris figured we should leave and get onto the Haskell clue, so we didn't pursue him. All I know is the little bit he told us before he left. It was in Tulsa. Ashe is about twenty-seven or twenty-eight years old."

Alex tapped one finger against his lips. "Tulsa. Twenty-eight years ago."

"He said you were there for two weeks," Cara prodded.

He sighed. "I've been in Tulsa a lot of times. Let me see... I was working on a deal with a wildcatter out of Tulsa in the early fifties. I think it was a year or two before we brought in the Hunter well in the Permian Basin."

"Ashe said his mother was blond and pretty."

A faint smile touched Alec's face. "There was a girl... What was her name? Sally? Cindy? Something like that. Maybe it was Vicky. She worked in the hotel, in the restaurant, I think. Yeah, I remember. I was there for two or three weeks. She was young, about twenty-three, single, blond. I don't remember her name being Harlan, though." He frowned in concentration. "Hell, I can't even remember her first name."

"He said you left her some money and a ring."

"Yeah, that's the girl. We were walking one evening after dinner, window-shopping downtown, and we looked at a jewelry display case. She saw a ring she liked and innocently pointed it out. She wasn't grasping, like some. So the next day I bought it for her. A little ruby thing. She was a sweet girl, cried when I gave it to her. I wish I could remember her name."

"Oh, Daddy!" Cara exclaimed. "You know the date and location of every well you ever drilled, but you can't recall the name of a woman you slept with for two weeks!"

He turned his unreadable blue eyes on her. "You don't understand, Cara. Women like that meant very little to me."

"It's obvious."

"I never loved anyone but your mother. Surely you realize that. Ginny was the only important one. All the others were just..." He shrugged expressively.

"If Ginny was so important, why did you run around on her?"

"Lord, Cara, I don't know. Because Ginny also drove me crazy, always fluttering around, forgetting this, losing that, never on time or certain of anything. Because I was away a lot. Because I enjoy women."

"You mean you enjoy the chase."

"That, too. Whatever the reason, I don't intend to sit here and rehash my marriage with you. What's relevant now is the kid. Do you think he's telling the truth?"

"I don't know. His mother was blond and pretty and worked as a waitress in the restaurant of the hotel where you were staying. It was in Tulsa, you stayed two weeks and when you left, you gave her money and a ring, which fits with the woman you remember. He doesn't look like you, except that Chris saw a resemblance in the eyes. And I think he has your walk."

Alec drummed his fingers on the arm of his chair. "I think I'll have a detective check out his background, find out when and where his mother worked and whether she was living with someone else. Then I want to talk to the boy. I'll fly him down from Canada." His eyes pierced Cara. "You've given me the most startling information I've ever received. If I actually have a son . . ." He broke off and shook his head. "No doubt it'll turn out to be a fabrication."

The intercom on his desk buzzed and Alec rose to answer it. His secretary's efficient voice stated metallically, "Mr. Durek's here to see you, Mr. Stone. You have an appointment with him at five."

"Yes, that's right. I'll be through in a second." He turned to Cara. "Thank you for watching Wozniak for me. And for everything you found out."

"Sure." Cara walked to the door. " 'Bye, Daddy. You'll let me know what you find out?"

"As soon as I have anything."

Cara entered the outer office, where Michael Durek waited in a plush brown chair. He stood up at her entrance and inclined his head slightly. "Miss Stone." He was a tall, lean man with brown hair and cold gray eyes. Cara had met him a couple of times before and didn't like him. He was as hard and powerful as her father, but without Alec's charm and occasional flashes of fire.

"Mr. Durek," she replied and passed him, walking swiftly to the elevators. She rode down to the underground parking lot feeling strangely deflated. After Chris had walked away, she had concentrated on going to Alec and telling him about the investigation and Ashe Harlan. Now the task was over, and there was nothing left to do except return to her empty apartment. Cara swallowed against the lump in her throat. Suddenly, achingly, a void yawned in her life. Chris was gone, and she knew she would never feel whole again.

During the next few days Cara was lonelier than she could remember. Her feelings for Chris were stronger and deeper than ever, if possible. She thought of him constantly, recalling his smile and speech, the way his green eyes tilted up when he was amused. Before, she had been able to soothe her lacerated emotions with hate, but now she felt drained of anger. Only the pain was left.

Without a job to occupy her, time hung heavily on her hands. It was more than a month until school started—too short a time to start another project, but far too long to endure patiently. She drove to a bookstore and loaded up on paperbacks, but when she returned home, she found she couldn't concentrate on them. She went swimming at the country club, but the noise and people annoyed her. Movies could not fill up the void, and when the intern she had dated asked her out again Cara quickly refused, feeling repulsed by the thought.

She tried to fill her days by visiting Morgan and playing with her nephew. A solemn-faced man in his thirties was there, Sam Burnett, the guard whom Alec had hired to watch his grandson. The only times he let Matt out of his sight were his periodic inspections of the grounds, doors and windows. His quietly waiting presence was unnerving, no matter how necessary it was. Alec had urged her to move into Morgan's house for the time being, so she would be protected also, but Cara refused. She could not stand to spend her heart-pained hours under Burnett's watchful gaze. At least she could have privacy in which to be unhappy.

One evening as she sat at home in her apartment, the phone rang, and to her delight, the caller turned out to be her mother. "Ginny!" she cried. "It's so nice to hear your voice."

Her mother laughed, pleased by the unaffected compliment, and for a few moments she chatted about the social activities that filled her life. Finally, however, she broached the reason for her call. "I received a letter the other day from George Washington University. It's addressed to you. What do you want me to do with it?"

Cara closed her eyes, remembering the sweet, unhurried day she and Chris had spent exploring the college campuses in Washington and the passion-filled night that had followed. She sighed. "Oh, open it and tell me what it says. It's probably about the application I sent them."

There was a rustle of paper as Ginny obeyed her instructions. "You've been admitted to their master's program!" Ginny exclaimed as she skimmed it, then went back to read the entire letter aloud to Cara.

Cara's heart began to thud painfully in her chest. She could go to school in Washington, be close to Chris, maybe see him again. Sternly she tried to repel the thoughts, but they buzzed around her head. "I . . . I see."

"Isn't that nice? Would you like to come here to school? You know I'd love to have you." Tactfully Ginny did not press her daughter, knowing her heart might yet be too sore for her to live so near Chris Wozniak.

"I'm not sure," Cara answered weakly, aware she should have given a firm no. "Let me think about it. I'll let you know, all right?"

"Of course. Now tell me, how is that beautiful grandbaby of mine?"

Cara launched into an account of Matthew's activities, carefully expurgating any mention of the man who guarded him. She and her sisters had agreed that there was no reason for Ginny to be worried by the threats against Matthew, wrapping her, as everyone had done most of Ginny's life, with protection. Finally Cara had related enough amusing anecdotes to please even a grandmother, and Ginny hung up, leaving Cara alone to face her doubts and desires. The thought of seeing Chris again made her hands tremble, and she crossed them beneath her arms to stop the shaking as she began to pace her apartment.

All her life she had been cool, rational Cara, not as lovely as one sister or as bright as the other, but certainly the one with both feet firmly on the ground. She saw people with a clear eye and smiled at their foibles even as she loved them. She was not a creature of impulse, nor was she given to extravagances. It was the solidity, so different from her vibrant mother, and the calm acceptance of life, unlike her father's urgent ambition, which had made her such a puzzle to both parents. Yet now here she was, entertaining the idea of a move that would throw her entire life into shambles, eager to jump into a situation any idiot would know to avoid at all costs. She wanted to go to school in D.C., realizing full well that the next step would be to walk back into Chris's life.

It was ridiculous. Crazy. Not at all the kind of thing she would do. Cara had covered all the arguments before and made the decision to build a life separate from Chris. There was no future there; it was wrong. And yet . . . she wanted so badly to grab at the first slender excuse to see Chris again. With a muffled sound of disgust, Cara grabbed her keys and jammed her feet into sandals. She would talk to Morgan. Morgan would make her see sense.

Morgan was surprised to see Cara so late in the evening, but one look at her troubled face stilled any questions. They went into the quiet living room, where they would be undisturbed. "Oh, Morgan, I'm such a mess," Cara began, and her sister's green eyes opened wide. This wasn't like Cara at all.

"Honey, what's the matter?" she asked anxiously. "What are you talking about?"

"Well, you know there's been something wrong since I returned from D.C. I couldn't talk to you about it. I don't know why."

"That's okay. I understand."

"You probably guessed it was about Chris Wozniak." Morgan nodded helpfully, and Cara began the long, twisting story of their relationship, ending with their trip to Canada.

Morgan reacted predictably, her eyes glowing dark emerald with anger. "That . . . oh, I can't think of a word bad enough to describe him. They all sound too old-fashioned, like *cad* or *blackguard*."

"No, Morgan, really, I believe him now," Cara hastened to assure her. "He's tied to a loveless marriage." A quirked eyebrow conveyed Morgan's disbelief, but she made no comment. "But that's not the problem. I know I can't have Chris. He'll stick with Monica until the day she dies. He's set on it. I don't know if it's self-punishment or what, but he'll never change. I can't fool myself. When he left for D.C. last week, I knew I'd never see him again. I made that decision."

"Then what's the problem?" Morgan leaned forward and took Cara's hands. "Has he called you? Asked you to come back? Is he trying to push you into an affair with him?"

"No. I haven't heard from him. Chris isn't applying any pressure. It's me! *I* want to go to Washington. *I* want to see him again. It's insane. I never thought I'd miss him this much, that I'd want so to be with him again. Morgan, I dream of him all the time. I want him! Sometimes I feel like a sex maniac. All I can think about is going to bed with him. Ginny called tonight and told me George Washington University had accepted me. It was as if an alarm went off in my head. I thought, here's my chance. I can return to Washington. And pretty soon I'd find some way to run into him."

"Cara, no!"

She smiled wryly. "I know, I know. I'd be throwing myself right into the fire. But all of a sudden I have no desire to be sensible."

"Look, Cara, from the very first that guy's been bad news. He deceived you, hurt you, left you and then came back to do it all over again. If you go to him you're asking for more of the same." She paused and frowned. "If you ask me, he sounds just like Daddy."

"No, he's not," Cara cried. "I'm not wrong about Chris. I know I'm not. When he first left, I tried to hate him, but even then I had my doubts. I couldn't understand how I could have been such a bad judge of character. But now I don't think I was. Oh, he has faults—he's ambitious, even ruthless sometimes: his work is all in all to him; he's carrying around a huge guilt complex about his wife. But essentially he's a good man. He's honest. I know it sounds funny, but in some ways he's downright moralistic. He's not like Daddy. He has principles, and he doesn't indulge in countless meaningless affairs while claiming to be madly in love with his wife."

"How do you know?"

"I just know! If you were around him for a few days, you'd believe it, too. Damn it, Morgan, I love him! And I'm miserable. That's what it all boils down to. Whether I'm wrong or right, it's tearing me apart not to be with him. How much worse off could I be with Chris than I am without him?"

"It'll last longer. Before long it would eat you up, knowing you saw him only on borrowed time, saying good-bye to him every weekend when he runs home to his wife, having no rights to him—"

"I don't need that," Cara interrupted. "Or want it. What I want is Chris, not rights and appearances. Maybe there's more of Alec Stone in me than I ever realized. I feel like seizing what I want out of life, and to hell with the consequences."

"The way your jaw is set, you look like him," Morgan teased gently, and a trace of tears sparkled in her eyes. "Oh, honey, I don't mean to upset you or say you're wrong. But I hate for you to make yourself unhappy."

"Tell me this. What if Nick were in Chris's situation? What if he were married to another woman and felt he couldn't leave, although he loved you. What would you do? Go to him or cut him out of your life?"

Morgan settled back in her chair, and a faint smile touched her lips as she considered the thought. "Nick? Nick would never get into such a situation." Slowly the smile faded, and her eyes turned thoughtful. "It's funny. I never thought of it like that . . . Nick wasn't married, of course. But he was in love with Alexis, or at least he had convinced himself of the idea. And knowing he loved someone else, that I'd never have any importance in his life, I fell for him anyway. I was very *sensible*. I ran headlong into an affair with him, just asking to be hurt." She smiled ruefully. "I guess I don't have any business telling other people what to do. In fact, now that I think about it, I remember discussing my problem with you once. And who was it who told me to let loose and throw myself into the situation, to seek my happiness as hard as I could, no matter the odds?"

Cara grinned. "Me, I'm sure."

"Well, I took your advice. I got burned. But eventually I came out with more love and happiness than I ever expected to receive." She sighed and studied her hands. "Frankly I don't know what you ought to do. All my mother-hen instincts tell me to protect you and not let you go to D.C. because you might get hurt. But you're a grown-up now, not my baby sister any longer, and I realize you have to take some risks. The only advice I can give you is to follow your heart. That's what I did... and Alexis, too. It leads you down some pretty rocky paths, but I hate to think where I'd be if I hadn't stuck with it."

Cara studied her silently for a moment, then burst into a grin. "Thank you, Morgan. I think you've given me the answer I need."

Chris shifted impatiently in his chair as he waited for the dessert and coffee to be wheeled in. As always, the Sunday-noon meal was served with irritating formality. They sat in the dining room at the table designed to seat eight people, the vast mahogany expanse covered by a snowy tablecloth and centered by a low arrangement of flowers in a silver bowl. China, crystal and silver glittered against the cloth, as elegant and cold as the silver-blue-and-white patterned wallpaper above the white wainscoting. There were no guests. He and Monica sat in splendid isolation at each end of the table. He flicked a quick glance down the length of it at his wife.

She sat stiffly upright in the armed dining chair, her

wheelchair relegated to the corner of the room. She wore a blue silk blouse above a blue-patterned long skirt. The blouse was adorned with a soft feminine ruffle running down the front and around the high, upstanding collar. He had come to realize lately that she wore such frills and ruffles to hide and soften the wrinkles that were beginning to traverse her long, elegant neck, just as she wore long sleeves to disguise the muscles that three years of pulling herself in and out of the wheelchair had developed in her slim arms. Ironically he wouldn't have noticed either change if she had not taken such pains to hide them.

She was still a lovely woman, every feature perfect, her long blond hair silky and sparkling, the sherry brown eyes framed by delicately arched brows. But years of discontent and invalidism had taken their toll, eating away at what had been great beauty until only the remnants remained. The lips that had once curved so sensually had tightened into a thin line, and grooves had etched themselves grimly beside her nose and mouth. In her determination not to grow fat in her immobility, Monica had starved her face into dry, pinched thinness. Her eyes were hard as stone, accusing and angry, and her upswept hairdo did little to soften her face.

"I don't know how you convince Evelyn to come in on Sundays to fix and serve dinner," Chris commented. He would have liked to say that he found the whole charade of the formal dinner a deadly bore and a waste, but he knew better than to start up that old argument again. So he chose a safer topic on which to vent his irritation.

"Evelyn is one of the *few* people who still understand the importance of loyalty," Monica answered smoothly, her voice as cool as her carefully made up face.

"I presume your remark is a dig at me?" Chris realized with a start that he was actually looking for an argument, continuing a conversation that was pointless except to flex their tempers. In fact, he had started it. Usually he maintained peace by keeping his mouth shut. There was little in their lives anymore that was worth fighting over. He was simply itching for a battle to relieve the bitter tension of the past few days. Curbing the impulse, he began again. "I imagine it's more money than loyalty that inspires her devotion, don't you think?"

"With what you give me, I could hardly pay a dog for its devotion, let alone a housekeeper," Monica retorted, her mouth curling. "Thank God I have parents who can't bear to see me live on the edge of poverty."

"Poverty?" His eyebrows quirked. "I didn't realize a house with a sauna and indoor pool, which, by the way, you never use, qualified as poverty."

"Those are essential because of my condition, and you know it. How can you of all people throw up that expense to me?"

"I didn't throw it up to you, Monica. I simply pointed out that you aren't about to go on welfare, and you don't do your exercises. You were a trifle melodramatic."

"Yes, you pay for the house and the food—" she spat.

"And Evelyn's salary."

"But you refuse to hire a nurse for your crippled wife! I have to pay Mrs. Schrift with money from Mama and Daddy."

"From your grandmother's trust fund, you mean. You're right. I won't pay the general slavey you euphemistically call a nurse. She is not a medical person, which you don't require, anyway. You aren't wasting away like Camille."

"No, I'm not at death's door, although I'm sure you wish I were. I'm simply crippled for life."

"You are paralyzed in both legs, but you are able to lift yourself in and out of your motorized wheelchair. You have an elevator so that you can use both floors and every gadget conceivable to reach whatever you need. Not to mention the fact that you have a full-time housekeeper. The only reason you want poor Mary Schrift is to fetch and carry and bear your bad temper, which you don't dare let loose on Evelyn for fear she'd quit."

The door from the kitchen swung open, and the middle-aged black housekeeper wheeled in the tea cart on which sat a sliced cheesecake, two cups and saucers and a silver coffee service. While Evelyn served slender pieces of the rich dessert, spooning strawberry sauce on top, and after-dinner coffee, Monica stared down at her clasped hands. Chris moodily watched the housekeeper's movements and wished he had not yielded to the impulse to reply to Monica's stinging comments. It was crazy to fight with her. No one won in their battles. He would go back to Washington with a sick, impotent churning in his stomach, and she'd settle down to a week of resentment and plans for retaliation next Saturday and Sunday. The whole situation was idiotic. Why did he come out here every weekend? Why subject himself to the frustration and anger? They'd both be better off if they lived completely apart instead of participating in this farce of ritual togetherness. They hadn't been truly man and wife since before her accident.

It was a rhetorical question, of course. He came because it was Monica's last-ditch demand, her desperate clutching at the remnants of pride. As long as he returned to the house on weekends, people couldn't say for sure that their marriage was over, that he didn't care a bit for her. And she could have the double-edged satisfaction of sinking her claws into him again for two days a week. He agreed to it because it seemed such a small thing to offer against the unending bleakness of her paralysis. No, admit it, he told himself, as Evelyn returned to the kitchen, and Monica raised her head, great tears glistening artfully in her eyes. He came because it was his hair shirt, his penance for all the wrongs he'd done her—marrying her; not divorcing her; loving his job; being the cause of her miserable, invalid state. And this weekend he sought the penance doubly because the taste of Cara lingered on his mouth and skin. But God, it was so much harder than the three Our Fathers and nine Hail Marys old Father Jadlowski used to give him on Saturday mornings.

Monica was a master performer, he thought cynically, watching the drops fill her eyes without spilling over to mar her makeup. Her voice throbbed with pathetic hurt. "It's easy for you to say I don't need a companion because it's possible for me to take care of myself. But I need someone to talk to. I get lonely out here all by myself."

"You're the one who insisted on living here. And your friends visited you before you drove them away with your petulance and demands."

"Oh, no, pity-inspired visiting doesn't last long. They came a few times and then quit because it was too much trouble to drive all the way to the country to see someone who can't do anything or go anywhere."

"Monica, we've been through this routine a million times in the past three years. You have a wheelchair, and I've offered to buy you a custom van with a lift for it and hand controls. You could go to movies, visit, shop—anything you wanted to do."

"And make a spectacle of myself? No, thank you. I have no intention of playing the noble invalid."

"Good, since you've hardly succeeded in that role," he commented dryly.

"And," Monica went on, not to be diverted, "since my friends won't come, I need a companion to at least *be* here, even if she isn't the most scintillating creature on earth. Especially since my husband doesn't deign to visit me during the week . . . or even on the weekends half the time."

"Is that where all this has been leading? The fact that I wasn't here last weekend?"

"Or the one before that."

"I called you before I left and explained I'd be in Texas for a few days working on a story. I didn't expect to be there as long as I was, but something came up."

"Some black-headed something named Cara Stone?"

His head snapped up at her words, and his eyes flashed green. "What are you talking about?"

"Really, Chris, did you think I wouldn't find out? You must be slipping. You used to hide your affairs better."

"I didn't have any to hide," he growled.

She laughed bitterly. "A man like you? Don't make me laugh. You haven't graced my bed in years, but I know you aren't doing without. I remember when I first knew you. You'd wake me up two hours after we made love because you were so hot. Oh, maybe you've slowed down. Men do as they get older, I've heard. But stop entirely? Surely your Texas honey isn't the first to get you—"

"Shut up, Monica." His voice was coldly threatening as he rose to his feet.

"Tell me, how old is Cara? I've heard she's just a child."

"Who told you this tripe?"

"Come, come, you ought to know better." Monica smiled tauntingly. "I'd never reveal my sources. But don't think I don't still have some. I know you had a little fling with her a few months ago, even took a trip into Virginia. Tell me, did you take her where we used to go? The cozy little cabin in the Shenandoah Valley?"

"You know I sold it long ago. I don't know why you delight in this sort of scene, but I'm not going to stay here and take it. What I do is my own business. And I won't have you maligning Cara Stone."

"Oh, no!" she mocked. "I mustn't do that. A good wife must never malign her husband's latest whore."

His hands clenched, and for a moment red swam before his eyes. He wanted to fling himself at Monica's throat and choke her to silence. Grimly he clung to his control, his jaw tightening, and turned to leave the dining room.

"Did you think I wouldn't find out?" she shrieked after him. "Did you think I wouldn't know why you went running off to Texas?" There was no answer from him except the final slamming of the front door. Monica picked up her fragile coffee cup and flung it against the far wall, her face contorted with rage.

The Jaguar roared out of the circular driveway, spewing gravel backward beneath the wheels. Jaw set, hands clenched around the steering wheel, Chris pressed the accelerator to the floor, speeding down the street as if he could leave the anger and pain behind him in the white colonial house with his wife. Damn Monica and her spying ways!

Her cuts about the woman he loved—Cara—made him
burn with rage. He had come closer to striking Monica than
ever before in their stormy marriage. It made him sick to
think of her acid tongue slicing at Cara. What if she should
take it into her head to write to Cara . . . or even to phone
her? There was almost nothing he wouldn't put past Monica
in one of her jealous fits. If she invaded Cara's life, hurt
her somehow. . . . He swallowed convulsively and forced
himself to calm down.

Monica wouldn't do that. Not knowing how very much
he cared for Cara prevented Monica from attacking her
directly. All Monica wanted was to make him suffer, to
goad him, to prod him into the arguments that were the only
remnants of their old relationship. He released a slow sigh
and eased back on the pedal, his hands loosening their death
grip on the wheel. Indifference was the only way to combat
Monica. If he could control his temper and simply smile
sardonically at her, she would soon drop the subject. If he
didn't, she'd return to it again and again. He knew Monica
well enough that he should have realized that and not fallen
into her trap. He wouldn't have jumped so hard at her
spurring if he hadn't been living on the edge of hell for the
past few days, thinking about Cara.

Chris had hoped he would be able to bury himself in
work when he returned and gradually ease his sense of loss.
However, although he had plunged into the search for Vern
Haskell, he still couldn't keep Cara out of his mind. She
was a constant, dull ache inside him, a feeling that never
left. He thought of her during the day, imagining her smile,
her walk, her clear laugh, the soft accent tinging her speech.
He recalled in detail every moment of their lovemaking,
each curve and swell of her body. He would dream of her
and wake up sweating, the sheets twisted around him. At
times he wanted her body at any cost. At other moments
he thought it would be enough simply to be with her and
talk to her. More honestly, he had to admit he wanted all
of Cara all the time. He was as taut as a stretched-out wire,
and it required every bit of his self-control not to pick up

the phone and beg Cara to come to him. He tortured himself by wondering whether she would.

When Chris reached his Georgetown apartment, he went to the den to map out his week. Howard should be back with his police drawing of Haskell—provided the surly Harlan kid had cooperated, of course—and that would open up a whole new dimension in his search. Chris's concentration on his task was poor, however, and he soon flung up his hands in frustration. He paced the living room, now and then glancing at his watch. The hands crawled with agonizing slowness. Not yet four o'clock. Too early for a relaxing drink. Besides, if he started drinking over Cara, he'd probably become an alcoholic before he erased her from his memory. He thought of calling Dean, but he hated to spoil his friend's weekend with his wife, whose job so often kept her away from him. Perhaps it would be best to sit down and abandon his mind to Cara and let it dwell on her until he grew tired of thinking about her. Not that it seemed a very likely possibility.

The buzz of the doorbell startled him from his thoughts, and he started toward the door eagerly, thankful for the diversion. He swung it open and stopped, his hand frozen on the knob. For a moment Chris thought he had become delusional, that he had summoned up the figure on his doorstep through wishful thinking. She was beautiful, her blue eyes sparkling, her cheeks flushed, the silken hair tumbling about her bare tanned shoulders. In a pink halter and matching casual skirt, she looked crisp, cool and delightful. His throat clamped tightly on any words he might have said, and he could do no more than stare.

Her light laughter tumbled out nervously. "Hello, Chris. Aren't you even going to invite me in?" Cara teased.

Chapter 14

Chris had to wet his dry lips before he could speak. "Yes, of course." He stepped aside to allow her entry and closed the door behind her. "I'm sorry. You...surprised me."

"Did I?" Cara turned, and he saw for the first time that her hands were tightly clasped in front of her. Her voice quavered a little. She was frightened, or at least nervous.

"Did something happen to Matthew?"

"No, he's fine as far as I know." She looked away, and an awkward pause stretched between them.

Finally Chris cleared his throat and asked, "Cara, what are you doing here?"

She didn't look at him, and her hands clenched more tightly. "I'm going to graduate school in D.C. this fall. George Washington University accepted my application."

"How nice." His voice grated on the words.

Cara glanced at him and away again, but he caught a sparkle of tears in her eyes before she turned. "I...I'm sorry. I didn't think about whether you—that is, when I decided to come, I didn't even consider how you would feel. That you might not want to see me."

"Not want to see you? Of course I do. It's all I've been able to think about."

"Really?" Cara's face shone, and her eyes met his with the full force of their azure glow.

His hands began to tremble. "God, Cara, how can you doubt it? I can't sleep. I can't work. Seeing you on my doorstep was like having the one thing I most desire materialize."

She beamed. "Good. For a minute, when you acted so stiff, I thought maybe you didn't like my coming here."

"I don't!" he growled. "It's sheer torture. I need more than just to look at you."

Cara moved forward, her hands going out. "Then do what you need."

He whirled away and strode to the window, gazing out until he could command his breath and voice. "What are you trying to do? I can't stand this. I'm too old to play games."

"I'm not playing games!" She drew her brows together in a baffled frown.

"Then what are you doing? All I can see is that you're teasing me with what I can't have."

"But you can. I wouldn't have come here if I didn't intend to sleep with you. Chris, I love you. I want to be with you for as long as you want me. I mean sex, love, companionship—whatever you want."

His body went rigid. "Cara, you don't know what you're saying."

"Oh, yes, I do. Ask anyone in my family. I don't change my mind easily."

"Nothing's different. I'm still married."

"I know it. I accept it."

"That's crazy!" he exploded, trembling all over in the effort to subdue his longing. "I have nothing to offer you."

"You have all I want—yourself. Which is exactly what I'm offering you. Don't you want it?"

"Of course I do! If I thought of nothing but myself, it would be sheer heaven. It's all I can do not to drag you into the bedroom and make love to you right now."

"Then why don't you?"

"Because I am supposedly a mature, responsible adult! Cara, I can't give you what I want to. I can't divorce Monica. Don't think you'll be able to twist me around to doing it. You'll be my mistress, that's all."

"I know it. That's enough."

"It's not."

She shrugged. "Maybe not. But it's better than nothing, which is what I had sitting at home in Dallas. Chris, I'm aware you'll spend time with Monica. She's Mrs. Wozniak, and if we're seen together, people will know exactly what my role is. I know you can only give me part of yourself. I'll have to be content with the share not given to Monica or your work. I've thought it through. I'm not a child making a rash decision. What other people think doesn't bother me. Being a Stone gives one a certain amount of saving arrogance. And the forms—a ring on my finger, your name on a wedding certificate—are things I can live without . . . as long as I have your heart."

"You'll always have that."

"Maybe it's morally wrong, but I'm beginning to think morals don't mean much more to me than they do to Daddy. All I care about is you and being with you. I don't want to cry my eyes out and be miserable for the rest of my life, just so I can say I've done the 'right' thing."

"I don't want to hurt you." His words were low.

"Then don't turn me away. Let me be happy with you." She raised her arms to him, tears spilling silently onto her cheeks.

"Oh, Cara!" He crossed the room in two quick strides and pulled her hungrily into his arms. His lips sought her moist mouth, and she clung to him, her momentary qualms vanished. Cara was certain now that he wanted her as much as she wanted him.

Chris swung her into his arms and carried her into the bedroom. Her hands were busy unbuttoning his shirt and exploring his chest. Cara giggled at his quickly indrawn breath and curled her fingers into the thick mat of hair. He laid her carefully on the bed and stepped back to rip off his encumbering clothing. Cara disrobed as eagerly, and soon they were together on the old-fashioned bed, touching and tasting, discovering anew the wonder of their bodies. His hands on her skin were dry and hot as a man in a fever, igniting rivers of flame throughout her. She thrust up against him, reveling in the scratch of his curling hair against her tender, engorged nipples, and he groaned, sliding down her body. One by one, he kissed the rosy tips of her breasts into hardness, and one hand crept down to open the satiny bud of her femininity, slick with desire. Cara trembled and moved against him, crying out softly. Chris shifted and moved into her, his strokes slow, building the need thrumming within her and stretching her taut. His breath rasped, searing her neck, changing abruptly into a hoarse moan of pleasure as he scaled his peak. The tension broke in Cara, turning to liquid fire, and her body eased, having found the fulfillment it had sought since Chris left.

"I love you," she whispered.

They dozed and woke to make love again, more slowly this time, savoring every pleasurable moment. Afterward they lay together in quiet, calm companionship, her head nestled into the hollow of his shoulder, his arm curved lovingly around her. They drifted in and out of conversation, content to be with each other. He told her about looking for Alec's extortionist, describing the dusty search through business tomes that yielded the names of executives and major shareholders of various oil companies.

"Oh, Chris, do you suppose I could help you? I mean, I could go through books and lists."

His eyebrows rose in surprise. "You mean you'd like to?"

"Sure. It's for Matthew's sake, after all. And besides, I'd like a chance to see more of the work you do. It's interesting. I kind of enjoyed what we did in Canada."

"Sure. I'll be happy to give you all the work you can handle. You may be sorry you expressed an interest."

"I doubt it." Cara snuggled closer to him, a happy smile on her face.

"After I finish collecting all the names, I'm going to check out their life histories. You can certainly help me there. We'll need to examine the pasts of the men your father considers to be enemies. Hopefully I'll turn up some more overtly criminal activities than the usual oil deals on one of them. Finding Vern Haskell is by far the better bet, though. I sent Howard Cantrell to talk to Ashe Harlan. He's the artist I told you about, the one who does police sketches. When he gets back tomorrow, I'll have a portrait of Haskell."

"Provided Ashe will be cooperative," Cara added dryly.

"Yes, it's a big *if*. I told Howard to offer him money if Harlan gets stubborn. Maybe that will move him if nothing else will."

"I told Daddy what Ashe said—about being Daddy's illegitimate son. Alec remembered being in Tulsa about that time and also recalled a woman he'd had an affair with. The story fit with Ashe's, but Daddy couldn't remember her name. He was definitely intrigued and decided to fly Ashe to Dallas to speak to him."

"What does he plan to do about him?" Chris asked idly, curling a strand of her hair around his fingers. He was largely indifferent to Alec Stone's plans for his possible son, but he enjoyed lying there listening to Cara's soft voice. "I mean, if he decides the guy is his son."

"Who knows? Daddy might take it into his head to do almost anything. I suspect if he believes Ashe, he'll pull out all the stops—bring Ashe into the business and groom him to be president one day, set up a trust fund, that sort of thing. It's funny. I've been seeing Daddy in a new light lately."

"What do you mean?"

"Well, two things, really. One is that I've discovered more and more of his traits in myself. It's almost scary. I never thought I resembled him in the least—on the inside, I mean. But I've found I'm as stubborn as he, as determined to get my way and rather careless about right and wrong when it comes to what I want."

Chris chuckled. "I wouldn't worry about turning into a female Alec Stone if I were you. I hardly think you qualify as ruthless."

She smiled. "No. I didn't really mean that. But in the past I felt so separate from Daddy, unlike him and unable to like him. And now I can see him in me. I've felt sorry for him this past week. He's frantic about Matthew's safety. When he told me how much he'd always wanted a son and never had one, I actually pitied him. It may not sound amazing to you, but to me, Alec was a rock, a super being apart from the rest of us. I didn't think he ever felt or hurt or loved. I still don't understand him or why he treated Ginny the way he did, but at least he's become a human being to me."

"Is this where I'm supposed to point out to you that you're growing up?"

Cara giggled. "No. It's always a kindly uncle or grandfather who does that . . . not the man you're lying in bed with."

"Oh, forgive my faux pas. You'll have to excuse me. I'm Polish, you know."

"Well, don't you Poles ever get hungry? I'm starving to death."

"After the important things of life, we do take time out to eat now and then." He slapped her playfully on the rump. "Get up, and I'll take you to one of the sidewalk cafés that are all the thing now in Washington."

They showered and dressed, then drove to the towpath along the Chesapeake and Ohio Canal. Several small shops, art galleries and restaurants were clustered together there in a semblance of an English village. They sat down at an outdoor table at Port O' Georgetown in a rustic, tree-shaded setting and dawdled through a leisurely meal of soup and sandwiches, watching the pedestrians who passed by. Afterward they strolled down the towpath hand in hand. Looking up at Chris, seeing his face relaxed and happy, without the hard tension she had always seen there before, Cara knew she had done the right thing. It couldn't be wrong, it simply couldn't; not when they felt like this.

The following days continued in the same vein of lazy happiness. For the first time the strain was gone from their relationship, and they were able to enjoy one another completely. They made love often, sometimes quickly, sometimes with shivering slowness, stoking the fires of their love until it burst into devouring flames. Chris was by turns tender, ardent, forceful, even impatient in his lovemaking, and Cara gloried in trying every possible mood. But there were many times they spent together when they did not make love. They stretched out on the couch one evening and simply held each other for a long, long time. They joked and teased, laughing like children.

Cara helped him with his research, squinting her way through columns of names and adding to the ever-growing list of possibilities. When she finally closed a book with a thud and declared she was going blind, he set her to scanning old newspaper articles about each of the people on her list. Her fingers grew black from newsprint and her eyes ached from staring at microfilm. The newspaper's library had little on some of the names and a great deal on others, but nothing that looked remotely like indicators of a future extortionist.

Chris brought her the sketch of Vern Haskell as soon as he got it. It was the picture of a heavyset, jowly man with thick eyebrows and thinning hair. His eyes were small and his nose fleshy, his mouth wide with a full lower lip. The face was strong, even stern, despite the pudginess. Cara sighed. He looked like a man who could work for an extortionist, but unfortunately she had never seen the face before.

"Does he look at all familiar?" Chris prodded.

Cara shook her head. "No. I'm sure I don't know him."

"I didn't expect you to recognize him. It would be too much to ask for. But I'll send a copy of this to your father in the hope he might know him. If not, he can at least use his influence with the Dallas police. Maybe they can dig up something on the guy. With a picture and a name, it's possible."

"I hope so." Cara looked at Chris almost tearfully. "Sometimes I think we're getting absolutely nowhere. None of these people seems like an extortionist. Ambitious, aggressive, yes, even a little slippery with the law now and then. But not the kind to threaten a baby's life in order to steal another company's well!"

"I know. Sometimes I think we're barking up the wrong tree entirely. But who else could benefit from Stone closing its Canadian well? The whole thing doesn't make sense unless there's a profit to be made that we're overlooking."

"But how are we ever going to find it?"

"Good question." The lines of his face shifted, and he grinned at her. "Enough of this gloom. I think a nice walk would do us both good." As he pulled her from her chair, Cara had to smile at him. Just being with Chris was enough to lift her blackest mood.

They drove to East Potomac Park and strolled among the trees. The day had been hot, but the sun was setting and a faint breeze fanned them. Cara had to agree it was good to get outdoors after days spent hunched over books. "I think I'll take a day off tomorrow and visit Ginny. I feel guilty. I've been here four days and haven't even called to let her know I'm in town."

He smiled, quirking an eyebrow. "You've been busy."

"I thought I'd spend the weekend with her—that is, if you're going out to . . . see Monica." Firmly Cara stifled the ache that rose in her as she said it. She knew this was as much a part of the deal as the past few days of love and laughter.

His face darkened, and he glanced away. The last thing in the world he wanted to do was spend even two days with Monica . . . and away from Cara. But if he didn't, Monica would start snooping again. And he wanted to keep Cara's presence in his life from Monica as long as possible. She'd be certain to find out one day, and then there'd be holy hell to pay, but the longer he could delay the moment, the better. He ignored the insidious, pleasure-seeking voice urging him to stay with Cara and replied, "Yes, I suppose I'll have to."

Cara kept her voice expressionless. "Then I thought it would be a good time to visit Ginny. We can go apartment hunting."

He turned toward her, surprised. "Apartment hunting? But I thought you would stay with me. Why do you need an apartment?"

Cara warmed at the thought that he wanted her to live with him. "No, I think it would be better if I had a place of my own to live in. It's rather an awkward situation, my staying in your apartment."

"Awkward? How? If you think I care whether anyone knows you're there, you don't know me very well."

"Chris, you're hardly an anonymous person. People will talk, and it will get back to Monica. It's bound to."

Resentment tore through him. "Let it. She'll find out anyway. I don't give a damn if she knows."

"You don't want to hurt her, do you?"

"Monica hurts herself as well as everyone else she can get in her grasp. Believe me, as far as her finding out, your feelings are all that matter to me. Any tenderness I had for Monica died long ago."

"I find that hard to believe when you stay married to her."

"I explained it to you. I thought you understood. Love, even kindness, doesn't enter into it."

"I know you don't love her. It's largely guilt that keeps you tied to her. I understand that. But there must be some sort of feeling for her."

He snorted. "It'd burn your ears to hear what I feel for her."

Cara frowned, puzzled, then shrugged. "Well, Monica aside, I still think I should get a separate apartment. Living together can be a strain on a new relationship. You work at home, and pretty soon I'd begin to get in your way. I'll have schoolwork to do. And sometimes I may have to stay late at school. It'd be easier to go back to my apartment. Otherwise we'd be bumping into each other and getting irritated over little things."

"You don't know that."

"I don't want anything to jeopardize our relationship. Why wait until it's too late to realize it was a bad idea to live together?"

"Why are you so sure it will be?"

Cara looked away, reluctant to explain. Finally she began. "Chris, I need someplace separate. I need . . . a life of my own, an identity apart from you. I know what I'm getting into. I'm willing to risk it. But I don't want to be completely involved in your life, so absorbed in you that I have nothing outside of you. Do you understand what I mean? As it is, I love you so much it scares me. But at least I can say I have interests and a place of my own. If we lived together we'd be as close, as intimate, as sharing as if we were married . . . only we're not. And every time you went to your wife or I was somehow reminded that I'm merely your mistress, it would hurt much more. This way I can maintain a little saving distance."

His face was still, expressionless. He shrugged. "Perhaps you're right. For a while there I was dreaming I could have everything. But you're right. Do whatever you want. I won't object. I'm hardly in a position to make demands."

"Chris . . ." Cara began tentatively, suddenly afraid she had hurt him. "You do understand, don't you?"

He smiled at her sadly. "Sure, I understand. Cara, I want you to do what's right for you. I just wish you didn't have to be so strong. I wish you didn't need to be protected from me."

The following afternoon Ginny was predictably delighted to find her daughter on the doorstep. Cara was immediately guilt-ridden because she hadn't come earlier. She'd been so happy with Chris she hadn't wanted any interruptions, even from her loving mother.

Ginny hugged Cara enthusiastically and pulled her inside,

asking dozens of questions without pausing to let Cara answer. Finally she drew to a halt and laughed merrily. "Here I am bursting to know why you're here, and I keep talking so much you can't get a word in edgewise. I'm sorry. I'll stop. Now you tell me what's going on."

"Well, I've decided to go to school here."

"Marvelous! I was hoping you'd say that. It will be such fun. It's been ages since I've lived close to any of my girls."

"I thought we might look for an apartment this weekend."

"Certainly, if you'd like to. But did you drive all this way by yourself?"

Cara nodded. "I wanted to see the South, and this seemed as good a time as any. I drove across through Tennessee, North Carolina and Virginia. The scenery was beautiful."

"You went through the Blue Ridge?"

"Yes, and then up through the Shenandoah Valley. It was gorgeous. When I see things like that, I wonder how the pioneers could bear to leave all that beauty and move west."

"The Blue Ridge Parkway is lovely in June when all the rhododendron are in bloom. But you can see them next year. I'm so excited I hardly know what to do. I can't wait to tell Wilson. After you left last time, he told me he missed you. He said he'd forgotten how nice it was to have a daughter around the house. His is twenty-six, you see, and has been away from home for years. Here, let's sit in the den. Now, tell me all about Morgan and the baby. And how's Alexis doing?"

Cara obligingly described Alexis's condition and looks and gave a long account of Matthew Fletcher. Ginny drank in her news avidly, stopping her incessantly to ask questions, and they passed away a couple of hours catching up. As they talked, however, Ginny sensed a time discrepancy in Cara's leaving her apartment and arriving on Ginny's doorstep. Her lovely forehead wrinkled. "But honey, I don't understand. Why did it take you so long—"

"It didn't." She sighed. "I might as well get it over with.

You're not going to like this. I got into Washington last Sunday afternoon. The reason I didn't come here any sooner is—"

"Chris Wozniak."

"You're right, naturally."

"Oh, Cara." Ginny's sunny face pulled into sad lines. "Why? Do you really think it's the right thing to do?"

"I don't know," Cara replied. "Maybe not. A lot of things have happened since I was here." She related Chris's visit to Dallas, and his explanation of his marriage, although she did not include their side trip to Canada.

Ginny, unlike Morgan, did not disbelieve Chris's story. She shook her head. "How sad. It's nice, really, to think a man today has enough sense of duty to stick with his wife like that. But when there's no love between them, it must be an awfully hard, lonely life. They'd be better off apart."

"They practically are apart, anyway. They only see each other on weekends. In my opinion, they might as well be divorced. He could continue to support her financially, and they'd both be free to find someone else. But that's not the way Chris sees it. His conscience drives him to continue it. He feels guilty because his job was responsible for her injury, and she hated his work. I think it's his pound of flesh."

"Well, it seems rather a strict view to hold when it takes your flesh, too. That's what I don't like. Sorry as I may feel for him—and her—you're the one I hate to see hurt."

"I know." Cara smiled warmly at her mother. "You're so sweet and understanding. How many other mothers wouldn't dump a big pile of guilt on me?"

"Honey, I can't condemn you, any more than I can Chris. I certainly made a botch of my first marriage, so I can hardly be holier-than-thou when it comes to relationships."

"*You* didn't botch it up."

"No, that's not fair. Alec was the one who cheated on me, but it takes two people to make a bad marriage. I loved him, but I wasn't right for him. It was the same with him.

If I had been more independent, less scatterbrained, less pliable, maybe he wouldn't have sought other women. I didn't meet some need in your father."

"That's true," Cara agreed with a mock serious face. "All Alec really wanted was perfection. It should have been easy enough for you."

Ginny grinned. "Cara, you wicked girl, to talk about your father that way. Besides, you're leading me off the subject, and probably on purpose. What I want to know is, are you going to be happy with Chris this way? Or are you throwing yourself into a situation where you'll be miserable?"

"I keep asking myself the same question. Right now I'm so much happier than I was without him. I don't think I could be more depressed than I was then. Who can say what the future holds? It may all come tumbling down around my ears, and I'll wish I'd never done it. But I talked to Morgan about it—"

"And she recommended you go to Chris?" Ginny interrupted, amazed.

"Not exactly. But after I'd explained how I felt, she admitted it wasn't dissimilar to the decision she'd made to date Nick despite his love for Alexis. And she told me that the most important thing was to follow my heart. So that's what I did."

Ginny curved an arm around Cara's shoulders and gave her a quick squeeze. "Morgan has good, practical instincts. I agree with her. No matter what happens, you have to give love every chance you can."

Chapter 15

Chris idly shuffled through a stack of index cards, his mind hardly registering the words flipping past his view. He glanced at the clock for the fourth time in the last hour, even as he told himself he was being ridiculous. It was late Sunday afternoon, and he had returned from Monica's two hours ago. It had been the usual stiffly formal meeting except for their occasional acerbic exchanges. It had been harder than ever to endure Monica's presence, coming as he did from Cara's light, loving warmth. He compared her every word and gesture to Cara's, and found Monica achingly wanting. Yet, oddly enough, it was easier to ignore her stinging comments, for his mind was focused not on Monica and her words but on Cara.

He missed her. She had been in his life hardly a week, but already he was bereft without her. He yearned for her soft body in his bed, her passion, her laughter, her unselfish caring. So he had left immediately after the noon meal, rushing home to envelop Cara in his arms, only to find that she was not there.

He had spent the past two hours waiting for her, reminding himself she didn't know he was already back, then arguing that she could easily have called to find out. He imagined her in a wreck, helpless and bloody. Yet he knew she was probably lingering over coffee with Ginny. Then he became certain she had decided not to return at all, even though they hadn't discussed returning at any specific time. More than once he started to phone Wilson Decker's house, only to draw back his hand. Chris knew he was being foolish, and he wasn't sure how Cara's mother would react to his calling. She must hate him for the way he had treated her daughter, for the mess he had allowed Cara to get into.

The doorbell rang, and he rushed from the study. He flung open the door and saw Cara, smiling and natural. Instantly he swept her into his arms, giving her as bone-crushing a hug as if she had been absent a month. Cara seemed content to remain in his steely grasp, wrapping her arms around his neck and kissing him softly on the ear and neck. "I've missed you," Chris whispered as he let her slide gently from him.

She smiled. "I missed you, too." They kissed, lips clinging, and Cara stepped back, her face flushed, her voice a trifle breathless.

"I was worried," he confessed. "I was afraid you'd decided not to come back."

Cara stared. "Why would I do that? Heavens, Chris, it's only five o'clock. I didn't know when to expect you."

"I know. And I didn't give you a key. You couldn't have gotten in if you'd come home before me. I realize all that. But I was still anxious. You could have found an apartment and decided to move in right away, or wanted to stay with your mother for a few days. Or decided you made a mistake in coming here to begin with."

"Well, none of those things happened." She stretched to brush his lips with a soft, brief kiss. "I did find an apartment, but it's not available until September first. So you'll have to put up with me a little longer."

"I think I can handle it." He looped an arm about her

shoulders and guided her to the sofa, where he sat and she snuggled happily against his side. "Tell me about it. How was your weekend? What's the apartment like?"

"Oh, just an apartment. It's nice, but nothing special. Tan carpet, white walls, a tiny kitchen, but not far from school. No personality, but convenient."

"Good. You won't spend much time there." She cast him an appraising sideways glance but made no remark. "How's your mother?"

"Fine. She was very nice and understanding about us. Ginny's a marvelous person. Most mothers would have let me have it, but not Ginny. She truly wants me to be happy."

"You mean she didn't even call me a cad?"

Cara giggled. "Not once. Ginny's a soft touch. She thought your situation was sad. But also, being practical, she was of the opinion that you should cut your losses and run."

They fell into silence, and Cara cursed her impulsive tongue. She had sworn she wouldn't nag Chris about a divorce. No matter what her own thoughts on the subject, she knew he would do precisely as he pleased, and any comments from her were more likely to engender resistance than agreement. Wetting her lips, she asked noncommittally, "And how was your weekend?"

He snorted. "Not exactly what you'd call pleasant. A few minor skirmishes, but otherwise an armed truce."

"Meaning?"

"We don't talk much, and when we do, we argue. That's the pattern of my weekends. But not the next one."

"Why not?" A sudden fear clutched at her throat. Had he decided to try once more to make the marriage work?

"I'm taking you to Marble Falls to meet my sisters."

Cara stared at him in astonishment. "Chris! We can't go to see your family. What would they think? You told me you come from a very strict, religious family. You can't take a mistress into their house."

"My parents would have minded. The rest of us aren't quite as rigid, particularly my younger sisters. We'll stay with Mary Helen. She's two years younger than I am and has always adored me. Believe me, whatever I do is right as far as she's concerned. And if the others object . . . well, they need something to talk about. It's been too long since the last family scandal."

"Chris, you can't be right. Surely your sisters would be upset, to say the least."

"I promise they won't be," Chris assured her. "They resented saying the rosary on their knees on the cold wooden floor at five o'clock every morning as much as I did. Nor did they enjoy bruised knuckles from the sisters rapping their hands with rulers. None of us is an ardent Catholic. Also they suffer from the delusion that I'm stupendous. I'm the only one in the family with a college degree. To them I'm fabulously famous and wealthy, and they're proud of me. I'm also considered different and excused my little peculiarities."

"Such as bringing a woman other than your wife to visit?" Cara asked skeptically.

"They despise Monica. She looked down on them. The few times we visited Marble Falls, she did her best to make them feel inferior. They were in awe of her at first, but it didn't take long for them to realize she wasn't worth liking, let alone worshipping. Besides, they know my marriage is a farce, and being loyal sisters, they blame Monica entirely. They've all been urging me to get a divorce for the past five years."

"Well, if you're sure . . ."

"Tell you what—I'll call first, and if Mary Helen seems reluctant, we won't go. That is—I'm not giving you much choice, am I? Would you like to go?"

"As long as I'm not an intruder or the family's 'scarlet woman,' sure, I'd love to. I want to meet your family and see where you grew up."

"Good. It's settled, then. I'll phone Mary Helen, and we'll go this weekend."

* * *

They drove northwest from Washington, cutting through the awesome mountain beauty of West Virginia into southwest Pennsylvania. Cara gasped at the unfolding scenery one moment, only to cry out in dismay when they rounded a curve and came upon ugly slag heaps or a coke plant belching smoke. Once Chris left the main road for a side trip through a small coal town. Ramshackle buildings lined the narrow street, and abandoned mine shafts dotted the landscape. Occasionally they passed a person sitting useless, idle, dull-eyed.

"What happened here?" Cara exclaimed.

"Mines played out. It became unprofitable. You can blame it on oil or greed or the lack of foresight, whatever you want. But the fortunes of western Pennsylvania rose or fell with steel and coal. It almost happened to Marble Falls, but fortunately the town was smart enough—or lucky enough—to avoid it. The wire mill was our main industry, but it stopped in the early sixties. Some light industry was attracted, which saved it. Now there's an electronics plant and a chemical plant, plus a couple of other smaller ones. But the land here is so laced with mine shafts that it's likely to cave in if heavy buildings are put on it."

"Chris, this is awful. It looks like something out of a war zone. Why do people remain here?"

He shrugged. "Nowhere else to go. They've probably lived in this town all their lives. People waited for years for the coal company to come back. They were sure the mines would start again. It had happened before. They couldn't believe their livelihood had vanished."

"How sad."

He ran his hand gently across her cheek. "You're softhearted. The history of this area may be too much for you."

"Why?"

"It's full of misery. Immigrants were shipped to the coal mines and steel mills like cattle, literally sold by agents to the owners. They worked for starvation wages. The practices in effect then would make ruthless men today cringe. They lived in company towns that were sometimes surrounded by barbed wire. Company police patrolled the streets and searched anyone who entered to make sure union organizers stayed out. The people lived in filth, and their pitiful salaries were often paid in company script that was spent at the company's stores."

"It sounds like a concentration camp."

"It *was* a prison, of sorts. Nobody could build up savings to leave. Children had to work in order to keep the family afloat. By the time a man was forty, he was past his prime. The really horrifying thing is that it wasn't so long ago. The unions didn't make a breakthrough until the great 'steel wars' of the 1940s. My father and uncles went through it not long before I was born."

"How horrible."

"Enough gloom for the day. Let's drive on to the Falls."

Marble Falls was a "ravine" town set beside the wide, muddy Monongahela River. The huge, brown, brick wire mill dominated the flat access to the river, and the rest of the town straggled up the sides of the bluffs. At the top the more elegant homes boasted a panoramic view of the river. Cara looked about eagerly as Chris pointed out places of interest. "That's the old wire mill. What's left of downtown. Not very prosperous, I'm afraid. The newer plants are north of town. Here's my old high school."

He turned and drove into a residential section. Row after row of similar brown brick houses lined the streets, postage-stamp lawns adorning the fronts. The once-white trim had blended into dirty tan over the years. "Everything's so brown!" Cara exclaimed, then stopped guiltily, afraid she sounded critical. She might have to curb her tongue if she wanted to gain the goodwill of Chris's sisters. After all, they disliked Monica because she was snobbish. It might have been remarks like the one she just made that had aroused their antagonism.

But Chris simply laughed. "That's soot and dirt. Years of accumulation of smoke from the mill. You're no longer in Texas, my love."

He pulled to a stop in front of a house that was indistinguishable from the rest, his Jaguar absurdly incongruous in the blue-collar neighborhood. The front door banged open, and a swarm of children tumbled down the steps and across the lawn. Chris stepped out of the car and swooped them up one by one, swinging them high over his head. Cara watched him tenderly, noticing the gentling of his face, the easy smile.

A woman in her early thirties appeared on the small porch and called to the children, "Enough! Enough! You'll kill Uncle Chris. Come back into the house and behave." She smiled across the yard at Chris. "Well, don't just stand there. Come in. I'm dying for a look at Cara."

Chris laughed as the children darted into the house, and he held out a hand to Cara. "I think it's safe to get out now," he joked. "How's that for a herd?"

"Are all of them your sister's?" Cara asked, awed.

"No. Four. The other two are her husband's by a previous marriage. Six in all."

"Goodness."

"Leaves you speechless, doesn't it? Well, if anybody can handle it, Mary Helen can. She's the calmest person in the world. Come meet her."

His sister was a tall woman with short, curly brown hair and eyes the same hazel-green color as Chris's. Her face was wide and angular, her expression curious and merry. When Chris introduced them, she shook Cara's hand firmly. "I'm glad you're here early. I wanted a chance to visit with you before the others arrive." She turned to Chris and greeted him in Polish: *"Jak się masz."*

"Fine," he replied in the same language, then asked, "What do you mean? What others? Is the whole tribe showing up?"

"No. But I called the girls in Pittsburgh and Irene, since they live close enough to come. I thought they'd like to see you."

"Like to see Cara, you mean," Chris corrected, his eyes twinkling.

Mary Helen shrugged eloquently. "Anyway, you know

Irene. She'll be here this evening with all her kids as soon as she gets off work. The oldest one, Barbara, has a new baby, and Irene's dying to show off her grandchild."

"Irene's my oldest sister," Chris explained to Cara. "She lives in the Falls, too. Married Andy Kowalski."

"And Sophie and Annie are driving in tomorrow from Pittsburgh."

"Angela's not coming?"

"Maybe, but you know Paul. If he decides he doesn't want her to, she won't come." She sighed and shook her head at the thought that any Wozniak could be so accommodating.

Again Chris turned to Cara in explanation. "Angie's married to Paul di Nardo, a cop. Mary Helen didn't want to say it, but what she really dislikes about him is that he's Italian."

"He's a slob," Mary Helen protested indignantly. "What are you talking about? *I* married an Italian the first time around."

"I know. That's why you hold it against Paul."

She swung at him playfully. "You're going to make Cara think we're awful."

"It won't take more than meeting all of us for her to figure that out."

"All of you?" Cara squeaked.

"No, not really," Mary Helen hastened to reassure her. "Just Irene, Sophie and Annie. Maybe Angie."

"Most of the others don't live as close as Pittsburgh. Stef's in Philly, and so is Tracy," Chris explained.

"Don't you have any brothers? Are they all girls except you?"

"One brother. John. He's a steelworker in Pittsburgh. But he's not the type to run to a family reunion. He's the tough guy of the family."

"All these names are confusing me."

"I'll help you."

Mary Helen ushered them into the living room and hustled off to find soft drinks. Chris settled comfortably onto the couch, propping up his feet on the small coffee table. "I'll have to take you to Irene's home. It's very similar to my mother's—full of religious pictures, cramped and dark. The younger girls have gotten further and further away from the old traditions."

"Your sister has more of an accent than you."

"Yeah. I lost a lot of mine at college. I felt like an idiot saying *tick* instead of *thick*. *Trough tick and tin,*" he mimicked. "When I'd come home in the summer, the guys around here would accuse me of trying to talk better than them. I was just trying not to get laughed at the rest of the year."

"Tell me about your sisters. Sophie and Annie?"

"They're the two immediately older than I. Anastasia is Annie's full name. She's married to an insurance agent, and Sophie's married to a stockbroker, of all things."

"What happened to all these blue-collar workers?"

"Those are the older girls. Stef's husband is a longshoreman, and Tracy's is a plumber. Is that better? Andy used to work at the wire mill until it was closed. Now he runs a convenience store."

Mary Helen reentered the room with glasses of Coke. "Guess what. Sophie's got a Mercedes. She drove it down here last month. Now everybody in the neighborhood will really think I'm something, with both a Mercedes and a Jag in front of the house," she teased.

"You'll have to learn to live with us high-society types," Chris said with a laugh.

"Huh!" His sister snorted her low opinion of his statement. She settled into a chair near the couch and took a sip of her drink. "Mm, that's good. I haven't had a minute to sit down all day. The kids were bugging me to death about when Uncle Chris was coming. I hope you realize you're expected to spend most of your time playing softball with them."

"Sure. Provided you fix me *goląbki* while I'm here."

"Can't you smell them cooking?" she retorted with a grin.

"I fell into that trap." Chris heaved a false sigh. "All right. I might as well do my duty now. Cara?" He rose and turned to her questioningly.

"What?"

"Do you mind? If I leave you alone for a while to play ball with the kids?"

"Heavens, no. Should I?"

"Just checking." He touched the tip of her nose in a playful, loving gesture and left the room, calling out to the children, "Okay, where's a ball and glove?"

There were a few minutes of tumult as the children gathered up their equipment before the gang burst out the front door, covering the small lawn and spilling over into the street. Cara twisted to gaze out the window at them as Chris ran and caught and threw with the kids. Cara smiled at his enthusiasm. He wore a black Pirates T-shirt and ragged denim shorts, which left little of his well-muscled frame to the imagination. Cara's eyes roamed over him, caressing the tight buttocks and rock-hard chest. There was nothing heavy about Chris. He was lean and compact. Yet when he moved, muscles flared tautly under his skin, rippling sensually. A hot quiver of desire darted through her, and she blushed, remembering his sister's presence.

"Isn't he a hunk?" Mary Helen echoed her thoughts, standing behind her to watch the scene.

Cara glanced up, startled, and grinned. "I think so. Obviously."

"In high school I was very popular with all the other girls, and pretty soon I realized it was because Chris was my older brother. Back then I couldn't see it. After all, he was only Chris and didn't have the perfect Paul Newman face I adored. But now I understand." Her face sobered. "I tease him, but when it comes down to it, I think he's the greatest guy in the world. That's why I hate Monica."

Cara groped for a reply, uncertain as to how to react to the woman's honesty. "I don't...uh, know Monica."

"You're lucky." Her eyes flashed. "Oh, I know she's crippled and all, and perhaps I should feel sorry for her.

But I don't. I feel sorry for Chris. She's trapped him but good. Monica's capable of doing a lot more for herself than she does, but she won't try because it's handier and nicer to make Chris responsible. He's got a noble streak a mile wide, and she milks it for all it's worth."

"He seems very adamant, though, about sticking with her."

"That's Chris for you. He'll take any amount of punishment if he thinks he's right. It's kindness he can't bear. When he called to ask if he could bring you, I was thrilled. You're the first woman he's shown any interest in since Monica. I thought maybe now that he's found someone to care for, he'll realize the insanity of staying married to that cold—" She waved her hands, incapable of describing the full depths of her disgust with Monica.

"I don't know," Cara demurred. "I wouldn't set my heart on it if I were you. He's told me he won't leave her, in very plain terms. I'm living with a situation I can't change."

"Don't give up. He's hard to convince, but not impossible."

"But how do you know I'd be any better?"

Mary Helen grimaced. "Anybody would be an improvement. Besides, I could see at a glance that you love him. I could also tell you're a warm, loving person, which puts you miles above Monica. He brought her here right after they were married, and she looked like she'd just stepped out of Saks. She gave Mom's house an inspection, you know, like this." Mary Helen raised her head and swept the room with an arrogant gaze, her lids lowered. "Like she smelled a garbage dump or something. Mom turned red as fire, and the veins in her neck practically burst." She paused. "I could take it if it was just disliking the family. After all, we're a far cry from the Virginia fox-hunting society she was raised in. But she made Chris miserable, and I can't forgive *that*. She's jealous, petty, conniving—" Mary Helen broke off and sighed. "Oh, hell, let's not discuss her. I'd rather learn about you. Are you really from Texas?"

They spent the next hour chatting pleasantly until Mary

Helen's husband, Bob, came home from work. The baseball team followed him in, all demanding food at the top of their lungs. Mary Helen introduced Cara to Bob, a husky man who seemed to grin constantly at life. Quickly they sat down to eat at the long table, where Mary Helen had crammed in two extra places. She set a huge casserole on the table and lifted the lid to reveal the *gołąbki*, which Cara discovered was cabbage rolls stuffed with meat and rice and smothered in tomatoes. Chris dished her out an ample serving and topped the rolls with sour cream. Cara dug in eagerly and found them delicious. Mary Helen, not content with only one dish for supper, also served up links of Polish sausage, salad, cauliflower and green beans. The meal was topped off with apple slices fried in a sweet batter, which were so good Cara groaned for her figure.

"Pretty soon we'll have you with the shape of a babushka," Chris teased, his smile a warm caress.

Cara had never seen him appear so relaxed, his face so free of tension and worry. It was as if the pressures of Washington had fallen from him during the course of their trip. Throughout supper he joked with the children and traded laughing reminiscences with his younger sister, recalling carolers and the *torun*, a man masked as a fearsome goat who had come to their house every year when they were children and chased them around the yard, and the Christmas Eve opening of presents followed by the Midnight Mass. "We'd wear our new clothes to Mass that night to show them off. Didn't matter if they matched. We'd put on everything we'd gotten and traipse to church proud as peacocks. 'Course, no one noticed what anyone else had on because we were all so busy being proud of our own acquisitions."

Mary Helen laughed. "Well, at least I didn't sleep in my new clothes." She turned to Cara in explanation. "This character couldn't bear to take them off. Once he even tried to wear his new shoes to bed."

Cara smiled at Chris, her love an ache in her chest, and squeezed his hand. Chris kissed her forehead. "Careful," he warned his sister, "you'll make Cara cry. She's too tender-hearted for us Polacks."

The meal was noisy, filled with clatter and talk and exuberant laughter. Cara, who had never eaten with a large family, took in the proceedings with amazed joy. It was so different from her own sedate background. Surely no one from a family such as this felt the lonely isolation she had known as a child, the echoing stillness of a huge house that swallowed childish laughter. Poor little rich girl, she mocked herself inwardly. No doubt Chris and his sister would laugh at her envy and swear they'd have traded places, but she knew they possessed something special that she had not experienced. Their early years might have been a struggle, but she would have gladly traded her expensive toys for a few rambunctious siblings near her own age.

After dinner Irene came over with her husband, their three children and their spouses in tow. She was shorter than Mary Helen, darker haired and obviously many years older, but the unmistakable Wozniak features were stamped on her face—the wide cheekbones and slightly tilting eyes, the definite slash of eyebrows and the firm nose and mouth. Similar, too, were the exuberance and fast bantering.

"Now you can see why I'm quiet," Chris said as he indicated his sisters with a nod. "I never had a chance to get a word in."

"Unfair!" Mary Helen said with a laugh. "You're not the only quiet one. So are Stef and Angie."

Irene noted his remark with merely a disdainful lift of her eyebrows and continued to regale Cara with the many wonders of her first granddaughter. That important personage lay in the arms of her mother, a slender, quiet girl who resembled her tall, spare father more than Irene. Cara's eyes lit up at the sight of the five-month-old child, who sputtered pleasantly at her and reached for her hair.

"Would you like to hold her?" Barbara asked shyly.

Cara took the child, beaming down at it. She turned to Chris, smiling. "Isn't she adorable?"

"Of course. She's a Wozniak." He held out his arms,

and Cara placed the infant in them. He bent over the baby, smiling and muttering nonsense at her. The child crowed with laughter, reaching up at him with wildly swaying arms. Chris laughed as if he had just discovered something rare and wonderful, and his face glowed. Pain stabbed through Cara's chest as she watched him. Chris loved children. It was obvious from the way he acted around Mary Helen's kids and this baby. He should be a family man, with a loving wife and children of his own. Instead he was tied to a cold woman who did her best to make his life unbearable, who had had an abortion when she was healthy and now used her crippled condition to keep him in a desolate marriage. Cara burned with anger. Why wouldn't Chris leave her and reach for some happiness? If only he loved Cara enough to leave.

Chapter 16

Sophia and Anastasia arrived the next morning with their children, swelling the crowd. They had the physical characteristics Cara was coming to recognize as common to the family. However, Annie was short, bouncy and vivacious, whereas Sophia was a tall, striking-looking woman dressed in sophisticated clothes, rather silent and self-deprecating. The rest of the day was spent in a happy family gaggle of gossip and memories. For the most part Cara simply listened, enthralled.

After supper, when the summer day was gradually fading into dusk, Chris took Cara by the hand and led her out of the house to his car, promising her a tour of the Falls. First he drove her past his childhood home, a small, decaying frame house squeezed up against others just like it. "It was in better shape when I lived there," he remarked rather sadly. "It's changed hands a couple of times since Mom died, and it's been neglected. This is still the Polish section, of course. North a couple of blocks is the Italian neighborhood, which looks exactly the same."

He took her past the old mill, a vast collection of crumbling buildings encircled by a tall chain-link fence. It was an eerie, deserted place with a huge smokestack looming against the sky. "It gives me the shivers," Cara commented, and Chris nodded.

"I'll drive you to the newer factories, so you can see we aren't a ghost town." As they took the main road out of town, he pointed toward a red brick building a couple of blocks off the main street. "My high school. And up here is St. Mary's. That's the church, and the building beside it is the old grade school. In the back is the convent. It's empty now." He pulled into the crowded cemetery behind the church, and they left the car to walk down the rows of graves.

They passed among the old Polish markers first. "I don't think I've ever been in a cemetery where the tombstones were in a foreign language."

"You've led a sheltered life."

"Look at this name. How on earth do you pronounce it?"

He did as she requested, and added, "That family was related to my mother. I think his wife was her cousin. Over there are my parents' graves." Cara followed him. "Mom would have liked you."

"Why?"

"Because you're sweet and wouldn't have given her any lip, like some of her in-laws and most of her children."

"Were you close to her?"

He shrugged. "Sometimes I thought so. Other times we were miles apart. There were moments, after I went to college, particularly, when I felt like a stranger to my whole family. They looked askance at me, proud that I was educated but a little wary as well, as if they were wondering— is he really one of us? I wasn't too sure myself. I had different dreams from the others. I was more ambitious. I wanted to see the outside world, to travel, to experience another kind of life. Once you told me you were the odd one out in your family. In many ways I was, too." He

214

wrapped an arm around her shoulders, and they strolled to the car.

"Why did you go to college? When did you decide you wanted to?"

"Frankly, I hadn't thought about it until my senior year. Oh, I dreamed of receiving a baseball scholarship, but school wasn't interesting to me—only the idea of taking a step toward professional ball. During my senior year Father Jadlowski called me in one day and asked if I would like to go to college. I stared at him with a 'who, me?' sort of look, and he chuckled. He told me I had what it took to make it, that I was intelligent and curious, ambitious, a lot of things I'd kept well hidden from myself... and everybody else as well. Father Joe was the first person who'd shown any confidence in my abilities. I began to wonder about it, and I thought, well, hell, I can do that if those other guys can. I went back and told him I'd go, but that money was a problem. He scrounged around for a scholarship, and I made lots of applications. But when I graduated, I still hadn't gotten anything. I took a job at the mill. My grades weren't great, and I more or less decided it wouldn't work. Then I received a scholarship to Our Lady of Mercy, and all of a sudden I was gone."

"Were you scared?"

"Scared isn't the word for it. Try petrified. I was also excited, proud, embarrassed... you name it. I had every emotion in the book." He chuckled. "The first year I was a fish out of water. The work was hard. Nobody talked the way I did. I didn't know how to act, and I felt like an idiot. Yet it was so marvelously different. Our dorm rooms were tiny cubbyholes that had once belonged to seminarians, barely big enough for a single bed and a chest. But I'd never had a place all to myself. It seemed like heaven to be able to retreat into my room and close everybody out. I listened to the other guys, vicariously soaking up their experiences. It made me hungry to see more of what they'd seen, to go places and do things. I'd always known the Falls was a backwater, but I hadn't realized how limited it made me. Suddenly I wanted to expand my horizons. I took a job to earn extra money for side trips to New York and New England."

Cara raised his hand to her lips and kissed it tenderly. "I've never known anybody like you, with your drive and curiosity and desire to experience life. Most people are placid, content to rock along with what they have."

"I was eager to learn, all right—social things, at least. Scholastically I was in the pits. I'm surprised they renewed my scholarship the next year. My counselor was a very kind man, or I'm sure they wouldn't have. He understood my cultural shock. Then in my sophomore year I began to take hold in school."

"What happened?"

"Oh, I was settling down, mostly. Things weren't as foreign anymore. I was more at ease with the students and teachers. The immediate catalyst, though, was an incident in one of my classes. I had a professor who liked to ask long, complicated questions, then have one of the students research and report on the subject the next week. One day he asked who wanted to research a particular question. For some reason it interested me, and I volunteered. A smart guy who sat beside me stared at me as if I'd lost my mind. 'Jeeze, Wozniak, you can't do that. That's a tough question.' That was all I needed. I was determined I'd answer the question perfectly, no matter what. I lived in the library, looking up things, taking notes, trying to fit it together. At first I was scared. I didn't know anything about libraries or studying, but I plugged away. After the initial fright wore off, I began to understand what I was doing and where the question led. I became fascinated and pursued various aspects of the issue simply because I was curious. Anyway, I worked up the best damn answer I could to that question. The next week, when I started explaining it, everyone's jaw dropped, especially the professor and the kid next to me."

Cara laughed. "Serves him right."

"Oh, he wasn't a bad guy. He was trying to be helpful. He realized I didn't know enough about the subject to understand how tough the question was. But after that he was wary of me. I guess he thought I'd been putting something over on him by pretending to be dumb. Anyway, my hunger turned from the social to the intellectual. I studied for the first time in my life and actually found a lot of the stuff interesting. I threw myself into schoolwork and improved my scores considerably. My counselor was positively pink with gratification. I imagine I'd won an argument with the other counselors for him. I added culture to my list, hitting the museums and galleries every time I went to New York or Boston."

"How about girls? You haven't said anything about them."

He grinned. "I discovered how delightful it could be to date someone whose family didn't know me from birth or whose father didn't work with mine, who didn't attend the same church or didn't go to Mass at all. It was terrific." He had turned the car onto a winding road leading to the top of the bluff, and now he started along a narrow track that followed the edge of the cliff, overseeing a breathtaking view of the river valley and town by moonlight. Pulling to a halt, he said, "Speaking of girls . . . when I was a teenager, this was my favorite romantic spot. If I could manage to beg, borrow or steal a car, that is."

"You used to park here?" Cara leaned across him to peer at the view. "I imagine you looked at the scenery a lot."

He grinned. "Of course."

"Is this where you lost your virginity?"

Chris pulled back, his face stamped with mock horror. "I didn't lose it. I struggled very hard to get rid of it. Innocence was not one of my goals."

"Do tell." Cara settled back into the curve of his arm with a sigh. How could it feel so secure to nestle against the rigid bone and muscle of Chris's chest . . . and yet so exciting?

"This wasn't the location of my first sexual experience, though. That was behind the stadium, before I drove a car."

"You must have been precocious."

"I had a reputation to consider. With so many sisters, I had to fight not to be thought of as one of the girls."

"More likely that being accustomed to girls, you were more fun to be around than most awkward, tongue-tied teenage boys."

"Maybe." He kissed the top of her head, then slid down to her ear, his hand kneading her scalp gently as his lips caressed her earlobe. "I don't think there's a place on your body that doesn't turn me on. How would you like to use this spot again, for old time's sake?"

Cara tilted her head at him, a mischievous grin forming. "Okay. Shall we move to the backseat?"

"No need." He nibbled at her neck, his hands coming around her from behind to cover her chest.

She melted against him, her breasts already swelling with desire, the nipples rigid at his touch. Chris turned in the seat to lean against the door, pulling Cara between his outstretched legs, her back against his chest. His burgeoning manhood prodded her hips, and she wriggled against him. He uttered a soft, wordless noise of passion and, still nuzzling her neck and ears from behind, tugged her skirt up until he could slip a hand beneath it to stroke her legs. His free hand played over her breasts, arousing her through her clothes. Cara unfastened her bra and reached to pull off her silk blouse, but Chris stopped her hands. He rubbed and squeezed the lush globes, using the material of her blouse against her skin to heighten the throb of her nerves. Cara ached to feel his fingers on her flesh, and her hunger was multiplied by the sensual, smooth touch of the clothing. She moved eagerly within the circle of his arms. His other hand caressed her thighs, traveling to the joinder of her legs. Cara gasped as his hand slid over the silken smoothness of her panties, lightly teasing the bud of womanhood until it throbbed.

Her head fell back, exposing the soft flesh of her throat to his voracious mouth and tongue. Kissing and nibbling, his lips fiery with his own unfulfilled desire, Chris again continued the gentle, sensuous massage of her nipples. The material of the blouse both aroused and frustrated her, while his other hand explored the satin fire between her legs with agonizing slowness. At first he used the cloth of her delicate underwear as he used her blouse, until she moaned and writhed beneath his touch. Then his fingers slipped between the silk and her flesh, and the roughened skin of his fingertips thrust her even higher into delight. It seemed as if his mouth and hands were upon her everywhere, sweetly, leisurely arousing her whole body to a wild, pulsating longing. Cara arched against him, crying out mindlessly for release. Chris buried his face in her neck and his hand tightened, hurling Cara at last into a white-hot explosion that tore through her body and left every limb trembling and weak. She knew he had conquered her in some inexplicable way with this lovemaking, giving her unequaled pleasure as he stamped his ownership of her body. She was wholly his, and he would be part of her forever.

They returned to Washington the next day after a typically warm, noisy sendoff by the Wozniak family. "Were they too much for you?" Chris asked, smiling, as they sped through the beauty and the glaring industrial ugliness of western Pennsylvania.

"Oh, no!" Cara responded. "I loved them. They're so strong and capable. So outspoken! Well, you know what Ginny's like. In our house everything was sweetness and light or she pretended it didn't exist. You must never hurt anyone. I longed for a little bluntness in a conversation. Besides, it's fun to be with a big, noisy, loving family. Loneliness was always my bugaboo. 'I haven't got anybody to play with.'" She mimicked a child's whine.

"I never lacked for companions." He laughed. "I'm glad you liked them. I was afraid they might overwhelm you.

Sometimes my sisters have all the subtlety of a steamroller."

She giggled. "No, it was fun. It's fascinating to hear about your childhood and the culture you lived in. My background is so unrelievedly Waspish it bores even me. I like the experience of meeting different people. Not only that—I got to eat *gołąbki.*"

He grinned. "Well, certainly, that makes it all worthwhile." His face softened as he studied her. "Cara, you're a dream. You're open, loving, generous." He turned abruptly back to the road and settled his gaze on the horizon. Cara was sure he had been about to say something else and had stopped himself on the brink. Finally he continued in a lighter voice. "Didn't you know oil heiresses are spoiled and insular?"

"Oh, I'm sorry," Cara retorted in the same vein, swallowing her curiosity and a sudden flicker of hope. "I didn't realize my education was lacking. I promise next time I'll try harder to be a snob."

The rest of their trip was spent in light conversation and gentle raillery. Cara marveled at how content they were with each other, how at ease, with none of the tension she had experienced in other relationships. Why, even with her own family she was less open and relaxed. What an odd twist of fate that she and Chris Wozniak, so different in all the externals most people considered important, should fit together so well.

A letter from Alec Stone awaited them at Chris's apartment. He tore it open eagerly, but after a moment his face sagged in disappointment. "He doesn't recognize Haskell from the drawing," Chris explained to her. "He's shown it to the police and put on the pressure, but so far no word from them." He sighed and sank onto the sofa. "I guess we'll start our search again tomorrow. Maybe the time off will have given us a fresh outlook and we'll spot something we overlooked before."

"I hope so." Yet doubt rose insidiously in Cara's chest.

How could they ever discover Haskell's boss? The longer they worked at the task, the more impossible it seemed.

However, on Wednesday Chris returned from a meeting with a wide smile curving his face. "Good news. My friend at the police department finally dug up something. The cops in Florida have one misdemeanor charge on Haskell, which was dropped. They didn't have a decent case so they used the charge to detain him while they tried to round up proof that he was involved in a nursing-home swindle. The name he used in Florida was Samuel Harrison."

Cara's face lit up. "Great! So we have another name to add to his aliases. We can look for that, too."

"Better than that, Ken also discovered another party interested in Samuel Harrison—the F.B.I."

"What!"

"Yeah. He cropped up in another investigation. He was pretty minor in the Florida scheme, but if they had something good on him, they might make him squeal on the others. I asked Ken to arrange a meeting with an agent on the case. Perhaps we can trade a little information with them."

"I want to go with you."

"No."

Cara's brows drew together at his peremptory tone. "What do you mean, no? This is far more important to me than to you."

"You can't get involved. When I began working on it, you promised you wouldn't get into anything dangerous. Remember?"

"My father promised, not me. Besides, you're just meeting someone from the F.B.I. How dangerous could it be? I mean, surely he won't shoot me on sight."

"Don't be silly. I don't want your involvement to be obvious. There's no telling who might see us with the agent. *They* may have somebody following *him*, you know."

"Oh, don't be so cloak-and-dagger."

"Besides, the guy may object to your being there."

"Why?"

"Because he'd rather have fewer people around if he reveals something secret."

"Chris, I have to know. If he's really so reluctant to tell you anything with me there, I'll leave. But I at least want to try, not sit at home like a good little girl waiting for you to tell me what happened. It's *my* father who's being threatened and *my* nephew."

Chris glared at her for a moment, then sighed and shrugged. "All right. All right. God, you're stubborn."

"Persistent," Cara corrected. "I know a few other people with the same quality."

He shot her a sideways glance. "Point taken. When Ken phones to set up a meeting, I promise I'll let you know."

The call came early the next morning, and the meeting was set for two o'clock that afternoon at the Reflecting Pool in front of the Lincoln Memorial. Cara and Chris arrived fifteen minutes early and waited patiently for twenty minutes for the agent to appear. He was of medium height, dressed in a suit and carrying an innocuous black briefcase. Cara, glancing at Chris in his well-fitting slacks and a casual white knit top that revealed the swell of muscles in his arm, decided he looked like a more dangerous character than the agent. The man walked toward Chris, noticed Cara and paused. Chris rose and stepped forward to meet him. "Mr. Ingram? I'm Wozniak."

"Yes. I recognized you from the photo Ken showed me. Hello." The man shook hands, and Cara thought it appeared prosaically like a business meeting. "I don't understand . . ." He turned toward Cara.

"This is Cara Stone. She's the daughter of the man being extorted. Did Ken explain it to you?"

"Not really. He simply said you had information on Samuel Harrison, also known as Ben Lydle."

"Or Vern Haskell. That's the name we know. He works for a man who's threatened Miss Stone's father." Ingram looked askance once more at Cara but allowed Chris to lead him to the steps where she sat. Setting down his briefcase, Ingram listened intently to Chris's description of the threats that had been made against Matthew Fletcher and the price the extortionist had demanded to leave the baby safe.

Ingram frowned. "This is a case for the authorities. Why are you involved in it, Wozniak?"

Chris explained Alec's reasoning, adding with a shrug, "Who knows? He may be right. So far I haven't dug up much, but at least the head man might not suspect me immediately, as he would a cop. Anyway, that's the way Mr. Stone wants it. Cara and I discovered some information about Vern Haskell—Samuel Harrison that might help you. I have an informant, someone I think would testify well, who claims Haskell offered him a bribe to sabotage one of Stone's wells."

"What's his name? I'll check up on it."

"Frankly, in return for the information, I was hoping you'd be able to help me a little."

"Are you trying to sell the information?" The agent raised his eyebrows, his voice cold and forbidding.

"You know I wouldn't try that. I simply wanted to finish my story before we got into specifics."

"Look, Wozniak, this is pretty flimsy information. I don't even know that your Haskell and Harrison are the same man."

"Ken ran a check on him. Here's a police drawing of Haskell." Chris tossed a folded piece of paper to the agent.

Ingram opened the sheet and studied it before he handed it back to Chris. "It looks like the same man, and if Ken's run a check . . ."

"My informant is the kind who'll show up great in court. A hardworking young man, no record, thrifty and honest. He's not the usual sleazy informant. Plus, if I can prove Haskell's connected to the Stone extortion, you'll have more charges with which to threaten him."

"Well, of course I'll do what I can to help, provided the information won't endanger our case."

"It shouldn't mean anything to your investigation. All I want is whatever you find that might have a bearing on the extortion threat—say evidence of a payoff not connected to your case or the name of an influential person, preferably in oil, whom you photographed meeting Haskell."

"I don't want you beating it down there to question him," Ingram stated flatly. "He doesn't suspect we're onto him yet."

"I won't need to question him if you give me the dope on his boss's identity. He's the man we want."

"Offhand, I'd say it's not one of the men we're investigating. They have nothing to do with oil. But I'll see what I can find out. Now, what's your informant's name?"

"Ashe Harlan."

"Where is he?"

"Bow Lake, Canada, at the moment. He's the tool-pusher on one of the Stone rigs."

The other man flipped open a small ringed tablet and jotted down a few notes. "Okay. Good. I'll see what I can do for you. But I'm telling you right off I won't give you Harrison's address."

Cara had remained silent throughout the conversation, anxious not to make Chris regret bringing her, but now she had to speak up. "Mr. Ingram, a child's life is in danger. If Chris could talk to this man and find out who's behind the threats, wouldn't it be worth it? Even if he does get suspicious, with Chris's information you could force him to testify against the others, couldn't you?"

Ingram frowned, and Chris laid a warning hand on hers.

"Miss Stone, I am working on a very complex scheme that not only swindled several investors out of their money but also hurt thousands of senior citizens and involved the bribery of state and federal officials. I can't afford to jeopardize it. I doubt very seriously whether even Chris Wozniak could convince the man to talk. All the visit would do is alert Harrison to the fact that someone's onto him."

Cara longed to retort, but Chris squeezed her hand, and

he words. They couldn't afford to antagonize
o could give them their only lead on Vern Has-
realize that," she forced out. "But I'm extremely
rned about my nephew."

"Of course. Believe me, I'll let you know if I turn up
anything of use to you. However, I must strongly advise
you to turn over this matter to the legal authorities. It's not
a situation for amateurs."

"I'll tell my father," Cara promised demurely. The man
shook Chris's hand again and strode off briskly. She
watched him leave, her mouth twisting in a grimace. "Do
you think anything will come of it?"

Chris shrugged. "It's the best chance we've had. The
F.B.I. won't have concentrated on anything except what
relates to their case, but if we're lucky a stray piece of
information will float by, and Ingram will recognize it as
being related to our case. I wish I could get hold of their
information, though. I'm afraid there might be a clue there
Ingram won't spot, not being familiar with the case."

"Do you suppose Daddy would have any influence with
them?" Cara pondered.

"More threats and bribes?" He grinned, then shook his
head. "I don't know. Anyway, I'm not sure it would do any
good. It might stiffen Ingram's resistance. I gave him a nice
bit of information, and he knows it, no matter what he says.
He'll help us, on the hope that we'll discover something
useful."

"If only you could talk to Haskell."

"It would help," Chris agreed. "What I'd really like,
though, is to put a tail on him to find out if he's meeting
one of our thousands of suspects." He shrugged and stood,
extending a hand to her. "That's the breaks. I had a feeling
I wouldn't get an address out of him."

They walked hand in hand to Chris's car, Cara brooding
over the meeting. If only something would come of it . . . a
name, an address, anything. The investigation had been
dragging on for almost a month, and they had nothing to

show for it except Haskell's name and description. How long would the extortionist wait before he struck at Matthew? Despite the continuous guard, she was worried about the baby. How hard could it be to overpower one man? An army around Matthew would hardly be enough for her. Yet she could do nothing but wait, slog through the paperwork and hope Chris would somehow engineer a breakthrough. Cara glanced up at him surreptitiously. His stern face was thoughtful, his mind obviously miles away. Somehow, simply looking at him made her feel better. He would find a way to solve it, she was certain. Funny how her outlook had changed. Once she had sworn Chris was the most untrustworthy man alive. Now all her hopes and trust were pinned on him. He held her heart and mind as surely as he had captured her body.

Chapter 17

Although neither mentioned it, Cara knew Chris would go to Monica's for the weekend. So on Friday morning as he was about to leave the apartment for an interview, Cara announced, "I'll be at my mother's until Sunday. So I probably won't be here this afternoon when you get back."

A shadow crossed his face, but Chris said nothing, avoiding the subject of his own plans as assiduously as she did. He fumbled in a drawer in the kitchen and pulled out a second key to the apartment. "Here, in case you get back earlier than I do."

"Thank you." Her hand closed around the cold metal. Would it remain this strained between them every Friday? Cara wanted to be cool and matter-of-fact, but she couldn't stop the quivering jealousy rising in her stomach. Chris didn't love Monica. And yet ... it was Monica he would be with during the next two days, not her.

After Chris left, she called Ginny. Her mother responded enthusiastically, paused, and continued uncertainly. "Honey, would you mind terribly coming earlier? Say, before one or two this afternoon?"

"Sure, whenever you want. Why?"

"Well, that's the part you won't like. Remember Lucille Caldwell?"

"Of course." How could she forget the gossip who had revealed Chris's marital status to her one shattering spring afternoon?

"She's been driving me crazy ever since she learned you were in Washington. She wants to take us to a friend's house for coffee. I told her I'd check with you and maybe we'd go the next time you came to visit."

"Oh, Ginny, no."

"I know, I know. What could be worse than an afternoon with Lucille, except an afternoon with Lucille and one of her friends? I'm sure it will be a deadly bore. But you wouldn't believe how often she's called me about it. Frankly I'd rather get it over with this afternoon. If we don't, she'll keep on until she wears us down."

"You, you mean," Cara laughed.

"Don't think you'll get out of it that easily. I guarantee she'll be over here as soon as she spies your car in the driveway."

Cara sighed. "Okay, I give up. I'll go. Who is this friend, anyway?"

"I haven't the foggiest idea. I'm sure she's told me about her in detail, but you know I'm not the best listener in the world. And I tune Lucille out half the time. Apparently it's someone she thinks would love to meet you. I don't know. Maybe she's a nurse or something."

"I can hardly envision Lucille with a friend who's a nurse."

Ginny reflected. "Me either. Oh, well, it doesn't matter. I'm sure it will be a total loss, whoever she is. You're a doll to even come out here, after I dump this on you."

"I'll pack now and, hopefully, I'll be there for lunch."

"Good. Lucille will probably come unglued when I phone

her. I'll fix a little treat to compensate for the afternoon ahead."

In deference to the impending outing, Cara dressed in a tan skirt with a soft, sleeveless, peach-color top and a short, military-style jacket instead of her usual blue jeans and T-shirt. She packed a few casual clothes in an overnight bag, dabbed on mascara and lipstick and, slipping into low-heeled brown sandals, left for Arlington.

Ginny whipped up a lunch of chicken salad and fresh asparagus, finishing with the treat she had promised, a frosty crème de menthe parfait. "Ahhh," Cara sighed, scooping the last morsel from the tall glass. "That may have been worth going out with Lucille."

"Isn't it marvelous? The only problem is, now we have to pay up." Ginny carried the glasses into the kitchen. "I'll run upstairs and put on something a little dressier." She returned twenty minutes later in an ice blue dress with full, sheer sleeves, looking utterly cool and feminine. Cara smiled, thinking, not for the first time, how lovely her mother was. Fifty years old and she could still put almost any other woman in the shade. It wasn't surprising that Ginny was the only woman her father had loved. Cara doubted whether his present wife knew one-tenth of the passion he had felt for Ginny.

"How can you be a grandmother?" Cara joked. "You aren't nearly old or harried enough."

Ginny smiled. "Flatterer."

"Not a bit."

"The secret is to have children who don't give you a moment's worry."

"Oh, come on. Surely we weren't that perfect. Close to it, I'll admit..."

Ginny chuckled and led her out the side door, crossing the lawn to the door-size gap in the hedge between her house and the one next door. "The people who lived here before us must have been great friends with the Caldwells to leave a pass-through in the hedge. Personally I'd prefer it seven

229

feet high and four feet thick, clear to the back of the property."

As they had expected, Lucille was delighted to see them. "Oh, I'm so glad you could come today. I called my little friend, and she was absolutely ecstatic about your coming. Just a minute—let me grab my car keys, and we'll go." She bustled about finding her purse and keys, then herded them out to the car.

"Who is it we're going to see?" Cara asked as she settled in the backseat.

"Oh, you'll love her!" Lucille gushed, starting the engine and backing into the street. "Such a beautiful woman—a few years older than you, but still gorgeous. And the tragedies she has endured! I tell you, it would make a saint quail. But she still has a lot of interest in people. When I told her about you, she was insistent that I bring you out to meet her. She doesn't get into the city much herself." Lucille babbled on, extolling the woman's house and wardrobe and arm-long pedigree. Cara stopped listening and gazed out the window.

They soon left Arlington and were driving through the Virginia countryside, which was hot under the August sun despite the large, spreading trees. They turned into a suburban development, where the homes were set back on half-acre verdant lots. The tires crunched on gravel as Lucille pulled into the semicircular driveway of a graceful, two-story white colonial. "How lovely," Ginny enthused.

Cara had to agree that it was beautiful, with its clean lines and sparkling white brick, a border of hot pink flowers providing a touch of color in front of the porch. But the manicured lawn, neat rows of flowers and carefully kept home were almost too much, too... antiseptic. She could imagine the owner—a trim, elegant, middle-aged woman who wore her hair in a smooth bun, not a strand out of place or a wrinkle in her dress. They would no doubt perch on elegant furniture and take coffee or tea from a silver pot. The china cups would rattle fragilely on their saucers, and Cara would struggle to balance the cup, linen napkin and dainty cookies. She would smile and say little, while Ginny attempted to infuse some sparkle into the lifeless conversation. After an hour of stiff talk and a smile held so firmly in place that it hurt, they would finally leave. That moment couldn't arrive too soon, Cara thought.

A pale, frizzy-haired woman answered the door at Lucille's ring. She smiled nervously, and one hand fluttered to her hair, then down to her breast. "Hello, Mrs. Caldwell. Mrs. Wozniak is waiting for you in the living room."

Mrs. Wozniak! Cara's heart skipped a beat. It *couldn't* be. In her mind there was only one woman named that. Absurd. Such a coincidence couldn't happen. Or was it a coincidence? She swiveled a glance at Lucille to find the woman watching her, a quickly concealed slyness in her eyes. Lucille turned away, and Cara wondered if she had imagined the expression. Ginny, after one initial twitch at the name, assumed an expression of serenity and walked beside her neighbor into the adjoining room. Cara plodded numbly after them.

The living room was floored with a thick, dusky pink carpet, and one wall was papered in off-white with climbing flowers of the same beige-tinged pink. The furniture was French provincial, feminine, as delicate as the watercolors lining the walls. A woman sat in a wheelchair beside the couch, a soft, thoughtful smile on her face. Pale and fragile as the room, she wore a green caftan that fell in folds across her immobile legs. Pearls glowed softly in her ears and around her throat. A diamond flashed on the ring finger of her left hand. Her golden hair was pulled up and tied at the crown, falling loosely to her shoulders. Although it was obvious that she had once been beautiful, her looks were leaving, not fading gently but shrinking in upon her as if eaten away by acid, leaving her features too sharp, too precise.

There was no doubt now. This was Chris's wife. Cara had never thought people really fainted from emotional shock, but now she understood. Her knees locked, and she felt as if someone had landed a blow to her solar plexus.

Her breath would not come, and she heard the same faint roaring that had sounded in her ears when she had broken her hand years before. The others were speaking, but the words made no sense. Then Ginny grasped her firmly by the elbow and propelled her forward. Cara wouldn't have thought there was such steel in Ginny's whole frame, let alone her slender fingers.

"And this is my daughter Cara," Ginny said. "Dear, this is Monica Wozniak." Ginny sat down on the sofa, pulling Cara with her. "What a lovely home you have here, Mrs. Wozniak. So tastefully decorated. Did you do it yourself?"

"Yes." Monica preened slightly. "Thank you. Please call me Monica."

"Of course, I'm fond of decorating, too. My first husband used to say he never knew if he had come home to the right house, I changed the decor so often."

Ginny's blatantly absurd statement penetrated Cara's daze, and she almost smiled. Alec had never noticed anything about the house. Ginny could have painted it orange, and he wouldn't have said anything. Her mother continued to chatter about interior design, then leaped to fashion with hardly a pause for breath, artfully dominating the conversation until Cara was somewhat recovered. The frazzled, nervous woman who had answered the door poured coffee into thin china cups and offered dainty cookies from a tray. Cara gradually figured out that the woman was a nurse-companion who rarely entered the conversation, effectively blending into the furniture.

Cara sipped her coffee and nibbled at one of the cookies. Both were tasteless to her. Funny how close to reality her mental picture of the gathering had been...and how horrifyingly different. From time to time, as Ginny prattled on, subtly encouraging Lucille to ramble also, Cara saw Monica studying her with intent, sherry-color eyes. Each time Cara wanted to shiver. She would never again think brown eyes were warm. Why had Lucille tricked her into coming today? What did Monica hope to accomplish? Was the sick feeling in Cara's stomach satisfaction enough, the chill that permeated her feet and hands? Or was it a macabre joke Lucille had played on them both—bringing the mistress and the spouse together, both unwitting? No, Lucille was merely a pawn, an accomplice. Cara knew when she looked into Monica's hard, cold eyes that the woman was aware of her relationship with Chris. She hated Cara.

"I understand you're from Texas, Cara," Monica cut into Ginny's speech, and Cara saw Ginny's lips become thin. She had fought a holding action as long as she could. Monica was no longer to be sidetracked.

"Yes, I am," Cara replied firmly, without inflection, raising her chin a trifle and meeting the woman's gaze steadily.

"My husband was recently in Texas." Monica's eyes remained steadily on Cara's face, and Cara had to restrain her fingers from curling into claws around the thin cup. "Do you know him?"

Ginny's silvery giggle sounded. "Monica, there are so *many* people in Texas."

"But Ginny," Lucille interrupted, "you know Chris Wozniak. You and Cara asked me about him several months ago."

"Did I?"

"Yes," Cara replied smoothly. "You remember—he was at a party you and Wilson gave."

"Oh, yes, of course; a nice-looking young man."

"And I happened to meet him again in Dallas. He interviewed Daddy," Cara continued boldly. Better to meet the truth head-on than to scuttle away.

"Really?" Monica drawled, her eyes sliding from Cara to the far wall and back again. "How fortunate."

"You mean he's after Alec now?" Ginny asked her daughter, her tone bordering on laughter. "Well, that should be some match-up." She turned to address Monica. "Alec is the most stubborn man alive. If Chris can get any information out of him, he deserves a medal."

"Actually, Daddy liked Chris."

"No doubt that applies to all the Stones," Monica slipped in.

"Why, yes," Cara met her gaze blandly. "Alexis thought he was very sharp. I'm not sure Morgan met him, though. They're my sisters."

"Well, perhaps you'll get to see Chris again, since you're living in D.C."

"Yes, isn't it nice?" Ginny gushed, and Cara could have hugged her mother for her persistent efforts to divert the conversation. "I love having Cara home with me again. She's my youngest, and I'm afraid perhaps I'm too possessive of her. Do you have children of your own?"

"No," Monica returned shortly.

There was a long pause, and Cara wondered what was running through her adversary's mind. Would she continue this cat-and-mouse game, or would she launch a full attack in front of the other guests? Cara didn't know how she could endure either tactic. Before Monica could say anything, however, a car door slammed outside, and moments later a key turned in the front door. All the women turned instinctively toward the hallway. A feeling of numb horror rose in Cara's throat. No, she couldn't stand it—it would be too much.

Chris stepped into the foyer, a frown on his face as though he were deep in thought. Pulling the key out of the lock, he closed the door and headed toward the staircase without glancing through the wide double doorway into the living room.

"Chris!" Monica's imperious voice stopped him, and for the first time he swung in their direction. He froze when he saw Cara sitting on the edge of the couch, her blue eyes wide and stricken, her face white with shock. For a moment nothing made sense to him, and even his impassive face revealed supreme surprise.

"Chris, come in and meet my guests. You remember Ginny Decker and her daughter, don't you?"

He walked stiffly into the room, his eyes fastened on

Cara, his mouth grim. "Yes, of course. How are you?" He turned toward his wife, meeting her smug gaze, and his eyes glowed bright green with anger. "Monica." His voice was clipped. "Sorry to break up your party, ladies. If you'll excuse me, I'll go up to my room." He left without glancing again at Cara, his back straight, his tread on the stairs firm and unhurried.

Cara sneaked a look at Monica. Her mouth drooped petulantly. Cara suspected she had not received the reaction that she had expected from her husband. Had she hoped Chris would fly into a rage or reveal their affair? Cara's fingers trembled, and she laced them together firmly. She had to leave. She couldn't take much more tension.

As if on cue, Ginny exclaimed brightly, "Well! Isn't that nice? A husband who comes home early. I think it's about time we left, don't you, Lucille? No doubt Monica would like to be alone with Chris." She stood, forestalling any protest from Lucille, and picked up her purse.

"Nonsense," Monica murmured. "You mustn't go yet."

"Oh, yes, I'm afraid we must. The time has simply slipped by. I've enjoyed so much meeting you and seeing your lovely home."

"Lucille, why don't you and Mary take Ginny out to the garden behind the house? I'm sure she'd like to see it before you all leave. Cara can stay here and chat with me."

Ginny hesitated, but there was no polite way she could either refuse to go or insist that Cara come with her. With a brittle smile she acceded and followed Lucille out the door, determined to make a very brisk tour of the garden.

Cara's heart began to trip madly, but she did her best to arrange her face in placid lines.

"Well," Monica said as she let her eyes sweep over Cara. "You certainly aren't what I expected."

"Really?"

"Yes. I thought you'd have more flash. A blonde, maybe. Nor was I aware Chris had taken to robbing the cradle." Cara stared blankly, lifting her eyebrows a trifle. "Come, come, there's no need to pretend ignorance with me. I know all about your tawdry little affair with my husband. You aren't the first, you know, and I'm sure you won't be the last."

Cara rose. "This is insane. I'm leaving. Tell my mother I'll wait for her in the car."

"Running from the truth?" Monica taunted. "No doubt it hurts, but you might as well face it. Chris can't be content with one woman, but he loves *me*. He'll stay with me the rest of his life. If you think you can get your hooks into him, you're terribly naive. Chris is mine and always will be. He'll never divorce me. Never!"

"No doubt you're right!" Cara spat back, shaking with anger. "He's too full of guilt and duty to free himself and be happy."

"Guilt? Don't be silly. That man never felt a moment's guilt in his life. The truth is, he can't get me out of his system, no matter how hard he tries. I suppose you think he has a separate room and all the other soothing lies he tells his amours. Don't believe it!" she snarled, her face twisting into a mask of fury. "He still crawls under my covers when he comes home."

"If that were true, you wouldn't need to proclaim it to the world," Cara retorted coolly.

"Sure of yourself, aren't you?" the other woman said with a snort. "Well, don't be. I own that man. He'll pay the rest of his life for what he did to me. I pull the strings, and Chris Wozniak dances. Don't forget it."

"Once I felt sorry for you because I was *stealing* your husband. But believe me, not any more. Having seen what a vulture you are, I don't regret for a minute giving Chris what little happiness he's known since he married you!" She swung on her heel and marched away.

Monica screeched unintelligibly after her, but Cara did not turn or respond. She merely continued out the front door and down the steps to Lucille's Buick. The vehicle was baking hot inside from the sun, but Cara opened the door and sat down, her knees feeling too wobbly to stand. Her brain was still whirling when at last Lucille and Ginny returned. Lucille inquired solicitously whether she felt well, but Cara didn't bother to answer. She left any attempt at conversation to Ginny and leaned her head against the window, blindly watching the houses and trees slide by.

When at last they reached the safety and solitude of her own house, Ginny collapsed in the first chair she came to. "What a ghastly situation! I could cheerfully throttle Lucille Caldwell. How could she? I'll never speak to her again as long as I live."

Cara remained standing, not listening to her mother's angry exclamations. She wandered aimlessly about the room for a few moments, then turned to her mother. "Ginny, if you don't mind, I think I'll go back to the city."

"But honey, why?" Ginny's voice vaulted with concern.

"I want to be by myself for a while. Please?"

"Will you come back? I hate to think of you all alone after this."

"Maybe. I don't know. I just have to think." Ginny did not argue, although her face crinkled with worry as she followed Cara to the front door. Cara flashed her a brief smile before she got into her car. Hardly aware of the traffic around her, Cara drove slowly to Chris's apartment. Opening the door, she stood for a moment gazing at the room as if she were seeing it for the first time. Slowly she walked through the apartment, trailing her fingers over the furniture, hardly aware of what she was doing. Finally she sank into his favorite chair, huddling her arms around her bent legs and resting her head on her knees. Abandoning her iron control, Cara burst into a flood of tears.

When Chris heard Monica's voice rise in a demented shriek, he dashed from his room and down the stairs, where he found his wife livid with fury, her fists clenched in her lap. Cara was gone. Without speaking, he strode to the front bay window and pulled aside the sheer curtains to see Cara getting into the car. He started to go to her, but at that moment Ginny and Lucille entered the hall from the rear. Chris stopped, trapped into politely listening to their good-byes. He watched their departure, then swung back to his wife. Mary Schrift stood uncertainly in the hall, sensing the wrath crackling between the Wozniaks and not anxious to come under its fire.

"You can go home now," Chris snapped at her, and she scurried away. Again his attention centered on Monica. "What the hell were you trying to pull?"

"Why, what do you mean?" Monica replied with false sweetness. "Just having a few friends over for coffee. I thought you wanted me to see my friends."

"Cara Stone and Ginny Decker are no friends of yours."

"No, I suppose not. They're my enemies, aren't they?"

"I'd say quite frankly they don't give a damn about you one way or the other. You're the enemy around here—to everyone, yourself included. What did you hope to accomplish with such a stunt?"

"I simply wanted to see your latest girl friend. Is that so abnormal? I think any wife would be curious about the woman her husband's sleeping with. Woman, did I say? *Child* would be a better description."

"She is more mature than you'll ever be. Monica, I won't put up with it. Leave her alone."

"My, how protective you are. The primitive Polack comes out." She pouted in what had once been a pretty gesture but was now rendered shrewish by overuse. "Really, Chris, I must confess I was surprised. If the girl was a beauty like her mother obviously used to be, I could understand it better. But this! A mop of black hair hanging everywhere, no makeup to speak of...Why, she was practically plain!"

"Shut up!" Chris snarled. "I don't want to hear a goddamn word from you about Cara. You aren't worth the tiniest part of her. She is genuine, loving, warm. And beautiful. You can't understand natural beauty...or perhaps you merely wish to deny it."

Monica's upper lip curled. "I told her the truth—that you'd never leave me."

"She knows it."

"But she seemed unaware that you still love me and seek my bed at night."

"What! Is that what you told her? You lying bitch!" His face flamed with rage for an instant, and Monica shrank back in her chair, honestly frightened. He clenched his fist, slamming it into the wall with an inarticulate cry of frustration and anger. When he pulled back his hand, there was a gaping hole in the delicately papered wall. He unclenched his fist, drew a deep breath and faced Monica coldly. "It grows more pointless every weekend. I won't be coming here anymore."

Monica gasped. "A formal separation?"

"Call it whatever you like. I'll continue your support, of course, and you can still be Mrs. Wozniak—for what it's worth to you—but I'm not living in the same house with you, even for two days a week."

"You can't do that! After what you did to me, you can't leave me alone in this huge house."

"Move to a smaller place if you want. I have no objection."

"You're tossing out your crippled wife?"

"I'm simply ending a farce."

Her hands gripped the arms of her chair like claws. "You don't dare leave me! How would you like the world to know that Chris Wozniak, champion of truth and justice, is really a philanderer? That he sleeps around on his invalid wife, the wife who's in that condition because of him?"

Chris shrugged. "Go ahead, if you want people to feel sorry for you for a few days. It'll be the usual nine-days' wonder, and then something else will come along to snare their interest."

"You think so? Not when your latest mistress is the daughter of Alec Stone, the oil man on whom you're doing an article. The reading public may not care about your sexual peccadilloes, but when it relates to your integrity, they'll sing a different tune. And how will little miss heiress enjoy being exposed to the public eye for what she is? The reporters and photographers, the sly smiles, the gossip at parties..."

His face turned cold and hard as rock, and he advanced slowly to where she sat. Leaning down, Chris stated quietly, ruthlessly, "If you ever... *ever* hurt Cara Stone in any way, I promise I'll divorce you. I suggest you hold onto what you've got or you'll lose it all."

He walked away from her and out the front door. Monica sat frozen, staring after him in frightened disbelief.

Chapter 18

A key rasped in the lock. "Cara?" Chris stepped into the darkening room and flipped on the lights. Cara's head snapped up and she uncurled from the chair, dabbing at the tear streaks on her cheeks.

"Chris! What are you doing here?"

"Did you think I'd stay there when I didn't know what you might be thinking or feeling? I was so angry with Monica I could have strangled her. I'm not going back there anymore. I wouldn't be able to control myself after what she put you through today." He knelt beside the chair and took both Cara's hands between his. His forehead was knotted with concern. "Are you okay? Whatever she told you, I promise it was said out of spite and anger. It wasn't true."

"You mean when she said you still sleep with her?"

Chris nodded, his eyes searching her face.

"No, I didn't believe her. She was too vicious and eager to tell me. Besides, I trust you, and you swore you didn't." She smiled weakly. "If I don't keep my faith in you, Chris, my whole world falls apart."

241

He kissed her hands tenderly. "I'm sorry you had to go through it. I left shortly after you did, but I thought you'd be at Ginny's and I went there first. She told me you'd returned to town, so I came home. But I was afraid you were just driving around or had checked into a motel room."

"No. I wanted to be here, where I feel more secure. Oh, Chris, it was so awful!"

"I know. Tell me what happened. How did Monica manage to get you there?" He lifted her out of the chair and sat down, reseating her on his lap.

Cara cuddled against him, soaking in the warmth and feel and smell of him. There was nothing as comforting as Chris's arms around her. "Ginny's next-door neighbor, Lucille Caldwell, is apparently a friend of your wife's. She's the one who originally told me you were married. Anyway, she's a busybody and a gossip, and she had been bugging Ginny for us to go with her to a friend's house. We figured she wouldn't let up until we gave in, so we agreed to go this afternoon. I asked Lucille her friend's name, and she began to talk about what a wonderful person the woman was and how much I'd like her, and she never answered the question. But it didn't seem suspicious. I mean, why would I be suspicious? When we walked in and she introduced us to Monica Wozniak, I nearly went through the floor. I was stunned."

"I know. I felt the same when I saw you sitting on the sofa. For a second I thought I was hallucinating. Did Monica abuse you?"

"No, not till the end. But from the way she looked at me when she dropped your name into the conversation, I was sure she knew about us."

He sighed. "I'm not too clever at deception. When I got back from Dallas, she informed me that she knew about our weekend in Virginia. I don't know what kind of spy network she has, but it certainly is effective. Lord, Cara, I hate to drag you into this."

"It would be hard for me to avoid it. I knew it was possible that she'd confront me. I decided to take the chance when I came to you. I can hardly gripe about it now."

"No, you have every right to complain. I shouldn't have let you into such a mess."

"It wasn't pleasant," Cara admitted. "At first I was shocked, then scared and numb all at the same time. Even though I love you, I couldn't help thinking I was the other woman coming face to face with the wife. I wondered how Ginny would have reacted if she had met one of Daddy's girl friends at a party."

"It's not the same."

"I know. But no matter how much I reminded myself that we love each other and that Monica has given you nothing but grief, I felt wrong and guilty!"

"Oh, baby," he said, and his voice cracked. He buried his face in her hair.

"I was also embarrassed and angry because she had tricked me into such a situation. She managed to get rid of Ginny and Lucille, and then she informed me that she knew all about us. She said I'd never take you away from her, that you still love and desire her. She was vicious. The hatred poured out of her—more for you than for me, I suspect. Her venom stiffened my spine some. I realized she wanted to hurt you through me. She was playing an ugly game with us. A confrontation with an outraged wife is one thing, but her manipulation of us was cruel, and I despise her for it."

"Good for you."

Cara shrugged. "I stood up for myself as best I could. I tried not to let her see how she had shaken me, but I was in such turmoil. A thousand conflicting emotions rushed through me. I had to come here after we left that house. I couldn't be around anyone, not even Ginny. I drove to the apartment and walked around touching things. I felt like someone had died."

"I'm so sorry." Chris sighed, easing Cara off his lap. He began to pace the room, stopping once to gaze out the window at the street below. Cara watched him, empathizing with his anguish. Finally he turned to her and spoke, his voice low and constricted. "Cara, I was foolish and wicked to let you stay with me. I should have sent you home immediately. But I wanted you so much I couldn't act rationally. Now I have to face it—I've been the cause of a great deal of pain to you. I may hurt you worse in the future. Maybe . . . maybe you ought to return to Texas."

"Do you want me to leave?" Cara asked, the breath catching in her chest.

"No!" The longing ripped out of him. "But I'm a monster to ask you to stay. You'd be better off far away from me."

Cara ran across the room and threw her arms around him. "No, I don't want to go. Please don't make me. No matter how badly this afternoon hurt, it couldn't possibly give me as much pain as never seeing you again."

She choked on her tears, and Chris crushed her to him, burying his lips in her soft hair. "I love you. Cara, believe me, I don't ever want to hurt you. God, I'm insane not to insist that you leave, but I couldn't bear it either."

He covered her face with small, eager kisses, finally coming to rest on her lips. The honeyed sweetness of her mouth pierced him anew, and his tongue thrust in to caress hers. Cara moved against him suddenly, sharply wanting the full force of his love. They sank to the floor fused together, his hands tangled in her hair, their lips clinging. Trembling, they pulled apart only long enough to jerk away their clothes. Then they melted together again, hot and demanding, hands and mouths seeking possession of each other and satisfaction of their own quivering need. Mumbling breathless, incoherent words of love, they rushed eagerly to the joining. They moved as one in an ecstacy that was almost torment, bursting at last into a shattering unity, their cries mingling in the empty air.

Cara looked up from the book in front of her to rest her eyes from the minute print and rolled her head to ease the stiffness in her neck. She was finding out how much drudgery was involved in Chris's work, broken only rarely by flashes of excitement. Yet she could understand the pull of the investigation, too, the drama and the pure need to know, which kept him going through the sluggish parts. She enjoyed helping him and listening to him explain his job, a fact that never ceased to amaze him. Often he would stop in the middle of a sentence and query, "Are you *sure* you're interested in this?" He seemed hardly able to believe his good fortune, after Monica's active dislike of reporting.

As she rested, she saw Chris in the doorway and smiled at him. He grinned back, but there was a tense alertness in his face that was not usually there. Something was up. Cara's stomach tightened. Was it Monica, or something to do with Matthew? Chris strode rapidly to her table and wrapped his fingers around one arm, hauling her up from the chair. "Let's go outside. I've something to tell you."

She followed him at a half trot out of the library and into the summer sun. "What is it?"

"Ingram phoned awhile ago to say he had a piece of information related to our case." He propelled her to a secluded stone bench, and they sat. "They're monitoring Ben Lydle's checking account. That's one of Haskell's aliases. Anyway, he deposited a check for ten thousand dollars."

"Wow. Sounds like a payoff. Who wrote it?"

"Here's the really weird part. It was a Stone Oil Company check."

"What!" Cara gaped at him.

"Yeah," he commented dryly and extended a piece of paper to her. "Here's a photocopy of the check. I picked it up at Ingram's office. Hopefully your father can trace it inside his office and find out who ordered the check drawn."

"What does its being a company check mean? Is someone within the organization sabotaging it?"

"Looks that way. Maybe someone is seeking personal revenge because of being passed over for a promotion or something. Or the Stone employee could have been hired by someone else. In other words, he could be a middleman, like Haskell."

"I see. It has a nice ironic touch, paying Haskell with Daddy's own money."

"Doesn't it, though? Gives us a clue to the guy's personality, although I haven't figured out what. Let's call your father to give him the details."

When Cara dialed Alec's number, his secretary put her through immediately. "Cara?" his strong voice boomed through the receiver. "Do you have something?"

"Yes, but you'll have to figure out what it signifies. Chris managed to discover some aliases of Vern Haskell, one of them being Ben Lydle. The F.B.I. is after him on a different charge, and they've gone through the checks he receives as Ben Lydle. He got a ten-thousand-dollar check last week."

"Who paid it?" he asked quickly, his voice tense with excitement.

"Stone Oil."

There was a stunned pause on the other end of the line. "What are you talking about?"

"It's a Stone Oil Company check made out to Ben Lydle in the amount of ten thousand dollars. Chris hoped you could trace it."

"Sure. Every check requires an authorization slip, and for that amount it would have to come from someone high in the organization." His voice was grimly efficient. "Give me the number and date."

Cara did so, adding, "It has your signature and the treasurer's."

"Doesn't mean anything. If there was authorization for it, we would have signed automatically." He sighed. "Any other information?"

"No. Just the new names and the check."

"Okay. I'll let you know what I find out." He paused. "Uh, Cara, I don't want to frighten you, but something's happened here. We think someone tried to get to Matthew three nights ago."

Cara gasped, her eyes becoming round with fright. "Oh, no! What happened?"

"Somebody tried to open one of the downstairs windows in the middle of the night, and the alarm Morgan installed went off. The police came, but whoever it was had already gotten away. Of course, it could have been a simple robbery, but the odds are it was an attempt on Matthew. That's why it's becoming more vital every minute that Wozniak find this man."

"Of course, Daddy. I just know if you can find out who authorized that check, we'll have him."

"I hope so. I'll call you back soon."

Three days later Alec phoned them. Cara knew as soon as she heard his voice that the search had been fruitless. She had never before heard such defeat in her father's voice. "You didn't find it."

"No. I immediately sent a memo to accounting. They called Mrs. Jenkins and said the authorization slip for that check was missing. I let them have it, told them it was a direct order from me and they better come up with it. This morning the head of accounting informed me that they'd searched every possible location, and it simply wasn't there. Obviously our friend got to their files first and removed it."

"Oh, Daddy," Cara moaned. "Everything we turn up just leads to a dead end."

"At least we know someone within the organization is in on it. It can only be one of a small number of men. I'll have them all investigated."

"It might be someone lower on the totem pole, you know," Cara suggested. "Someone could have forged a signature on the authorization slip."

"You're right, of course. That enlarges the number of people who could have done it, but we're dealing with a finite number." He paused, then began tentatively, "Cara, I was wondering if you would fly home for a couple of days."

"What? Why?"

"I told Greeson to send Ashe Harlan to me. He'll arrive day after tomorrow. I thought it would ease the situation if you were present when I meet him. After all, he knows you."

"Well, he doesn't like me one bit, so I don't understand how I could help. Daddy, it would be better if you saw him alone. Why do you need a third person there?"

"I disagree. You're the only bridge between Harlan and me. For all we know, you may be his sister."

"The thought occurred to me. But I can't say I feel a strong familial tie. Ashe was rude and nasty, and I don't want to subject myself to him again. Anyway, it's time for school. I have to register in a few days."

"All the more reason to come home for a last visit with Morgan and Matthew. When school starts, you'll be too busy. Besides, I'd like to see you. I didn't know you'd left until Morgan mentioned it to me. Why didn't you come to say good-bye?"

"I didn't think. I'm sorry."

"Cara, it'd be a big favor to me. You'll pick up Harlan at the airport and bring him to the office. If it's too awkward, you can leave. Please."

Cara closed her eyes, wavering. "Okay. I'll catch a flight out tomorrow."

"Good. Tell Wozniak I'll continue to work on the Stone Oil angle. See you tomorrow."

She turned to Chris. He raised one eyebrow. "I take it he wasn't successful?"

"No. The guy apparently covered his tracks well. But Daddy's going to investigate all his employees for a connection with another company. He sounded really low, which isn't like him."

"What was the rest of the conversation about? Are you flying to Dallas?"

"Yeah, for a couple of days. For some crazy reason Daddy wants me to introduce him to Ashe Harlan."

"Is Alec acknowledging him?"

"I think he's just curious. I have no idea what Alec hopes will transpire. Maybe he believes he'll recognize Ashe or know definitely Ashe isn't his son. Nor do I understand why he thinks I'll improve the situation, since Ashe flatly disliked me."

"He made a great *effort* to dislike you. However, something impelled him to reveal Haskell's bribe."

"Well, whatever his reasoning, Daddy asked me to be there, and I couldn't refuse. I can't remember Daddy's asking me for a favor before. He even said please. And it'll be nice to see Morgan and Matt again before I get bogged down in classes." She didn't add that a few days' absence from him might help ease the tortured emotions she had been suffering since meeting Monica.

"Maybe it'll do you good to get away," Chris said, seeming to read her thoughts. She glanced sharply at him, and he smiled. "You think I don't know you've been unhappy the past few days?"

"No, not unhappy," Cara hastened to deny.

"Troubled, then."

Cara shrugged. "It's nothing, just an overload of emotion from the other day. My system isn't built to take so much excitement."

Chris took her hands, his wide face softening with love. "The last thing in the world I want is for you to be hurt."

"I know."

"So take a few days off from all of us here in Washington. Then, when you come back, if you're still unhappy you know I won't try to hold you."

"No!" Cara shook her head fiercely. "I won't leave you. I'll never want that."

Chris drove her to Dulles the following morning, and she landed at Dallas Fort Worth Airport three hours later. Cara rented a car and drove into Dallas. Her first stop was Morgan's house, where her sister fell on her with cries of delight. They spent the afternoon talking and laughing, catching up on the latest news of Alexis and each other. Cara exclaimed over Matt's growth since she had last seen him and quickly renewed their friendship.

"Matt's grown so fond of Sam," Morgan indicated the silent guard. "I don't know what we'll do with Matt when he leaves. Although the way things are going, he may become a permanent member of the family."

"I know. Chris hasn't dug up one solid lead. Everything that looks promising runs straight into a blank wall." She described the latest discovery of the Stone Oil connection to Haskell.

Morgan frowned. "Somebody within Stone Oil is paying this guy?"

"It's got Daddy stumped."

Morgan chewed thoughtfully at her lower lip. "You know, there's something peculiar here. I can't put my finger on it, but I sense . . ."

"What?"

Morgan sighed. "I don't know. That's the problem. But I feel we're overlooking something obvious." She frowned, then shrugged, clearing her brow. "Oh, well, perhaps it will come to me if I don't think about it. So tell me about Chris. How are you two doing?"

"Wonderfully. I get crazier about him every day. We have fun, we laugh, we talk. It's perfect, except that on the weekends he goes home to his wife. Before I went to Washington I thought I loved him as much as it was possible to love someone. I expected to get an apartment, go to college, have a life of my own, just as I always have. I would see Chris whenever we could and enjoy what we had together. I wasn't prepared for getting so wrapped up in him!"

"What do you mean?"

"I mean, he's not simply the man I love, separate and apart from my life. He *is* my life. Not that I have nothing else to do or that I spend all my time with him. But somehow he's become a part of the very essence of my being. Am I making sense?"

"Perfectly. Nick and I may not be together all day, but in a sense I'm never apart from him. We know each other so intimately and our love is so strong that I'd be half a person if I lost him."

"Exactly. No matter what happens between Chris and me, I could never feel this deeply for another man. Perhaps

I'd be able to love again, but Chris would remain in my heart and mind. And it's hell to think he'll always be another woman's husband."

"I'm sorry, honey."

"Oh, I got myself into it. And I don't regret it. I wouldn't want not to experience it. I'm just greedy. I want it all."

"You're not greedy. You're normal." Morgan reached out to squeeze her hand.

At the thud of feet on the stairs, Matthew threw up his hands and took a few toddling steps before reverting to quick crawling. Nick stepped into the room, picked up his son and swung him above his head until the child shrieked with laughter. Then, settling Matt into the crook of one arm, he turned toward his wife and saw Cara for the first time. "Cara! What are you doing here?" He bent down to place a quick kiss on her cheek.

"What about me?" Morgan demanded. He smiled and kissed her full on the mouth. She breathed in the deliciously familiar scent of him, a combination of cologne, paint and warm flesh. "That's better."

"When did you arrive, Cara?"

"About four hours ago, right after lunch," Morgan volunteered. "If you'd stick your head out of your studio sometime, you'd discover such things."

"Did we know you were coming? I realize I'm getting forgetful in my old age, but . . ."

"No, it's a surprise. I came on the spur of the moment because Daddy asked me."

A spark touched Nick's dark eyes. "It's about Matt?"

"No. Unfortunately we're going down blind alleys on it. This concerns Ashe Harlan. Remember him?"

"Ah, yes, the long-lost bastard son."

"Nick!"

"Well, isn't he?"

"Maybe. But it's no joking matter, at least not to Alec," Morgan stated. "Since Cara told him about Ashe Harlan, he's been worried. Between that and Matthew—honestly, Cara, I think he's grown grayer overnight."

"What does Harlan have to do with your coming to Dallas?"

Cara explained her father's request, and after a long silence Nick finally said, "Do you think he's really Alec's son?"

"I don't know. I thought I saw some similarities between them. Their eyes, their walk, certainly their aggressiveness. And Daddy knew his mother."

"Wouldn't it be weird to suddenly have a brother?" Morgan commented.

"Believe me, he doesn't act in the least brotherly. He hates us. I don't know what Daddy will accomplish by meeting him. Which reminds me—I'd better call Daddy and find out when and where to pick up Ashe tomorrow."

"If he's not utterly hostile, bring him by here after Daddy sees him. I'm dying of curiosity."

"I won't promise anything," Cara said with a laugh as she walked to the phone. "He's about as predictable as a tornado."

Alec was still at his office and quickly gave Cara the flight number and airline on which Harlan would arrive. As she expected, he had no news about the traitor within Stone Oil. After she hung up, Nick suggested they dress and go out for dinner. Morgan and Cara willingly adopted the idea, and soon they sailed out the door bent on an evening of fun. Nick and Morgan were entertaining companions, and Cara thoroughly enjoyed the outing. She did not specifically think of Chris, but she was viscerally aware of his absence. Even when he wasn't present, he was with her.

Cara waited by the low railing separating the departure lounge from the wide hall of the airport, watching the passenger arrivals. She almost decided Ashe had chickened out when she finally spotted him. He was dressed in jeans, boots and a tan Western-style shirt, his sun-streaked hair and deeply tanned face out of place among the paler city dwellers. Ashe saw Cara, and his stride checked before he continued toward her. Her stomach tightened in excitement and anticipation. Could this man honestly be her brother, his flesh and blood as akin to hers as Morgan's and Alexis's?

"Hello, Ashe."

"Are you the family representative, or what?" His blue eyes were piercing, his face disdainful.

The small swelling of warmth that had risen unbidden in Cara died instantly. "You're charming as ever. Let's get your luggage." She swung away, marching to the baggage-claim area. Ashe followed silently, and they stood solemnly watching the empty, circling carousel until the suitcases began to pop out onto the belt. She sighed with relief. Her possible half-brother was not an easy man to be with.

He grabbed a canvas duffel bag and slung it over his shoulder. "Okay, let's go."

Moments later he tossed the bag in the rear seat of the car and got in. Cara started the engine, dreading the long drive to Dallas with him. She maneuvered along the airport roads and headed for the south gate. Ashe stared moodily out the side window, and Cara stole surreptitious glances at him, searching for a resemblance between them. Was the line of his jaw like Alec's? His mouth? It was so difficult to see a similarity to oneself or the familiar members of one's family. Of course, perhaps none existed. Maybe the walk was coincidence, or simply her imagination. And lots of people had blue eyes.

Her gaze dropped to his hands, resting on his denim-clad leg. Suddenly her heart began to hammer, and she looked away quickly. There was something disturbingly familiar about Ashe's hand. She glanced back and realized what had caught her eye. The right thumbnail was slightly dented. Halfway above the curving white moon, a narrow white line ran across the nail, as if something had hit it hard in child-hood and left a permanent mark. However, she knew that it was no accident but a natural curve of the nail imprinted on his chromosomes. A mark exactly like it was on her right thumbnail, also. Several years ago she had noticed that Alexis possessed the same dent, although a trifle more marked, and, intrigued by the wonders of genetics, Cara had searched other family members' nails. It had stood out clearly on her father's thumbnail.

Cara gripped the steering wheel, stopping automatically at the exit toll booths to pay the parking fee, although her mind was far away. He was Alec's son. Surely it couldn't be mere coincidence for Ashe to have such a trait.

"Why does the mighty Alec Stone want to see me?" Ashe's voice broke into her reflections.

"You certainly go out of your way to be disagreeable," she commented. "I told Daddy what you'd said, and he wanted to meet you."

"Why? To warn me not to spread around the nasty facts of my birth? To pay me off? To tell me I'm a liar?"

Cara grimaced. "Too bad Daddy didn't know you existed earlier. You wouldn't have grown up to be so obnoxious if you had three sisters to take you down a tad." Her words effectively silenced him, and she continued, "Did it ever occur to you that Daddy might simply want to see you and talk to you?"

"Why should he?"

"That's a pretty stupid question. What if you'd spent your life not knowing your father's identity instead of building up hate and prejudice against Alec? Then if someone informed you that Alec was your father, wouldn't you have the least curiosity or desire to see him? Feeling as you do about Alec, don't you wonder about him?"

Ashe shot her a blazing blue glance, and Cara knew she had struck a chord in him. He was quiet for a few minutes, but when they approached the outskirts of Dallas, he began to question her about various buildings, his voice noncommittal, almost pleasant. Cara answered, chatting away merrily, glad he was making a bit of an effort. If she could manage to keep him in a receptive mood, maybe the explosion she feared when he came face to face with her father wouldn't occur. She would have liked to ask him to tread easily with Alec, to give him a chance instead of throwing up an impenetrable barrier, but she knew that would only increase his stubbornness and make him even more defiant.

When Cara exited from the expressway and turned into the parking garage of the towering, blue glass Stone Oil building, the slight ease and friendliness in Ashe's manner faded. Cara parked the car, and they rode the elevator to the top floor. With each step closer to Alec, as he took in the mirrored elevator walls, the plush carpet and heavy furniture of the executive floor, the soaring view of downtown Dallas through the plate glass windows, Ashe's face grew stonier and his body stiffer. Cara clamped her teeth together in frustration. Why did he have to be so darned prickly?

Mrs. Jenkins smiled and buzzed Alec's office, her eyes carefully assessing Cara's companion without appearing to do so. Alec's voice rumbled over the intercom, and his secretary waved them inside. Cara walked past the heavy door, Ashe following.

Alec rose to meet them. Cara stepped aside to give him a clear view of Harlan, and Harlan stopped, his body tense, as if he might break and run at any moment. Alec came around his desk and hesitated, his eyes searching the younger man's face. For a moment the identical blue gazes locked.

Chapter 19

Alec stepped forward, his hand outstretched to shake Harlan's. "I'm Alec Stone."

"Ashe Harlan," he responded, clasping Alec's hand briefly.

"Sit down, sit down." Alec motioned toward the chairs and returned to the seat behind his desk. Cara instantly knew her father had made a disastrous move. Behind his desk he looked authoritarian, powerful, impersonal. It would set Harlan's back up more. If only he had remained where he was or sat down with them . . . but Cara understood why he hadn't. Alec was scared. It was an amazing thought, that her father was scared—not reasonably frightened while retaining control as he had been regarding the threat to Matt, but terrified of the emotional undercurrents that lay between himself and this young man. It was as if he wanted Harlan to like him yet had to protect himself by slipping into his familiar, powerful role.

Harlan perched stiffly on the edge of the chair, saying nothing to ease the atmosphere. Alec stirred and picked up a gold and leather letter opener to toy with it. "Cara told me about your claim."

Ashe frowned. "I made no 'claim.' She asked me why I disliked you, and I explained. That's all."

"However you want to phrase it, you said you were my son."

"Yes."

"It came as something of a surprise to me, since your mother never informed me of your birth."

"If you had bothered to learn more about her, it wouldn't surprise you. She felt it was her own burden and didn't want to put any restraints on you or harm your marriage."

Alec slid his fingers down the letter opener, turned it over and repeated the motion again and again, his concentration seemingly fixed on the movement. He continued as if the younger man had not spoken. "Several things Cara told me rang a bell. I couldn't remember the woman's name—" He glanced up briefly at Ashe's noise of disgust. "But I remembered some of the details—the ring, for instance. Do you . . . do you have it with you?"

Ashe dug in his pocket, his lips tight with fury, and flung a key chain across the desk. Alec picked it up and studied the small woman's ring attached to it. "Yes, I remember it." He extended the chain toward Harlan, who snatched it from him.

"You remember the ring, but not the woman you gave it to," he snarled.

"It was quite a few years ago," Alec retorted sharply, stung by the man's tone. "And I said I couldn't remember her *name*. I remember your mother quite clearly."

Ashe's mouth curled. "Then you admit you had an affair with her."

"Yes. After Cara's revelation, I sent an investigator to Tulsa to check out your story."

"You what! How dare you pry into my life?"

Alec ignored him. "He discovered that Vicky Harlan worked in the hotel restaurant at the time I was staying there, and that you were born approximately eight and a half months later, a week before her scheduled due date. The name of the father on your birth certificate is Andrew Alexander, and since my middle name is Andrew, it would indicate that she believed me to be the father and was attempting to protect me."

"Wonderful. So now you're convinced. Is this why you called me down here?"

"I'm convinced you're Vicky Harlan's son, and she is the woman with whom I had an affair in Tulsa many years ago. She believed you to be my child. My investigator could find no evidence that she was having an affair with anyone else during the time I knew her, but of course there is a possibility. Which is why I'd like you to take a blood test."

"No!" Ashe shot out of his chair. "Absolutely not! I don't have to prove I'm your son, and I won't submit to your legal games."

"There's a great deal at stake here!" Alec retorted, also rising, his hand planted firmly on the desk top. "We're not talking about some penny-ante operation. If I brought you into the business and groomed you for advancement, acknowledged you as my son and one of my heirs——"

"I don't give a damn about your company! I didn't ask to be acknowledged as your son. I'm not here hat in hand, begging favors. Frankly I'd as soon have nothing to do with you. I needed a father when I was a kid, but goddamn it, I don't need you now!" He whirled and strode toward the door, pausing to toss a parting shot over his shoulder. "I'm not at your beck and call, Mr. Stone. Don't bring me down here again."

Alec stared as Harlan stormed out the door. "But——" He swung to Cara, his eyes suddenly bleak. "I handled it badly, didn't I? I didn't mean to antagonize him. I simply wanted to make sure. It's something I've wanted so much that I'm scared of it turning out to be a lie."

His words touched Cara, and with a stab of surprise and dismay, she realized her father was getting older. All her life he had seemed an indestructible force, ageless, in control. Now, for the first time, he looked his age. Cara hesitated for an instant, then darted out the door after Ashe. He stood beyond the glass doors of the outer office, impatiently waiting for an elevator. Cara hurried to him.

"Wait a minute! Where are you going? I'm the one with the car, remember?"

His brief glance dismissed her. "I don't need a Stone to chauffeur me."

"Really? And here I thought it would tickle your proletarian sense of humor." He didn't respond to her quip, and Cara sighed. "Did you have to be so defensive? Just because you're convinced you're his son doesn't mean it's as clear cut to the rest of the world. Daddy owns a big business and is very wealthy. When somebody turns up saying he's Alec's son, don't you think he has a right to be suspicious? He'd have to check it out. You can't expect him to throw his arms around you like you're the prodigal son."

"I don't expect anything from him!"

"Maybe not, but Daddy wants to give it. He's yearned for a son all his life. Your mother did you a great disservice by not telling Daddy about you. He'd have been ecstatic and done everything he could for you."

Ashe snorted. "Sure. I'd have been a regular member of the family. All of you would have loved that."

"You're the most maddening person! You don't know the first thing about me or my sisters, but you make sweeping judgments about us. How can you be so sure we wouldn't have liked a brother? The life you lived wasn't our fault. We didn't have any idea you existed. You can hardly blame us for not giving you money or an education or whatever it is you wanted. It was what your mother chose for you!"

"Don't you dare say a word against Mother. She slaved her whole life to keep me in food and clothes. There's not a Stone worth a tenth of her."

"Look, I can emphathize with your mother a lot more

than you think—probably better than *you* can. I fell in love with a married man, too. I understand her pain. But I also realize she made a conscious decision to do it. She chose the same thing I did—to grab her moment of love and accept the consequences. I certainly don't blame her. But she wasn't an innocent victim. She knew Daddy was married. He didn't deceive her. If anyone was wronged in the deal, it was *my* mother. If Daddy is to blame for your birth, so is your mother. And she made another decision—to keep you and raise you alone. Again, I'm not saying she was at fault. Maybe it made her feel better to protect Alec. If she knew Daddy well, she was probably afraid he'd take you from her because he desired a son so badly. But whatever her reasons, *she* chose that life for you, not him."

The cold blue fire in Ashe's eyes told Cara she'd pushed him far enough. The elevator door opened and he stepped inside without looking at her, but Cara reached out to hold the door. "You mean you aren't finished?" he snapped.

"No, I'm not. You're something Daddy's wanted all his life. He's scared you'll turn out to be false, simply because he hopes so much your story is true. That's why he'd like you to take the blood test. I know my father, and believe me, if he didn't think you were telling the truth, you'd have been out on your ear long ago. He wouldn't have flown you here to talk. Alec is reaching out to you, and I've never seen him do that. He's not simply talking business when he says he'll bring you into the company. He's offering you what has been his whole life, more important than us or my mother or his second wife. God knows, Alec isn't an easy man, but he's your father. Yet you won't take a single step toward him."

He glared. "Get out of my life, Cara Stone. I never asked for you or your father. I don't need his money or his love. And I sure as hell don't need you telling me what to do. Leave me alone!"

Cara's eyes blazed. "Don't worry, I will. You're a pig-headed, stiff-necked, compassionless fool! Thank God

Daddy didn't know about you earlier. I'd hate to have had a brother like you."

She released the door and swung away, hearing the swish of the elevator closing behind her. A heavy wooden door on the other side of the hall opened, and Michael Durek stepped out, impeccably dressed and coldly handsome. Cara suppressed her anger and forced a frigid smile onto her face. "Mr. Durek."

"Why, Cara," he seemed surprised. "I thought you were in Washington."

"Yes, I'm living there now, but I came to see Daddy for a couple of days. I'm flying back tonight."

"Oh? Well, enjoy your trip. Nice to see you." He opened the glass door for her, and she passed through, nodding her thanks. With quiet interest Mrs. Jenkins watched her cross the outer office and disappear into Alec's office.

He was standing at the large ceiling-to-floor window, staring out. Deep grooves were etched beside his mouth and ran from his eyes. His hair seemed to have grown grayer. Cara wondered if she hadn't noticed his aging over the years or if it had suddenly descended on him during the past few months. Heaven knows, she thought, between worrying about Matthew and struggling with Ashe Harlan, it was no wonder he looked older. "I tried to stop him, but it didn't work. He's very proud."

"And full of resentment," Alec added, turning to her. His eyes were bleak, almost hopeless, and impulsively Cara went to hug her father. Alec returned the hug fiercely. "If Wozniak hurts you, I'll ruin him," he whispered.

Cara gave him an extra squeeze, surprised, and he released her. She stepped back awkwardly, her eyes filled with an unaccustomed moisture. "How did you know about Chris?"

"I didn't when I sent you to Canada with him, or I wouldn't have. Morgan told me." He added sternly, "If it weren't for Morgan, I wouldn't have any idea where you are or what you're doing. I didn't know you were in D.C.

until you'd been there a week. Whatever compelled you to—no, I won't ask you that. The reason's all too familiar to me."

Cara smiled. "You and I don't seem to handle our love lives very successfully."

He returned her grin, a slight cheerfulness returning to his face. "Tell me what you think. Is that kid my son?"

"Well, if I needed anything to convince me, it was the sight of you two glaring and shouting at each other. He looked like a carbon copy of you."

"Did he?" Alec seemed pleased. "He's too unreasonable, though, to be like me. I'd never have thrown away an oil company. Oh, well, he'll come around. I won't give up easily." He sighed and sank into his chair. "If only I could resolve the thing with Matthew."

"Have you discovered anything about the person inside the company?"

"Not a clue. I've had investigators going through my people's backgrounds with a fine-tooth comb. We've covered every employee, even the secretaries and the errand boys. Nobody has any connection with any other oil firm except for two or three whom we hired away from other places. Why would they want to do me in? It's insane."

"If Chris finds anything, I'll let you know immediately," Cara promised. "I'm flying to D.C. tonight."

"So soon?"

She shrugged. "Registration is Monday, and I have several things to do in the meantime. Besides . . ."

"I know, I know, you want to get back to your reporter. What taste my daughters have. Didn't any of you ever think of falling for a hardworking young man who'd *like* to be affiliated with Stone Oil?"

Cara laughed. "I guess not, Daddy. You'll have to look to Ashe or Matthew for your succession." She kissed him on the cheek and left his office in a happier frame of mind than when she'd entered it a few moments before. Alec might have experienced a setback with Ashe Harlan, but he wasn't about to give in. He wasn't crumbling before her eyes, as she had feared for a moment.

She drove to Morgan's house, where her sister waited eagerly for a blow-by-blow account of the meeting between Ashe and Alec. Then Cara packed and left to catch her return flight to Washington. She would barely have time to make it, she thought as she backed out of the driveway, what with having to return the rental car to its separate parking lot and then travel to the terminal in a computerized rail car. Waving a final good-bye to Morgan, who stood on the front steps, she headed for Stemmons Freeway. As Cara drove, a faint uneasiness began to swell in her. She glanced in her rearview mirror and at the cars on either side. If someone had asked her to explain the sudden feeling, she wouldn't have been able to. She had just felt, strangely, that someone was watching her. Yet the other drivers stared ahead at the road, totally unaware of her.

Minutes later she looked again in the rearview mirror. It was not the same car behind her. Perhaps the white one two cars back had been there earlier, but she couldn't be sure. Anyway, why shouldn't it be there still? He had as much right as she to be on the expressway. Cara took the 183 fork, and the white car followed Stemmons. She breathed a little easier, telling herself she was getting paranoid. But by the time she passed Texas Stadium, the uneasy feeling had returned. This was crazy. Who would want to follow her? She forced herself to ignore her uneasiness. After all, she couldn't keep glancing in the mirror every few seconds.

It was, as always, a long drive to the airport, which lay halfway between Dallas and Fort Worth. Finally she reached the turnoff and entered the smooth, wide airport road. Pulling into the far left lane, she took the rental-car exit and soon turned into the wide, car-filled lot. Looking at her watch, she hurried to park and get out, bending over to lock the door. Then, grinding her teeth in frustration, she unlocked the door, leaned across the seat and fished the rental papers from the glove compartment. Out of the corner of one eye, she noticed a car creep down the aisle between the rows of cars and stop behind her. No doubt it was making for the empty slot beside hers, and she was blocking the way with her open door. She grabbed the papers and slid out of the car, slamming the door and bending once more to lock it. Hearing footsteps, Cara straightened to turn and smile an apology when suddenly her waist was encircled like steel and both arms were pinned to her sides. A hand clamped over her mouth.

Cara froze in astonishment. This couldn't be happening, not in broad daylight. Where was the lot attendant? Her second thought was of rape, and finally she began to struggle, kicking back with her heels and trying to wrench her arms free. A needle pricked her arm, and she struggled harder as a man dragged her backward toward the waiting car.

There must be more than one man, Cara thought. The man holding her couldn't have given her a shot, too. Why the needle? A drug, of course. Did rapists subdue their victims with drugs? It seemed unlikely. Did they run in pairs? Did they follow one from home all the way to the airport? But she knew it wasn't rape, although her mind was growing groggy now. The man holding her swung her around, and she had the impression of a dark green vehicle. Then she was pushed into the backseat. There was no one sitting in front. Cara hadn't yet had a glimpse of either man. Her attacker threw her facedown on the seat, his arms still around her, and lay on top of her, his weight crushing her. Her face was shoved into the vinyl upholstery of the seat, and she could hardly breathe. She couldn't keep her eyelids open, and there was a humming in her ears. It wouldn't be long, she knew, before she slipped into unconsciousness. Her mind examined the fact coolly and found that she really didn't care. She should fight to stay awake, but it seemed too much trouble. So much easier to slide down into warm darkness.

She blinked and swallowed, forcing her brain to concentrate. She knew the motive. Think about that. These men were part of the plot against her father. They were kidnapping her to force Alec to close the well. She wondered if the security around Matthew had been too tight, making them switch to her. Or were they even now taking Matthew, too? The thought sent a chill through her, and Cara revived to struggle again. Her assailant's grip had relaxed, and she managed to land an elbow in his stomach. With a grunt and a muttered curse, his arm tightened around her until she couldn't breathe. Black spots danced before her eyes, joining the numbness in her limbs and mind, and she passed out.

Chris took a final bite of lasagna and settled back in his seat with a sigh of contentment. "Sheer heaven," he commented to his friend, Dean Lowenstern, seated across the table from him. Dean's wife, Cynthia, was out of town on another legal job, and he was as much at loose ends as Chris was without Cara. Funny, Chris thought, he had lived by himself for so long, and yet in a matter of weeks Cara had made her presence in his life felt so firmly that he hardly knew what to do when she was gone. He glanced down at his watch. "Six-thirty. I'll have to run soon. Cara's plane arrives at seven-thirty."

"How is she?"

"Fine, as far as I know. Well, I told you about Monica's trick. I think it shook Cara up pretty badly. I could have strangled Monica."

"Probably a good thing for all concerned," Dean replied. "Although I believe it's easier to get a divorce."

Chris shot him a warning glance. "Don't start in again."

"My lips are sealed. I'll talk about something more pleasant—Cara."

Chris smiled. "I have no objections."

"You have a lovely girl there. Too good for you, if you want to know the truth."

"Probably. But I've been careful not to let her in on that secret."

"How long do you think she'll put up with this kind of life? I mean loving you, lavishing all her time and attention on you, only to have you run home to Monica every weekend."

Chris frowned. "I told you, I let Monica know she'd seen the last of me."

"Will that make everything all right for Cara?"

"Of course not, but she's aware—"

"Who cares if she's aware? I'm aware that people are starving in India, but that doesn't mean I like it. You have a beautiful relationship there, and you're going to throw it away for the sake of a bitch who cares for no one but herself."

"I don't think you really changed the subject, Dean." Chris ran an impatient hand through his hair. "You're not saying anything new. I realize Cara is the best thing that ever happened to me. She's beautiful, loving, generous, sexy. When I'm with her, I'm on top of the world. She deserves a lot more than I can give her. When we were at my sister's, I watched her holding Bab's baby, and she looked so natural with it, so happy. I knew I ought to let her go—no, force her to leave. She should fall in love with someone else—a man who's free and who can give her a home and a family."

"You can do that right now."

Chris shook his head. "Dean, we've been through this a million times. I can't divorce Monica. She's an invalid, and—"

"You're right. I've heard you before. I know all your arguments. I also know how much they're worth, which is nothing. Look, you no longer plan to keep up a pretense of marriage by living with Monica on weekends. What's the difference between this total separation and divorce? Huh? All you're doing now is supporting her financially. You can pay her just as much money when you're divorced, if it will ease your conscience, though why you find it

266

necessary is beyond me, since she's wealthy. Her parents have more money than you do, and they love to lavish it on their perfect little girl." He raised his hand. "Okay, I won't get into that. Go ahead and pay for her support, but divorce her. Is she crazy about having your name? Hell, she can keep that, too, when you're divorced. What else are you giving her except the satisfaction of knowing she's ruining your life?"

"Maybe that's my reason," Chris put in grimly.

"Terrific. The big guilt trip. Isn't three years long enough to expiate your sins? Do you *need* to be miserable? It wasn't your fault! It was an accident. True, if you were not a reporter who happened at the time to be threatened by a hoodlum, she wouldn't have been shot. On the other hand, if she hadn't been standing in the yard making a nuisance of herself, neither one of you would have gotten a bullet. Her own bad temper brought it on her just as surely as your job did. Why punish yourself and Cara? And if you felt so strongly that you needed to pay her off with your mental anguish, why didn't you quit reporting and take the job Monica wanted you to? You could have immolated yourself entirely. That would have been nice and saintly."

"This conversation is going nowhere. We've been through it before."

"Yeah, when it was just you and your freedom we were talking about. You didn't have a girl who loves you and whom you love waiting in the wings. But now . . . you have a full and happy life as an alternative, and I can't bear to see you destroy it."

"Dean, please, I've got to go or I'll be late for her plane. Continue the harangue some other time, okay?"

"No, one last thing." Dean reached out to catch his sleeve as Chris rose. "This is very important. I've made a discovery about you. It's not all guilt that ties you to Monica. Or duty, or all the other virtues they taught you in catechism class."

"What is it, then, Dean?" Chris urged with heavy sarcasm.

"You're just plain scared."

"What?"

"Monica's invalidism is an excuse, a shield. You're safe as long as you stay married to her. You can't commit yourself to another person. And commitment is what terrifies you. The first time around your marriage was such a bad experience that now you're gun-shy. You don't want to get deeply involved again. You're afraid to give your heart into another woman's keeping."

"I've already given Cara that."

"Not totally. You haven't jumped in feet first and said, 'I love you and want to spend the rest of my life with you.' That's what you're avoiding. Someday Cara will grow tired of the mess and move on. You'll be upset, but safe, still whole. You're positively racked with fear that if you divorce Monica and marry Cara, you'll have the same unhappy experience."

"You're crazy," Chris growled. "You had too much wine with your spaghetti. I've got to go now."

"Monica is insulation for you," Dean warned as Chris snapped open his wallet and tossed a tip onto the table. "Think about it."

"It won't keep me awake at night." He strode away from the table, scowling blackly.

Chapter 20

Chris stared moodily at the stream of arriving passengers, his mind still festering with Dean's words. The file of people slowed and eventually stopped altogether. Chris stared into the empty tunnel leading to the plane. Where was Cara? A few moments later a stewardess strode out of the metal walkway, and Chris stopped her. "Have all the passengers gotten off?"

"Why, yes, sir," she answered, her brown eyes friendly. "This is the end of the run."

"Thank you." Where was Cara? Chris was sure he hadn't missed her. He'd been there before the plane taxied up to the entrance, and he'd watched every person who disembarked. If by some chance he had missed her through a moment of inattention, surely she would have spotted him. He turned back down the hallway and strolled into the airport hub, head down, hands jammed into his pockets. She had missed the flight. It was as simple as that, but disappointing. Probably Alec had found something else for her to do. A spurt of jealousy surged through Chris.

He had Cara paged, but after fifteen minutes, when she

still had not answered the red courtesy phone, he gave up. Last night he had called her at her sister's. The number was still tucked away in his wallet. Digging out the slip of paper, he went to the nearest phone booth and dialed. When Morgan answered, he recognized her sunny voice from his call the evening before. Funny, despite the difference, there was the faintest tinge of Cara's speech in her voice. "Morgan? This is Chris Wozniak. Is Cara there?"

"Cara!" she repeated. "Heavens, no. She left hours ago. I thought you were supposed to pick her up at the airport."

"I was. That's where I am, but Cara wasn't on the seven-thirty flight. Did she miss it? Is she coming on a later flight?"

"Not that I know of. She left here four or five hours ago. She should have caught her flight. She wasn't late, although she was probably slowed down by turning in the rented car. If the plane left exactly on time, she might have missed it . . . but I can't imagine that happening."

"Well, she's not here."

Morgan sounded worried. "Do you suppose anything could have happened to her?"

"I'm sure she was just late and couldn't reach me at home. I guess I'll go back there now in case she calls."

Morgan hung up, a frown on her face. Nick, who sat on the couch reading a book to his son, looked up and caught the expression. "What's wrong?"

"Nothing, I guess. That was Chris. He said Cara wasn't on her plane. He thinks she missed it, but if she did, why wouldn't she have called me?"

Nick shrugged. "If she could catch a later flight, there'd be no point in driving back here. Why call? What could you do about it? Cara's very self-reliant. I'm sure she grabbed a bite of supper and bought something to read."

"But if she'd phoned me, I could have told Chris when she was coming in."

"Maybe she didn't think of it. She probably tried to get hold of him, couldn't, and decided to take a taxi when she arrives in Washington."

"I think I'll call the airport and have her paged. Maybe she's still there." Morgan opened the thick Yellow Pages and thumbed through it until she found the airline's number. She asked for Cara to be paged, then sat down to wait. Twenty minutes later she was still waiting, her fingers clenched in her lap. Matthew, bored by the books, wriggled from the couch and toddled off to noisier pastimes.

"Still worried?" Nick asked.

"Yes. It sounds silly, I know, but I'm scared."

"Her second plane probably left soon after the other one. That's why she isn't at the airport. Also why she didn't call you. She'd have had to run to catch a train to one of the other terminals."

"I guess." Morgan sounded unconvinced. "She might have had car trouble on the way and never got there."

"You know she would have called if that had happened."

"Not if somebody stopped to help her and then carried her off to rape or kill her."

"I tell you what." Nick crossed to the phone. "I'll call the rental agency and find out when she returned the car. Then you'll be certain she got to DFW."

"That's a wonderful idea." Morgan beamed at her husband.

It took several minutes of Nick's charm to convince the desk clerk at the rental agency to reveal whether one of their clients had returned a car that afternoon. However, a few moments later she said, "No, sir, we have no record of Miss Stone turning in a car. She didn't come to the desk to leave the papers and the key."

"She didn't?" Nick repeated, stunned. "Are you sure?"

"Yes. I checked, and that key hasn't been dropped off. If you'd like, I can have the lot checked."

"Please," Nick responded, although he was sure it was futile. He gave her his number and hung up, reluctantly turning to Morgan. "She hasn't shown up."

Morgan jumped up. "Something *did* happen to her. Oh, Nick, what can we do?"

"The girl was going to look in the parking lot to see if the car had been returned."

"What good will that do? How could the car be there and not her?"

"Maybe she was in a hurry, knowing she was late for her plane, and she forgot to stop at the desk. It's possible. Let's wait for the clerk to call back. Then we'll drive to the airport and look for her car along the way."

"Oh, honey, I'm scared." Morgan leaned against him. "What if something's happened to her? What if they couldn't get Matt so they took Cara instead? I should have gone with her."

Nick wrapped an arm around her shoulders, his voice soothing, although he couldn't quite still the quiver of alarm that ran through him. "If that's what happened to her, then they would just have grabbed both of you. What could you have done to protect her?"

"I don't know," Morgan mumbled. "But she's my little sister."

He guided her to the couch, and they sat down edgily to await the phone's ring. When it came, they jumped, and Nick grabbed the receiver. The same clerk's voice came through the earpiece, this time with a note of puzzlement. "Mr. Fletcher? This is a little odd, but the attendant found Miss Stone's car in the lot. I can't understand why she didn't come to the desk. She'd already paid for the rental. And unless we know the car has been returned, we have to continue to charge for it."

Nick sighed with relief. He must have been right about what Cara had done. "She was probably in a hurry. She was late for a flight."

"There was something else, though. The door was locked, but the key was left in it." Nick's heart began to thud uncomfortably. "The attendant opened the trunk just to look over the car, because the key in the door seemed weird. There was a suitcase in the trunk."

"Her suitcase was there!" Morgan sat bolt upright at Nick's startled exclamation.

"Yes. At least the tag had her name on it."

"Uh, this sounds melodramatic, but tell the attendant not to touch the car again. We may have to call the police."

He hung up and shot a worried glance at Morgan, who had turned white and whose eyes were twice their normal size. "The police!" she whispered.

Nick frowned. "I don't know what else to do. It just doesn't seem like Cara not to stop at the rental counter or to forget her suitcase in the trunk, even if she had to rush to catch her flight." He frowned. "I'll call Wozniak, just in case he's heard from her. Do you have his number?"

Numbly Morgan found her address book, where she had jotted down the number Cara had given her, and handed it to Nick. Quickly he dialed. Chris's deep voice answered on the first ring. "This is Nick Fletcher."

"Have you heard from Cara?"

"No. Morgan tried to page her, but no luck. Then I phoned the car rental agency, and they told me something weird. Cara didn't check in at the counter, but she returned the car to the lot. The key was in the door, and her suitcase was still in the trunk."

An icy hand squeezed Chris's heart, and he replied dully, "Something's happened to her."

"Yes, but what? I was hoping you'd heard from her."

"No." He stared numbly at the wall and repeated, "No."

"I'm afraid it's connected to Alec and the threats he's received. I think I'd better call him and get the police in on it."

"Yes. Of course. I..." Chris's brain was blank, numb. What was the best thing to do? "I'll catch the next flight to Dallas. Hopefully there'll be another one tonight."

"Okay." Nick replaced the receiver. "He hasn't heard from her. Honey, I'm going to have to tell your father."

Chris remained in the same position, staring at the phone for several minutes after Nick hung up. Finally he roused himself enough to call the airport, only to find that there were no flights to Dallas on any airline until the red-eye flight the next morning at six. Chris made a reservation and went into the bedroom to pack. The task was soon finished, and he had nothing to do except sit and let his mind roam free. He pictured Cara dead, frightened, hurt, a thousand terrible things, and blamed himself for letting her go. When he first began the investigation, he had retained the good sense to protest her involvement in it. But the past few weeks had been so happy that he'd allowed the thought of danger to slip from his mind. He should have realized that the extortionist would try something else as the truth drew closer. The check from Stone Oil would doubtlessly point a clear finger at someone if he kept after it long enough. The extortionist had decided to act quickly and, though Matthew was closely guarded, Cara had been available, wandering around Dallas alone. Stupid. Stupid.

The telephone rang, and Chris grabbed for it, his heart pounding with hope. A muffled voice, barely understandable, asked, "Wozniak?"

Chris straightened, instantly alert. "Yes?"

"We got your girlfriend."

"Let me speak to her," Chris demanded, his palms damp with the sudden sweat of excitement and fear.

"No. It's nighttime, and she's asleep."

"Then how do I know you have her?"

"I guess you'll have to take my word for it, huh? The old man's calling off the investigation, so you're out of a job. But there's something you got to do, too, if you want Miss Stone back alive."

"What?"

"I want all the notes you've made on this investigation, originals and copies. Your entire files."

"Then you'll let Cara go?"

"Yeah. Once you drop the stuff."

"All right. Where?"

"In Dallas, at three o'clock tomorrow afternoon." The voice gave him the location of a trash dump container, and Chris grabbed a pen to jot it down.

"Okay, got it. But I want to speak to Cara first."

"Like I told you, she's asleep. Can't do it."

"Tomorrow, then, before I drop off the material."

"I plan for her to sleep a long time."

"I have to be sure she's all right."

"You'll know it when you see her." The man hung up with a final click.

Chris gripped the receiver tightly, staring at it as if it could reveal the answers to his questions. Slowly he put it down. All his notes and information on the investigation. No doubt they guessed he would continue it whatever Alec Stone told him, after what they'd done to Cara. Chris walked mechanically into his study and began to pull the relevant material from the file cabinets and table, gathering it into a compact bundle. He sat down at his desk and stared at the pile. How would the extortionist know he had been given everything? Suppose Chris were to make and save copies of everything he dropped off tomorrow? When Cara was released he could begin the investigation again. And if she wasn't—well, he wouldn't give up until he'd nailed every person involved, and it would be easier if he didn't have to start over from scratch.

The only way the extortionist could be sure he had all the research would be to search Chris's apartment while he was in Dallas. Perhaps he was gambling on Chris's not having the time to take his files to be copied tomorrow before he left for Dallas. Chris glanced at the small copier he had bought the year before. It had already been worth every cent he'd paid for it, and now it would prove priceless. He could make the copies tonight and hide them securely before he left tomorrow morning. He doubted he'd get any sleep tonight anyway. Grimly he picked up the pile, placed it beside the copier and turned it on.

It was after two o'clock before he finished making the copies. He took out a box and filled it with the originals and copies he would drop off in Dallas. Carefully he bound it with twine and set it beside his suitcase. He put the copies he had just made into two smaller boxes, and tucking them under his arm, he left his apartment and went quietly up the stairs to the third floor. Three apartments had been fashioned from the old town house. The top floor was occupied by an artist who had installed skylights in the roof and made a studio out of half the attic. However, the other half was used by all the tenants for storage.

Chris halted in front of what appeared to be a small closet door on the third-floor landing and unlocked it. Inside, a narrow set of twisting stairs led upward. In the pitch-black attic he groped for the long string connected to the lightbulb above and jerked on the light. It sprang into dim life, partially revealing the boxes, trunks and suitcases scattered around the dusty floor and casting eerie shadows around them. Chris stored an empty trunk here, but he preferred one belonging to another person, preferably one filled with other material. The first two he tried were locked, but the third had no fastening. Chris opened it, revealing old clothes reeking of mothballs. Perfect. Removing the contents, he laid the two boxes on the bottom, filled the trunk again and shut the lid.

When he returned to his apartment, Chris stripped off his now dusty pants and shirt, thrust them into the hamper and took a shower. Clean and dressed again, he looked at his watch. Three-thirty. Still over an hour to wait before leaving for the airport, and nothing to do to stave off the terrifying images of Cara's kidnapping. With a sigh he sank into his comfortable leather chair and settled himself to sit out the long, dark hour ahead.

The dreams seemed to go on without end, strange and jumbled, but Cara was aware they were dreams and wasn't frightened. It was bothersome more than anything else, and even in her sleep she grew irritated. Most annoying was that she wanted to wake up and end the bizarre flow of images but could not. Slowly she floated nearer and nearer the surface of consciousness. Cara could hear noises nearby but she could not identify them, and sometimes they became part of her dreams. There were voices and movements and then a cessation of both. Dead silence. Cara's eyelids floated open blearily and closed almost immediately.

Yet there was still the desperate need to awaken, and soon she opened her eyes again. Her head hurt, and her mouth was dry and foul-tasting. She wanted a glass of water, but when she moved to sit up, her head went spinning, and she fell back, closing her eyes. She dozed, then drifted once more into faint consciousness. This time her brain worked better, and she did not attempt to sit up. Instead, her feet and legs slid off the bed and she rested on her knees beside it. The world was tilting slightly, and she felt sick, but she found that if she simply let the rest of her body slide off the bed, she could crawl on all fours. She knew she had to do it.

Cautiously Cara groped her way to a door and through it into a bathroom. She knew it was a bath because there was the cold hardness of tile beneath her hands and knees instead of soft carpet. Cara pulled herself up at the sink and turned on the faucet, catching water in her hand and gulping it down. It eased the thirst and the acrid taste in her mouth. But her stomach revolted, and she staggered to the toilet to retch violently. Afterward she washed her face in cool water from the sink and realized she felt better, less foggy. She washed her face again and sipped more slowly from the faucet.

Where was she? What was going on? Cara felt terribly confused, but she was positive something was wrong. She had to get out. That much she knew with every fiber of her being. She lurched out of the bathroom, weaving across the darkened room and running painfully into the bed frame. Palms out, she felt her way around the bed. There was a faint light coming from one wall. Windows, she thought. It was enough to reveal the outline of a door against the adjoining wall. She stumbled across the floor and opened it, only to find blacker darkness. Carefully Cara extended her hand and stepped forward. Her hand came into contact with a wall. She patted around the wall and discovered she was in a boxlike structure. A closet. Of course. Cara backed out, closing the door, and groped again, finding and opening another closet door. She kept on, turning a corner, and there was another door. She turned the handle, but it did not open. Vainly she tugged at it, turning the knob first one way and then the other. She pushed against it, but it wouldn't budge.

It was the way out, Cara was certain. And it was locked. However, she continued her tour of the rest of the walls. With every stumbling step her mind grew clearer. She was in danger. There was something about the car and a man behind her. A struggle and then slipping into unconsciousness. She couldn't remember exactly what, but something was very, very wrong. She had to get away and back to Chris.

Cara made her way to the faint light and pushed aside the curtain. It was dark outside, night, but there were lights below. She stared out, trying to orient herself. A parking lot, and beyond that, buildings. She was in an apartment, but not her own. And she was on the second floor, too high to crawl out the window to escape. There was a small balcony outside, and the windows went all the way down to the floor. A sliding glass door. She could step outside. Maybe the night air would revive her. She tugged at the handle, and when it did not move, she groped for the lock and shoved it up with a satisfying click. However, the door still remained in place.

Tears sprang to her eyes as she continued to pull the handle without success, until finally she leaned her face against the cool glass. She was weary, and everything seemed set against her. Slowly her knees bent, and Cara slipped down along the door to rest on the floor. She was so tired, and she wanted desperately to return to the hazy world of sleep. Why was it important to leave? Why must she get away? One hand touched a small metal box attached to the track of the door. There was a keyhole in the middle of it. Of course. The door was locked at the bottom, and she didn't have the key. Cara leaned her head against the door, her throat closing with tears. She felt as she had when she was a child and had had her tonsils removed—the same druggy, hazy, achy feeling. She'd wanted to cry but had been afraid to because her throat hurt so much, and she hadn't known where she was or what was happening. There had been a lot of white, and nurses who took her temperature and pulled open her eyelids, until finally a voice said she could be taken back to her room. There had been the same confusion, but then she had known Mama waited for her in her room, and Daddy, too. Once she got there she would be all right, because Mama would give her all the comfort she needed, and Daddy wouldn't let anybody do anything else to her. Her eyelids closed, and she drifted back to sleep.

Cara awoke to the sound of voices. She kept her eyes shut tightly, too scared to move. A man exclaimed and jerked her up, carrying her to the bed. Her head was clearer now. She remembered standing by the car, and then a man's arms around her, and being shoved inside. They had given her a shot. That was why she felt so drowsy and out of control. She could vaguely remember staggering around the room last night like a drunk, unable to escape or to help herself. If only she kept her eyes shut, maybe they would leave her alone again. Then she could try the door or break the window if there was any hope of escaping that way. As long as they believed she was still asleep.

"I told you you should have given her another shot last night," a gruff voice complained.

"Don't be stupid. She didn't go anywhere, did she? She was just walking around in her sleep," another man said. "People do it all the time. She didn't wake up. Besides, where could she go?"

"Nowhere, but she might have woken up and seen us when we came into the room. Then she'd be able to identify us."

"Would you stop griping?"

She was on the bed again, and the man who had carried her stepped back. The other one came closer, bending over her. Cara forced her muscles to relax. She must appear asleep. Could he tell she was awake by the movement of her eyelids? Her breathing? There were noises she could not identify, then the jab of a needle in her arm. Involuntarily she flinched, and it was all she could do to keep her lids from flying open. Mustn't do that. Safer if she couldn't identify them. The two men withdrew, and Cara heard the door close behind them, then the rasp of a bolt being shoved home. No wonder she had been unable to open the door last night.

Cautiously she opened her lids and glanced about, then rolled over to survey the rest of the room. Empty. They had left no guard behind. She sat up and stared at her arm in despair. There was a drop of blood where the needle had pricked it. Damn! The drug was already in her system, and she would soon pass out again. She was already wobbly and unclear from the first shot. This one would send her under immediately. If only she could get away before it took effect. But how?

Cara glanced around the room. It was bare except for the bed and a chair. She stood up and walked shakily into the bathroom. She eased open the medicine cabinet. Nothing. There was nothing she could use in the whole bathroom. Unless she could jerk the towel bar from the wall and smash the glass door with it. But the door led only to a balcony. What would she do once she got out there? Cara staggered back into the bedroom and over to the window. Pulling aside the curtain, she gazed out. It was daylight now, but the view outside told her little more than it had last night. A parking lot and apartment buildings. She wasn't even sure she was in Dallas. Her eyelids grew heavy and closed. She pulled them open again, almost sobbing with frustration. The drug was taking effect. She couldn't clear her mind to think. There must be something she could do. If she broke the glass, went out on the balcony and screamed, surely someone would hear the commotion and call the police. At least someone would complain to the manager. Would anything come of it? Would it not be better simply to wait and hope that the men would release her? They wouldn't worry about her describing them unless they planned to let her go. If she screamed, they'd come in and subdue her. In the struggle she would see their faces. Would they release her if that happened? But who knows what would happen if she didn't get out or attract attention?

Right now she had to sleep. She could hardly keep her eyelids open. After she slept for a while, she would wake up again, and then she could plan better. Maybe this evening would be the best time to scream, anyway. More people would be home. She'd wait until dusk. Cara weaved back to the bed and fell heavily onto it. Almost instantly she plunged into a deep, black sleep.

Chapter 21

Alec stepped into the kitchen and poured a steaming cup of coffee from the pot. Laraine prepared the coffee maker each night so it would be ready for him to turn on before he showered and dressed early the next day. He had automatically pushed the button this morning, although his actions today were anything but routine. He was clean-shaven, his suit as immaculate as always, but his face was gaunt and strained, his eyes sunk in his head. He looked ten years older than he was, and he felt as if he were a hundred.

When Laraine followed him into the kitchen, he turned in surprise. Usually she slept long after he left for the office. But now here she was, belting her flowing blue robe, hair uncombed and face not made up. Alec couldn't remember when she had appeared downstairs without her makeup on and her hair swept up elegantly.

"I heard you down here," she said to explain her presence. "I thought I'd make you a bit of breakfast."

"No need. I'm not hungry."

"You really should have something. It'll be good for you."

"Why is it that women think food is the cure for every sort of emotional ill?" he asked, not unpleasantly.

She smiled. "I guess because it's something we can offer to help." She went to the coffeepot and poured herself a cup, adding saccharine and a dollop of creamer. "I don't suppose you've heard anything further."

He shook his head. "I expect the call to come to the office. I'd just as soon be there, anyway. I'm no good sitting around here."

Laraine stirred her coffee, a frown creasing her forehead as she studied her husband. She had never seen him look this bad in all the time she'd known him. Her heart ached to ease his burden, but she realized it was impossible. She had no children herself and was not particularly close to Alec's, but she knew how she would feel if something had happened to Matthew, the baby who had become her chief joy in life. There would be nothing anyone could do or say to diminish her fear and despair. She sipped the hot liquid and asked, "Have you told Ginny yet?"

He frowned. "No. She couldn't take it."

Still protecting Ginny. It was something she'd fought for years. When Alec had divorced Ginny and married her, Laraine had believed she possessed all his love. He had been sad over the divorce, and now and then longings for his first wife crept out, but Laraine thought in time she would banish such things from his heart. After all, she was younger and almost as beautiful as Ginny, with her golden hair and sky-blue eyes, her creamy complexion and carefully guarded figure. Moreover, she was an excellent hostess and a tasteful housekeeper. She could handle any social situation, and never flew into quavering flights of uncertainty. Alec would realize how superior to Ginny she was. However, as the years passed, Laraine came to understand that she could not take Ginny's place, let alone surpass her. Despite the faults Alec had carped about, he loved Ginny, and no other woman could come so close to him. In time

Laraine became resigned to holding only half her husband's heart. She was convenient, she fit his needs, and he respected her. He enjoyed her company in bed, and he appreciated the absence of complaints. He was comfortable with her and loved her in his own way. With that she had to be content.

But it was still hard to take when he shielded Ginny as carefully as if he were married to her. There were times when Laraine wanted to scream with jealousy, but today her innate fairness overrode even her envy. "But Alec, that's not right. Cara is Ginny's child, too. She deserves to know."

"Cara will be back soon, and Ginny need never hear about it."

"Honey, Morgan says she's much stronger than she used to be. She has a husband to help her. Surely it won't damage her irreparably. I mean, she doesn't have a weak heart or anything."

"You've never understood about Ginny," he snapped.

"Good Lord, Alec, she's a grown woman! I'm sure it will frighten her, but she has a right to know. How would you like it if I kept something like this from you?"

He grimaced. "That's an entirely different matter. I'm more capable of handling things than Ginny."

Laraine raked a hand through her unkempt hair, feeling as if she'd like to pull it out by the roots. She had slept no more than Alec last night, having lain awake listening to his pacing. She wanted to comfort her husband, but he rejected all solace, and now he insisted on thinking of Ginny first, as always. Why didn't he take her in his arms, pour out his fears and allow her to comfort him? But no, such was not the tenor of their marriage. And there was no point in arguing with him in his present state. She would discuss it with Morgan later. Perhaps Morgan would tell her mother about the kidnapping. "All right. I don't mean to plague you."

"I know." He set down the empty cup and started for the door. "I'm going to the office now. I'll call you when I learn anything." Then he was gone. Laraine tossed the residue of her coffee into the sink and placed the delicate cup on the counter. She watched as Alec backed his car down the driveway past the kitchen window, and tears filled her eyes.

It was seven o'clock, Alec's usual time to drive to work. The traffic along Central was not yet at the standstill it would reach in thirty minutes. It was a short distance to his building, and normally he traveled it without noticing the surroundings, his mind lost in contemplation of a business problem. Today, however, he observed the cars around him, the buildings, the absurdly narrow expressway. He was aware of the exit he took and the turn into the underground parking lot of Stone Oil Company. He wondered how many more times he would travel this route. Not many. What did one do when one retired? He had never seriously contemplated the matter. After all, he was not yet fifty-five, and he had planned to work long past normal retirement age. Ah, well, he'd soon find out.

He parked his silver Cadillac in its slot and rode the elevator to the top floor. No one was there, and he unlocked the glass doors to the executive suite, flipping on the lights. He continued into his office, turning on the light switch and tossing the newspaper he had picked up out of habit onto his desk. Alec started to open the drawers and pull out the files and papers he was working on, then stopped. It was pointless. He'd get nothing done today, anyway. He was capable only of waiting to hear about Cara. He slumped into his chair and stared at the view of downtown Dallas through the plate-glass window.

He didn't know how long he sat that way, but he was roused by the sound of Mrs. Jenkins coming into the outer office and arranging her desk. He was familiar enough with her routine to know she would brew a pot of coffee and bring him a cup when it was ready. He swiveled back to his desk and opened the newspaper. He wasn't interested in it, but he didn't want to arouse his secretary's curiosity by sitting idly at his desk when she came in.

As he had expected, there was soon a rap at his door,

and it eased open. Mrs. Jenkins held out a cup of coffee, and he nodded. She set it down on his desk. Alec told her, "When Mr. Durek comes in, tell him I want to see him, please."

"Yes, sir. Anything else?"

"Not right now. Oh, yes, I'm expecting Chris Wozniak sometime this morning." Nick had said Chris was leaving D.C. on the first flight he could. Since he hadn't yet heard from him, Alec presumed Chris had been unable to catch a flight last night and would arrive early this morning. He sipped at his coffee, a familiar anger against Wozniak curling in his stomach. When he had learned that Cara had gone to Chris, a married man, Alec had almost exploded in rage. It infuriated him to think that a man would use his youngest girl, take her to his bed while remaining married to another woman. Yet Alec knew there was nothing he could do to change it. He'd discovered that much with Alexis and Morgan when he had opposed their choice of husbands. He simply had to accept that Cara had made the worst choice of the lot. Nick Fletcher was an idle playboy and Brant McClure a righteous jackass, but at least their wives were happy with them. Alec could see nothing ahead for Cara but heartbreak. He didn't want to dwell on it, but he realized she'd chosen a man like himself. For all his philandering, only his wife had counted, and Alec was sure Chris Wozniak felt the same way. Cara was being taken advantage of. He grimaced. No point in thinking about it now. The important thing was to get Cara back.

His intercom buzzed. "Mr. Wozniak is here, sir."

He pressed down the button. "Send him in, please."

Chris entered, carrying a large box under one arm, and Alec had to revise his opinion of the other man's feelings for Cara. Chris looked as haggard and drawn as Alec. Obviously he had not slept the night before, either. Gray shadows were smudged beneath his lids, and above them his eyes stared out as if from behind a wall, stark and haunted. Alec motioned him toward a chair.

"I just got in," Chris explained. "The first flight I could

get was at six this morning." He rubbed one hand across his face, flopping into a chair and dumping the box beside him. Alex looked at it questioningly.

"Those are my notes, originals and copies, on your sabotage story. Last night a man phoned and demanded them as ransom for Cara. I'm supposed to drop them at this address this afternoon." He extended a piece of paper to Alec.

Alec glanced over the paper without surprise. "Yes, I know where this is. I'll have someone drive you there."

"Have you heard anything about Cara?"

Alec shook his head. "Nothing since last night. Right after Nick called, they phoned me. My ransom, of course, was to shut down the well and call off your investigation."

"Did you?"

"Naturally. I called Greeson right after I talked to the kidnapper and told him to shut it down immediately. There was nothing else to do. I didn't call the police. The caller warned me not to."

"When will Cara be released?"

"He wouldn't say. Nor would he let me speak to her. God knows if she's all right." His eyes flashed. "If she's not, I'll have his head on a platter." He paused, searching for his former calm. "I presume we'll have to wait until he learns that the well has actually been shut down. I told Greeson to begin dismantling the equipment as quickly as possible. We may have to clear out entirely before he lets her go."

Chris blanched at the idea. They could be talking about days. To keep his mind off the thought, he asked, "What do you intend to do after Cara returns? You could start the well again."

"Yes, but I won't. I'd be open to the same blackmail. It's too expensive a proposition to continually set up the equipment and then remove it. I'll leave the well alone. In fact, I plan to retire."

"What?"

Alec shrugged. "What else can I do? I make Stone Oil

too vulnerable. I have three daughters and a grandson. Soon I'll have another grandchild. I can't keep them guarded all the time. I've yielded once, and they know I will again. The only way I can thwart them is to retire and turn over the handling of the company to Durek. I'll probably sell out to him gradually. None of the girls is interested in the company. For a while I hoped Ashe Harlan—but he wants no part of me or my company. I intended to hold it for Matthew, but I'll be an old man before he can take control. Besides," a flicker of a wry smile crossed his face, "if he's like my children, he'll decide to be a doctor or an actor instead."

Chris studied the other man in silence. No wonder he looked so grim. Not only was he worried about his daughter, he was also facing the loss of his life's core, the work on which he had spent most of his years and which he loved fanatically. Chris wondered if he would have the same strength. For Cara? Yes, of course, he'd ditch his typewriter tomorrow.

The morning passed slowly. The two men sat staring at each other or into space, mired in lonely misery by their thoughts. Stone instructed his secretary to put no business calls through to him, but she interrupted now and then with an unidentified caller or a personal call. Each time the phone rang, both men went taut, and Alec would grab for the phone as if it were a lifeline. Two or three calls turned out to be business, and Alec dismissed them quickly. One was from Morgan, asking if they'd heard anything. Another was from Alexis, wanting to know the same.

"No, nothing yet," Alec told her.

"Daddy, shall I fly to Dallas? Brant and I have been talking about it. Maybe we should come, guard and all."

"No, there's no need. What could you do? Besides, this isn't a time for you to be traveling."

"Don't be archaic. I'm still three months away from delivery. I can make a trip. Wouldn't it help you if I were in Dallas?"

He sighed. "I think you're safer there. After all, Cara

was kidnapped at the airport. I'd be even more nervous knowing you're waltzing around, making yourself an open target."

"Okay, if it'll make you feel better, I promise I'll stay here. But remember to call as soon as you hear anything."

"I will."

Mrs. Jenkins buzzed to say that Michael Durek had arrived, and Alec went to Durek's office to inform Durek of his impending retirement. Chris left his chair and stretched out on the heavy red leather couch that sat against one wall of the expansive room. Hands locked behind his head, he gave way to thoughts of Cara, remembering their first meeting, the rush of emotion he'd felt when he saw her, the sudden hot longing. He'd known better than to do any of the things he did, and yet he had been unable to stop himself. Idly he wondered if even his investigation of Stone Oil had been more an excuse to see her again than a necessary part of his oil story. He smiled faintly as he recalled the details of the time they'd spent together, even though it squeezed his heart like a vise.

Alec's entrance a few minutes later jerked him from his memories, and he sat up quickly. Alec was more drawn than before, and Chris guessed how much the conversation with Durek had cost him emotionally. Again they resumed their watchful, waiting positions, jumping when Mrs. Jenkins buzzed the intercom again.

"Mr. Harlan is here, sir. Are you free to see him?"

Alec blinked in surprise. "Yes, send him in."

The young man entered hesitantly, an almost shy expression giving his face a youthful quality Chris hadn't seen there before. Harlan looked surprised to find Chris in the office, but he made no comment. He glanced at his feet and back up, clearing his throat, then pausing interminably. Chris felt a faint twinge of curiosity. Harlan was obviously finding it very hard to say whatever he had planned to tell Alec. Alec watched him mildly, too concerned about Cara to experience the hope and fear he had earlier with Ashe.

Finally Ashe began. "I came because—well, that is,

after I left yesterday, Cara ran after me—" He did not notice the increased tension of the other two men at the mention of her name. "And, well, frankly, she told me off pretty well. I thought a lot last night about what she'd said—how it wasn't your fault, since you didn't know about me. It's true. I always put all the blame on you and none on my mother. She was so good and hardworking, sacrificed so much for me—I couldn't admit she might have been wrong. But I shouldn't blame you for her separating us. Yesterday I refused to listen to what you had to say. But I decided to return and hear you out, give you a fair chance. I meant it when I said I didn't want any of your money, but if you still want me to take the blood test, I'm willing. I'd like . . ." He swallowed. "I'd like for you to be certain you're my father."

His blue gaze shot briefly toward Alec, then went to the window, his face tightening to receive Alec's rejection. Alec stared at him, his numbed brain slow to take in the man's words. Finally he began, "Well, yes, of course, if you're willing, I'd like to prove it, too." A weary, almost sad smile touched his lips. "Cara told me all the proof she needed was seeing the two of us yelling at each other."

A grin broke across Ashe's face, routing the usual hard suspicion that rested there. Alec went on. "I want to talk to you more at length, but right now I'm too fuzzy to make sense. It isn't a good time. All I can think of is Cara, and I—"

"Cara?" Ashe interrupted quickly. He glanced from Alec to Chris, noting for the first time the weariness and anxiety his own embarrassment had hidden from him. "Is something wrong? Is she sick?" The sudden alarm that leaped in him at the idea surprised him. He'd never thought he could have any liking for the Stones, but as before in Canada, he felt the prick of family feeling.

"She's been kidnapped," Chris answered for Alec, playing a hunch. He'd suspected Harlan hadn't revealed all he knew. Perhaps, faced with Cara's danger, he'd give them information that might help.

"Kidnapped!"

"Yes, by the same man who asked you to sabotage the well."

"Vern Haskell? But why—Oh, you mean they're using her to force you to close the Michaelson Number Two. It didn't work with the little boy."

Chris leaned forward, quivering with anticipation. He mustn't alienate Harlan and mess it up now. "Ashe, is there anything you didn't tell us before, something you might have forgotten?"

"No, I told you. Haskell approached me and—" Ashe stopped abruptly, his eyes turning blank with thought. "There *was* one other thing. I met Haskell at an apartment here in Dallas. I couldn't remember the address, so I didn't think it was any use to tell you."

"Do you recall where it was? How you got to it?"

"You think they might have Cara there?"

"It's possible."

"I can try." He pointed out one window. "We went up that expressway past a big white shopping mall and a couple of gold towers."

Alec nodded eagerly, his face blazing with renewed hope. "Yeah, I know where you're talking about."

"We got off on a nice-size street, named . . . something beginning with an *r*. Regal?"

"Royal." Alec's voice was flat, but he was already rising, eager to begin the hunt.

"Yeah, that's it. We turned left over the expressway, went a couple of blocks and turned off on a side street. I think I could find it if we drove out there, although I can't remember the exact address."

"Then let's go." Chris was instantly out of his chair and opening the door. Alec left his secretary hasty instructions about answering his calls. Impatiently they rode down in the elevator. When it opened on the garage, they tumbled out, racing for Alec's sleek silver car. With Alec driving, the car roared out of the lot and burst onto Central, speeding north past the twin gold towers and North Park mall, which

Harlan had mentioned, exiting at Royal and following
Ashe's directions down the street.

"That's it!" Ashe exclaimed softly. "We just passed it.
I'm almost sure that's the side street." Alec whipped the
car around to make the turn. Ashe stared intently at the
buildings as they crept by. "Yes, this is it. Turn in at the
second entrance. There! The mailboxes. It's the next building on the right."

"Can you find the apartment?" Chris asked as Alec
parked in one of the numerous empty spaces.

"Sure. It ended in an eight, I think. Anyway, it was the
last one on the right side at the far end. Second story. Let's
go." He made a move to open the door.

"Wait." Chris put out a restraining hand. "We have to
decide how to proceed. We can't all barge in there. It could
endanger Cara's life."

"Well, what do we do, then?" Harlan asked impatiently.
"We can't sit around out here, either."

"First we ascertain whether Cara's actually there," Alec
stated, years of command in his voice. "One of us could
go up and scout it, but we don't know whether the crooks
would recognize us."

"It wouldn't matter if they recognized me," Ashe volunteered. "You two are obviously their enemy, but they
don't necessarily know I am. After all, they asked me to
help them a few months ago. I could go up and tell them
I want to see Vern Haskell, pretend I've decided to sell out
after all. Maybe I could get inside the apartment and find
out if Cara's there."

"It's chancy," Alec mused. "But we don't have much
choice at the moment. Okay, go ahead. But remember,
don't take any risks."

"Sure." The daredevil grin on his youthful face belied
the reassuring answer. Ashe opened the door and slid out.
Hands nonchalantly in his pockets, he sauntered across the
asphalt and up the stairs.

Alec watched him go. Then his gaze slid to the large

black wrought-iron numbers adorning the side of the building. "There's something familiar about this place."

"You mean you've been here before?"

"No. But that address," he pointed to the numbers, "rings
a bell in my head for some reason."

"Could it be one of your employees'? The one who's
double-crossing you?"

"Maybe, although I don't know where I would have seen
an employee's address. I'll put Mrs. Jenkins on it. If it's
anything to do with Stone Oil, she'll find it." He picked up
the telephone that was concealed in the dashboard of the
car and dialed his office. Tersely he told his secretary to
check the employee records for the address of the complex.
After he hung up he continued to stare at the building, his
forehead wrinkled with thought. "It's a good address.
Hardly seems like a hangout of kidnappers."

"These aren't ordinary kidnappers," Chris reminded him.

They sat up straight when Ashe ran lightly down the
stairs and strode across the lot to the car. He opened Chris's
door and leaned in. "Nobody there. Or at least nobody
answers the bell. I listened at the door and window, but I
couldn't hear a sound."

"Let's find the manager. I'll convince him to open it for
us."

"Too iffy. And it takes time. If they're gone they could
return at any moment. I'm for breaking in," Chris voted.

"How?"

Chris grinned, adrenaline pulsing through his tired body.
"Investigative reporters acquire some odd talents."

The men took the stairs two at a time, hurrying along
the concrete walkway with Ashe in the lead. Chris knew
they were acting foolishly. The trio was unarmed and had
no idea whether the kidnappers were inside the apartment
or had weapons. They were risking their lives and perhaps
Cara's as well. The intelligent thing would be to call the
police, get a search warrant and let the cops break into the
place. But with the possibility of action before him, Chris

could not resist. He was sure Alec felt the same way. They were not used to standing by and watching things take place. Rather, they were accustomed to being the movers of the action. His heart pumped blood furiously, and it thundered in his head, while adrenaline shrieked along his nerves. He might be only a few steps from Cara, could see her, hold her, save her.

Ashe stopped before the last door. "This is it."

Chris saw Alec studying the number on the door, filing it away with the address in his memory. He ran his eyes down the door frame. "Good. A credit card will do this one." He flipped open his wallet and extracted one, then slid it between the door and the jamb, moving it down and thrusting the metal bar back into the door. It opened quietly beneath his fingers, and just as silently he slipped inside, with Alec on his heels. Ashe waited at the front door to warn them of anyone's approach.

The richly furnished living room was empty, hushed with the silence of vacancy. Chris moved toward the hall and glanced down it. Open doors on either side. He glided past them, flicking a quick glance into each. Bedroom, bathroom. And there, the last one—closed, and with a shiny bolt holding it firmly locked.

Chris glanced at the others, seeing on their faces the same realization of what the bolt meant. He thrust it back, and it made a loud click in the stillness. Shoving the door open, he burst in, not knowing quite what to expect, possibly to be met again by silent emptiness. But this time a figure lay sprawled on the bed, black hair flowing across the spread.

"Cara!"

Chapter 22

Cara did not move even at his hoarse exclamation, and for one heart-stopping minute Chris thought she was dead. Then he saw the slow, steady rise and fall of her chest, and he exhaled in relief. He crossed the room in two quick strides and lifted her to a sitting position. She lay flaccid and inert against him. "Cara," he repeated, patting her cheeks gently. She did not move, not even a flicker of an eyelid.

"She's out cold," Alec barked. "They've doped her. We'd better get her to a hospital."

Chris lifted her from the bed, carrying her like a baby in his arms. Alec and Ashe trailed him out of the apartment and down the stairs to the car. Gently he positioned her on the backseat, cradling her head in his lap. Alec started the ignition and wheeled out of the parking lot, tires screeching, his mind busily deciding on a hospital. The closest? The best? Was time a factor? Which one dealt best with drugs? There was the answer.

Firmly he pushed down on the accelerator, speeding along Central. Parkland was the primary emergency hospital, the one that handled Saturday-night shootings and stabbings and overdoses. It was farther away, but at least it could be reached by fast expressway.

They reached Parkland in record time and whipped into the emergency entrance. Chris stepped out of the car with his burden, and almost instantly an attendant with a gurney appeared for Cara. They walked beside the cart into the hospital as Alec related a terse account of the cause of her unconsciousness. Then the men were excluded as a nurse directed the cart into a separate small room, closing the door in their faces. The three sat down, stunned, the reality of their situation only now beginning to soak in. Cara was free. And in a hospital. She didn't seem to be in too bad a condition. An antidote, a pumped stomach—they could save her.

A young intern left Cara's room, and all three jumped to their feet. "We've drawn a sample of blood and sent it to be analyzed. Do you have any idea what she's taken?"

"She hasn't *taken* anything!" Alec growled.

"All I know is that when we found her," Chris burst in, "she was out. I saw two bruises on her arm, and I assumed she'd been given an injection. We have no idea what the substance was," Chris informed him. The intern glanced at him oddly.

"Someone did this against her will?"

"Of course!" Alec's brows drew together, and Chris realized he was about to explode with all the anger and uncertainty that had been stewing inside him since yesterday evening. Ashe saw it, too, and firmly steered him away from the intern. Chris attempted to explain the situation to the doctor, whose eyebrows rose.

"I think this is one for the police, don't you?" he inquired.

The police were duly called, although Alec made certain the order filtered down to the patrolmen through his preferred channels. Therefore, the two uniformed men who questioned them were affable and polite, jotting down Chris' and Alec's story with only a calm reminder that the police should have been called in earlier.

"We'll need to speak to Miss Stone, of course," one of them said. "She may be able to provide a description of her kidnappers."

The police continued the vigil with the others as they waited for another appearance by the intern. In due course he came, his smile telling them immediately that their worries were over. "She's fine. She was only given a sedative. No overdose. She's been out for several hours, and from the movements she's making, she should be awake soon. I'm sending her up to a regular room. We'd like to keep her under observation for a day."

"When can we see her?"

"As soon as she wakes up and is coherent. They're moving her now, if you'd like to accompany her."

They followed Cara's inert form on the cart down the hallway to the elevator. It carried them to another floor, where she was wheeled into a private room. One policeman stationed himself outside the door, and the others were herded into the waiting room. Chris sank wearily onto the sofa and leaned his head back. All the energy had drained from him as soon as the doctor announced that she would be all right. He was suddenly, acutely aware of the weariness that invaded every corner of his body. He hadn't slept in more than twenty-four hours, and his shredded nerves screamed for rest. His eyes closed, and instantly he was asleep.

There were the dreams again, fleeting and strange, but she was unable to awake. There were voices and a great deal of movement, the squeak of wheels and a feeling of floating in mid-air. Then it stopped, and there were only more dreams. A woman's voice said her name, and she touched Cara's cheek lightly. She wanted to answer, but her tongue was too thick to speak and her lips were sealed dryly. Desperately she tried to force open her eyelids but couldn't. The woman left, returning twice to speak to Cara, and each time it was impossible to answer despite her struggle to do so.

Finally, after the woman left the third time, Cara's lids briefly fluttered open. After a while she was able to look about and grasp that she lay in a white room. There were steel bars around her. It seemed stranger than ever, and she shut her eyes. Later there was the woman's voice again, and this time Cara raised her lids. The woman who bent over her was fuzzy but dressed in white, a cap on her head. A nurse. Of course, she was in a hospital. That made sense. But why had she fallen asleep on the job? Probably the nurse was telling her to get up and get to work, but Cara knew her muscles wouldn't respond. She smiled weakly and murmured, "Sorry."

The next time she awoke her mind was clearer, and she looked over her surroundings. She was in a hospital room, no longer in that apartment. What had happened? Had the mysterious men brought her here? A nurse came in a few minutes later and, seeing her awake, asked a few simple questions, including her name and age. Cara frowned, puzzled. "What am I doing here? Don't you know who I am? Was I found somewhere?"

"Oh, no, just seeing if some of the grogginess has gone," the nurse assured her brightly. "Your father brought you in."

"Alec?"

"Yes. Do you feel up to seeing him?"

"Of course." Cara struggled to sit up as the nurse left. So Alec had brought her. Had he found her? Paid a ransom? Her mind whirled with questions. She hadn't realized confusion could make one's head ache so. The door burst open, but to her surprise, it was Chris who rushed in, with her father several paces behind him. "Chris!" Tears sprang into her eyes and she held out her arms, suddenly struck with how frightened she had been, how much she had longed to go to him.

"Cara." In an instant he was beside her, letting down the side bars to sit on the edge of the narrow bed and pull her into his arms. "Oh, baby." His voice was muffled against her neck, his grip tight, almost desperate. "God, I've been

so worried. They said you were all right, but when you
didn't wake up for so long..."

"Someone gave me a shot," Cara explained.

"I know. A sedative."

"What are you doing here? What's going on?" She gazed
over his shoulder at Alec, who was standing at the foot of
the bed, his face tired but creased with a grin. And beyond
him, shifting uncomfortably in the doorway, was Ashe
Harlan. "What's going on?"

Reluctantly Chris released her and sat back. She held out
one hand to her father and with her free hand motioned for
Ashe to come inside. Chris began to explain what had happened in the past day, with Alec chiming in from time to
time to add or clarify. Cara listened, wide-eyed, her still-
numb brain hardly able to take in everything they said. It
seemed unreal, inapplicable to her, like something from a
movie. Out of all the facts one solid thing emerged, and
she grasped at it eagerly. "So, Daddy, you know the address
of the apartment? Then you can find out who's behind it!"

Her father sighed. "Yes, it seems familiar, but for the
life of me I can't remember why or to whom it belongs.
Wozniak here guesses it's someone in Stone Oil, the same
one who authorized the check. Maybe he's right. My mind
is so foggy now I can't come up with anything clear."

Cara yawned widely, then chuckled. "Me too. I think
we all need a nice nap."

"My opinion exactly," Alec concurred. "I've arranged
for a private security guard to remain outside your door until
you're released from the hospital. There should be a policeman in the hall guarding you, too."

"Daddy, really, do you think they'd try again? And in
such a public place as a hospital?"

"An airport isn't exactly deserted. Besides, I'm not taking any chances. Knowing you're safe, I can go home and
sleep. Tomorrow morning maybe I'll be able to piece this
all together."

"Good idea."

He leaned forward and kissed her cheek. "I'll leave now

and let you get some rest. Chris?" He turned toward the other man.

"No. I'll stay with her tonight to make sure."

"But Chris," Cara protested, taking in his weary face and sunken eyes, "you need sleep, too, and there's nothing but a chair here."

"I'll manage. Please, Cara, don't make a fuss. I simply can't leave you alone."

Her face softened at his words, and she smiled. "All right, if you want to."

When Alec left the room, Ashe stepped forward hesitantly. "Uh, I'm glad you're all right."

"Thank you for finding me."

"It wasn't anything, really. I should have described where it was earlier. If Mr. Stone knows who lives there, it might have saved all this trouble."

"You couldn't have known."

He smiled. "You're more forgiving than you were yesterday."

"Was I too hard?"

"No. I suppose I needed it. That's why I came back this morning. I kept thinking about what you'd said, and I realized you'd hit the nail on the head. Anyway, I . . . I'm glad you're okay."

Cara recognized the inchoate, unfamiliar emotions that lay beneath his simple words, and she reached out to squeeze his hand. "Thank you."

He followed Alec from the room, leaving Chris alone with Cara. He gathered her into his arms once more. They luxuriated in the pleasure and certainty of their embrace for a long time. Finally Chris kissed the top of her head and eased her down onto the pillows. "Now it's time you went to sleep."

"That's all I've done for almost twenty-four hours," Cara protested.

"And you need more of it. You aren't entirely free of the drugs."

Cara nodded submissively, her eyelids suddenly too

heavy to argue. Chris retired to the heavy chair at the foot of her bed and watched until her eyes closed. Then he leaned back and fell into an exhausted sleep.

The sound of the breakfast tray against the bed table brought Chris awake with a snap. He blinked, orienting himself, and Cara chuckled. She was sitting upright, her face bright and alert. "You look like you've been on a three-day drunk," she said.

He scratched his jaw, smiling ruefully. "I haven't shaved in two days. I imagine I do look pretty scruffy." He stood up and stretched, his joints cracking from the awkward position in which he had slept. It had been far from an uninterrupted sleep. First the policeman had disturbed them to ask Cara questions. She was able to give only highly unsatisfactory answers, and he left. Then an intern appeared to examine Cara. He pronounced her progressing well, although he insisted on keeping her in the hospital through the night. Things had settled down for a while until Morgan and Nick came in, full of hugs and cries of glee at her escape. The nurse had finally bustled them out and tried to eject Chris, also, but he managed to wangle an okay to remain through the night. After that Chris fell asleep, although every entrance of a nurse had jerked him awake instantly.

Cara ate her breakfast, sharing it with Chris, and before long Alec arrived. They went through the long procedure of checking out of the hospital, which was further delayed until a doctor could examine Cara again and pronounce her perfectly healthy. At last she was released. Alec bundled her into his car and headed for his Highland Park home.

"Where are we going?" Cara asked.

"To my house, of course. You and Hargrove here," he jerked a thumb in the direction of Cara's newly acquired private guard, "are going to spend a few days there. You, too, Chris, if you want."

"Thank you, I have a hotel room. Besides, I have to go to Washington."

"Me, too," Cara chimed in.

"Absolutely not. You need a few days' rest, and—"

"But I'm fine. You heard the doctor. I've recovered completely. Anyway, I've had more than enough rest lately."

"And," Alec waded on as if she had not spoken, "I want you where I can keep an eye on you."

"Daddy . . ." Cara began to protest.

"Your father's right. Until this is settled you need protection," Chris added.

"I can be protected in Washington. I have to register. School starts in less than a week."

"We'll discuss it later," Alec said with finality, and Cara subsided, contenting herself with a heavenward roll of her eyes. She was sure it wouldn't be long before the attraction of the mother-hen role palled for Alec. Once he returned to work, she'd be able to leave.

Laraine had coffee and a second breakfast ready for them when they reached the mansion. Chris and Alec dove into the food, while Cara nibbled at a sweet roll, eyeing the new wallpaper Laraine had hung in the dining room. After the events of the preceding days, everything seemed absurdly normal. When Chris's appetite was satiated, he lit a cigarette and turned toward Alec, all business. "Have you come up with anything on that address?"

Alec grimaced with exasperation. "Not a damn thing. I've drawn a blank. However, I phoned Mrs. Jenkins and told her to go through all the employees' addresses for the past couple of years. Hopefully she'll find something. I've reached the point where the more I think about the address, the more the memory recedes."

"What's happened with you and Ashe?" Cara asked curiously.

Alec smiled. "He took a blood test yesterday when we were at the hospital."

"And?"

"Type A positive, same as me."

"And quite a few other people," Chris pointed out.

"I know. It's common enough. It doesn't prove I'm his father, but at least I know it's not an impossibility."

"I think you are," Cara put in positively.

"I think so more and more myself." He sighed. "However, he's still not cooperative. I tried to get him to come into the organization, but he's adamant. He's determined to do it on his own, without any help from me." He shrugged. "But he'll agree eventually. I don't intend to give up."

"I didn't figure you did," Cara murmured with a smile and an amused sideward glance at Chris.

Laraine put on her small half-lens glasses and began to sort their mail, slitting the letters and studying the contents. The conversation continued desultorily, wandering from Ashe to Cara's kidnapping to lighter topics. Laraine flipped open a square envelope, read it and asked casually, "Alec, dear, shall we accept this invitation to the Cobrells' beach house? It's two weeks from now. They're having a big smash down there."

"The Cobrells'? Where is it?"

"Outside Corpus Christi. You remember, we went to it last year. It's not theirs, exactly. It belongs to his company. Supposedly it's a business party."

Alec stared at her, his face frozen in a look of stunned discovery. Laraine raised her brows. "Darling, what is—"

"Goddamn!" He swung his fist down on the table, rattling the dishes. The other three gaped at him as he shoved back the chair and strode to the phone, jabbing out the numbers with a murderous expression on his face.

"What in the world?" Cara murmured, and Laraine removed her glasses to stare at Alec, as if that would make his actions more comprehensible. Chris rose from his seat in quick, gut-level anticipation.

"Mrs. Jenkins," Alec barked into the phone, "go into my office and pull the merger file. I want the list of assets for Durcom Oil." He waited impatiently.

"What's that?" Cara asked.

"Do you know who owns the apartment?" Chris overrode her voice.

Alec, glowering, held up a hand. "Just a second. I have to make sure." His secretary had obviously returned, for he spoke again into the mouthpiece. "Is there an apartment listed there? What's the address?" There was another pause, and he said grimly, "Thank you. No, that's enough."

With the care of a man barely in control, he replaced the receiver and turned to the others. "Durek."

"What?"

"Your partner?"

"What are you talking about?"

A chorus arose from the other three, and he made a quieting motion. "Mike Durek's company owned that apartment when we merged. It was one thing he retained personally. It didn't become an asset of Stone Oil."

"You mean you think Mike is behind the sabotage?" Laraine gasped.

"Why?" Cara exclaimed. "He owns part of the company. Wouldn't he lose as much as you from the shutdown of the well?"

"No, because it was your father's decision," Chris explained, his mind leaping to the conclusion. "Of course. I knew I was overlooking something. None of us suspected him, but he definitely had something to gain."

"Sure. Yesterday morning I told him I'd have to resign and offered to sell the company to him under a long-range purchase plan. I bent over backward to be fair. It was what he was aiming for. He hoped I'd realize how open I would be to similar threats in the future and would offer to step down. But if I didn't, he could use my decision against me with the board of directors—a power play to prove I was no longer capable of running the company."

"I can't believe it—your own partner!"

"Yeah. My own partner." Alec's face was set, his blue eyes blazing with an unholy light. "I'm going over there and face that son of a bitch." He yanked his suit coat from the back of a chair and thrust his arms into it. "When I'm through with him, he'll not only be out of Stone Oil—and on my terms—he'll be finished in oil, too."

He charged out of the room without a backward glance for the others. They gazed after him in a state of shock. Finally Chris ran one hand through his thick hair and turned to Cara. "I guess that's it, baby. Villain identified and captured."

"It's so strange. I feel... well, almost let down. It's over, but I can't quite absorb the idea. I was beginning to think we'd never discover who was behind it."

"And to find out it was Mike Durek," Laraine added. She cocked her head thoughtfully to one side. "What should I do about that fellow lurking out in the kitchen?"

"You mean the guard?" A bubble of laughter rose in Cara's throat. Trust Laraine to consider the proper procedures. "I don't know. I guess leave him there until Daddy tells him what to do."

"I'll get a taxi and run back to the hotel," Chris said abruptly. "I need to shower and shave."

"I'll come with you," Cara offered immediately, jumping up from her seat.

"Of course," Laraine agreed. "Why don't you take the station wagon? No need to get a taxi."

"No," Chris vetoed the idea. "I'll manage. You're supposed to remain here under protection, remember, not go traipsing around town with me."

"But we know who did it now! There's no need to stick with the guard."

"You and I know the game's up, but do Durek's men? They're probably combing the streets for you."

"Nonsense. Durek's bound to realize it's only a matter of time till he's caught. You all found me at his apartment, and he'll know Daddy'll figure it out. I imagine he's trying frantically to cover his tracks, not kidnap me again."

Chris sighed. "Okay. I know better than to argue with you. Come on."

* * *

Cara reclined on her elbows on the bed, listening to the sound of Chris in the bathroom. It was pleasant simply to lie there and hear the familiar, curiously stirring masculine noises of a shower and shave. The realization the danger was over for herself and Matthew was beginning to sink in. Chris would stay here for a while, getting the information on the oil business her father had promised him, and then they would return to Washington, with nothing more disturbing on their minds than each other.

Chris emerged from the bathroom, nude except for a towel around his slender hips, his toweled hair standing out in dark spikes over his head. Cara observed him silently as he combed and dried his hair, enjoying the play of muscles across his back and chest and the sight of his long, slender legs covered by a fuzz of black hair. A feeling she knew well stirred in her loins.

He pulled a shirt and trousers from his suitcase and re-closed it. "Aren't you going to unpack?" Cara asked, wondering at his action.

"No, I'm returning to D.C. as soon as I can catch a plane. Call the airlines, will you, and find out when there's a flight available."

"But what about your story? Aren't you going to stay for the inside scoop about the oil industry?"

"If you'll remember, I'm not the one who discovered Durek."

"But if you hadn't gotten the information out of Ashe originally . . ."

He shrugged. "Actually you did that. Anyway, it doesn't matter. I've realized my story isn't the most important thing in the world. I couldn't write one that might injure someone you loved. See, you've compromised my integrity." He flashed a crooked grin at her.

"Well, at least wait for me to get my luggage. It's over at Morgan's."

"I don't want you to go back with me."

A sudden knot of fear tightened her stomach. She knew

with dreadful certainty that this was it. He was ending their affair. Her hands turned icy and her mouth dry. How was she to combat this? She simply couldn't lose him. How would she live if she did?

"What do you mean?" she asked, stalling for time.

He glanced up and saw the fear imprinted on her face. "Oh, baby, I didn't mean it like that. Of course I want you. But I don't want you to fly into D.C. with me today. In fact, I think it would be better all around if you stayed here for a while."

"I can't. School," she managed to croak out. "Chris . . ."

He came to her quickly and knelt before her, taking her hands in his. "Your hands are frozen. Don't look so worried. Cara, I'm going home to see my lawyer. I'm filing for a divorce as soon as possible."

She stared, her mind whirling. This was the last thing she had expected him to say. "What?"

"I did a lot of thinking the past couple of days. When I learned that you had been kidnapped, I thought I'd lost you forever. And I knew there was nothing left for me without you. You've turned my life around. I used to live in a little cage, running around and around like a white rat, going faster all the time so I wouldn't catch onto the fact that I wasn't getting anywhere. My marriage was a penance, a sacrifice to my guilt. Dean accused me of using it to cut myself off from love. Maybe he was right. I was scared of marriage, of commitment, of opening myself up to another person and risking getting slashed to bits again. So I imprisoned myself in that narrow world. But you unlocked the door. I experienced wonderful, painful emotions—stronger than any I've ever known. I *lived* again."

"Oh, Chris." Tears sprang into Cara's eyes and she blinked them away. "Oh, honey, I love you." He stood up, pulling her against his chest, his arms wrapped tightly around her.

"You're the cornerstone of my life. I'm committing a far greater sin than any wrong I did Monica by denying us the full life we could have. Monica won't allow herself or me to live more than a partial life. I'll support her financially, but I won't allow her to destroy my life any longer."

Cara stood on tiptoe, and their lips blended in a soft, searching kiss. Chris released her and moved away. "But I don't understand. Why can't I go with you?" she asked.

"Monica won't let me go easily. She'll fight every inch of the way and bring you into it. She'll do her best to make us both miserable. So until I get my divorce, the less we're seen together, the better. In fact, I'd prefer for you to stay here and avoid the whole mess."

"But I have to go to school. I'm not abandoning my career plans to keep out of Monica's grasp. I'm made of tougher stuff than that. When I met her earlier, I felt wrong and guilty, but now . . . Now I can face anything." She made a grandiloquent gesture, her face glowing with happiness.

He grinned. "I know. You could conquer the world. But I want you to exercise some caution. You're moving into Ginny's house until you can take possession of your apartment. It'll be hell, but we've got to avoid each other."

"You mean I can't see you?"

"See, yes. But sleep over, no. She'll have ten detectives following me everywhere. I know her. And I want you safe. I won't let her drag you through the mud to wreak a little vengeance on me. It'll be hell, but that's the way it has to be."

Cara studied Chris, her head tilted to one side. A slow grin spread across her face. "All right. I'll agree to follow your plan. But tell me, does that ban on, uh, *physical relations,* start immediately?" She held out her arms, her curving mouth and warm eyes promising sensual delights.

He smiled. "No." He unfastened the towel with a single snap.

About the Author

For *Summer Sky*, Kristin James based much of the hero's life on that of her handsome husband Pete, who is of Polish extraction. She was pregnant throughout the writing of this story and delivered her first child—Stacy—the day after she completed her work on the novel. That is what an editor calls a cooperative baby and a dedicated author.

Yet dedication and self-discipline are nothing new to Kristin James, a licensed attorney who gave up her practice in favor of writing books. Not only is she the author of the popular *The Golden Sky* and *The Sapphire Sky*, but she is also the bestselling historical romance writer Lisa Gregory.

Her next exciting contemporary romance will be a departure from the Stone family. So if you would like to read more books about these dynamic people, please let us know.

GLORIOUS BATTLES OF LOVE & WAR

Romances of Strange Lands and Distant Times

Read about the dazzling women and bold men whose passion for love and excitement leads them to the heights and depths of the human experience—set against flamboyant period backgrounds.

Look for Richard Gallen Romances from Pocket Books—